Dee Williams was born and brought up in Rotherhithe in East London where her father worked as a stevedore in Surrey Docks. Dee left school at fourteen, met her husband at sixteen and was married at twenty. After living abroad for some years, Dee moved to Hampshire to be close to her family. She has written thirteen prevous sagas including HOPES AND DREAMS, A RARE RUBY and KATIE'S KITCHEN.

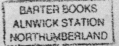

# PRIDE AND JOY

## Dee Williams

**headline**

First published in 2003
by HEADLINE BOOK PUBLISHING

First published in paperback in 2004
by HEADLINE BOOK PUBLISHING

10 9 8 7 6 5 4 3 2 1

ISBN 0 7553 0099 8

Typeset in Times by
Letterpart Limited, Reigate, Surrey

Printed and bound in Great Britain by
Mackays of Chatham plc, Chatham, Kent

Headline's policy is to use papers that are natural, renewable and
recyclable products and made from wood grown in sustainable forests.
The logging and manufacturing processes are expected to conform
to the environmental regulations of the country of origin.

HEADLINE BOOK PUBLISHING
A division of Hodder Headline PLC
338 Euston Road
LONDON NW1 3BH

www.headline.co.uk
www.hodderheadline.com

I would like to thank Allison and her mum for putting me in touch with Carole Hiorns at the Autistic Society. Many thanks to you all for your information on this subject. Also, thanks again to Ron Brown from the *News*, who has helped me to learn more about Portsmouth's history. And I must add Charles Weatherby from the Havant and District Writers' Circle. He discovered so many details for me about the asylum in Portsmouth as it was in 1935. Thank you, everybody, for helping to bring a little realism to a work of fiction.

I would also like to say a big thank you to my daughter Carol and my son-in-law Gez for the wonderful surprise party they gave for Emma, their daughter, my granddaughter, on her eighteenth birthday – not forgetting the four others whose birthdays we celebrated that night. It took six months to plan and was enjoyed by everyone. This book is dedicated to both of them, and to Emma and Samantha: you are indeed my *pride and joy*.

# *Chapter 1*

**June 1934**

It was Saturday afternoon and Mary Harris and her best friend Liz were walking home from the biscuit factory in Rotherhithe where they worked. It was their half-day and, as ever, they were deep in conversation. As they neared the docks they could see a group of men laughing at a small figure sitting in the gutter. To Mary's horror, she realised that the object of their amusement was her four-year-old half-brother Eddie. She knew from the state of him that he'd been begging for food: he had jam in his hair and all round his face. The dockers were taking great delight in throwing him sandwiches, laughing when he missed catching the bread.

'Eddie!' shouted Mary. 'Come here!' As she started towards the boy, she saw her friend Liz turn and hurry away, obviously embarrassed by the situation.

Eddie just grinned at his sister, but when she started to get closer he got up and began to run on his stubby little legs. When she finally caught hold of him, to her shame, he spread himself on the ground and started screaming and pounding the pavement with his fists. Mary had to physically drag him to his feet.

'For Gawd sake, girl, leave the poor little sod alone,' yelled one man. 'Daft Eddie ain't hurting anyone.'

The other dockers joined in, urging Mary to leave Eddie be.

Finally she got a strong grip on Eddie's arm and they started to make their way home. As they struggled along, Mary's thoughts went back to four years ago. For the first two years after his arrival, Eddie had brought her family a great deal of happiness. With his big blue eyes, blond hair and funny little ways, he was idolised. He was a beautiful boy, but somehow he was different to other children his age. He was always behind them when it came to learning new things, and he never grasped how to talk. But he was a good-natured child and seemed happy in his own little world. Over the past two years or so Eddie had changed, and not for the better. He still didn't talk, although he'd learned the word 'no'. When he got frustrated he'd sit and bang his head, and he had terrible tantrums. The only peace her mother had found was during the few weeks that Eddie had been at school. But it didn't last long as the teachers had sent him home saying they couldn't control him. He had been naughty and he'd upset the other children with his shouting and strange noises. No one knew what to do with him when he was like that, and smacking him and locking him in the outside lavatory only made him worse.

After much pulling and shouting Mary finally got him home.

'Thank God you found him,' said her mother when Mary stepped into the passage. 'I've been worried sick as to where he'd got to. I've been running up and down the street looking for him. I even sent Sadie's kids out as well.'

'He was down at the docks.'

Sarah put her hand to her mouth. 'Oh no. Thank God he's safe.'

Eddie was shouting.

'Shut up! Why is he so naughty?' asked Mary, who had lost

all patience with Eddie after her ordeal.

'I only wish I knew.'

The shouting got louder.

'Please, Mum, make him stop,' pleaded Mary. 'You've got to.'

'How? Mary, I'm at my wits' end.'

Mary looked at her mother and felt full of guilt. She knew Eddie was driving his mother, as well as herself, to despair. She began to cry.

'Come along, love. That's not going to help,' said her mother.

'I'm sorry. Was I like this?'

Sarah smiled. 'No, love, you were the perfect baby.'

'I wish we could understand why he's this way.' Mary ran her hand under her nose.

'We will one day,' said her mother.

With tears running down her cheeks, Mary helped her mother as they battled to tie him in the chair. He was getting very strong and had begun to fight back; soon her mother wouldn't be able to control him.

'If Gran was here she'd soon make him behave,' said Mary, holding down Eddie's hands as he tried to hit out.

Mary had idolised her gran. They had lived in this house with her all Mary's life. She had never known her granddad, who had died before she was born, and she was only two when her father died. She didn't remember her dad but her mum said she'd inherited his dark hair and eyes. Her mother had had to go out to work and it had been Gran who had looked after her while Sarah wasn't there. Mary remembered when her mother used to work in the shirt factory; she was a very good needlewoman and always made Mary's Shirley Temple-type frocks. They had all been very close. But when Mary was eight her gran had died. The bottom had dropped out of Mary's world. The loss was something she never thought she would get over; the house seemed very empty without Gran. Then, a few years afterwards, her mother brought a man home.

Mary thought about when she'd first met Ted. She hadn't liked him. She hadn't wanted anyone to come between her and her mother. It had taken a while for her to come round, but he'd been patient and kind. He had taken her out and with his lovely warm smile and generous ways he'd soon got round her.

Mary glanced at her mother. Sarah had married Ted Harding almost six years ago. Mary had been adamant about keeping her own name. It had upset Sarah at the time, but that feeling had long passed. Ted was a tall handsome man with fair hair and piercing blue eyes. Some had said: Change the name and not the letter, marry for worse and not for better; but her mother had been very happy. Sarah Harding had been a great beauty in her younger days; she was still attractive, with a mop of dark hair now streaked with grey. But for the past year or so her dark eyes always seemed to have a melancholy look about them.

Mary knew it was because of Eddie. Ted, who had always been thoughtful, had at first idolised his son and put his wild ways down to simple high spirits. Back in those early days, somehow he had managed to get through to Eddie even though he couldn't speak. Now the only word they could understand was no, which he'd repeat over and over again. Most of the time he'd gabble and grunt or scream; he'd bang his head against the nearest surface or sit rocking back and forth when things didn't go his way. It was very distressing for Mary and her mother. At first Ted said it was because he was frustrated and he'd grow out of it, but this past year even Ted began to find him impossible and most of the time either

4

shouted at him or just ignored him. The atmosphere in the house was often strained.

Sarah went into the scullery and busied herself doing the potatoes. She let her thoughts stray to happier days. For most of these past six years her life had been perfect, but things seemed to be changing now. She remembered when she had first met Ted. He'd been so loving and thoughtful: always worrying about her. When he first came into her life she'd felt like a woman again. After Ben's death, she'd never thought she would be able to love again, but Ted had been so understanding. She never felt she had betrayed Ben; she knew he would have approved of her choice. As he lay so very ill, he'd told her many times that she should marry again, but that had been the last thing on her mind. After he'd gone, her life had been a struggle; thankfully she'd had her mother to look after Mary, who was still a toddler, while she went to work at the shirt factory. Her mother had never known Ted but Sarah knew she too would have approved of him. It had been hard for Mary after her gran had died; it meant her coming home from school and being alone till Sarah finished work. Sarah was very close to her daughter and at first she knew Mary resented Ted coming into their lives. Acceptance had taken time; he was very good to her. When Eddie was born life took on a new meaning. Ted was overjoyed with his son, who was the image of him. Sarah was thrilled that she could be home all day with this baby, giving him all the love he deserved. They were comfortably off now and Sarah didn't have to make every penny count any more. She would hate to go back to those days again.

She had met Ted when she was assisting in the general strike. Ted had been helping to keep the transport moving; he'd said he enjoyed being a conductor on the trams, it was a change from being stuck in an office poring over columns of boring accounts. He was charming and Sarah had been swept off her feet. Ted was very clever; he worked in an office in the City and used long words she didn't always understand. Sarah smiled as she remembered when Ted proposed. She'd been very apprehensive and thought long and hard before she accepted. Her biggest worry had been: would Mary accept him? But she loved him and it was lovely to be in a man's arms again.

It wasn't long before they were married and Ted moved in with them in their typical back-to-back terraced house. Number sixty Doyle Street, Rotherhithe, had two bedrooms; the third had been turned into a bathroom, but they still had to use the outside lav. It was after Ted had had his name put on the rent book that he went to see the landlord about having that alteration done. Downstairs was a front room, which was only used on Sundays, the kitchen being the main room of the house; beyond that was a scullery. Ted didn't have a home as he had lived in rooms after he came out of the navy. Doyle Street, like most in this area, had a couple of shops in the middle: the newsagent and the dairy. There was a pub at one end; at the other, high above the arches, were the railway lines. The infant school was round the corner.

It wasn't a posh house, but Sarah kept it sparkling clean. Ted was always saying they would soon be moving out of Rother-hithe and into the suburbs, but so far that hadn't happened. They would have to move one day, when Eddie got bigger and needed a room of his own. Although Mary loved him Sarah knew her daughter wasn't willing to share her bedroom.

Mary came into the scullery with Eddie in tow. 'He wants the lav.'

Sarah watched them go out into the back yard. That was one thing Sarah was pleased about. Although he couldn't speak he didn't like to be wet or dirty and made sure

6

everybody knew when he wanted to go. He would shout and, holding himself, jump up and down. It had taken Sarah years to teach Eddie he had to hold on until he reached the lavatory.

Mary went with Eddie to the lav. 'I hope you learn to do this on your own one day.' She laughed. 'I don't fancy being in here with you when you're going to work.'

Eddie laughed with her.

'Mary, don't tell your father you found him at the docks,' said Sarah when they returned to the scullery.

'No, all right.' Once before, when Mary had told Ted about finding Eddie down there begging for food, he had got very angry with her mother for letting him get out.

'If he had got past the gatekeeper he could have drowned going there on his own. What were you thinking of, woman? You must be more careful,' he'd shouted.

That was the first time Mary had ever heard him raise his voice.

'What can I do to keep him in?' Sarah had retorted. 'I'm at my wits' end with him now he can reach up and open the front door.'

'Lock him in a room. Tie him to a chair or something. I don't know. Use your loaf, woman.'

Mary's mouth had dropped open at this conversation. She had never heard her mother or stepfather utter a cross word until then; now their son was driving a wedge between them. Why didn't her mother tell him how Eddie behaved when he wasn't here? Eddie had got crafty; he was very different when his father was around. He didn't throw so many tantrums or hit out; he would cower down and simper. Mary knew her mother worried about Eddie, but when she asked if there was anything wrong with him, her mother quickly dismissed it. But surely there must be something amiss? He certainly wasn't like other children.

7

Mary sat him in the chair and watched him banging his head against the back of it. 'Eddie, stop that,' she insisted.

As ever, he grinned and looked away, then his big blue eyes filled with tears.

Mary went over and with difficulty held him close. How could she get angry with him?'

He shook his head vigorously, shouting what Mary always said was: 'No. No. No.'

Her mother came in the kitchen. 'Is he being silly again?'

'I don't know. Does Dad know why he can't talk?'

Sarah shrugged. 'He thinks he's just lazy and looking for attention. He was talking about taking him to see a specialist, but that costs a lot of money.'

'I thought Dad got a decent wage.'

'He does, but it don't run to things like that.'

'I could give you a few shillings more, if that would help.'

Sarah smiled. 'You're a good girl. I take more than enough off you now. You look after your money. You'll need it for nice clothes one of these days when you start walking out with a young man.'

Mary laughed. 'Mum, I'm only sixteen. And besides, just where am I gonner find one of those?'

'You'll be seventeen very soon and you never know. Could be someone at work in the packing room. What about all these new young drivers they've got now?'

Mary screwed up her face. 'Don't like the look of any of *them*. Some of 'em have got spotty faces.'

Sarah smiled. 'Looks aren't everything, my girl.'

'I know, but it helps to start with.'

Eddie put his head back and began shouting.

'Somebody feels he's being left out. Mary, there are some jam crusts in the scullery. Bring them in for him.'

In the scullery Mary put the crusts on a plate. She stood

8

looking at them for a moment or two and thought about what her mother had just said. She would like to meet a nice young man and walk out with him. In fact, that's the thing she and Liz talked about most of the time. Mary had known Liz ever since she started working on the line packing biscuits into the large boxes. She'd been at the factory for nearly three years, and she liked it there. She especially enjoyed listening to the girls and women talking about what they got up to – though it shocked her when they told her what they did with their boyfriends. Mary thought she could never do things like that, not till she was married. It was Liz whose company she enjoyed the most. She was just a month older than Mary and they went to the pictures and dancing together. Liz was one of four; she had two younger sisters, but it was her brother, who was four years older than her and in the Royal Navy, that Liz was always on about. Mary had never met Billy, he had been away for two years, but she had seen a photo of him. He was tall, and looked a bit like Liz, but unlike Liz's mousy-coloured hair his was dark. And he had a cheeky grin. In his picture his sailor hat was perched on the back of his head. In some ways, he was quite nice-looking.

'He's got greeny-grey eyes,' Liz had told her recently. 'Not a bit like my pale blue limpid pools.' She had laughed and fluttered her eyelashes.

Mary had laughed with her. 'Limpid pools! Where'd you get that from?'

'Thought it sounded rather grand.'

'You read too many magazines. You sound like one of their heroines.'

'So what? It does sound good. Don't know who our Billy takes after, must be the milkman.'

'Don't let your mum hear you say that.'

9

'I'd soon get a clip round the ear if she did.'

Liz had told Mary that Billy's ship was coming back to Portsmouth soon and she had asked her friend to go with her to meet him. To Mary, going to Portsmouth did sound very tempting. The only seaside she'd been to was Southend on the factory's outing. That had been a very boozy affair with many of the older ones getting very drunk and being sick all the way home. Liz did say that Billy liked the girls and probably had a girlfriend in every port.

'Mary? Where are those crusts?'

'They're here,' she said, coming back from her daydream.

That evening, before Ted came home, Sarah said again there wasn't any need to mention Eddie being down by the docks. 'Don't want to worry him.'

Mary knew her mother wanted to avoid another row.

'Are you going out tonight?' Ted asked Mary after they'd finished their tea.

'Yes. The pictures with Liz.'

'That's nice,' said her mother.

Ted stood up. He put his hand in his pocket and, taking out a shilling, gave it to Mary.

'What's this for?' she said, looking at the shilling resting in the palm of her hand.

'Treat yourself. I know the lad here can be a bit of a problem at times and you're a good girl helping your mother out.'

'But, Dad—'

'Shh, before I change my mind.' His piercing blue eyes sparkled.

She threw her arms round his neck and kissed his cheek. 'I'm so glad my mum married you.'

'Not nearly as glad as I am.'

Sarah Harding smiled, but somehow Mary could sense she was troubled.

'If we can get in the sixpenny seats I'll bring back the change.'

'No, treat yourself. Bring the lad back a bar of chocolate if you've got any over. I had a good afternoon on the horses today.'

Both Mary and her mother knew he liked a flutter on the horses and dogs; sometimes he'd even taken Mary to the dog track. She'd got almost as excited as he did when the greyhound he'd backed had won. Ted also liked a drink or two, but there was nothing excessive about Ted Harding and Sarah never went short of money. Not like some that lived round this way. In fact, he was very generous.

Mary stood in front of the mirror that hung over the fireplace and brushed her short dark hair. She patted it into place and, wetting her finger, made a cute little curl to nestle on her cheek. As it was a warm June evening she didn't have to bother with a coat to cover her frock. It was blue, and pretty enough, but she was hoping to get one of the fashionable short frocks she'd seen in the magazines. It was something she'd asked for for her birthday in August. That and pointed toe shoes with a neat little heel. She was so lucky, she thought; it had been hard and very lonely for her and her mother after Gran died. With her mother working long hours Mary had had to come home from school and start the tea alone. There is nothing sadder than coming home in the winter to a dark empty house. Now they didn't want for anything. Life was so much better since her mother married Ted. If only something could be done to help Eddie.

# Chapter 2

June had slowly moved into July. It was a fine warm evening and they settled down to their evening meal. But for some unknown reason Eddie, who had been quite happily lining up his wooden trains, decided to throw a terrible tantrum. Ted was home early and this was the first time for a while that he'd witnessed such a display. Normally Eddie had had his tea and was ready for bed before his father appeared, but tonight he was still about.

First Eddie slapped the dinner with his hands. When Ted told him to stop, he laughed and squeezed it through his fingers; he then threw his enamel plate down. It landed with a loud clatter on the lino, spilling the rest of the contents over the floor.

'Stop that at once, young man,' shouted Ted.

Eddie shook his head. 'No. No. No.'

Ted stood up and, standing over him, told him to behave. This only seemed to make the lad worse and he screamed and screamed and began rubbing the dinner in his hair. Sarah went to hold her son's hands down. He grabbed her hand and bit it hard. She yelled out in pain as spots of blood appeared. She sped into the scullery to run her hand under the tap; Mary, frightened, watched Ted snatch Eddie off the chair and tuck him under his arm. With a lot of shouting, kicking and arm-waving, they left the room.

'Mum, are you all right?' Mary asked, following her mother into the scullery.

Sarah smiled. 'Yes. I'll just put a bit of rag round this.'

'Is it very bad?'

'No. I was silly to make such a fuss. Do you think you could tie this for me?' She held out her hand to Mary.

'Mum, it's gone very quiet. Do you think Eddie's all right?'

'Of course. Ted knows how to handle him.' Her mother went back into the kitchen and Mary set to and helped her clear up the mess that Eddie had left.

It was a while before Ted returned to the kitchen – alone.

'I'm so very sorry, my dear,' he said, going up to Sarah. Taking her bandaged hand, he kissed it.

'It's nothing,' she said, giving him a loving look. 'Is the boy asleep?'

'Yes. He's spark out. I think he just exhausted himself.'

'I'll go and make sure he's all right.'

'No, leave him. We don't want him waking. Let's finish this delicious meal in peace. What's for pudding?'

'Apple pie.'

Yet as Sarah dished up the pie she couldn't tear her thoughts away from Eddie. What if he was crying? She couldn't hear him so Ted must have closed the bedroom door. Now he'd taken to chewing his clothes, would he choke? Sarah desperately wanted to go to her son.

'Don't look so worried, my dear. The boy's fine.'

Sarah gave Ted a slight smile. 'I'd feel better if I could go to him.'

'No. Sit down. You must let him see that you can't be at his beck and call all of the time.'

Reluctantly Sarah sat down, but she only picked at her food; she had lost her appetite. What was to become of their son? He couldn't go on like this for ever. What about when he got older and bigger, how would she control him then?

Mary looked from her mother to her dad. She didn't like the tension between them.

The following morning, for the first time in months, when Mary opened her eyes she didn't hear Eddie shouting or rattling the bars of his cot as he usually did. When she quietly looked round the door of the bedroom that he shared with his parents he appeared to be sleeping soundly.

'He's still asleep then,' said Mary, walking into the kitchen.

'Yes, don't wake him, I could do with a few more moments of peace and quiet.'

As Mary and Liz walked home from work that evening, Liz was once again talking about her brother Billy. He was coming home.

'You will come to Portsmouth with me, won't you?'

'Do you know when?'

'No, Mum's still waiting to hear. It could be next month. Let's hope it's over the bank holiday; perhaps we could stay down there for a couple of nights. Mary, please say you'll come with me, it'll be really great. With all those sailors, who knows, we might find ourselves a boyfriend!'

'Yes, it would be nice.'

'Is that it? I'd thought you'd be a bit more enthusiastic.'

Mary smiled at Liz. 'I'm sorry. I'd love to come.'

'I've told Billy all about you,' said Liz.

'You haven't. Why?'

'I thought it might be a good idea.'

'Oh, did you? I hope it was all good.'

'Course it was.'

'And what did he have to say?'

'He reckons you sound a bit of all right.'

14

Mary laughed. 'Cheeky so and so. Mind you, I'll miss going to the fair on Blackheath.' Every bank holiday since they had been at work the girls had gone to the fair on Blackheath. It was always the highlight of any bank holiday weekend.

'So will I. Who knows, they might have one down there.'

However, try as much as she could to get enthused, it was Eddie that was filling Mary's mind. 'Liz, do you think there's something wrong with Eddie?'

'I don't like to say it, but, well, if you ask me, he don't seem all there.'

'I wish I could help him. I wish there was someone I could go and see.'

'Don't think a doctor would be any good.'

'No. But there must be someone.'

'You wonner be careful who you talk to. They could end up putting him in a loony bin.'

'Liz, don't say that.'

'Well, just you be careful then. Here, I hope it don't run in the family.'

'Thanks. So you think I'm daft as well?'

'No, course not. But what about your stepdad's family?'

'Don't really know that much about them.'

'Where did he come from?'

'Up north somewhere, I think.'

'He don't talk like Edna, she comes from Scotland.'

'That's true. I'll ask him. He was in the navy in the war.'

'Was he? D'you know what ship he was on? I might be able to find out something from Billy.'

'No. He wasn't on a ship. He said he was in the dockyard in Chatham.'

They continued chatting, as they walked, until it was time for them to part.

'See you tomorrow,' yelled Liz as she turned the corner into Bray Street.

'I hope so.' Mary waved, then carried on, deep in thought. She was worried at what Liz had said about Ted. Was there something bad in his background? She hoped she was wrong as she did love her stepfather.

When Mary walked into the house she found Eddie sitting on the floor. He had his back to her and was concentrating on lining up his wooden trains, a task that took up most of his time. This afternoon he was very subdued and didn't shout or throw a tantrum when it went wrong.

'Hello there,' Mary said, ruffling his hair.

Eddie turned and Mary gasped. He had a multi-coloured bruise down the side of his face.

'How did he do that?' she asked her mother.

'It happened in the night. Ted reckons he must have thrown himself against the bars of his cot.'

'Was it there when you went to bed?'

'No. At least, I don't think so. He was lying on that side. Ted suggested that I didn't take him out shopping today, as we don't want people thinking that we did it. It should have nearly gone be Monday.'

'Your poor little mite,' said Mary, going to him and hugging him.

He stood up and, putting his arms round her neck, grunted and kissed her cheek.

'I love you,' said Mary with tears in her eyes. 'Why can't you always be like this?'

Eddie was smiling broadly.

'He can be such a little charmer when it suits him,' said her mother.

'Mum, do you think he should see a doctor?'

'Whatever for?'

'That bruise.'

'No. I was talking to Sadie and she said it'll go in a couple of days. And she should know, she gets enough of 'em. She gave me some tincture of arnica to put on it, seems she's always got some of that indoors.'

'I was wondering if a doctor could find out why he won't talk,' said Mary.

'He will in time. He's a little slow, that's all. Look how long it took him to walk and to be clean.'

'I thought Dad was going to take him to see someone?'

'He will when he gets the time. Now stop trying to see things that don't exist and lay the table. Eddie has had his dinner so he can go to bed when we have ours.'

Reluctantly Mary went into the kitchen and took the knives and forks from the drawer of the oak sideboard that lined the wall one side of the fireplace. This must have been one of the few houses round this way that had a bowl of fruit on top. This room didn't have a lot of furniture, just the table with four chairs under. When they weren't having a meal the table was always covered with a green chenille cloth. All the while Mary was laying the table she smiled and chatted to Eddie, hoping to convey to him the fact that she loved him and wanted him to talk to her. 'Look, Eddie, fork. Say fork.' She said it very slowly, holding up a fork, but he just turned away. 'I know if I keep on you will talk one day.'

Mary was going outside to the lav when Sadie who lived next door called her over. She removed the pegs from her mouth. 'Hello, Mary. How's young Eddie now?'

'He's got a nasty bruise, but it don't seem to worry him.'

'I know. I saw it this morning when him and yer mum come out in the garden.'

Mary smiled and looked round the yard; you could hardly

17

call this bit of dirt and concrete a garden.

'I gave her something to put on it.'

'So she said. Sadie, you've got enough kids to know if something was wrong with one of 'em, haven't you?'

Sadie looked over her shoulder and moved closer to the odd bits of wood that served as the fence. She put her hands in the small of her back. 'This one seems to be a proper live wire.' She patted her large stomach.

Mary smiled. 'Would you be worried if Eddie was yours?'

'I don't like to say, but I think he should be saying proper words be now. And I'd be worried he might do himself more harm, not just bruises now he's getting bigger. Yer mum said you found him down the docks again. That ain't right. He could come to a lot of harm down there.'

'I know. I do worry about him.'

Sadie smiled. Although she was one of the poorest in Doyle Street she had a heart of gold and Mary and her mother thought a lot of her. Often when Sarah saw her hanging the pitiful rags she called her washing on the line she would keep her head down, and Sarah would realise she had another black eye. Sometimes Sarah passed food over the fence saying she'd cooked far too much. It was sad, Sadie tried so hard to keep her family fed and clean.

Mary's old gran also used to worry about their next-door neighbour, especially when her husband, Wally Fellows, came in drunk and smacked her about. He couldn't find work so he hung about on street corners scrounging a few bob from anyone daft enough to give it to him. Through the thin walls they could often hear the furniture being thrown about and the kids screaming out in fear.

Gran would sit in her chair tutting. 'He'll end up killing her one of these days. If it's not with his bare hands, it'll be by keeping putting her up the duff.'

Sadie had six kids and another on the way. 'You're a good girl, Mary,' she said now. 'Got a way with kids. My lot finks the world of you.'

Mary blushed. 'Thanks. I'd better go and have a wee before I wet me knickers.'

After checking for spiders, she sat on the wooden seat. The thought that was continually running through her mind was, if Ted wasn't going to do anything about Eddie, then she'd try and find out something herself. She glanced at the scrap of newspaper she was holding and something about Shirley Temple, her idol, caught her eye. She started looking through the cut-up squares of newspaper, which had been threaded with string and hung up on a nail, for the rest of the story, but gave up when she couldn't find it.

That evening when Ted came home he didn't look very happy. The moment Eddie saw his father he ran to Mary and, scrambling on to her lap, buried his head in her shoulder.

Ted kissed Sarah's cheek, then threw his newspaper on to the table. 'Have you seen this?'

'No, love. What is it?' Sarah picked up the paper.

'That Hitler appears to be doing just what he likes over there in Germany. The paper says that he ordered the killing of the Brownshirts.'

'What's the Brownshirts?' asked Mary.

'You must have seen them in the newspapers, they stand on street corners shouting,' said Ted.

'I've seen 'em but never took a lot of notice of 'em. Why does he want to kill 'em? Are they the same as the black-shirts?' asked Mary. She'd seen Hitler on the newsreels but wasn't that interested.

'No, the blackshirts are fascists. Hitler reckons the Brown-shirts were hatching a plot to kill him. I can't see that, not

19

with the amount of bodyguards he's got.'

'Should we be worried?' asked Sarah.

'Depends on how much power he wants. How's he been today?' He nodded towards Eddie.

'Fine. He's been fine.'

'That's good. I couldn't stand any more of his tantrums, not tonight. Not after the day I've had.'

'What's happened at work then, dear?'

'Just found out they could be laying some off.'

Sarah gasped. 'Oh no. Would that affect you?'

'No. But I could be the one that has to tell the poor blokes.'

With the atmosphere charged as it was, Mary knew this wasn't the right time to talk about Eddie. 'Shall I put him to bed?'

'Yes, that's a good idea. Say goodnight to your father, Eddie.'

Mary held Eddie's hand and gently pushed him towards Ted.

Eddie yelled out, 'No. No. No.'

'Eddie, don't be silly,' said Sarah.

'Leave him alone,' said Ted. 'Just take him on up and make sure he can't get out.'

Mary took his hand and led him upstairs. As she undressed him she talked to him all the while. 'I *am* going to make you talk, you know!'

He put his arms round her and held her tight.

'Say Mary.'

He giggled and kissed her cheek.

She hugged him back. 'You will say Mary one day.'

# Chapter 3

For the past week the girls on the packing line had talked non-stop about what they were going to do August bank holiday Monday.

Those who worked near Liz and Mary were envious of them going to Portsmouth tomorrow.

'You wonner be careful of all those sailors down there,' yelled out Bet. 'They love 'em and leave 'em, you know.'

'How d'you know?' asked Lil, who worked next to her.

Bet touched the side of her nose. 'I wasn't born yesterday,' she said with a wink.

Lil grinned. 'Silly cow don't know what she's talking about.' And, waving a packet of biscuits at her friend, said to all within earshot: 'She ain't been any further than Southend and her old man'll kill her if she ever went near a sailor, or anybody else for that matter.'

Bet tossed her head in the air and said with a laugh, 'But it don't stop me dreaming though, does it?'

'Just as long as you keep yer drawers on you'll be all right,' said Lil.

'They might have more fun with 'em off,' said Bet.

Everybody shrieked with laughter.

Mary and Liz were very excited as they left the factory. The girls were shouting after them, wishing they were going with them tomorrow.

Liz squeezed Mary's arm. 'You won't be late in the morning, will you?'

'What do you think? I've almost packed.'

'Won't take me long. I ain't got that much.'

'Just as long as you make sure you've got your clean drawers.'

They giggled as they made their way to their homes.

'Now, you're sure you'll be all right?' Sarah asked as she watched her daughter put her clean underwear, nightie and frock into a small suitcase.

'Course. I'm really excited about it. Liz said she thinks they may have a big fair down there.'

'You sure you ain't thinking more of meeting her brother?'

Mary laughed. 'Oh Mum.' She gave Sarah a saucy grin. 'I don't know though. He does sound rather nice.'

'Well, don't get up to any mischief,' said Ted, poking his head round the bedroom door. 'Be careful. After all, you know what they say about sailors.'

'I do – everyone keeps telling me! Mum said you was a sailor in the war.' Mary tried to sound casual.

'Yes, but I was only stuck behind a desk. I didn't get the chance to sail the seven seas.'

'Mary, you will take care, won't you?'

'Course, Mum. We're only going for one night. And Liz's dad will be with us to make sure we get a decent lodging.'

'I expect there are places down there that young girls shouldn't go.'

'Oh Ted. Don't say that, I'll be worried.'

Mary grinned. 'So how do you know about those places then, Dad?'

'Bound to be, anywhere where there're sailors. I dare say

this Mr Thomas has got his head screwed on.'

'I hope so. It's a pity the boy's mum can't get to see her only son.'

'Yes,' said Mary. 'She's really upset about that, but they can't afford the fare for all of 'em and Mr Thomas will only get a cheap day return, he can't stay the night.'

'Surely the lad will get some leave? After all, you said he's been away for two years,' said Sarah.

'Yes, he will,' said Mary. 'Liz said it's because it's Navy Days and he has to stay with his ship all week. King George and Queen Mary will be there as well. I hope I get to see them. I really am looking forward to it.'

Sarah smiled. 'And I shall really look forward to hearing all about it. What is Navy Days?'

'Liz was saying it's when they open the docks to the public and anybody can go and see over the ships. There'll be ever such a lot of boats there.'

'Sounds very exciting. You'd better take a towel in case you want to have a paddle. Have they got a beach?'

'I would think so. Don't know if it's sand though.'

'It's very stony,' said Ted, settling down with his newspaper.

'Have you been there, dear?' asked Sarah.

'No. I've just read about it.'

Later that evening, when she was getting ready for bed, Mary remembered Eddie would still be fast asleep when she left in the morning, so she went in to see her brother. 'You look so peaceful,' she whispered. 'I'll bring you something back.' She kissed her finger and gently touched his forehead. He gave a long sigh and turned over.

The following morning Mary kissed her mother and Ted goodbye and hurried to the bus stop. She was so excited, she just hoped she wouldn't be sick. This was the first time she'd ever been away from home for a whole night.

When Mary caught sight of Liz and her dad she waved and Liz came bounding up to her. She gave Mary a huge smile and, after hugging her, slid her arm through her friend's.

'Hello there, young Mary,' said Mr Thomas. 'Here's our bus. Looking forward to going to the seaside?'

'I should say so. Is it like Southend?' she asked, clambering aboard the bus.

'Dunno. Ain't never been to Portsmouth before. Go upstairs, love, I wonner have a smoke.'

'I loved it when we went to Southend with the firm. I'd never ever been on a charabanc before, or seen the sea,' said Liz, settling down next to her friend.

'Yes, it was a good day out,' said Mary.

'And the sing song we had on the way back,' said Liz, trying hard to sit still.

'Didn't like it when some of the blokes had too much to drink.'

'Some of 'em did get a bit silly,' agreed Liz.

Soon it was time to leave the bus and enter the station. Mary had never been to a railway station on a bank holiday weekend before and was taken aback at the chaos. Waterloo appeared to be full of people shouting and rushing about. The noise was deafening. Carriage doors were being slammed and the loud hissing from the trains letting off steam all added to the confusion.

'Keep close together,' yelled Mr Thomas. 'Don't wonner lose you.'

The girls tottered along in their high heels, pushing and shoving in order to get to their train through the crowds and luggage that was piled high on the platform.

'I hope we can get a seat,' said Liz, panting for breath. 'Don't fancy standing all that way.'

'Good job your dad's gone racing ahead to try and get us one. Let's hope we can find him.'

'In here, girls,' shouted Mr Thomas, who had his head hanging out of a window frantically waving his trilby. He opened the carriage door and they fell into a seat.

And then they were on their way. The only other occupants in the carriage were a mother with her two children. Gradually they saw the houses and tall buildings give way to green fields.

'How long will it be, Mum, before we see Dad?' asked the girl, who was about ten.

'A couple of hours.'

'My dad's on a big ship,' said the boy, leaning forward to address Mr Thomas confidingly. He was a little younger.

'That's nice,' said Mr Thomas. 'My son's on a big boat as well.'

'You gonner see him?'

'Yes, son.'

'My dad's on the *Rodney*. What's your man on?'

Mary and Liz grinned at each other: these children were as excited as they were.

'My boy's on the *Marley*.'

'Is it big?'

'I think so.'

Mary was studying the little boy. 'And how old are you?' she asked him.

'I'm six now.'

'I have a young brother, his name's Eddie. What's your name?'

'I'm Charlie and my sister's called Amy. How old is your brother?'

'Four.'

'Does he go to school?'

25

Mary quickly glanced at Liz. 'Not yet.'

'Dad, d'you think we could have our sandwiches?' said Liz.

'That's a good idea,' said her father. 'I'm starving. What you got in yours, Mary?'

'Only cheese.'

'I'll swap you a fish paste,' said Liz.

Mary handed over one of her sandwiches. 'I thought I might be too excited to eat, but I'm starving.'

Everybody was smiling. The children were also enjoying their packed lunch. As they ate, they struck up a conversation with their mother and discovered she was very knowledgeable about Portsmouth; she had been there many times. When Liz told her they were going to stay the night she asked them where they were lodging.

'Don't know. Me dad's gonner find us a room for the night. It's gotter be cheap. Don't fancy sleeping under the pier.'

'Do you want a word of advice?' asked the lady.

'Yes, please,' said Liz.

'When you get out of the station turn to the right and head towards the High Street. There're a lot of side streets down there and quite a few of the sailors' wives do bed and breakfast this week. You don't want to go the other way, as there are places there that cater for other things.' She blushed as she added softly to Mr Thomas: 'You know what I mean?'

'Yes. Yes, I do. Thank you,' said Mr Thomas.

With the warm sun streaming through the window and the steady rhythm of the train Mr Thomas was soon nodding off. Liz and Mary were too busy looking out of the window and at every station they watched the people get on, admiring the fashionable clothes many wore.

'I can't see the sea yet,' complained Liz after a while.

'Do we get out here?' asked Mary, jumping up when the train pulled into Portsmouth and Southsea.

'No, it's the next stop,' said the lady.

At Portsmouth Harbour the train slowly came to a halt and everybody spilled out on to the platform. Liz and Mary followed, then stopped on the station, looking completely bewildered.

'Just follow the crowd,' said the lady kindly.

Mr Thomas doffed his hat. 'Thanks very much for all your advice. Right, girls, best foot forward. I think that first of all we'd better try and find you a room,' he said. 'So keep your eyes peeled for any houses that have got a "Rooms To Let" sign in the window.'

Soon they were swallowed up in the mass of people.

They passed several houses that looked dirty and unkempt, but then Mr Thomas stopped outside one of the terraced houses with a 'Room To Let' sign in the window. The brass doorknocker shone in the bright sunlight. Mary looked at the curtains. Her mother always said you could tell the sort of woman who lived there by the state of her windows and her curtains. This house had sparkling windows and the lace curtains gently moving in the breeze looked fresh and white, so Mary knew her mother would have approved of it. The doorstep on the pavement was also white.

A warm friendly woman who introduced herself as Mrs Johns took them upstairs to their room. It was clean, homely and bright, and the twin beds were covered with pretty floral bedspreads.

'The other room is mine. I do let it out when I have a family staying, but your father said he's not staying the night?'

'No, he has to get back,' said Liz, walking over to the window.

'Would you like a cup of tea?' asked Mrs Johns.

'Thank you, that would be very nice,' said Mary.

27

'This is lovely,' said Liz, bouncing on one of the beds as soon as they were alone. 'You can sleep near the door.'

'Thanks,' said Mary, putting her small case on the bed. Oh, she *was* going to enjoy these couple of days!

When the girls went downstairs they found Mr Thomas drinking his tea.

'This is grand,' said Mr Thomas, looking round the front room. 'I think you've landed on yer feet here, girls,' he whispered.

Mrs Johns came into the room. 'I'll tell you how to get to the best places to see the ships. You say your son's on the *Marley*?'

Mary and Liz didn't really want to worry about tea, they wanted to go out and join the throng of people. They were beside themselves with excitement. But they swallowed their impatience, and after tea and a bit of social chit-chat they were on their way to the docks where the sight of the big ships took Mary's breath away.

'Look at the size of all these boats, and look at all these sailors!' said Mary as her head turned this way and that.

'Well, you'd expect to see 'em down here,' said Liz.

'Look, Liz.' Mary pointed at a very old ship. 'I think that's called the *Victory*. I'd like to go over that.'

'We'll have to ask Billy, that's if we can find him in this lot.'

'I'll ask someone to tell us where his ship is,' said her father.

Mr Thomas went and spoke to a sailor with peaked cap and gold braid up his arm.

'I reckon he's an officer,' said Liz, nudging Mary. 'He looks a bit of all right.'

'A bit old,' said Mary.

'S'pose he is.'

The girls watched Mr Thomas and the officer talking. After a lot of pointing, Liz's dad came back.

28

'Right, girls. This way.'

When they reached the ship, they looked up at its tall sides in awe.

'Can we go on it?' asked Mary.

'Course. That's what Navy Days is all about.' Mr Thomas began to walk up the gangplank and the girls followed.

They were getting plenty of looks from the sailors and one or two winked at them. Mary felt silly and giggly. She had never seen this many nice-looking young men before.

'Welcome aboard,' said the young man at the top.

'I'm looking for me son. Billy. William Thomas.'

'Sailor,' he called out. 'Go and find Able Seaman Thomas. He's down below.'

'Yes, sir.' The sailor saluted, turned smartly and quickly walked away.

A few moments later Billy came in view. He looked so handsome, Mary felt her knees buckle.

'Take your family down below, sailor.'

Billy gave a smart salute. 'Yes, sir.' He gave the girls a grin. 'Follow me.'

Mary was so happy. She knew she was going to enjoy these two days and meeting Billy was already a bonus.

# Chapter 4

'How's Mum and the kids?' asked Billy over his shoulder as they made their way down below.

'They're fine. Looking forward to seeing you again, son.'

'Me too. This way. We can go in the mess; they've laid out tea for relations. I say, little sis, I can see that now you're growing up you've not turned out to be bad-looking; I'll have to watch out for you, I can see some of this lot are giving you the eye.'

Liz giggled. 'You don't look half bad yourself, you look taller. Was it a good trip?' she asked, walking close to her brother.

'Not bad.'

'You look ever so smart in that uniform.'

He rearranged his hat. 'I should hope so. That's why I joined the navy, so that I could have all the women swooning over me. You should see me in me whites, I look dead handsome.'

'What's yer whites then, son?'

'It's the uniform we wear in hot countries. We wear shorts so we get our knees all lovely and brown.'

Mary's heart skipped a beat as she imagined him dressed in white shorts.

Billy pushed open a door. 'In here.' As Mary passed him he said, 'And you must be Mary.'

She nodded.

'I've heard a lot about you.'

'All good, I hope.'

'Sis, you didn't tell me what a looker she is, she's even better-looking than you.'

Mary blushed.

'Billy. Sit down and tell us all about where you've been and, what's more important, when will you be home?' said Mr Thomas.

'At the end of the month, I've got twenty-one days' leave, so watch out, Mary, I shall be calling round your house to take you out.'

Mary was on cloud nine.

'See? I told you what he was like,' said Liz. 'Me and Mary are staying down here for the night so can you get tonight off and show us the sights?'

'I should say so. You staying as well, Dad?'

'No, I've got to get back. But you look after these girls.'

'I will. Where are you staying?'

'I've got them in with a woman in Oyster Street. She seems a nice little old lady. It looks very homely.'

'That's all right then. Right, how about a cuppa?'

'Can't you show us round?' asked Liz.

'I can show you round this ship, but I can't leave till I get off duty tonight.'

'That's fine. We'll have our tea, then we can see what you do on this boat,' said Mr Thomas, settling himself down.

'She's a ship, Dad. Never call it a boat.'

Mary giggled.

'And she's a she.'

When they finished their tea and walked out of the mess Billy touched Mary's arm. 'I'm glad Liz brought you down here.'

31

She could hardly speak. His touch had thrilled her in a way she had never known before. 'So am I,' she said, smiling up at him. Billy was head and shoulders taller than her; his dark hair was lighter than his photograph.

They had their tour of the ship, then Billy told them what were the best things to see while they were here in the dockyard.

'I must go, I'll see you two at the gates after six.' He hurriedly kissed Liz's cheek and disappeared.

Mary watched him stride away. He was so poised and sure of himself but not in a show-offy kind of way.

'He seems to be enjoying himself,' said Mr Thomas.

'Sounds like it,' said Liz. 'That'll please Mum, she worries about him so much.'

'Well, he certainly liked being in the Mediterranean,' said her dad.

'It must be nice being a boy and to be able to go off like that seeing the world,' said Mary. She was looking back at the ship, hoping to catch sight of Billy.

'And get paid for it,' said Liz.

'It ain't all honey, you know, he has to work hard,' said her father.

'I know, but it still must be better working in the sun and not stuck in a factory day after day.'

'Could be. Now, where to, girls?'

'You choose, Dad,' said Liz. 'You've got to go back tonight, we've got all day tomorrow to see what we want to.'

'I'm really looking forward to going to the fair tonight,' said Mary.

Liz hugged herself. 'Me too. Billy made everything sound so exciting.'

Mary would have liked to add: it's even more exciting now I've met your brother.

32

For the rest of the afternoon they wandered round admiring the ships.

'What train are you catching, Dad?'

'Why, you trying to get rid of me?'

'No, course not.'

'I'll leave about eight.'

'You're not coming to the fair with us then?'

'Why's that, frightened I'll cramp your style?'

'No,' said Liz petulantly.

'I just want to see Billy again, that's all. You know, take him for a drink.'

He wasn't the only one who wanted to see Billy again. Mary was really looking forward to it.

They made their way back to Mrs Johns's house. Inside they rushed up to their room to get ready for their big night out. They giggled as they got dressed.

'What d'you think?' Liz asked Mary as she stood in front of the mirror, smoothing down the skirt of her blue frock.

'It's lovely. I like those little sleeves. Are you taking a cardie?' said Mary.

'Better.'

'What about mine, is it all right?' Mary twirled round to give Liz a full view of her delicate floral frock.

'That's really nice. Did your mum make it?'

'Yes. She was a bit worried about this boat neckline, what d'you think? Does it lay flat?'

'Yes. I think it's really nice. Now, you ready?'

Mary nodded.

'Well, let's go.'

Mr Thomas was sitting outside on a wall waiting for them and when they came out he wasn't happy about the time they had taken.

'But, Dad, we've got to look our best.'

'Don't take this long, does it? Come on, I'm starving.' He ground his cigarette end under his boot.

'Don't be such an old grouch,' said Liz as she tucked her arm through his.

'We've got time to get a bite to eat before we see Billy. Mrs Johns said there's plenty of cheap places round and about. Fancy a bit of fish and chips?'

'That's fine with me,' said Liz.

'Me too,' said Mary.

After they'd eaten they strolled back to the docks. It was a warm evening and Mary was feeling full of anticipation.

When the sailors poured out of the docks, it was a swarm of blue. Everyone looked alike. Many ran into the arms of girlfriends and wives. Billy spotted them before they saw him.

'I must say you two look nice. It's gonner be a real pleasure taking you out tonight. I did think of bringing a mate, but decided I wanted to be seen with two lovelies on me own.'

'You rotten thing.' Liz playfully punched her brother's arm. 'It would have been nice to have another bloke with us. I quite fancy going out with a sailor.'

'I'll see what I can do for you.'

'D'you fancy a drink, lad?'

'I should say so. Thirsty work on a ship.'

'I did see there was plenty of pubs about.'

'That's one thing, you could never die of thirst round here. Mind you, there are some you steer clear of, that's unless you fancy getting in a fight.'

Billy took them to a pub away from the docks. Mary felt very grown up; this was the first time she'd been inside a pub. Billy told them this was one of the better ones – well, Mary thought as she looked around her, if that was so, she dreaded to think what the others were like. The floor was sticky with beer, and it looked as if the dog ends had been ground in for years.

'Right, girls, what you drinking?' asked Billy.

'Get them a ginger beer,' said Mr Thomas. 'They're both under age.'

'Oh, Dad,' said Liz.

'I don't care. I promised your mother I'd look after you.'

'I ain't getting meself arrested if you're both under age, so you'll have ginger beer,' said Billy. 'Go and sit outside and I'll bring it out.'

They did as they were told.

'My dad's rotten not letting us have a proper drink.'

'I don't mind.' Mary sat on her hands and leaned forward. 'It's really lovely sitting here looking at the ships. To think, somewhere out there are the King and Queen. I'm so glad you asked me to come with you.'

'It is nice down here,' said Liz. 'Me mum wouldn't have let me stay if I'd been on me own. I wonder what fun we'll have tonight?'

Mary giggled. 'I'm glad that Mrs Johns gave us the key.'

'So am I. I wouldn't fancy waking her up.'

'She's all right.'

'Not if she was woken up.'

'P'r'aps not.'

Billy and his dad came out with their drinks.

'Well, here's to you,' said Billy, raising his glass. 'Happy holiday.' He gave Mary a wink and her stomach churned.

They chatted companionably until it was time for Mr Thomas to leave. After taking him to the station they said their goodbyes, then they made their way to where Billy said they could catch the tram to the top of the hill.

'Is that where the fair is?' asked Mary.

'That's right.'

'Is it very big?' asked Liz.

'You'll have to wait and see. Here's the tram.'

It was very crowded and as Billy ushered them along the lower deck he put his arm round Mary's waist to steady her when the tram swayed.

Mary turned this way and that, eager not to miss anything as the tram left the city and chugged up the big hill.

At the top Billy said, 'Right, girls. This is it.'

They stood looking at the fair with its big swing boats, musical horses and other hurdy-gurdies. Liz squeezed Mary's arm. 'It's ever so big. I think it's even bigger than Blackheath.'

Mary thought her face would split in half she was smiling so much. 'Look at the view,' she whispered. 'It's wonderful.'

'Wait till it's dark, it's really smashing up here.'

'You been up here much then, Billy?' asked Liz.

'A few times.'

Liz laughed. 'And I bet you wasn't on your own.'

'I was to start with.'

Mary felt a pang of jealousy. But she knew she wasn't going to be the first girl Billy had been out with.

They went on all the rides and laughed so much that Mary thought her head wouldn't stop spinning. She was so happy.

'Look,' yelled Liz, trying to make herself heard above the hurdy-gurdy music, which was belting out. 'Madam Za Za. She'll tell you yer future for sixpence. Shall we have a go?'

Billy came up to Mary. 'I can save you sixpence. I can tell you yer future.'

'Don't listen to him,' said Liz. 'I bet he says that to all his girlfriends.'

'She can see right through me,' he said, laughing.

Mary was a little upset at that. 'You go in first,' Mary said to Liz.

'All right.'

After a few minutes she came out smiling. 'You'll never guess. She said I'd be going out with a sailor. And I'll have a long and happy life.'

'She saw me and I reckon she thought we was sweethearts. Right, your turn, Mary, and I bet she tells you the same thing,' said Billy.

'Well, she ain't gonner tell me I'm gonner drop dead next week, is she?'

'No,' laughed Billy. 'If she does you'd better ask for yer money back.'

Mary was full of apprehension as she went inside the dark tent. Madam Za Za was sitting at a round table covered with a dark cloth; she had a glass ball in front of her. She was draped in what looked like old rags. On her head was a band with jangly bits like coins hanging down. Her fingers were covered with rings; the stones caught the light from the flickering candles, and her many bracelets jingled when she moved.

She held out her hand. 'Sixpence first.'

Mary handed her money over.

'Sit down, love, and give me your hand.' She took Mary's palm in her own gnarled, bent fingers; she studied it for a moment or two, then looked up. 'You're not very happy, are you?'

'Yes. Yes I am.'

'You seem to have a very heavy burden on your young shoulders. It's to do with your family.'

Mary shuddered.

The old lady said, 'It's going to take time to resolve itself, I'm afraid. I see a very rocky road ahead for you.' She looked up again and smiled. 'But it will all turn out well in the end. Very soon you are going to meet a dark, handsome man. You both have something in common and you will be very happy.'

She patted Mary's hand. 'Believe me, it will work out fine for you but you must give it time. You are a sensitive and loving young lady.' She sat back. 'That's it.'

Mary sat for a moment or two taking in what had been said to her.

'You can go now. The reading's over.' Madam Za Za began straightening the cloth in front of her.

'Thank you.'

'Well, what did she tell you?' asked Liz.

'She said I had a burden. But it will all sort itself out.'

Liz laughed. 'That it? What about meeting a bloke?'

Mary smiled. 'She said I'd meet a dark, handsome man and we'd have a lot in common.'

'Well, that's something, I suppose.' Liz nudged Mary. 'My brother's dark and handsome and you both know me, so that's it. Come on, let's have a go on the chair-o-planes.'

'Why not.' Mary wasn't going to mention the rocky road. Could Madam Za Za have been talking about Eddie? 'Where's Billy?'

'Talking to that sailor over there. He looks a bit of all right. I hope he brings him over.'

Then Billy turned and caught sight of them; he waved and sauntered over. To Liz's joy he brought his friend over as well.

'Liz and Mary, this is Pete. He's on our ship.'

'Hello,' said Liz and Mary together.

'Just to get things straight: Liz is me sister and Mary's me girl.'

Billy took her arm possessively. He had called her his girl. Mary knew then that this was going to be a wonderful weekend.

# Chapter 5

For the rest of the evening they laughed and joked as they went on all the rides. The boys managed to win them a cuddly toy each on the darts, and coconuts on the coconut shies. After failing to prove their strength by hitting a block with a hammer to make the bell ring, they wanted to show them how tough they really were when they stood outside the boxing booth, but the girls objected. The man with the big cigar was urging the boys to come in and fight the two thin, weedy, ugly-looking men who were up on the stage dancing about in front of them.

'Don't you dare,' said Liz to her brother. 'I ain't carrying you back to your boat.'

Billy laughed. 'Ship.'

'Whatever it is, I ain't carrying you back.'

'And I don't want you coming round to my house if you end up looking like those two.' Mary pointed to the men.

Billy held up his hands. 'All right. You've just talked me out of it. They've probably got tougher blokes inside.'

They moved on and the girls had a lot of fun running pennies down a wooden slope, clapping and squealing with excitement when they landed on a square that won them money. Mary thought that Blackheath was never like this; she never had a good-looking sailor standing close to her there.

'The girls will like this,' said Liz, holding up the toy dog Pete had just won for her.

'And Eddie will love this,' said Mary, cuddling a teddy bear to her. 'Thank you,' she said to Billy.

'Who's Eddie?' asked Billy.

'My young brother.'

They wandered around and, although it was dark, the lights and the tinny music from the fairground organs were magical. After a while, exhausted through laughing and being thrown about on so many rides, the four walked away from the fair and stood on the hill looking over Portsmouth with all the lights flickering below.

Billy had his arm round Mary's waist. 'Not a bad view, is it?'

'I think it's wonderful. You must have seen some lovely sights on your trips.'

'We have. New York is great when it comes into view with that massive Statue of Liberty. Some places ain't so good, they're hot, noisy and stink, but it's a great life and I wouldn't swap it for a job on land.'

Mary sighed with contentment as she watched Liz and Pete, with their arms round each other's waist, move a bit further away. They stopped; Liz had her arms round Pete's neck and was letting him kiss her.

'Looks like they're enjoying themselves,' said Billy, holding Mary closer. 'Can I kiss you?'

She held up her face.

It was a warm soft kiss that he gave her.

'Can I take you out when I get home?'

'Yes, please.'

Billy laughed. 'I've never had a girl say that to me before.'

'What do they normally say?' asked Mary, feeling embarrassed.

'Now that would be telling.' He kissed her again; this time

with a little more passion, which she enjoyed.

'I think we'd better get back,' said Liz, coming up to Mary and Billy. 'Will we be able to see you tomorrow?' she asked her brother.

'Only for a while. What train're you catching?'

'Don't know. We don't have to go till the evening, we ain't got to go to work on Monday.'

'Can't you stay till Monday?' asked Pete.

Liz smiled. 'No. Me mum'll be worried if we don't go home. Besides, we can't afford it.'

Mary stood close to Billy. 'I wish we could stay,' she said softly.

'Me too,' he said, squeezing her round the waist. 'Look, me and Pete will take you back to your lodgings.'

'That's good,' said Liz, putting her arm through Pete's.

Once again they found themselves on the tram and heading back into Portsmouth.

They stood a while saying goodnight at Mrs Johns's door, then the girls let themselves in. Quietly they began to creep up the stairs, but they had only gone a few steps when the kitchen door opened.

'You're back then,' said Mrs Johns.

'I'm— We're sorry, did we wake you?' asked Mary cautiously.

'No, I was just sitting listening to the wireless. D'you fancy a cup of cocoa?'

Mary looked at Liz. 'Is that all right?'

'Yes, that'll be very nice. Thank you,' said Liz.

'Come in here and tell me all what you did tonight. Have you been out with your brother?'

'Yes, we went up to the fair.'

'Thought so. They look nice,' she said, pointing to the cuddly toys and the coconuts.

'The boys won them for us,' said Mary. 'We had ever such a good time. We went on all the rides.'

'That's nice. Used to go up there with me husband. He passed away a few years back. I still miss him. Never had any kids. He was in the navy. I take in visitors to help out. You seem a nice family,' she said to Liz as the kettle boiled. 'I don't usually take in young girls on their own. Always worried they might be up to no good.'

Liz giggled. 'Don't think me dad and brother would stand for that.'

'No, that's what I thought when I saw him. I normally have families, but the kids can be a bit of trouble, specially if they wet the bed.' She pushed the cups of cocoa in front of them.

'I can promise you we won't do that,' said Liz with a grin.

Mrs Johns smiled. 'It's nice to have well-behaved young ladies around. It's a pity you're only staying the one night.'

'We would have liked to stay a bit longer, but our mums will be worried,' said Mary.

'Well, if you ever come down this way again, come and see me.'

'We will,' said Mary.

When they'd finished their drinks they said their goodnights and went up to their room.

'She don't seem a bad old stick,' said Liz as she pulled her nightie over her head.

'No, it'll be good to have a place to come to if we ever come down here again. I really like it. I'd like to live here. Perhaps I could get Dad to move to Portsmouth. He's always talking about moving from Rotherhithe.'

'That'll be good, then I'd have somewhere to stay and it wouldn't cost me,' laughed Liz.

They turned out the light and despite the day's excitement they soon settled down.

'Do you really like my brother?' Liz's voice came out of the darkness.

'Yes, I do. Do you like Pete?'

'Yes. I'm gonner write to him.'

'That'll be nice for you. Where does he live?'

'Didn't ask. I'll write to him on board. Here, d'you reckon Billy's the one that Madam Za Za was talking about? You know, you'd meet someone and you'd have a lot in common?'

'Dunno.'

'It would be lovely if you and him got together.'

Mary didn't answer. It suddenly came back to her what she'd been told about having a heavy burden to bear that was to do with the family. But how could Madam Za Za know about Eddie?

The sun was streaming through the window when Mary opened her eyes. There was a faint knock on the door.

'Are you awake, girls?'

'Yes,' said Mary, rubbing the sleep from her eyes and getting out of bed. She opened the door. 'Good morning,' she said to Mrs Johns, who was standing in the doorway holding two cups.

'Good morning. I've brought you both a cup of tea and there's some hot water to wash with.' She nodded towards an enamel jug sitting on the floor.

'Thank you, that's very kind of you.'

'Come down when you're ready. Your breakfast is in the oven.'

'What's happening?' asked Liz, sitting up. Her hair was all over the place and she still looked half asleep.

'Mrs Johns brought us some tea.' Mary took the tea and went back for the jug of hot water. 'We'll be down soon,' she called as Mrs Johns walked down the stairs.

Mary went over to the window. They were in the front bedroom and Mary looked up and down the road. 'It's a smashing day and listen to them seagulls, don't they make a racket?'

'Are you always as cheerful as this in the mornings?'

Mary laughed and sat on Liz's bed and started to drink her tea. 'I am when I'm happy. What shall we do today?'

'Let's go and explore the beach.'

'That's sounds a good idea.' Mary quickly finished her tea. 'I'll wash first.' After taking the pretty china jug from out of the matching basin, she carefully poured some hot water from the enamel jug into the basin and began to wash. When she'd finished, she poured her dirty water into the empty china jug. 'Your turn,' she said to Liz, who had snuggled back down under the bedclothes.

Liz stood up in her petticoat. 'This is a nice room, and I love this washstand.' She ran her hands over the marble top. 'I wish we had something like this.'

'You might get one when you're married.'

'And a room of me own. That's something I'd really like. You're very lucky like that.' Liz peered in the mirror that hung over the washstand and pulled a face. 'Mind you, I won't mind sharing it with a handsome man. I hope someone will make me his bride.'

'They will one day.'

'Let's hope it'll be soon.'

'Why, you're not fed up at home, are you?'

'No, but it would be nice not to share a room with two of your sisters.'

Mary laughed. 'It'll come one day.'

The beach was very crowded with holidaymakers and the atmosphere was wonderful: kids playing; mums and dads paddling and shouting at the kids when they ran off; small boats bobbing about and taking people for trips round the harbour. The girls spent the day exploring the beach, finding shells and having a paddle. Then they sat on the pier. They watched the children playing on the beach and Mary's thoughts went back to Eddie. If only he could be like these children, laughing and running about enjoying himself.

'I shall be sorry to go back home,' said Liz.

'So will I.' Mary turned to face Liz. 'Could we do this again, before winter?'

'Dunno. Not sure I could find enough money. It's all right for you, you don't have to give up as much as me.'

'That's true.' Mary knew Mr Thomas didn't earn as much as Ted and they had three kids at home, including Liz, to feed.

'We could save up and come back at Easter. Pete said they might only be gone on a short trip this time, so they could be back here in Portsmouth.'

'That would be great.' Mary sat back and closed her eyes, letting the warm sun comfort her. She was so content.

When the boys left the ship they walked to the station with the girls. Liz and Pete fell behind and were deep in conversation. All too soon they were on the platform waiting for their train to take them back home.

'I'll see you at the end of the month,' said Billy as he kissed his sister. 'And you,' he said to Mary as he held her close.

'I'm really looking forward to that.'

The noise all around and the steam gushing from the train was so loud as they got on board that, even though they were shouting, they had trouble hearing each other. The girls hung out of the window and as the train slowly pulled away the boys ran with it.

Mary laughed as she tried to hold Billy's hand but all too soon his fingers slipped away and he was left behind.

She plonked down in the seat. 'I can't ever remember having such a good time.'

'Or me,' said Liz. 'By the way, Pete lives in Surrey, it sounds a bit posh.'

'Is he going to see you again?'

'He said he wants to. I really like him, Mary.'

'Liz, he's the first bloke you've been out with.'

'I know, but don't you believe in love at first sight?'

Mary wanted to admit that she did.

They were unusually silent as they watched the countryside give way to buildings; eventually they were rushing between houses crammed close together. Despite her happiness, Mary couldn't help thinking about what awaited her at home. Had Eddie been good, or had there been tears and tantrums today? If only Eddie could be like other children, then her life would be perfect.

# Chapter 6

The kitchen door burst open as soon as Mary had pulled the key through the letterbox.

'Mary!' called her mother from the kitchen doorway as she hurried along the passage to greet her daughter. 'You're home.'

Mary kissed her mother's cheek.

'It's good to see you. I did miss you. Did you have a nice time? You've caught the sun, look at your nose.' She ushered Mary into the kitchen. 'Look, Ted, Mary's caught the sun.'

'You certainly have, young lady. Did you have a good time?'

'Yes, I did. It was wonderful. I've got you a stick of rock, Mum, and Billy, that's Liz's brother, won this for Eddie.' She took the teddy bear from her bag. 'Is he in bed? Can I go and see him?'

'No, leave him, he's been a very naughty boy since you've been away, hasn't he, Ted?'

'I'm afraid so. Much as I didn't want to, I had to take my belt to him this time,' said Ted.

Mary gasped.

'But it was only lightly. You didn't really hurt him, love, did you?' Sarah gently touched Ted's arm.

'No, but I had to show him who's in charge.'

'What did he do?' asked Mary softly.

'It doesn't matter now,' said her mother. 'Tell us what *you* did.'

Mary began to tell them about Mrs Johns, Billy, the fair and even about Madam Za Za.

'You didn't waste your money on that kind of rubbish, did you?' asked Ted.

Sarah laughed. 'Oh, don't be such a spoilsport. Everybody wants to know what the future has in store for them.'

'I don't.'

'Take no notice of old Grumpy. What did she tell you?'

Mary was careful what she said; she didn't want to tell them about the problems she might have at home, so she told them she was going to meet someone who had the same interests as her.

'See, I told you it was just a waste of money.'

Mary smiled. 'But it was all part of the fun.' She tried to laugh but her heart wasn't in it. She wanted to see Eddie. Had Ted hurt him?

'And what about Liz's brother? Was he nice?'

Mary blushed. 'Yes, he was.'

'Do you think he was the one that woman meant?'

Mary shrugged.

'She would say that if she saw them together.'

'Ted, stop it. Is this boy coming home?'

'Yes, he'll be here at the end of the month.'

'And will you be seeing him again?'

'*Mum.*'

'Sarah, don't be so inquisitive.'

'I only asked.'

'He did say he would like to take me out again.'

'Good for you, girl,' said Ted. 'Now, Sarah, give it a rest.'

Mary grinned at her mother. 'He may change his mind when he gets here.'

'He'll be a fool if he does,' said Ted.

That night Mary lay thinking about Billy. Would he change his mind when he knew about Eddie? She hoped not.

The following morning Mary heard her mother moving about downstairs. When she heard the front door close, she knew Ted had gone over the road to get his paper. She looked round the door of her mother's room. The double bed and Eddie's cot were empty.

She quickly dressed and hurried downstairs. Eddie was tied in his chair. When he saw Mary he buried his head and made noises.

'Can I take him out, Mum?' she asked.

'Has he finished?' her mother called from the scullery.

'I think so.' She gently lifted him down. 'My, you're getting to be a big heavy lump.'

Eddie fell to the ground and held on to Mary's legs tight. She knelt down beside him. 'What is it? What's wrong? Look what I've got for you.' She showed him the teddy bear.

Eddie quickly hid from it.

'Come on, Eddie. Hold it.'

'No. No. No.' He was violently shaking his head and burying his head in her skirt.

'Leave him, love. He'll come round to it in his own way,' said her mother, coming into the kitchen. 'You know what he's like now with anything new.'

'Where did Dad hit him?' asked Mary as she looked over Eddie's legs and arms.

'I just think he tapped him, he didn't do any harm.'

'What did Eddie do?' asked Mary.

'He threw his shoes down the lav.'

Mary wanted to laugh. 'And he got the belt for that?'

'Ted had had a bad day. I think he lost some money on the horses.'

'Oh.' Mary was upset. She wanted to say that just because Ted had lost some money, he shouldn't take it out on his son. But she decided to hold her tongue, and began telling her mother about Portsmouth again. 'It's really lovely down there. I wish we could move there. Eddie would love it with all the boats and the sea. Dad's always saying he wants to move.'

'Mary, you do have some wild ideas at times. We have to think of Ted's job; we just can't up and go on a whim.'

'I know, but I can tell him all about it.'

At that moment Ted walked into the kitchen with his newspaper under his arm. 'The news don't seem to get any better.'

'What's wrong?'

'Hitler is now head of state in Germany. I don't like the look of things.'

'Germany's a long way away, surely it can't possibly affect us?'

'That's what we said the last time and look what happened then. The Germans like war.'

'We won't have another war, will we?'

'Wouldn't like to say.'

Sarah preferred not knowing about things that were happening elsewhere. 'I'll get your breakfast,' she said, going into the scullery.

Mary didn't want to think about war either, and said, 'Dad, I was telling Mum how much I liked Portsmouth.'

'Oh yes.' He didn't look up from his paper.

'I was wondering if we could move down there?'

He lowered his paper. 'What? Whatever for?'

'It's very nice.'

'I dare say it is, but I wouldn't want to live there.'

'I just thought I'd ask.'

Sarah came in with Ted's breakfast. 'Perhaps we could go there for the day, Ted? From what Mary was saying it does sound rather nice.'

'Not the sort of place I want to visit.'

'Why's that?' asked Mary.

'Too many drunken sailors trying to throw their weight about. And what about the stink?'

'What stink?' asked Mary.

'Rotting fish and seaweed.'

'I didn't smell anything like that,' laughed Mary.

'It's there, believe me.' Ted picked up his knife and fork and began on his breakfast.

'It was just an idea . . .'

When they'd finished breakfast, Mary asked, 'As it's such a nice day, could we all go out somewhere later on?'

'You've only just come home,' said Sarah.

'I know, but I fancy going out today.' Mary knew she was pouting.

'You're getting very restless, young lady. Just be content with staying here and keeping your mother company.'

'But you'll be here.'

'I have to go out later.'

'What about me and you going out then, Mum?'

Sarah looked at Ted. 'No, I don't think so.'

'Why not?'

'I have things to do.'

But Mary really didn't want to be stuck in on such a lovely day. 'If you don't want to go out with me then perhaps I could take Eddie for a walk somewhere.'

'I don't know.'

'Please, Mum.'

'It's so unusual for a young girl to want to take her young brother out with her.'

Mary began picking at the tablecloth. 'Ain't got no one else.'

'Till the sailor comes home,' said Ted.

'That's not for a few weeks. I'll get his shoes,' said Mary.

'They're on the top of the gas stove. I think they've dried out. Mary, do you really want to take him?'

'Yes, Mum. Why?'

'Well, he's a bit of a handful.'

Mary smiled at her half-brother. 'I know, but he's all right with me.'

'Well, I'm not so sure,' said Ted, folding his newspaper.

Mary walked over to Eddie who was as usual sitting on the floor carefully lining up his trains. 'Don't worry. He'll be all right. I'll go round and see Liz.'

'But will Liz want to see him?'

Mary thought about that and decided against it. 'I expect she's busy helping her mum. But we'll still go out. I'll get his coat.'

Sarah stood at the door and watched them go. She loved her son, but he was causing problems all round. Please let him behave, said Sarah silently to herself.

Mary held Eddie's hand and they strolled up Doyle Street. Eddie's latest phobia was the joints between the paving stones. Mary made a joke of it as he carefully walked along trying not to step on them; she giggled and did the same as they made their way towards the park.

'Now, Eddie, say Mary. Come on, say Mary.'

He laughed and shook his head.

'Mary. Mary,' repeated Mary.

He said nothing.

'You will talk one day.'

'No. No. No.' He was still shaking his head.

'Yes. Yes. Yes.' She laughed and they went happily on their way.

'What time do you have to go out, Ted?' asked Sarah as she cleared the table.

'Very shortly.'

'That's a shame. Is it work?'

'Sort of.'

'I think it's wrong expecting you to work on a bank holiday. Will you be gone long?'

'Don't know. You must remember that things are getting bad and we have to be seen to be making an effort.'

'I know, but it's still such a pity. We could have all gone to Blackheath this afternoon.'

'You sound like Mary. Are you restless as well?'

'No. It's just that I do get a little tired being here every day with just Eddie for company. It wouldn't be so bad if he could speak.'

'He will one day, he's just lazy.'

'It would be nice if he would let me read to him. I used to enjoy reading to Mary when she was little. If he went to school then perhaps I could join a ladies' club or something.'

Ted stood up. 'We've tried that, remember, and they sent him home.'

'But what if we try again?'

'No.'

'Could we afford some kind of teacher for him?'

'My dear woman, d'you think I'm made of money? What have I just been telling you?'

'I'm sorry. I must be feeling a bit down.'

'Come on, Sarah. This is not like you. Has that daughter of

53

yours been putting silly ideas in your head?'

Sarah smiled. 'No, of course not.'

'Well, I'm off. I hope to be back fairly soon.'

Sarah studied her husband when he came back downstairs. He was wearing his dark grey suit and carrying his grey trilby. He was so handsome.

'You look very smart,' said Sarah.

'Thank you.'

'It must be somewhere special.'

'It is. I have to keep in with the boss.' Very slowly he brushed his hand round the rim of his hat and, standing in front of the mirror over the fireplace, put it on at a jaunty angle. He smiled at her through the mirror. He still made Sarah's heart flutter; he was such an attractive man. Sarah knew she had been so very lucky to marry him.

'You will be back for dinner?'

'I'll try.' He kissed her cheek and left.

Sarah sighed after he closed the door. For a while now she had noticed that Ted had changed. Was it her imagination that he didn't seem as loving, or was it because she was always tired these days? He did do a lot of extra hours at work and didn't have a lot of patience with Eddie; lately he hardly spoke to him except to chastise him. Was he ashamed of his son? Sarah had to admit he wasn't like other children and she knew Mary thought the same. She was a good girl; not many would be so devoted to a difficult child like Eddie.

Sarah sat at the table and began pleating the green chenille cloth. She knew Mary thought the world of her baby brother. But everything else was certainly very different. Slowly a tear slipped down her cheek. Perhaps it was her fault: was she neglecting Ted? Had she been too possessive with Eddie? But the boy demanded so much of her time . . . She brushed the tear aside and went into the scullery. Sitting moping wouldn't get the breakfast things washed up or the dinner prepared.

When they reached the park, Mary sat on the bench beside Eddie and took hold of his hand. He smiled, although not directly at her. He never looked anyone in the eye. Mary held his hand tight. He was such a good-looking boy and just lately had shown he could be very loving, but it appeared to be only with her. She sat thinking about the way things were at home. Eddie seemed to be frightened of Ted. Had her stepdad hurt him? And why did Eddie just ignore their mother? Was that because she got cross with him a lot? Mary knew that although her mother raised her voice, she would never raise her hand to him. Oh, how hard it must be for her at home with him all the time.

Mary watched the children around them laughing and playing.

'Do you want to play?'

He shook his head.

'You understand everything I say, don't you?'

He just smiled.

'Come on, let's put you on the swings.' But when Mary tried to sit him in one he screamed and yelled so much she had to take him out.

'If you ask me, you wonner give him a bloody good hiding,' said the woman standing next to her, who was swinging her little girl back and forth. 'That'll make him sit up. Kids, who'd have 'em? They're never grateful whatever you try to do for 'em.'

Mary quickly took Eddie's hand and, giving the woman a half-hearted smile, hurried away.

'Eddie,' she said when she was out of earshot. 'You're a naughty boy showing me up like that. I think we'd better go home.'

He was holding her hand tight and when she looked at him she saw tears sparkling like little diamonds on his cheeks. Her heart melted. She bent down and held him close. 'I can't stay angry with you for long, can I? Come on, let me buy you an ice cream.'

By the time they got home Eddie had ice cream all round his face and down his coat, but he was happy and smiling.

'Look at the state of him,' said Sarah when she caught sight of her son.

'Sorry about that, Mum, but at least his coat is washable.'

'Just as well. Did you have a nice time?'

'I tried to get him on the swings.'

'I've tried that. He hates anything different.'

'I know. Dad gone out?'

'Yes.'

'Anywhere special?'

'He didn't say.'

Mary felt a flash of unease at the way things were gradually changing. She didn't realise her fears mirrored those of her mother. She just knew that a few years ago they were always laughing and happy to be together, but now Ted seemed to spend more and more time at work or at the dogs; he rarely took her mother out even when Mary offered to stay home with Eddie. And there was that atmosphere Mary had sensed on more than one occasion.

'Will he be home for dinner?' she asked.

'I don't know. Mary, I'm not sure if Ted will be able to afford both a frock and shoes for your birthday.'

'Why? Are things that bad?'

'He did say we would have to be careful, what with a lot of the men being put off. He just hopes he won't be next.'

Although Mary was very disappointed she tried hard not to show it. 'That's all right.'

'We'll be able to give you the money for your frock, at least.'

'Don't worry, I can get the shoes. Mum, is something wrong? You're looking very sad lately.'

'No, I'm fine.'

But Mary wasn't so sure. There definitely was a kind of tension in this house.

# Chapter 7

It was Saturday and straight after work Mary and Liz were going to Brick Lane to get her new frock, a present from her mum and dad. On 27 August, Mary would be seventeen but as it was on Monday she would be at work.

'What do you think of this?' asked Mary as she held up a very stylish, sleeveless dress in pale blue. It had a dropped waist with an overlay of chiffon.

'It ain't very practical,' said Liz.

'I don't want to be practical,' said Mary.

'Will your mum and dad approve?'

'I don't know. Anyway, I don't care. I want to look nice for when Billy comes home.'

'Mary, please don't get your hopes up too much. Remember our Billy's a sailor and he ain't home all that often. Don't waste your money on something you can only wear once.'

Mary looked downcast. 'Has he said anything to you about me?'

'No. But I don't want you to get yer hopes up.'

'He is still coming home?'

'Yes. Mum had a letter today, as a matter of fact.'

'But he didn't mention me?'

'No.'

Mary looked at the dress and reluctantly put it back on the

rail. Was she being silly falling for Billy? Someone she had hardly met?

'What about this?' Liz was holding up a very nice navy blue one with a large white collar. 'You'll be able to wear this to go to the pictures.'

'I'll try it on.'

When Mary emerged from the changing room Liz grinned. 'It's lovely. And it fits you a treat.'

Mary twirled round. 'It is rather nice and a lot cheaper than the other one. I'll take it: now I can get some navy shoes to go with it.'

Mary arrived home with her packages, eager to show her mother what she'd bought.

'Mum. Mum,' she called out, going from room to room. There was no sign of Sarah or Eddie. Mary put the kettle on the gas and made herself some tea. Then she looked at the clock on the mantelpiece. It was six o'clock. There was a lot of noise from next door. Mary could hear the kids shouting and yelling; it sounded as if they were running wild in there. Where was everybody? Panic began to fill her. Had something happened to Eddie? Where was her dad? He should be home, unless he had gone off to the dogs: after all, it was Saturday night. Would Sadie next door know something? She hurried out into the yard and called for Sadie.

Rosie, Sadie's eldest daughter, came out. 'Hello, Mary, you looking for yer mum?'

'Yes.'

'She's in here. Me mum's having a baby and me and Iris have gotter look after all the kids and your daft Eddie as well.'

'I'll come round.' Mary raced round to their front door.

'Me mum's upstairs,' said Rosie, opening the door. 'It ain't been born yet. Nurse Fox is with 'em. Me mum ain't half making a racket.'

'Where's Eddie?'

'He's upstairs wiv 'em. Yer mum tied him in me little brother's high chair. He tried to run away when yer mum brought him in. He's a funny fing.'

Mary edged her way into the overcrowded passage, pushing her way past a large bassinet that had scruffy furry animals thrown in along with a couple of china dolls. One of the dolls had a cracked face; the other looked scary as the eyes had been poked out. A home-made wooden scooter and other bits and pieces were cluttering up the passage. Mary went up the stairs. Although her footsteps made a lot of noise on the bare treads it couldn't drown out the shouts and screams from the bedroom and downstairs.

Rosie was right behind her. 'Me mum's in this one.'

Mary pushed open the door and saw Eddie in the high chair, which had been pushed over to the window. He was quietly rocking back and forth, completely oblivious of what was going on behind him. Her mother and Nurse Fox were leaning over the bed. Sadie's screams and sobs were heart-rending.

'Mum, can I help?'

Sarah looked up, her face wet with sweat. She ran her hand over her face. 'Mary, thank goodness you're back. Get her out of here,' she cried out, catching sight of Rosie.

Rosie was wide-eyed as she tried to look past Mary at what was going on.

'Mary, you could go downstairs and see if the kids want some tea or something, then come back for Eddie,' said her mother as she went back to the job in hand.

Mary pushed Rosie outside before venturing into the room. Sadie, whose nightdress was pulled up around her waist, was lying on a stained feather mattress covered with bloody newspapers.

'She's worried about the kids' tea,' said Sarah.

'Is she going to be all right?' asked Mary softly.

Sarah didn't answer; she just wrung out a cloth from a chipped white enamel bowl and placed it on Sadie's damp forehead. Sadie's eyes were closed and Mary could see she was very pale.

'Shall I take Eddie now?'

'No, leave him for the moment. He's quite happy gazing out of the window. Just see to the kids.'

Rosie was waiting for her outside the bedroom. She ran her hand under her nose and sniffed. 'Is me mum gonner die?'

'No, course not.'

'She didn't make all this fuss when she had Brian.'

Mary gently eased her down the stairs. 'Let's go and see what we can find for your tea.'

'Ain't got much in the cupboard.'

'Where's yer dad?'

'Up the boozer.'

Mary stood in the doorway of the kitchen. She had been in here before, mostly when Sadie had a new baby to show off. There wasn't a lot of furniture. Two armchairs stood either side of the fireplace. The grate was full of ash and the fire hadn't been cleaned out for days. Odd chairs stood under the table, which had newspapers and old tatty books strewn over it. Sadie's place was always untidy, despite her best efforts, but now it appeared worse than ever.

'Right, let's get this place cleared up and then I'll get you some tea.'

Iris came up to her and tugged at her frock. 'Mary, we ain't got nothing.'

'Well, why don't you go over to the dairy – Mrs West

should still be open – and get three eggs and a loaf of bread. You'd better get some milk as well.'

'She won't give us any more stuff on tick.'

'Tell her Mary Harris sent you and that I'll settle up with her later.'

'Cor, d'you mean that?' asked Ron, who was the eldest of the brood, a tall, skinny, good-looking lad. He was almost fourteen, but mentally he was years older and very streetwise. He couldn't wait to leave school and get a proper job. He did the odd errand or two, but unfortunately when people found out his father was the drunk, Wally Fellows, they quickly sent him packing. Many times he'd told Mary that he hated his father and would leave home if it weren't for his mum. He loved her and didn't want any harm to come to her.

Mary nodded as she began clearing the table.

'Can we have some biscuits as well? We don't ever have biscuits.'

'Ron, stop being greedy,' said Rosie.

'I'll go next door later and get you some broken biscuits.' There were always biscuits in their house as the workers were allowed to buy the broken ones very cheap.

Mary went into the scullery and began to look for a pan. 'Rosie,' she called, opening cupboards that were stuffed full of chipped crocks and dishes. 'Come out here and help me.'

'I was going with Iris.'

'She can manage on her own. Now, where's a pan I can use to do some scrambled eggs in?'

Rosie rummaged in the cupboard and brought out a large iron saucepan. It was very heavy and Rosie had to hold it with both hands.

Mary smiled to herself. 'Is this all you've got?'

'Got one that's a bit bigger.'

'No, this'll do.' Mary could see it had been scrubbed and

polished: Sadie always kept everything clean, even if the house was in a permanent mess.

Mary cleared the kitchen table and asked Rosie where the cloth was.

'We ain't got a proper cloth, we use the old newspapers.'

Mary straightened out a couple of sheets of newspaper and put plates all around.

When Iris came back with the shopping she said, 'Mrs West said make sure you pay her as she don't want you to run up any bills.'

'I'll do that Monday. Now, sit everybody up and I'll do some scrambled eggs.'

As Mary whisked up the eggs and milk, she thought: Was this how Jesus must have felt with the fishes and the loaves? If only she could work miracles. She cut the bread and every plate had some egg and half a slice of bread. She had never seen food disappear so fast.

'When was the last time you had something to eat?'

'Last night,' said Rosie. 'We only had a bit of bread with some fish paste on, then Mum went to bed, she said she had a pain.'

'That could have been me dad she was talking about,' said Ron cheerfully. 'He can be a right pain.'

Mary tried hard to keep a straight face. 'When did my mum come in?'

'I had to run and get Nurse Fox very early this morning. Dad was still sleeping it off. When he went out Nurse Fox told me to go and get yer mum. She wanted to get a doctor but Mum said no, we can't afford it.'

Mary didn't know a lot about babies, but this one did seem a long time coming. 'I'm just going up to see if they would like a cup of tea.' Mary had noted there was some tea in the caddy. 'You twins, see to the washing up.'

Silently they slid from the table.

She gently knocked on the bedroom door. 'Mum. Mum, it's me.' She opened the door. Her mother and Nurse Fox were still standing over Sadie.

'Come on, girl, push,' Nurse Fox was saying to Sadie.

'Mum, would you like a cup of tea?'

'Later.'

'Shall I take Eddie home?'

Sarah looked at her son who was fast asleep in the high chair. She came closer to Mary and whispered, 'Yes, you could do. Have you fed the kids?'

'Yes. If Dad's home I'll come back.'

'All right, love. It shouldn't be long now.'

Mary took Eddie from the chair and led him down the stairs. He was rubbing his eyes and whimpering.

She went into the kitchen. 'I'm just going next door. I'll bring you some biscuits back.'

'Thanks, Mary,' said Rosie.

At home, Mary could see her father still wasn't around so she took Eddie upstairs and quickly undressed him. She gently sang to him and it wasn't long before he was fast asleep once more.

Downstairs she put some biscuits into a paper bag and took them into the yard. 'Rosie? Rosie!' she called.

Why hadn't they heard her? Why hadn't anyone come out? They weren't making that much noise any more – in fact it was strangely quiet.

Mary went back inside and checked that Eddie was still asleep, then went next door. She pushed open the front door and saw some of the kids sitting on the stairs crying.

Fear filled her. Quickly she sat next to Rosie and held her close. 'What is it? What's wrong?' She was dreading the answer.

'The baby. The baby's dead.'

'Oh Rosie, I'm so sorry.'

'We like having new babies, don't we, Iris?'

Iris nodded and after wiping her eyes on the bottom of her frock, blew her nose on it.

'But you've got little Brian.'

'I know, but we wanted a new one. He's getting too big to sit in the pram,' said Rosie.

'And he walks as well,' sniffed Iris.

'We all like the new ones, don't we, twinnies?' said Rosie, poking them in the back.

The twins, who were sitting on the bottom stair sucking their thumbs, nodded vigorously.

Mary couldn't find any words of comfort for these little girls who loved babies. She remembered when they used to take Eddie out in his pram – that was before he started screaming and shouting. Did they think having babies was like having real dolls because they didn't have any decent toy ones?

'Look, I've brought you some broken biscuits. Shall we go into the kitchen and share them out?'

The girls nodded.

When Mary walked into the kitchen she was surprised to see Mr Fellows lolling in the chair. His eyes were closed and his mouth open. He was making dreadful gurgling noises. Mary gave a little cough.

'Hello, girl,' he said, sitting up and looking up at her with his bleary eyes.

'Hello, Mr Fellows,' said Mary.

'Hope they ain't been making too much bleeding noise. I told 'em to keep it down.'

'No, it's fine.'

'Did you get the biscuits, Mary?' asked Ron.

'Yes. Now we've got to share them out fairly.'

'I hear you've been feeding me kids. You didn't have to do that, you know.'

'It was all right. I'm sorry about the baby.'

'No need to be. It would only be another mouth to feed.'

Mary got a plate and tipped the biscuits on to it.

'Cor, look,' yelled Ron, grabbing a couple. 'Some of 'em have got cream in the middle.'

Mary slapped his hand. 'I said we'd share them out properly.'

'That's it, girl, you tell 'em,' said Mr Fellows, grinning at her. She was aware of his dreadful teeth. His suit was stained and dirty. She suddenly felt sorry for Sadie having to live with this man.

'Have you been up to see Sadie?' asked Mary over her shoulder as she carefully divided the biscuits.

'Na. That's women's work, they told me they don't want me hanging about.'

Mary wanted to tell him that it was his wife upstairs and she had been through a terrible time, but she wasn't brave enough. 'Right, that's finished,' she said, straightening up. 'And I don't want anybody telling me that someone has pinched theirs. I'm just going up to see if your mum wants a cup of tea.'

She could hear Mr Fellows laughing as she left the kitchen.

Gently she knocked on the door and pushed it open. 'Mum. It's only me.'

Sarah came over to her. 'How's Eddie?' she whispered.

'He's fast asleep.'

'Is Ted looking after him?'

'No, he's not home yet.'

'What? What time is it?'

'Nine o'clock. How's Sadie?'

'Not good. She's lost a lot of blood.'

Mary looked round the room and saw a small parcel wrapped in newspaper on the floor. 'Is that . . .'

'A little girl,' whispered her mother.

Mary swallowed hard. 'Would you all like a cup of tea?'

Nurse Fox looked up; she had been washing Sadie. 'That would be very nice, thank you.'

'Mr Fellows is downstairs.'

'Yes, we know. He came up here, but Nurse Fox here soon sent him packing.'

'I'll go and make the tea.'

Sarah was thinking about Ted when Mary left the room. She was very cross with him. Where had he been all day? She needed him here. She hoped nothing had happened to him. She had to get home. 'Do you need me any more?' she asked Nurse Fox.

'No, Sarah, but thank you. I don't know how I would have managed without you.' Nurse Fox looked down at Sadie's pale face. She had her eyes closed and looked exhausted. Nurse Fox moved away from the bed and whispered to Sarah, 'It's a pity in some ways, the outcome, but I don't suppose that under the circumstances she's that bothered.'

Sarah gave her a weak smile. 'She would have loved this one just as much as she loves all the others. I'd better get back, just in case Eddie wakes up.'

'Of course. I understand.'

'I'll just tell Mary I won't wait for tea.'

As she went down the stairs Sarah was becoming more and more agitated. It had been a long day with a sad ending. And on top of the tragedy, what was happening to her and Ted? They had always been so happy. Why was he out so often and so late? If it was money he was worried about why couldn't he talk to her? Or perhaps it was Eddie? She knew he was bitterly disappointed with his son. Sarah was aware their son could be a handful, but Eddie needed the love and support of two parents, not just one.

# Chapter 8

Sarah quietly closed the front door and, after checking the kitchen and scullery, hurried up the stairs. She was pleased to see that Eddie was still fast asleep but there wasn't any sign of her husband. It was nearly ten o'clock. Where was Ted? Back downstairs she plonked herself in the armchair. Suddenly she realised how tired she felt. It had been an endless, emotional day. Rosie had come in for her just after Ted had left this morning. Poor Sadie. There were times when Nurse Fox had thought they were going to lose her as well as the baby. The baby, a lovely little girl, was in a breech position and couldn't be turned: the cord had strangled her. They'd really needed a doctor but Sadie had been adamant: they just couldn't afford it. Sarah had been continually running up and down the stairs carrying buckets of hot water for Nurse Fox (they didn't have a bathroom). She felt drained, but what of Sadie? The poor woman had been in a lot of pain and had lost a lot of blood, and it had all been for nothing in the end. It would take her a while to get well again. Sarah sighed, and said to herself: Then I suppose a few weeks after that she'll be expecting again. What sort of an animal is Wally Fellows? Hasn't that man any pride?

Although Sarah had been left a widow many years ago, she had been lucky: she'd only had Mary to worry about and while she went out to work her mother had looked after her daughter. Over the years Sadie had told her how bad things were for them with her husband out of work and only getting a pittance from the relief office. 'Won't be so bad when the kids go out to work,' she often said. 'Ron tries to help out, but finds it hard with everybody knowing his dad's Wally Fellows. I reckon that when he leaves school he'll have to go a bit farther afield to get a decent job.'

How Sarah admired this woman, always making sure that somehow she managed to scrape together the rent, nine and six a week; to her that was the most important thing: she had to keep a roof over her kids' heads.

Sarah had never had that worry since marrying Ted. But she had other concerns now. Mary still wanted him to take Eddie to see a doctor, but Ted was adamantly against it. Even more worrying was his reason. He'd said to Sarah: 'What if we were told it could be something hereditary?'

Sarah had frozen at the suggestion. How could Ted know about her past? She had never admitted how her father had died. She had been just thirteen. It had all been very hush hush. Sarah thought about the times he used to behave strangely. He'd shut himself under the stairs for hours on end saying he was getting away from his demons. Sarah shuddered at that childhood memory. Had he killed himself? She remembered that her mother had been so ashamed after his death that she would never talk about it, no matter how many times she had tried to bring up the subject. It was soon after his death that they moved house. Doyle Street never knew their secret. It was something she'd never told Mary or Ted. How could she tell her daughter something like that? What if she wanted children, how could she with a threat like that hanging over her?

She sat fretting for a while, before falling into an uneasy

doze. She was still asleep when the kitchen door opened. 'Mary,' she said, jerking upright. She winced with backache. 'I was hoping it was your dad.'

'He's not home then? You all right?'

'Just a twinge; been sitting funny. I'm so worried about him.'

'I hoped you wouldn't mind but I stayed and helped put the twins and young Brian to bed.'

'No, course not.'

'Would you like that cup of tea now?' asked Mary.

'Yes, please, and would you mind making me a cheese sandwich? I ain't had nothing to eat all day.'

They were sitting at the table having their sandwich when Ted walked in. He looked a little bleary-eyed.

'Where have you been? Look at the time!' Sarah's voice was raised with anxiety.

'I've been to the dogs and, for your information, woman, I've been with a friend. And we've had a few drinks.' He grasped the table. 'So I don't want any of your shouting.'

Mary sat silently looking on, puzzled. What was he talking about? She had never heard her mother shout at him and she wasn't shouting now, even though she'd had a very worrying day.

'But, Ted—'

'Don't start nagging. Can't stand nagging wives and if you don't like what I do you can get out of my house.'

Sarah looked shocked. 'How can you say that?'

'Remember, it's my name on the rent book' – he pointed to himself – 'and I'm the one who pays the rent.'

Sarah's face blanched and her eyes filled with tears as she sank into the chair.

Mary opened her big brown eyes wide in amazement. She wanted to yell at him: 'It ain't your house. We was here before

71

you,' but thought better of it. It would only make things worse. Instead she said quietly, 'I'm going to bed,' and left the room.

As she lay in bed Mary reflected on the day. Such a lot had happened. A baby had been born and died. Her father had been out drinking and had come home a little the worse for drink. But it was the way he'd spoken to her mother that upset her the most. Please don't let him get like Mr Fellows next door. She turned over. At least Billy would be home next week. 'Please let him like me,' she said out loud.

She heard Ted stomping up the stairs. Her next thoughts were for her brother. 'Please don't wake up, Eddie,' she whispered. But the house remained calm.

Sarah was busy in the kitchen when Mary walked in the following morning.

'Everything all right?' she asked her mother.

'Yes, of course. I'm just doing some porridge for next door, it's almost ready. You can take it in. Tell them I'll do them some soup for their dinner.'

'I hope Sadie's all right,' said Mary.

'I've just seen Rosie out in the yard,' replied her mother. 'She said her mother was getting up a bit later on. She should really rest, but I suppose with a family to worry about that's impossible.'

'Poor Sadie,' sighed Mary. 'I'll just get me cardie, it looks a bit dull out there.'

'Did you get your frock yesterday?'

'Yes, I'll show you when you've finished doing breakfast. Mum, was Dad all right?'

'Yes, why do you ask?'

'Well, he seemed a bit, I don't know, not like he normally is.'

'He told me him and his friend had had a few drinks, and,

let's face it, your dad ain't used to drinking, is he?'

Mary shook her head. 'I was worried he might do something.'

'Like what?'

'I don't know. Hit you.'

Sarah laughed. 'What, Ted? You can get that nonsense right out of your head. Your father loves us all and he wouldn't harm any of us.'

'What about when he hits Eddie?'

'That's for Eddie's own good. He can be a very difficult little boy at times. Now, let's not hear any more of this. Ted was being silly and he's very sorry.'

But Mary was still worried. She picked up the bowl of porridge and went next door.

'Me mum's made you some porridge,' she said, handing Rosie the bowl. 'How's your mum?'

'Not bad. D'you wonner come in?'

'No, I'll be back later. Me mum's doing you some soup for dinner.'

'Cor, thanks. That'll be lovely.'

Mary didn't think she could face Sadie. What could she say to her? What if Mr Fellows was still in the bed? That thought sent her scurrying back home.

When Mary got back Eddie was sitting on the kitchen floor. Ted walked into the kitchen and went straight up to Sarah and kissed her cheek. 'I hope I didn't make a fool of myself last night. Please forgive me.'

'You were a little the worse for drink.'

'I hope I didn't show myself up too much.' He smiled at Mary. 'I know. I should have come home hours before, but you know how it is when you meet a friend you haven't seen for years, you start talking about old times and the time simply flies past.'

'Do we know your friend?' asked Mary.

'No, he was in the navy with me. I was going to bring him home.'

'It was a good thing you didn't,' said Sarah. 'I was out all day as well.'

'You were? Where did you go?' His tone was a little sharp.

'Next door. I was with Sadie, she had her baby yesterday.'

'So they've got another mouth to feed.'

'No. The baby was born dead.'

'I'm sorry to hear that. Is Sadie all right?'

'Not too bad. She's a survivor. Mary, now you've finished your breakfast go and try on your new frock.'

As Mary left the room she wondered if her mother was right. Was she trying to see things about Ted that weren't there? After all, it wasn't like him to be out drinking. This was the first time she'd ever seen him a bit drunk and he had been with an old friend.

'It's lovely,' enthused her mother when Mary returned and twirled round.

'This boy is going to be very proud of you when he comes calling,' said Ted.

'I hope so,' said Mary, smiling. 'D'you like me shoes?' She held up her foot.

'They're lovely,' said Sarah.

'I'm really sorry I couldn't run to getting them as well,' said Ted.

'That's all right.'

'Trouble is, with the problems at work, I don't know who'll be the next to go and we've had to take a cut in salary. It's very worrying.'

Mary felt a pang of guilt. She shouldn't think bad things of Ted. He'd always looked after them and he was entitled to see his friend and have a few beers.

★ ★ ★

Mary was in a cheerful mood on Monday as she went back to work, which only improved when Liz gave her a birthday card and a bottle of Evening in Paris scent.

'You can use that on Sat'day when our Billy takes you out.'

'Is he home?' asked Mary eagerly.

'No, but Mum had a letter. He'll be home Wednesday. There was a note in it for me and he told me to tell you he'd see you on Sat'day, that's if you want.'

'What do you think? I've even got a new frock and shoes for the occasion.' Mary's eyes were twinkling with excitement. This was turning out to be the best birthday she'd had in years. 'You seeing that Pete?'

'No, worse luck. He's going home.'

'You never know, he might turn up.'

'I should be so lucky.'

To Mary, it seemed like Saturday would never come, but finally it arrived. It was six o'clock and Mary had been in the front room looking out of the window for the past half an hour. When Liz had told her Billy was home and still wanted to take her out tonight, she was over the moon. She had spent most of this afternoon titivating herself. Although she knew Billy wasn't coming for her till seven o'clock, she had been ready for ages.

When she finally saw him come through the gate her heart gave a little flutter. He looked so handsome in his uniform. She hurried to the door. 'I'm all ready,' she said. Turning, she called out: 'I'm just off, Mum.'

She edged Billy back through the gate.

'Hope you don't mind me being in uniform. I ain't got nothing else to wear.'

75

Mind? She was thrilled. She swallowed hard to gain her composure. 'Where're we going?' she casually asked.

'I don't mind. Do you fancy the pictures?'

'Yes, please.'

He laughed. 'Do you always say that?'

Mary blushed. 'It's the way I was brought up.'

'Sorry. Only teasing. It makes a nice change to go to the pictures. It's all right when we're in the States, they've got plenty of picture houses, but in some of the backward places it can be a bit boring being ashore.' He pulled her arm through his.

Mary felt so proud walking along arm in arm with this handsome sailor.

'I thought you might take me inside to meet your family? After all, they must want to know who's taking you out.'

'They know you're Liz's brother.'

'Liz was saying your brother's a bit backward.'

'Did she now.' Mary was thinking: How dare she? On Monday when she got to work she'd give Liz a piece of her mind; she should mind her own business. What else had she told him?

'What's wrong with him?'

'Don't know. He's not very good at talking, that's all.' Liz couldn't have told him that much.

'We had a bloke on the ship who didn't talk much.'

'And he was in the navy? Where was he from?'

Billy laughed. 'He came from Ireland, so he wasn't English and we couldn't understand him.'

'You are awful. The poor man.' Mary laughed with him.

After the pictures they went to a Lyons Corner House for tea.

'This is great,' said Billy, smiling as he took off his hat and sat down. His teeth were white and his dark hair shiny and clean-looking. To Mary everything about him was just perfect. 'Can we go out again tomorrow?' he asked, interrupting her thoughts.

'Yes—' Mary stopped and laughed. 'I was going to say yes, please again.'

Billy leaned across the table and touched her hand. 'Mary, I know we've only seen each other a couple of times, but I really like you, you're honest and fun to be with.'

Mary wanted her heart and stomach to stop doing somersaults. 'And I like being with you,' she whispered.

'I thought that tomorrow we could go up West. Would that be all right?'

'That would be lovely. Perhaps we could get a boat out on the Serpentine.'

Billy threw his head back and laughed.

Mary looked downcast. 'Why are you laughing at me?'

'You said get a boat out. I spend me life on ships.'

Seeing her error at once, Mary laughed with him. 'It ain't quite the same though, is it? You don't have to row that one.'

'No. I'll grant you that. In fact it sounds a very good idea.'

Mary was so happy. He wanted to see her again.


When they turned into Doyle Street, Mary could see the lights were on in the upstairs window. She knew her mother and Ted would still be awake.

'I won't ask you in as it's getting late,' said Mary, looking up as the curtains began twitching in her mother's bedroom.

'That's all right. Perhaps I can meet them tomorrow?'

She quickly changed the subject. 'I'll see you at eleven then.' She stood waiting for him to kiss her. She was sure he would and she didn't care if her mother was looking. In the pictures he had put his arm round her shoulders, and he did kiss her when they were in Portsmouth, so she was sure he would again. When he took hold of her shoulders she felt her knees go weak. His lips touched hers and she felt like jelly. She just knew this must be love.

After she closed the front door, Mary stood for a while in the passage trying to remember every single thing that happened tonight, and every single word he had uttered. She gently touched her lips. He was the most wonderful thing that had ever come into her life.

'He looks very nice,' said her mother, coming down the stairs. 'Why didn't you ask him in?'

'I thought you were in bed.'

'I'd just been up to check Eddie. Are you seeing him again?'

'Yes. Tomorrow.'

'You could ask him back for a cup of tea.'

Mary stopped at the kitchen door. 'But what about Eddie? What if he started playing up?'

Sarah pushed open the door. 'You've not told him about your brother then?'

'No, not that much,' said Mary.

Ted looked up from his newspaper. 'What's all this about?'

'She doesn't want to bring her young man home because she's frightened Eddie will play up.'

'Oh dear. Is this the beginning of you being ashamed of us?'

'No, course it ain't.' Mary was getting cross.

'You take Eddie out,' said Sarah. 'That doesn't worry you.'

'I know. But people out don't see what he's like at home.'

'Liz must have told him about Eddie,' said Sarah.

'Yes, she has. But I didn't ask him *what* she'd told him. He knew he was backward, that's all.' She turned to Ted. 'Anyway, you didn't bring your friend home to see us, did you?'

'Mary,' said her mother, 'don't speak to your father like that.'

78

'He ain't me dad.'

Sarah went to speak but Ted put up his hand to stop her. 'Mary,' he said softly, 'this is so unlike you. What's wrong?'

She wanted to say: 'I love Eddie, but I also love Billy and I don't want to put him off.' But she remained silent.

'We'll talk about this in the morning,' said Sarah. 'I'm going to bed.'

'Me too,' said Ted, folding his newspaper.

They left Mary alone. She sat at the table thinking about what had been said. Was she ashamed of Eddie? And why was she angry with Ted? Was it because he wouldn't do something about Eddie? She was very sorry for what she'd said, but she didn't want to lose Billy. He might be only her first boyfriend but she was sure this was love, real love.

# Chapter 9

The following morning when Mary walked into the kitchen Eddie came up to her and held her hand. She bent down and he wrapped his arms round her neck. As she held him close she whispered, 'Say good morning, Mary.'

He pulled back from her and grinned.

'Say Mary. Mary.' She repeated the words very slowly and deliberately.

He ran away from her, laughing, and plonking himself down on the floor began rocking back and forth. 'No. No. No,' he chanted.

'You will say it one day,' she said, straightening up.

'No. No. No.'

'Eddie, stop that,' said Sarah. 'What time are you meeting your young man?' she asked as she put Mary's breakfast on the table.

'Eleven o'clock.'

'If you want to bring him in I'll make sure Eddie's out of the way.'

'Oh, Mum. You're making me sound awful. Just give me a little while to explain to him about Eddie. I'm sure he'll understand. Besides, he might not want to see me again after today.'

'I'm sure he will. What has Liz told him about Eddie?'

'I told you. He knows I've got a young brother who's a bit backward, but I don't know what else she's said about him.'

'And he's never said any more?'

'No.' Mary smiled at Eddie who was once more busy trying to line up some of his wooden trains.

'Well, if you don't bring him in you've got nothing to worry about, have you?'

Mary could see her mother was upset about it. 'S'pose not,' she said petulantly.

All morning Mary was in a dilemma. Should she bring Billy in to meet her mum and dad and risk Eddie playing up? Her brother hated anything or anyone new. Or should she wait till she got to know Billy better? In the end she decided to wait. If Billy wanted to write to her, she would tell him then. But what could she tell him? He knew only that Eddie didn't speak much; she hadn't mentioned the terrible tantrums and the head-banging. But just to say Eddie didn't talk sounded like a very feeble excuse not to bring Billy home. After all, Billy wasn't going to be around for ever and, as she'd said earlier, he might not want to take her out again. She had to make the most of seeing him while he was here, because he would soon be off. But at the moment the last thing she wanted to do was frighten him away.

That evening when Mary said goodnight to Billy she was bubbling over with happiness. The day had been perfect in every way. They had joked together all the time. She couldn't ever remember laughing so much. Mary had seen everything around her with new eyes. She was so lucky: the envious glances she got from other girls made her so proud to be on Billy's arm. They had received plenty of wisecracks from the boatman when they took out the boat – he'd wanted to know if this was what the navy was coming to now? She'd lain back and trailed her hand in the water just like she'd seen film stars do. Her joy had been complete.

'I won't ask you in as it's late,' said Mary when they reached her door, just as she had done the previous evening.

'Can I take you out next Sat'day?'

Mary laughed. 'Yes, please.'

He pulled her close to him and kissed her. It was a harder, more passionate kiss than before. 'I really do like you, Mary.'

'And I like you,' she gasped as she came up for air. She wanted to say I love you, but thought that was being too forward. 'I'll see you Sat'day.'

Billy laughed. 'Yes, please. I'll be round about two. Is that all right?'

She nodded.

He kissed her again, lightly this time. 'Goodnight.'

'Goodnight,' Mary whispered. She stood at the gate watching him walk down the street. When he stopped at the end of Doyle Street, turned and waved, Mary felt ready to burst.

On Monday, Liz was over the moon when she caught sight of Mary walking to work. She rushed up to her and blurted out, 'Guess what? Pete's asked me to go out with him next Sunday. I had a letter from him this morning and he wants to meet me at Victoria Station.'

'That's really good. What time?'

'Ten o'clock. I've got to get up real early.'

'Liz, I'm so pleased for you. Where's he taking you?'

'He didn't say, it's gonner be a surprise.'

'You don't think he's gonner take you back to his house, do you?'

'I hope not. Now you've got me all worried. He might be too posh for me.'

'Don't talk daft. You're just as good as he is.'

82

'No, I'm not. I don't talk like him.'

'You don't have to. Just be yourself.'

'You and Billy seemed to be getting on all right.'

'Looks like it. Liz, has he said anything to you about me?'

'Only that he reckons you're a bit of all right.'

Mary felt her feet were skipping through the air. Suddenly, though, she remembered. 'Liz, have you said anything to Billy about Eddie?'

'I told him that he's a bit simple. That's all. Why? What's he said?'

'Not much. It's just I ain't asked him in to meet me mum and dad yet.'

Liz grinned and nudged Mary. 'This sounds serious. Here, you ain't gone and fallen for me big brother, have you?' She stopped and looked at her friend. 'Mary Harris, I do believe you're blushing.'

'I do like him.'

'Well, just you be careful. Remember he's a sailor and they do say a sailor has a girl in every port.'

'I know. Pete's a sailor, but that ain't stopping you from getting all starry-eyed.'

'I ain't daft like you.'

'Thanks.'

'Well, you can only see the best in everyone. Look how you got took in with that old Mrs Jenkins. She was dressed in rags and stank of dried pee. We told her to sling her hook, we all knew she was just hanging around the factory gates for a handout for booze, but what did you do? You gave her a shilling. A whole shilling, I ask you; what was you thinking of?'

'I felt sorry for her. She looked hard up and she had a baby.'

'Yer. We found out later that she borrowed her mate's baby

to get money, which you gave her and she went and spent in the pub.'

'All right, so I'm daft, but I can't help feeling sorry for people.'

'All I'm saying is that I don't wanner see you hurt.'

'And you think yer brother's gonner ditch me?'

'I don't know. He's the first boy you've been out with. You ain't the first girlfriend he's had, you know?'

Mary didn't answer. 'Come on,' she said. 'Let's get a move on or we'll be late for work.' But Liz's words had worried her. It was true, he was her first boyfriend, but surely it didn't matter? She loved Billy and that was that.

The week seemed to drag for Mary and Liz. All they could talk about was this coming weekend. Now at last it was here.

'Billy coming round this afternoon?' asked Liz as they walked home.

'Yes, two o'clock.'

'Where's he taking you?'

'I don't know, we didn't decide on anything. I expect it'll be the pictures tonight. You've still no idea what Pete's got in store for you tomorrow?'

'No. But I am worried he might wanner take me back home.'

'I wouldn't think so, after all he's only seen you for a little while when he was down in Portsmouth.'

'That's true.'

'What does Billy think?'

'He reckons he's gonner take me to some secret hideaway and have his wicked way with me.'

Mary laughed. 'What did your mum say to that?'

'She warned me not to bring any trouble home, then gave Billy a clip round the ear for being dirty.'

They both giggled.

'See you Monday,' said Mary, still laughing as they parted company.

'Don't do anything I wouldn't do,' Liz called out after her friend.

'As if I would. I shall look forward to hearing what you get up to!'

Liz just smiled.

'D'you fancy that picture *The Thin Man*?' Mary asked Billy as they were on their way to the cinema.

'Don't mind.'

Billy made sure they sat in the back row, and as soon as they settled down Mary knew it wasn't going to be to watch William Powell and Myrna Loy. Mary was thrilled and snuggled against Billy when he put his arm round her. He began by kissing her ear and after a little while he turned her head towards him and the kisses became wild and passionate. Then his hand began gently squeezing her breast. She didn't really mind that but when he slipped his hand inside her blouse she gently pushed it away.

'Don't,' she whispered.

'Why not?'

She couldn't really answer that.

Billy kissed around her ear again. 'Come on, let me have a feel? It won't hurt, no one can see us.'

'I don't want to.' It was a very feeble protest, as deep down she really wanted him to. 'What about the usherette?'

'I ain't doing no harm; 'sides, they're used to seeing all sorts of things going on back here.'

Once again he put his hand inside her blouse and squeezed her breast. Then his hand slid her skirt up, gradually moving up and over her stockings, then he was feeling round her suspenders. She quickly pushed his hand away and sat up. 'I'm sorry, but I don't want you to do that.'

'Why? I ain't doing no harm.'

Mary straightened her skirt. 'I ain't like that.'

'Please yourself.' Billy took his arm away and sat up.

Mary could feel a coldness had come between them and she knew it was her fault. Should she have let him touch her? Throughout the rest of the film, news and the second feature he sat bolt upright. Mary was confused. She wanted him to hold her but she didn't want him playing with her, not like that.

'Have you any idea where Pete is going to take Liz tomorrow?' asked Mary as they walked to her house from the bus stop.

'No. Don't really know him that much. He ain't been on our ship long. Got transferred from a destroyer when we was in the Med. He's a very clever bloke. Reckon he'll be an officer before long.'

'That'll please Liz. Going out with an officer.'

'What about you, would you like to go out with one?'

Mary shook her head. 'I'm more than happy with the sailor I've got.'

'You wasn't earlier on.'

Mary blushed. 'I'm sorry about that.'

'That's all right, but you can't blame a bloke for trying.'

She was pleased and relieved Billy hadn't stayed cross after they'd left the cinema.

All too soon they reached Mary's front door. The moment they stood in the shadow of the doorway, out of the street's gaslights, Billy pulled her to him and kissed her. It made her head reel.

Billy was holding her tight. 'Mary,' he panted in her ear as his hand went over her breast. 'Mary. I'd like to . . .' His hand

86

dropped and he tried to pull up her skirt again.

Mary pushed him away. 'Don't do that. I'm sorry, Billy, but I don't want—'

'What is it with you? I thought you liked me?'

'I do. But I don't want to . . . you know?'

'What you frightened of?'

Mary didn't answer. Her thoughts were racing. She wanted to so much. She felt sensations in her body that she never knew existed. But what if she did give in? What if she then found she was having a baby?

'I thought you'd be a bit more loving,' said Billy.

Her heart wanted to cry out that she did want to be loving, but not this way. To her it wasn't right.

'I'll be careful.'

What could she say when she so wanted to? Should she let him? Was this all he wanted? Then, much to Mary's relief, the light came on in the passage and floated through the fanlight, bathing them in brightness. They sprang apart. Mary straightened her hat and skirt and Billy pulled down his jacket.

'I'd better go in,' said Mary. 'Will I see you tomorrow?'

'No, sorry. I've got to go and see me gran.'

Mary was taken aback. 'But I thought . . . Will you be gone all day?'

''Fraid so.'

'Is Liz going as well?'

'Don't think so, she's meeting Pete.'

Mary was trying hard to think. If Liz wasn't going why did Billy suddenly have to? 'Can't you go in the week?'

'No. We're all going, all except Liz. We had to wait till Dad's home and the kids ain't at school.'

'Where does your gran live?'

'Essex.'

Mary was upset. Why was he treating her like this? Why hadn't he mentioned this before? 'Will I see you next week?'

'I'll let Liz know. Goodnight.'

Mary let him lightly kiss her cheek. She pulled the key through the letterbox and opened the door.

'Have you had a nice time?' asked her mother when Mary walked into the kitchen.

'Yes, thank you.'

'You sound a bit subdued. Anything wrong?'

'No. Dad in bed?'

'Yes, he's just gone up, I came down to put the kettle on – I'm gonner make a cup of tea. D'you fancy one?'

'No thanks. I'll go on up.'

As Mary lay on her bed looking up at the ceiling her thoughts were full of Billy. She knew what he wanted. Should she give in to him? She didn't want to lose him. That was something she couldn't even bear to think about. If he loved her, he wouldn't put her through this. But did he love her? He had never said so. Had he suddenly made it up about going to see his gran? She would have to wait till Monday to find out if it was really true.

# Chapter 10

On Sunday morning Mary was very apprehensive. She stood in the front room looking out of the window hoping Billy might have changed his mind. Last night it had taken her a long while to get to sleep: her thoughts had been turning over and over. She knew Billy wanted to make love to her, but nice girls didn't do that sort of thing, not in doorways before they were married. She knew she loved Billy; if he loved her, surely he would understand her feelings and not ask her to do that.

The front-room door opened. 'What time are you going out?' asked her mother as she came into the room.

'I'm not.'

'Oh. Why's that? Mary, have you had a row?'

She quickly turned away and shook her head.

'Do you want to talk about it?' asked her mother gently.

Mary could feel the tears welling up. 'There's nothing to talk about. He's had to go and see his gran.'

'That's a shame. But still, it's only natural. After all, he's not here very often, is he? Where does she live?'

'Essex.'

'Will he call round a bit later?'

'He might do.'

'You seem to be very fond of him.'

'He's good fun,' said Mary brightly. 'I'll take Eddie out for a little while if you like.' She didn't want to discuss Billy any more; she didn't want to show her mother her true feelings.

'That'll be nice, he'll like that. I'll get him ready.'

Mary held Eddie's hand tight as they walked along jumping over the cracks in the paving. Once more she was deep in thought. Where had Liz gone? Was she having a good time with Pete? Had Billy really gone to his gran's? Mary was tempted to go to his house, just to find out if he had been telling her the truth. If Liz had been at home she would have had a good excuse. She was past worrying about Billy meeting Eddie. She just wanted to go out with him again. What if he went back without ever seeing her or wanting to stay in touch? Her heart would break.

When they reached the park, Mary sat on a seat next to Eddie and patted his hand.

Eddie was trying to pull his laces out of his boots. 'Don't do that,' she said softly.

He grinned and carried on.

A large dog came up to them and sniffed Eddie. He screamed and threw himself at Mary.

'Eddie, stop being so stupid,' she shouted, slapping his hands as she tried to unwrap herself from him. 'And you, get that thing away,' she shrieked at the man who was coming up to them, calling the dog's name.

'Jack ain't gonner 'urt the kid,' said the man. ''E's a friendly old thing, ain't yer, son?' He fondled the dog's ears.

'Well, we don't know that, do we?' yelled Mary.

'Don't you shout at me.'

'Get it away from us then!'

'Come on, son. Bloody miserable bitch.' The man dragged the dog away, scowling back over his shoulder at her.

Eddie had stopped screaming immediately Mary started

shouting and was now looking at his fingers, his wide blue eyes wet with tears.

Mary was filled with guilt at bellowing at him – and in the street as well. And as for slapping him, she had never ever done that before. She held him tight. 'I'm sorry, Eddie. I'm so sorry.' Was it because of Billy that she was letting her feelings get out of hand?

Eddie began to rock back and forth. They almost fell off the bench he was rocking so hard.

'Come on. Let's go home and see Mum.'

He didn't look at her and Mary was crying inside. Why was she feeling this way? She knew it was wrong to take her worries out on Eddie. What had Billy done, coming into her life and sending her emotions all over the place? She wiped the tears away and they began walking home.

'Where's Dad?' asked Mary as she took Eddie's coat off.

'He had to go out, some sort of business.'

'What, on a Sunday?'

'It seems he forgot to tell me last night. Has he been all right?' Sarah asked, nodding towards Eddie.

'Yes. We had a bit of a do with a dog, but he's been fine.' Mary didn't mention that she'd slapped Eddie and began to set the table. 'That smells good,' she added, sniffing the air. 'Will Dad be back for dinner?'

'I hope so.'

The rest of the day dragged. Even her mother appeared to be clock-watching all the time. When she came down from putting Eddie to bed, Sarah sank down into a chair and admitted, 'I'm really worried about Ted. His dinner will be all dried up. I hope he hasn't got himself involved with that friend of his again. He seems to be a bad influence.'

'Mum, do you know that much about Dad's relations?'

'No, not really. Why?'

'Just wondered, that's all. Are his parents still alive?'

'No. His mother died when he was very young and his father was killed in the war.'

'That's a shame. It would have been nice to have relations to visit on a Sunday.'

'I think he's got a sister somewhere, but he don't talk about her. I think she was a bit of a black sheep.'

Mary sat up. 'I never knew that. You've never said anything.'

'Didn't see the point. We never talk about her.'

'Sounds interesting. What did she do?'

'Don't know, he's never said. I don't even know her name.'

'That's a pity. I would have thought you would have tried to find out about her.'

'Why?'

'It would be nice to have an auntie. Can't you ask him again?'

'No, certainly not. He told me that he didn't want to talk about her and I respect his feelings. So that's that.'

Mary was disappointed, but knew better than to press it.

At ten o'clock Mary decided to go to bed. As she kissed her mother goodnight she sensed Sarah was full of apprehension. 'Don't worry about Dad. He'll be all right.'

'I hope so. I'm sorry your young man didn't manage to get to see you today.'

'So am I.'

'When does he have to go back to his ship?'

'The Wednesday after next.'

'So you'll be seeing him again next weekend?'

'I would think so.' Mary wanted to add that he might not want to see her. 'Goodnight.'

''Night, love.'

Again Mary lay awake wondering where Billy had really gone and if Liz had had a good time. Well, she'd find out all about that tomorrow. And what about Ted? It was a surprise to find out he had a sister. Why didn't he talk about her? And why hadn't her mother tried to find out more? Once again she wondered about what was wrong with Eddie and what Liz had said a while back went through her mind. Could it be hereditary? Was Ted's sister silly? Was that why Ted didn't want them to meet her?

As Mary walked to work she eagerly looked out for Liz. When she caught sight of her friend she hurried towards her calling her name. 'Liz. Liz!'

Liz turned and stopped, waiting for Mary to catch up with her.

Breathlessly Mary said, 'Well, did you see him? Where did you go?'

Liz grinned and her blue eyes were sparkling as she linked her arm through her friend's. 'I had a smashing day. You'll never guess where we went?'

'No. Get on with it,' said Mary impatiently.

'He's got an aunt and uncle who live in this big posh house over at Greenwich and they had a welcome-home family party for Pete. I met his mum and dad and a lot of relations. It was lovely. I felt a bit out of place at first, but they soon put me at ease. I'll tell you, Mary, I ain't never seen such a smashing place and as for the food, it could have fed our lot for a week.'

'Lucky old you! But why did he take you?'

''Cos he likes me, that's why.'

'Sorry, I didn't mean it like that. Ain't he got a girlfriend?'

'He did have. But while he was away on his last trip she got married to another bloke. His mum said it almost broke his heart. That was why he joined Billy's ship after they'd sailed.'

Mary wanted to say she knew what it was like to have a broken heart.

'Anyway, when he met me down in Portsmouth he said he liked my company, said I was fun to be with. He told his mother about me and she said, "That's just what you need. Invite her along." So that's how I come to be there.'

'Lucky old you. Are you seeing him again?'

'Yes, next weekend. His mum's invited me down for the weekend. They live near Dorking. I can't believe this is all happening to me.'

'Don't get your hopes up too high. He might drop you.'

'I don't care. I've seen the other side of life and I'm going to make the most of it while it lasts.'

In some ways Mary envied Liz: she knew her friend'd never let her heart rule her head, despite her reading all those love stories. She was more sensible than that.

When they reached the factory gates Liz stopped and pulled Mary closer. 'Don't say anything to any of them. You know how rotten they can be.'

'All right then, girls?' yelled Bet.

'Fine,' called Liz in reply.

Mary wanted to ask about Billy, but it was too late, she would have to wait till they walked home now. She wouldn't ask at lunchtime because although the girls and women they worked with weren't a bad bunch, they could be a bit loud-mouthed, and the last thing Mary wanted was for them to say something nasty about Billy and why he hadn't taken her out.

All morning, every time Mary glanced over at Liz she saw her friend was smiling. Mary prayed that this Pete wouldn't let her down.

At last the hooter went for home-time. As they all rushed out of the gates, Liz waited for Mary.

'I was so busy telling you about my day that I forgot to ask you, did you have a nice time with our Billy?'

'We went to the pictures on Sat'day. But I didn't see him Sunday.'

'Whyever not?'

'He said the family was all going over to see your gran.'

'They did, but Billy told them he wasn't going with them. He said he'd see her in the week.'

Mary felt sick. So he had lied to her. 'You don't know where he went then?' she asked softly.

'No. But I bloody well will as soon as I get in. He was still in bed when I left this morning.'

'Liz, don't make a big thing out of it. If he didn't want to see me again, well, that's up to him.'

'But I don't understand. He was really keen to take you out. What went wrong?'

Mary shrugged. How could she tell her that her brother wanted to go a bit further than just kisses. 'P'rhaps I wasn't like his other girlfriends.'

Liz stopped. 'You trying to tell me that he wanted to . . . you know?'

Mary didn't answer.

'You wait till I see him, the dirty little sod.'

'Liz, please don't make a big thing of it. I don't want him to know I've told you.'

'You didn't tell me, I guessed. He should know we ain't all easy. And I bet he'll ask me if Pete tried anything on. If I said yes, Billy would threaten to flatten him.'

'Pete didn't, did he?'

'No, course not, but blokes think like that. Always got to look after their own, don't matter about other people. D'you know, I'm flaming. You just wait till I see him.'

'Please, Liz. Don't make a fuss.'

'You like him, don't you?'

'Yes.'

'Well then.'

'But I want him to take me out cos he likes me, not because his sister threatens to punch him. Besides, he's bigger than you.'

Liz laughed. 'He might be bigger than me, but I can always stand on a chair.'

Mary laughed with her, but deep down she really wanted to cry.

# Chapter 11

As soon as Liz walked through the front door she caught sight of Billy going upstairs. 'Billy,' she called sharply and, beckoning him to her, added quietly: 'I wanner have a word with you.'

Without questioning her, he pushed his sister into the front room. 'I know what you're gonner say.'

'Do you? So what is it then?'

'Why did I tell Mary I was going to Gran's yesterday and I didn't go.'

'Right. So why did you?'

'I was angry with her.'

'Was that cos she wouldn't let you get inside her knickers?'

'She told you?'

'No, I guessed. She's very upset. What was you thinking of?'

'You can't blame a bloke for trying.'

'Yes, I can. I don't know what girls you've been out with, but we ain't all like that.'

'Don't tell me that Pete didn't try his luck.'

'No, he didn't.'

'So where did he take you then?'

'To his aunt's house.'

Billy burst out laughing. 'Go on, pull the other one.'

97

Liz then went into great detail of what she had done yesterday. 'So you see, all blokes ain't like that.'

'I must admit I do feel a bit rotten about it now.'

'Well, I suggest you put yer hat on and go round and see her.'

'She might not want to see me.'

'She does, just as long as you don't try it on again.'

'It *was* a bit stupid of me.'

'Yes, it was. Now go on. And remember to say you're sorry.'

Billy picked up his hat. 'Thanks,' he said, kissing his sister's cheek.

'Where did you get to yesterday then, Dad?' asked Mary as they sat down to their meal. 'Mum was very worried about you.'

'It was a business meeting and I couldn't let your mother know when it went on longer than we thought. I couldn't leave as the boss asked me to have a meal with him and his wife. I tried to say no, but you have to be very careful these days. You don't want to upset anybody.'

Mary wanted to say that he obviously didn't mind upsetting his wife, but just left it in her thoughts.

'You must have been asleep when Ted came in last night. It was soon after you'd gone to bed,' said her mother, smiling. 'He didn't want his dinner so I gave it to Sadie this morning, they won't mind it a bit dried up. The kids'll enjoy it. Sadie said she'd make a bit more gravy for them.'

Mary could see her mother was just rambling on. Why was she trying to justify Ted's actions? Had he been drunk again? If he had, he'd been very quiet when he came in. Surely he should be strong enough to say no to his boss? But then again a lot of people were out of work, so perhaps he did have to be careful.

'How is Sadie?' asked Mary, changing the subject. 'Does she ever mention the baby at all?'

'No. That bit of her life is over.'

'Till the next time,' said Ted.

'According to Sadie there won't be a next time.'

A knocking on the door caused them all to look up.

'Who can that be?' asked Sarah.

'I'll go,' said Mary.

She wasn't sure what her face registered when she opened the front door. It was a combination of joy, disbelief and shock. 'Billy?' was all she could utter.

'As you can see I've come with cap in hand.' He held up his cap. 'Am I forgiven?' A cheeky grin swept across his face.

'Did Liz tell you to come round?'

'In a way. But I am sorry and I did want to see you again. Can I come in?'

Mary's heart was fluttering and she hurriedly looked behind her. 'I don't know.'

'Why's that?'

Mary was trying to think fast. If he had come back into her life she didn't want him to go away again. Eddie was still up. 'I'll get me coat and we can go for a walk.'

'Please yourself.'

Mary left him on the doorstep while she went back inside.

'Who was it, love?' asked her mother when she went into the kitchen.

'Billy. I won't be long.' She took her coat from the hook behind the kitchen door.

'You haven't left him standing on the doorstep, have you?' asked her mother. 'Ask him in.'

'It's all right. I'm off now.'

'We'd like to see this young man,' said Ted. 'Bring him in.'

Mary glanced at Eddie who was sitting quietly on the floor

with his trains. 'I suppose I could.' She went to the front door. 'They want to see you, so you'd better come in.'

Billy walked in. 'Hello,' he said rather loudly. 'Pleased to meet you all.'

Eddie looked up.

'And you must be little Eddie?' Billy bent down to him and was very close to him.

At that Eddie yelled out, 'No. No. No,' and rushed at Mary.

'Eddie, stop being silly.' Sarah tried to drag him away.

'Come on now, son, behave,' said Ted.

Eddie cringed and began banging his head against the wall.

'Eddie, stop that,' yelled Ted. He tried to pick him up.

Mary thought she was going to die of embarrassment when she caught sight of the expression on Billy's face.

'What's wrong with him?' he asked as he watched Ted wrestling his son out of the room.

'He gets nervous when he meets new people,' said Sarah, desperately trying to act as if nothing strange had happened.

'How old is he?' asked Billy.

'Four,' said Mary, quickly finding her voice. 'We'll be off now, Mum.' She didn't want to stay. What if Ted took his belt to Eddie again? She couldn't bear not to help him, but she also didn't want Billy to witness any of this drama.

When they got outside Mary said, 'I'm sorry about my brother's little performance.'

'You said he's four?'

Mary nodded.

'Don't say a lot, does he?'

'No.'

'Does he always bang his head like that?'

'No. Not often.'

'He's gonner do his brain an injury if he carries on like that.'

Mary gave him a half-smile. 'Don't let's talk about Eddie. What did you do yesterday?'

'Well, as you can guess I didn't go to me gran's.'

'I know. Liz told me.'

'I did feel rotten about it, but you see I'm used to getting me own way.'

'Not with me, you're not.'

'I know that now. And I'm deeply ashamed. Am I forgiven?'

'Don't know.'

'Would you like me to go down on bended knee?'

Mary laughed. 'Now that I would like to see.'

'Sorry, but I don't want to ruin me clothes.'

'So what *did* you do yesterday?'

'Nothing really. Just got in the way. I should have gone with Dad to Gran's, but I really didn't feel like it. I was wishing I was with you.'

'And I was wishing I was with you as well.'

'Was you?'

Mary nodded.

'I really am sorry. Liz was all ready to give me a right ear-bashing when she got home tonight.'

'Is that why you came round, cos your sister told you to?'

'No, honest. Don't let's talk about that any more.'

'All right. But I can't be out too long. I've got to get up early.'

'That's all right.'

'Sounds like Liz had a good time,' said Mary.

'Seems like it. Not that she said a lot about it to me, she was too busy telling me I've got to behave.'

'She's going to Pete's house next weekend.'

'Is she now?'

'Yes. And his parents will be there so don't go putting two and two together and making five.'

'No, ma'am.'

They laughed together, and Mary's heart was full of relief. Everything was going to be fine once again.

They went on strolling and chatting, but when they reached Mary's front door again Mary said she wouldn't invite him in.

'That's all right. I hope your brother's calmed down.'

'I expect he has be now.'

'I'll be round about two on Sat'day. That all right?'

Mary nodded. 'I'll look forward to that.'

They kissed, long and passionately. Billy didn't make any attempts to touch her again, but Mary knew that now he had come back into her life, she was going to have a problem keeping her own feelings under control.

It was very quiet and there wasn't any lights on when Mary pushed open the kitchen door.

'Mum? Mum!' she called out. Fear grabbed her when she didn't get a reply. She rushed up the stairs and stormed into her mother's bedroom. She stopped when she saw her mother lying on the bed with her arms round Eddie, who was fast asleep.

'Mum?' she said softly, going over to her.

'Shh,' said her mother, stirring. 'Don't make so much noise.'

'I'm sorry. What's happened?'

'I'll tell you downstairs.' She gently eased her arm from under her son and, without waking him, slipped off the bed.

'Where's Dad?' asked Mary as they made their way down the stairs.

'Gone out.'

'Gone out? Where?' Mary stopped abruptly and her mother almost fell on top of her.

'I'll explain when we get into the kitchen.'

'Well?' said Mary as soon as the kitchen door was closed. She could see her mother had been crying.

Sarah blew her nose. 'I followed Ted upstairs after you left.' She stopped to blow her nose again. 'I'm afraid I got very angry with him.'

'Who, Dad or Eddie?'

'Ted.'

Mary could feel the colour drain from her face. She sank down into the armchair. 'What did he do?'

'He lost his temper. You know how difficult Eddie can be.'

'I've only been gone a little while – what on earth did Dad do?' Mary asked again, with more urgency this time.

There was a long pause. 'I stopped him from giving Eddie the belt.'

Mary felt full of guilt. If Billy hadn't come in this wouldn't have happened. 'Did he hurt him?'

Sarah shook her head. 'I got in the way.'

'Mum!' Mary was shocked. 'Did he hurt you?'

Her mother didn't answer. 'I gave Eddie a drop of whisky to calm him down and help him sleep. I must have dozed off with him.'

'Where's Dad?'

'I don't know. He was so angry with me for getting in the way. Oh Mary, why has he changed so much? We used to be such a happy family.' She put her head in her hands and began to weep.

Mary stood up and held her mother close. She felt so helpless.

For the rest of the evening Mary and her mother sat waiting for Ted. From time to time Mary noticed Sarah looking anxiously at the clock. After a while she said, 'Look at the time. Where could he have got to?'

'Would he have gone to his mate's?'

'I hope not.'

'Mum, are you all right?'

Sarah smiled. 'Yes, of course. Now you go on up, no point in both of us losing our beauty sleep. But don't make any noise, love, I don't think I can cope with any of Eddie's tantrums tonight.'

'Will you be able to get him back in his cot?'

'I should think so.'

'Call me if he starts.'

'I will. Now go on up.'

Mary kissed her mother and left the room. 'I hope Ted comes home soon,' she said silently to herself. She hated to see her mother so upset. What were they going to do?

Sarah sat in the armchair quietly staring at the door. Would Ted come home tonight? She had never seen him so angry and Eddie was the cause of all this trouble. Sarah knew that as he got older she wouldn't be able to cope. Would he have to be put away? How could she tell Ted and Mary that she was afraid this could be a throwback to her father? Had he been mad? If only her mother were still alive, then she could help. Sarah put her head in her hands and wept.

# Chapter 12

Mary was surprised when she opened her eyes the following morning to find she'd had a good night's sleep despite all the previous day's trauma. She checked her clock. It was time she got up. As she went downstairs she thought the house seemed very quiet, but she didn't dare look in on Eddie: she didn't want to wake him.

'Mum!' she cried out as she pushed open the kitchen door and found her mother sitting in the chair looking tousled. 'What are you doing?'

Sarah opened her eyes and shifted painfully. 'Is that the time?'

'You ain't been sleeping in the chair all night, have you?'

Sarah nodded and slowly got to her feet. 'I ache all over.' Putting her hands in the small of her back she stretched and winced with the pain.

'I bet you do. Why didn't you go to bed?'

'I sat up waiting for Ted. I must have dozed off.'

'Didn't he come home?'

Sarah sadly shook her head.

'Have you checked the bedroom?'

'He would have come in here first, or at least he would have come looking for me when he found I wasn't in bed.'

'Mum, what's happening to us?' Mary was frightened at all these unusual goings-on.

'I don't know, love, I really don't know. I'll make a cup of tea.'

'Shall I go and get Eddie?'

'No. Leave him for a moment or two. I need to gather my thoughts.'

'I'll make the tea.'

'Thanks.' Sarah gradually eased herself out of the chair. As she slowly and painfully made her way upstairs her thoughts were on Ted. Where had he spent the night? After quietly checking to see if Eddie was still asleep, she made her way to the bathroom. Sarah gently eased her frock off her shoulders and looked in the mirror. The bruise on her back was now beginning to show signs of turning multi-coloured before the day was out. She knew Ted would be horrified when he saw it and he would never forgive himself. It was her fault he'd left the house last night – she had told him to go; but at the time she'd been beside herself with anger. She hated it when he chastised Eddie.

Sarah sat on the edge of the bath and wept. She desperately hoped Ted would return today. She loved him so much, she didn't think she could live without him. Where was he? She would never show Mary what he'd done. Sarah dabbed her face with cold water, then made her way back down to the kitchen.

All day as Mary automatically packed biscuits into cardboard boxes, her thoughts were on the situation at home. She could hardly wait till the end of the day. For once she welcomed the noise of the factory around her masking what the other girls were saying, and didn't struggle to try and hear it. As they walked home, Liz was very chatty and although she was grateful for Liz telling Billy to come round she found she couldn't talk about it too much as her mind was on other things.

'D'you know you've hardly said a word,' said Liz. 'I thought you might at least have said thanks for me sending Billy round.'

'Sorry, Liz.' Mary smiled. 'Of course I was pleased at seeing Billy again.'

'He said young Eddie was playing up.'

'Yes, he was, but it's all right.' She wasn't going to say anything about Ted not coming home all night.

'So you're seeing him Sat'day then?'

'Yes.'

'Going anywhere interesting?'

'I don't know, he didn't say.'

Mary was pleased when at last they parted company and she was able to run all the rest of the way home.

Eddie was playing on the floor and Ted was sitting at the table when Mary burst in.

Ted jumped up. 'Before you say anything I've explained everything to your mother.'

Mary was taken aback by his attitude.

'It's all right, Mary. Ted and I have sorted out our little problem.'

Mary was silent. What could she say?

'Had a bit of a rough night sleeping in the park,' said Ted, laughing.

'Did Mum tell you she sat up all night in the chair waiting for you to come home?'

'She did. I am very sorry and deeply ashamed of my actions.'

Sarah went to him and kissed his cheek. Smiling at her daughter, she said, 'So, as you can see, love, everything is fine.'

Mary thought: Yes, for the time being, but will it happen again?

For the rest of the week everything was fine and Ted was very loving towards Sarah. Even Eddie sensed the atmosphere and was almost well behaved when Ted was around. But Mary was still worried; to her things seemed to be very false.

On Saturday when Billy called, Mary was ready and didn't ask him in.

'Is that brother of yours all right now?' he asked as they waited for a bus.

'Yes, thanks.'

'You know he shouldn't bang his head against the wall like that.'

'I know.'

'He could end up knocking himself silly.'

'I know,' was all Mary could think of to say.

After a moment or two, Billy said, 'Mary, you seem to be very quiet.'

She knew she wasn't being her usual chatty self. 'Am I? Sorry.'

'Is something wrong?'

'No.'

'Look, I've said I was sorry for being such an idiot and trying it on. I promise it won't happen again.'

'That's all right. Here's our bus,' said Mary, smiling up at him as they got on board.

They went to the pictures and although Mary let Billy put his arm round her she pulled away from his kisses, and she sensed he wasn't having a good time. She tried to relax, but somehow things weren't the same.

Afterwards, they were having a pot of tea in the Lyons

Corner House and Billy said, 'Mary, are you sure you want to be out with me?'

'Yes. I'm sorry.' She began fiddling with a spoon. 'I know I'm not being very good company.'

'What is it? What's wrong? Is it your brother?'

Mary quickly looked up. 'What made you say that?'

'Dunno. Is there any trouble at home?'

'No.'

'Well, it must be me then?'

'No. Look, what shall we do tomorrow?' Mary stared at him anxiously; her heart was pounding. She wanted things to be as they were before, but there was a tension between them. Billy was worried that it was down to him, but Mary knew the fault was with her. She had to stop worrying about Eddie and her mother. She should be happy; Billy wanted to take her out.

'You choose something.'

'I don't know,' was all she could say. '*You* think of something.'

'I've got to go back on Wednesday. I don't know when I'll be here again.'

'Will you write to me?'

'Do you want me to?'

Mary nodded and smiled. 'Yes, please. I'd love to hear all about the romantic places you go to.'

'They ain't all romantic, but I could send you a picture postcard of every place we visit, that way you'll be able to see them as well.'

'Thank you. I'd like that.'

'That's better.'

'What?'

'You smiling. I was beginning to think you'd regretted coming out tonight.'

'No. I'll never regret that. I like being with you.'

'Good. Now, about tomorrow. I wouldn't mind having a boat out again, that's if you fancy it?'

'I'd love it.'

'Good, that's settled then.'

On the way home Billy walked with his arm round her waist and on the doorstep he kissed her. Although his kisses were deep and passionate, there wasn't any fumbling with him trying to get inside her clothes.

She stood for a moment or two behind the closed door after he left. She did love him, she was sure of that, and tomorrow she'd tell him her real feelings.

The next morning a banging on the front door woke Mary. Eddie was yelling and she heard her mother hurrying down the stairs. Quickly Mary followed her. 'Who is it?' she asked as Sarah opened the door. Beyond her mother Mary could see that it was one of Liz's younger sisters, Elsie, standing there.

'What's the meaning of all this noise?' said Sarah sternly. 'Don't you know it's Sunday?'

'Sorry, missis, but Billy told me to bring this round to Mary.' She thrust a piece of paper towards Mary.

Mary stepped forward and took the note. She could guess what was in it without opening it.

'Billy said he's sorry, but you see our gran is ever so ill. We're all going there, all except our Lizzy, she's gorn away with some bloke and we don't know where he lives. Not that we could get there. Lizzy will be ever so sad if Gran dies and she don't see her. Got to go.' With that she turned and ran away.

Mary stood and looked at the paper in her hand.

'I'm so sorry, love,' said her mother as she shut the front door. 'I know how much you were looking forward to going out with him.'

'He's going back to Portsmouth on Wednesday,' said Mary softly. 'I might not see him again for years.'

'Maybe you'll get a chance to go down there when his ship comes back? It might not be years.' Sarah gently tapped her daughter's shoulder and went into the kitchen.

Mary opened the note. It repeated everything Elsie had just told her. He had added that he was very sorry and he'd try to see her again before he went back. Slowly she made her way upstairs. It was good of Billy to worry about his gran and Mary hoped she would get well soon. But her thoughts were muddled. If she didn't see him before he went away she wouldn't have the chance to tell him her feelings. She would have to wait till he wrote to her, that's if he found the time and had the inclination.

On Monday morning Mary looked around for Liz, but she wasn't at work. That evening she went round to see her friend. She banged on the door but there wasn't any answer. After knocking a few more times she gave up and began to walk away, but stopped when the lady next door suddenly came out of her house.

'They've all gone to see the old lady,' said the neighbour. 'They said she was very ill. Don't know how long they'll be there.'

'Thank you,' said Mary.

'Shall I tell them who called?'

'No, it don't matter, I'll see Liz at work.' With that, Mary made her way back home.

It wasn't till Thursday that Liz finally came to work.

'How's your gran?' asked Mary as soon as she saw her.

'She died yesterday,' said Liz softly.

'I'm very sorry.'

'Mum and Dad and the kids are still there arranging the funeral and all that. At least Billy managed to say goodbye to her before he had to go back. She was pleased about that.' Liz sniffed. 'He said he was sorry he didn't get to say goodbye to you, but he's promised to write.'

Mary gave her a weak smile. 'Thanks.' She felt awkward. It seemed wrong to ask her if she'd had a nice weekend when her gran had just passed away. 'Is Pete going to write to you?' was all she could think of saying.

Liz blew her nose and nodded. 'He's got a lovely house and his mum and dad are ever so nice. They made me really welcome.'

'I'm pleased for you. He seems all right.'

'He is. Mary, I do like him.'

Mary smiled. 'Does that mean we might be hearing wedding bells?'

'I shouldn't think so. Remember he's just getting over one romance; I can't see him rushing into another.'

'Give it time.'

'When they come into Portsmouth again, we'll have to go and see them. His mum and dad have got a car. They drive down there.'

'That must be great. Will they take you?'

'Shouldn't think so. But we can go on the train again.'

'I'd like that,' said Mary.

'Well, at least we know where to stay now,' said Liz.

'Yes. That Mrs Johns wasn't a bad old stick,' said Mary.

'And her place was clean and cheap.' Liz laughed. 'Me mum wouldn't have been too happy if I'd brought back some fleas as souvenirs.'

The first letter Mary had from Billy had been posted at Portsmouth. As promised, inside was a picture postcard.

Sarah had laughed. 'Wouldn't have thought you would have wanted one from there.'

112

'Still, at least he's keeping his promise,' said Mary.

'It'll be interesting to see where he is next,' said Ted, who was studying the card.

Mary was pleased Billy hadn't sent a loving message on the back: it meant she could show it to Ted and her mother.

Mary answered his letter right away, but she kept her feelings to herself. Billy's letter was short and just told her they could be off to the Mediterranean again but they would know more when the ship sailed. She didn't want to frighten him away with a declaration of love and a message saying that she would wait for him for ever. She was just going to see how things developed. She had looked up the Mediterranean on the atlas; it was a very big sea.

For the two weeks following Billy's departure the Harding household seemed to be at peace. Although Eddie still had his tantrums, during the week Sarah managed to get him into bed before Ted came home, and at the weekend Mary succeeded in keeping him busy for most of the day and out of the way.

She was still trying to get him to talk and repeated her name over and over again. She was pleased the incidents at the docks had stopped but now he was going through a phase of chewing his clothes and being frightened of people. Was this because Ted had hit him?

The next weekend Ted said he had to work late on Saturday, so Sarah and Mary had their tea alone. When they finished they sat and talked. Although it was a perfect October, the nights were beginning to draw in; Mary found such evenings were the only times they could chat peaceably together.

'Is Sadie all right?' asked Mary. 'I haven't seen her out back for a while.'

'I don't think she's too well, although she does put on a brave face.'

'What's wrong with her?'

'It's her back. Sometimes, when I look out of the back bedroom window and she don't think anyone's watching her, I've seen her gripping the fence in agony. When I've asked her about it she just says it's her age. Her age, I ask you! She's years younger than me. Mind you, she's never been really right since that last baby.'

'D'you think she'll have any more?'

Sarah shook her head. 'No. Think a lot of damage was done at the time.'

'Poor Sadie.' Mary sighed. 'It makes me realise how lucky we are.'

'Yes, we are. Although Ted's very worried about his job with all this unrest in Europe.'

'I expect a lot of people are. Is that why he has to work late?'

'I think so.'

'I wonder where Billy will finish up?'

'Do you care about him?'

'Yes, I do.'

'I'm pleased for you. From what I've seen of him he seems a nice boy.'

'He is.' Mary wasn't going to let on about her true feelings to her mother just yet; Billy must know about them first.

# Chapter 13

Summer had long gone and Christmas was fast approaching. Life was very humdrum for Mary and there hadn't been too many unpleasant incidents at home. Ted still had his nights out and Eddie hadn't improved.

It was Saturday afternoon. Ted was home and had planned to put up the paper chains. The box was brought down from off the top of the wardrobe and Eddie was given some of the old ones to play with. He put them on his head and walked about with them, making Mary laugh.

'Come on and give the pudding a stir,' said Sarah, who had been busy at the kitchen table. 'I need to put it in the boiler all day tomorrow. Don't forget to make a wish.'

Mary took the wooden spoon and gave the wonderful-smelling mixture a stir. Three times she went round and then, closing her eyes and with a great flurry, plonked the spoon in the middle.

'What did you wish for?' asked Ted.

Mary laughed again. 'I ain't telling. It might not come true if I told you.' She had wished that Billy would come home and ask her to marry him. But she knew that she really was wishing for something that might never be.

'Right. It's Eddie's turn,' said Sarah, lifting him up to stand on the chair. She tied a tea towel round him and he giggled along with them. She gave him the wooden spoon and, holding his hand, showed him what to do. His laughter was a joy to hear and when Sarah let his hand go he banged the spoon up and down, so everybody soon had spots of Christmas pudding on them.

'I think that's enough, son,' said Ted, putting him back on the floor.

Mary was waiting for the tantrum, but it didn't come as Eddie was too busy licking the spoon.

Mary was sad that he wasn't like other children and couldn't understand about Father Christmas and the joy Christmas Eve would bring. She would have loved to have taken him to a big store to see Father Christmas, but that was something she wasn't prepared to risk.

The thing that did bring a fresh smile to Mary's face was the letter and Christmas card she received from Billy. This one had been posted in Gibraltar. Again there was a card with a view. Mary had told Billy that her mother had enjoyed these pictures as much as she did and this one was inside an envelope with just some information scribbled on the back.

'It looks a lovely place,' said Sarah, admiring the view.

So far Mary had been very careful not to tell Billy her true feelings, as his letters had been informative but not very loving. Even his Christmas card had just said, 'Love from Billy.' Nothing romantic at all. Mary knew that Pete was writing to Liz, and couldn't help wondering if his letters were different.

'Is he loving?' Mary asked when she showed Liz the card she'd received.

'I ain't telling. Is my brother?'

Sadly Mary shook her head.

'Give him time,' said Liz. 'I know he likes you.' And Mary had to be content with that.

'What say we go up West tomorrow afternoon?' said Liz as they walked home on Friday night. 'That might help to cheer you up.'

With Christmas just over a week away, to Mary that sounded a very good idea. 'I need to get my presents and it'll be nice to see all the Christmas decorations in the shops.'

'Good, that's settled. We'll go straight from work. What you getting me?' asked Liz.

'You'll have to wait and see.'

On Saturday, the atmosphere in Oxford Street put them in a happy mood as they were jostled and swept along with the crowds. They managed to find a space to stop and stare in one of the store's windows.

'Just look at that hat,' said Liz. 'Cor, I'd like something like that in me stocking.'

Mary was looking intently when a reflection of a man in the window caused her to spin round. He had just passed them and had now crossed to the other side of the road. For a brief second he looked at her. He appeared very agitated as he hurried away.

'What is it? What's wrong?' asked Liz.

'That was Ted.' Mary pushed her way to the kerb and was straining her neck to see over the crowds. 'I'm sure it was him.' Mary turned back to Liz. 'D'you know, he had a young woman on his arm?'

'What? Where?'

'He's disappeared in the crowd.'

'You sure it was him? A lot of blokes wear a trilby like he does and the way everybody's muffled up you could have been mistaken.'

'I don't think I was. He looked at me. What's he doing up here? He told Mum he was going to have to stay on at work.'

'Perhaps he did and then had to take his secretary out. I

don't know. He may be out getting your mum's present and needs a woman's opinion. Does he work near here?'

'Don't know. I only know it's in an office. I suppose it could be round here somewhere.'

'Mary, don't read too much into it. As I said, he might have a perfectly good reason to have a young woman on his arm, that's if it was him.'

'I hope you're right.'

But all the while they did their shopping Mary was more intent on looking for Ted than for presents.

Mary's first words when she walked in and plonked her parcels down were: 'Mum, I thought I saw Dad this afternoon.'

'Did you? Where?'

'Along Oxford Street.'

'It couldn't have been Ted, he was working.'

'It looked like him. Where does he work?'

'In an office by Victoria somewhere. Ask him when he gets home, but I'm sure you were mistaken.'

The more Mary thought about it the more positive she was that she hadn't been mistaken. She didn't think she should tell her mother about the young lady holding Ted's arm; she would wait to hear what Ted said first. But would he say who the woman was?

It wasn't till ten-thirty that Ted came in. Mary could see he'd had a few drinks.

'You're very late, love,' said Sarah.

'Been very busy.' His speech was a bit slurred.

'Would you like a cup of tea?'

He plonked himself in a chair and grinned. 'That'll be nice.'

'Ted, have you been drinking?'

'Just getting into the Christmas spirit with some of the boys, that's all.'

'Dad, did I see you in Oxford Street this afternoon?'

Ted laughed. 'Oxford Street? I wish. I was busy working.'

'It looked ever so much like you.'

'Poor bloke.' Ted took the cup from Sarah. 'Thank you, my love. Have you had a good day?'

'No different from usual.'

'How's the boy been?'

'Not bad.'

Mary was still sure she'd seen Ted, but there was no way she could find out if he was telling the truth. Perhaps he had been buying presents and would tell her so later when her mother was out of earshot.

On Christmas morning, as she made her way downstairs, Mary felt happier than she had for a long while. This past week Ted had been home most nights and her mother looked more relaxed. Even Eddie appeared to have picked up on the pleasant atmosphere and seemed less troubled. Last night after he'd gone to bed they'd decorated the tree with lights and baubles and filled Eddie's stocking. Mary had bought him a box of building bricks and her mother had given him a large thick picture book; Ted gave him sweets and a little car. Later on they had sat and played board games; the whole evening had been happy and fun. Mary loved it when they sat in the front room with the roaring fire and the wireless.

This morning Mary could hear her mother singing carols and Eddie making noises as if trying to join in. She stood outside the kitchen door for a moment or two. Her mother's laughter caused tears to fill her eyes. She was so lucky compared to the family next door. Sarah had made the Fellowses a cake and a Christmas pudding; later Mary was going in to take Sadie a box of biscuits and sweets for the kids. Now, she pushed open the kitchen door, calling: 'Merry Christmas!' She went up to her mother and gave her a hug and a kiss.

'And a merry Christmas to you.'

Mary then kissed Eddie who was banging a spoon on the table.

'The chicken is in the oven.'

'Has he seen the tree yet?' asked Mary, nodding towards Eddie.

'No. I thought I'd wait till I've lit the fire and the room's cosy and warm and we're all together. I've just made the tea, perhaps you could take Ted up a cup?'

'Course.' Mary took the cup and saucer and made her way upstairs. She knocked very gently on the door. 'Dad, it's me, I've brought you up your tea.'

The grunt from the room told her he was awake. 'Merry Christmas,' she said brightly, placing the cup and saucer on the table beside the bed. 'Come on, get up, you lazy thing. It's Christmas.'

'I know. I know. Tell your mother I'll be down in a jiff.'

'It's dark in here, shall I open the curtains?'

'No. I'll do it when me eyes are ready.'

'Have you got a hangover? You did have rather a lot to drink last night.'

'Don't you start, I have enough of that from your mother.'

Mary laughed. As she walked round the bed she fell over a jacket. 'And you don't hang things up after you.'

'Don't nag.'

Mary picked the jacket from off the floor and as she did so Ted's wallet landed at her feet and the contents spilled out. As she gathered together bills, money, photos and various other bits and pieces, Mary smiled to herself. She put the old wallet on the dressing table; it was tatty and the stitching had come undone – in fact, it was falling to pieces. Mary was pleased she had bought him a new one for Christmas.

'Come on, we're waiting to open our presents.'

'All right. Talk about no rest for the wicked.' He swung his legs out of the bed and, putting on his dressing gown, left the room.

Mary went to the window and pulled back the curtains. Then, as she turned to leave the room, she saw she had left some of the contents of Ted's wallet on the floor. She bent down and picked them up. There were a few more pieces of paper and a photo of a very pretty young woman. She had never seen this before. Mary sat on the bed and studied it. Could this be the sister he never talked about? Had her mother seen this? The photograph looked old and the edges were a little dog-eared. Mary turned it over and took a quick breath. The photographer was Palmer's and the address was Commercial Road, Portsmouth. Who had lived at Portsmouth? She sat staring at the photo. He said he'd never been to Portsmouth. Mary wanted to know more about this woman, but would it spoil the day if Ted didn't want them to know about her? After all, he'd never shown this picture to her, and her mother had never mentioned it. She heard his footsteps on the stairs; she had no time to get across the room and put it back in his wallet, so she quickly hid the photo in the pocket of her pinny. She would sort it out later.

'What are you up to in here?' asked Ted, coming into the bedroom.

Mary felt her face flush with guilt. Should she hand it to him? What would he say? Would he think she'd been snooping? She quickly turned away; she would put it back later. 'Nothing, just pulling the bed back to air.'

'Well, let me get dressed then, young lady. That's a pretty pinny.'

Mary's hand quickly went to her pocket. 'Yes. Liz bought it for me for Christmas.'

'So you've already opened your presents?'

'No, only this one, I knew what it was and I wanted to look nice for Christmas and I didn't want to spoil me frock while I'm helping Mum.'

'That's all right then. Now shoo.'

As Mary left the room she felt full of guilt that she still had the photo. Would he look for it? She decided to wait and see; when the right time came she could replace it.

'Mary, I thought we'd wait till after dinner this year to open our presents,' said her mother. 'It'll be nice to sit in the front room and not have to keep jumping up to see to the food.'

'That's all right. I'll pop into next door after breakfast.'

When Mary knocked on the door the kids came bounding up to her.

'Come and see what we made at school,' said Rosie. She pointed to the few paper chains they had draped around. 'And we didn't have to pay for 'em. Our teacher gave 'em to us as a present.'

'They've very nice. I've got you all some sweets.'

'Cor, thanks, Mary,' said Ron. 'I got a Christmas present from the bloke I work for. He gave me half a crown.'

'Thinks he's the king of the castle now he's got a job on Sat'day,' said Rosie, 'and it's only taking old ladies' shopping home for 'em.'

'I get to ride a bike though, don't I? When I leave school next year I can work for him all the time.'

'Stop it, you two. Forever arguing, they are,' said Sadie with a sigh.

Mary smiled. 'I've got you a box of biscuits, Sadie. Not that I reckon you'll sit and eat them all yourself.'

Sadie laughed. 'I don't think I'd get a chance with this lot. Still, I don't wanner get fat.'

Mary also laughed. Although Sadie looked older and worn out these days, she was always ready to have a laugh. But it would take more than a box of biscuits to put flesh on Sadie's bones.

Mary stayed a while and talked to the children. She was aware that Mr Fellows wasn't around and guessed he was at the pub. 'So what have you got for dinner then?' she asked.

'Been saving up for a bit of pork. It'll be nice with roast taters and veg. And for afters we've got the pudding your mum made us. I'll make a bit of custard to go with it.'

'And for tea we've got the cake,' said Rosie with her bright little eyes shining. 'This is gonner be the bestest Christmas we've ever had.'

'You said that last year,' said Ron.

'Well, just goes to show, they get better every year. And when you and me can go out to work proper, they'll be even better.'

Mary wanted to hug this dear little girl who was always willing to run errands for anyone in the street for a ha'penny. It was just a pity she wouldn't push Eddie out in his pram now – she used to like having a couple of pence for taking him out just for an hour; it had been such a help to Sarah, but that was all over now he was so much of a handful. Rosie was a survivor and in her mind she had their future mapped out for them.

'When I'm old enough I'm gonner join the navy like your bloke,' said Ron.

'He's only saying that to get a uniform,' said Rosie.

'Well, it's gotter be better than having yer arse hanging out of yer trousers all the time.'

'Mum, did you hear that? Our Ron swore. And on Christ's birthday as well. What did you get for Christmas, Mary?'

'We're not opening ours till after dinner, then Mum can sit and relax.'

'I couldn't wait that long. Mum made me and Ron a pair of gloves. They're ever so nice. Is that a new pinny?'

'Yes, my friend Liz bought it for me.'

'It's lovely.'

Mary smiled and touched her pocket; the photo was still there.

After a while she left. The girls gave her a hug, thanking her for the sweets and biscuits. Despite everything Sadie was doing a wonderful job with her kids.

The smell of the dinner filled Mary's nostrils when she pushed open the kitchen door. Eddie was sitting in his chair gently rocking back and forth; his presents were scattered round the floor. His face lit up when Mary walked into the room. He scrambled off the chair and Mary bent down and held him close.

'Look at these nice toys.' But Eddie turned away when she picked up the book. She turned the pages, persevering. 'Look, Eddie.'

He was content with burying his head in her shoulder. Mary's thoughts went to next door. Those kids would give their back teeth for Eddie's presents, but he didn't seem to notice them. He wasn't a normal child and she wished she could find out why.

After dinner they opened their presents. Ted was really pleased with his wallet. He sat turning it over. 'Thank you, Mary.' He kissed her cheek. 'This is something I really do need, a good leather wallet. I'll transfer everything later.'

Mary smiled. How was she going to get the photo that was

nestling in her pocket back before he missed it? Mary tore the paper away from her present. 'Oh, thank you,' she said excitedly. 'A new handbag. It's just what I wanted.'

'Look inside,' said her mother enthusiastically.

Mary opened the navy blue bag and found a small purse. Inside was: 'A pound note! Thank you.' She kissed Ted and her mother's cheek.

Mary watched her mother open Ted's presents. There was a scarf and gloves and a box of chocolates. There was nothing there he couldn't have got on his own. Mary had bought her mother stockings and a white petticoat.

Everybody was in a good mood and laughing and even Eddie joined in, busying himself tearing up the paper.

At three o'clock they settled down to hear King George's speech.

'I think it's wonderful that we can really hear our King speak,' said Sarah when it was over.

'That's progress, my dear,' said Ted, putting more coal on the fire.

It wasn't long before Ted and Sarah, who had had more than a drop of port, sat back and began to close their eyes. Even Eddie was quietly amusing himself. Mary decided this would be a good time to put the photo back upstairs.

She stood up and put her hand in the pocket of her pinny. Then she panicked. It had gone! It must have fallen out. But where? She sat back down and tried to remember. She had been out to the lav, in the scullery and next door. Making sure the fireguard was in place she went first into the kitchen and scullery and searched round the floor. Then, not having any luck, she went out to the lav. It was freezing cold but she carefully retraced her steps. She could feel the tears welling up. What if Ted had found it? Surely he would have said something if it was an innocent picture?

Who was the woman? Perhaps he never looked at it and wouldn't even miss it. She should never have taken it. She didn't want to cause any trouble. Mary went back into the front room. She sat on the sofa and after rummaging down the sides to no avail, she sat back and pondered. Where could it be?

# Chapter 14

They had finished tea and Mary was in the scullery helping her mother wash up.

'You all right, Mary?' asked her mother over her shoulder. 'You seem to be very quiet.'

'Yes, I'm fine.'

Ted came into the kitchen. 'I'm just going to take the boy up to bed. He seems whacked out.'

'Well, it's been a long day for him and with us all around him I expect he's feeling tired.'

'And bewildered,' said Ted. 'Would be nice if he could really appreciate everything that has been happening.'

Mary was pleased to hear Ted take an interest in Eddie and speak kindly about him.

'I think he does in his own funny little way. I'll just finish off here then I'll give you a hand. I'll bring our presents up as well, then I can put them away,' said Sarah. 'I'm really pleased with what I got this year.'

'So am I,' said Ted as he left the kitchen.

Mary froze. What if Ted wanted to put everything in his new wallet? Would he miss that photo? 'Mum, has Dad said anything else about his sister?'

Sarah turned from the sink. 'What a funny thing to ask. Whatever made you want to bring that up again?'

Mary shrugged. 'Don't know. Cos it's Christmas I suppose. He never gets any cards from her or shows us any photos of his family.'

'I don't think he has any photos.' Sarah turned back to the washing up.

Mary's mind was going round and round. So her mother had never seen that photo. 'Do you ever wonder what his family looked like and if Eddie resembles any of them?'

'No.' Sarah's mind was also turning over. She took a quick breath and tried to steady her nerves. What was Mary thinking? That Eddie's condition was due to something in Ted's side of the family? Deep down Sarah worried that it could be on her side. She threw the water away and wiped her hands. 'I'll just go up and give Ted a hand.'

Mary stood and gazed out of the scullery window, but she wasn't seeing anything. Where was that photo? Should she go next door and ask them if it had fallen out of her pocket while she was in there? It could have been when the kids were scrambling over her. She had to find it.

Mary went back into the kitchen and looked at the clock. It was almost eight o'clock, too late to call in next door; besides, Mr Fellows might be there and she didn't want him asking questions.

Ted came into the kitchen. 'That was very nice of you to give me a wallet, it was certainly something I needed. In fact I have lost a couple of things from the old one recently.'

'Not any money, I hope,' she said as light-heartedly as she could.

'No, just a bill and—' He stopped. 'And don't tell your mother, but I lost a photo as well.'

Mary took a sharp breath. 'Who of?'

'Why, your mother of course.'

'Mum? When did you lose it?'

128

'Not really sure.'

'Which photo was it? Perhaps I can find you another one.'

'It was the one she had taken at the seaside before I met her.'

It certainly wasn't her mother in that photo; besides, she'd never been to Portsmouth. Mary busied herself tidying up, and said, with her back turned, 'Have you any idea where you might have lost it?'

'No. It could be at work, but it might even be under the bed.'

'When did you have it last?'

'Don't remember. I'll have to wait till morning to look for it. It might have been when I'd had a drink or two.' He laughed. 'Don't tell your mother,' he repeated. 'She's always saying I'm untidy. Just popping outside.'

Mary, trying desperately to think clearly, watched him go outside to the lav. She was bewildered. Why had he bothered to tell her about the photo? Did he suspect she knew about it? But then she would know it wasn't of her mother. If she could find the photo she could put it under the bed and he wouldn't know she'd seen it. What excuse could she have to go next door? Suddenly the sound of crockery being thrown against the wall caused her to look up.

'I hope he don't wake Eddie up,' said her mother, coming back into the kitchen and looking at the wall. 'I wonder what poor Sadie's done now?'

'Might not be her. It could be the kids larking about.'

'Could be. I hope they don't make too much of a racket. I don't know how that dear little Brian sleeps through it all.'

'Must be used to it.'

Sarah was worried about Sadie, but tried to brush it aside. 'I don't want them waking Eddie,' she reiterated.

'He's gone off then?' asked Mary.

'No trouble.'

'I'm glad he liked his bricks.'

'At least it gives him something to do: piling them up and knocking them down again.'

'And it makes him laugh,' said Mary.

Another plate hit the wall.

'Why does he have to start tonight of all nights? There should be peace to all men,' said Sarah.

'He probably don't know the true meaning of Christmas,' said Ted, re-entering the kitchen. 'It's freezing out there. I hope the lav don't freeze up.'

'Those poor kids.' Sarah sighed. 'I'm surprised they're as sane as they are.'

'Do you think I should go in and make sure they're all right?' asked Mary.

'No, love. Best stay out of it.'

'Sadie's not going to thank you for interfering, Mary,' said Ted, putting his arm round Sarah's waist. 'Now come on, let's get back in the front room. It's nice and cosy in there.'

Sarah and Mary followed Ted through, but Mary couldn't concentrate on playing Ludo and her missing moves made Ted laugh.

'I think our Mary has had too much to drink. Her mind's gone all fuzzy,' said Ted.

Mary smiled. That wasn't what was blurring her mind.

The following morning Mary said she was going next door to collect the basin the Christmas pudding had been in.

'You don't have to worry about that,' said her mother. 'It can wait. I'm not in any hurry for it.'

'I'd really like to see if Sadie's all right.'

'She will be. She's used to him behaving like that, and she won't thank you for interfering. I know. I've asked before and got short sharp shrift. You could find out if Rosie could go round Silwood Street tomorrow for me. I'll be needing a bundle of wood; Mrs West sold out before Christmas and I can't see her getting any more for a few days.'

Mary smiled. 'I'm sure Rosie'll run round there for you. I'll take sixpence in.'

'Thanks.'

Mary very carefully retraced her steps looking in the gutter and every nook and cranny en route. There were plenty of dog ends and rubbish which she gently turned over with the toe of her shoe, but no sign of the photograph. She couldn't wait to get in next door but when Ron opened the front door the sight of the objects strewn about the passage made her cringe.

'Hello, Mary. Come on in.'

What if the photo was under all that lot? She'd never find it. She followed Ron into the kitchen and wasn't happy at seeing Mr Fellows sitting in the chair. As usual he was unwashed and unshaved but she had to hide a smile when he turned and she saw he had a bit of plaster stuck on his forehead.

Ron saw Mary quickly glance at his father and grinned. 'He chucked a plate at Mum; she ducked and chucked one back, and her aim's better than his.'

'Shut yer trap, yer saucy sod.'

'Hello, Mary,' said Sadie, coming into the kitchen. 'Rosie, get Sarah's basin,' she called out. 'We've still got a bit of cake left, so I'll bring the plate in later. I'll make sure it's out of his way,' she said, inclining her head towards her husband. 'So what can we do for you?'

'I've come to ask Rosie if she'll get Mum a bundle of firewood tomorrow. Mrs West sold out before Christmas, so she'll have to go up to the ironmonger's in Silwood Street. Is that all right?'

Rosie came into the kitchen. 'Hello, Mary. Course I'll go.'

Mary handed her the sixpence. 'Thanks.' Mary looked around. 'Did you have a nice Christmas?'

'Not bad. He was his usual self,' said Sadie looking at her husband.

Ron came up to them. 'That means pissed as usual,' he whispered, bending his head towards Mary, for he was as tall as she was now.

'You watch your mouth.' Mr Fellows stood up and came menacingly towards Ron. 'I'll swing for you one of these days, me lad.'

Ron just walked away, but Mary was terrified.

'I'm going out.' Mr Fellows lumbered towards the kitchen door and took his coat off the large nail. When he left the room he slammed the door after him, making Mary jump. Then they heard the front door bang.

'Sorry about that, Mary,' said Sadie. 'He won't be back till closing time.'

'Why do you put up with him?' asked Mary. 'Sorry, I shouldn't have said that.'

'That's all right. But I ain't got a lot of option. His name's on the rent book and if I clear off the kids will be put in care and I couldn't stand that.'

Mary sat down at the table. 'I don't suppose you found a photo yesterday, did you? I may have dropped one.'

'No,' said Sadie. 'Did any of you kids find Mary's photo?' she called out.

'No,' came back a chorus.

'Who was it of?' asked Sadie.

Mary was trying to think fast. 'Me mate's granma.'

'To tell the truth I ain't done much housework, but I'll look for it when I have a sweep round.'

'Thanks. I'd better be off.'

'I'll get the wood tomorrow,' said Rosie.

Mary made her way back home, hoping the photo would turn up soon. At least it didn't matter now if Sadie handed it to her mother, not if they thought it was Liz's gran. Just as long as Ted wasn't there. He'd know who it was and he'd ask how it had come to be at Sadie's. Then he'd realise that Mary had taken it.

Everyone at the factory was talking about the Christmas they'd had. Liz was thrilled she'd received a Christmas card from Pete's mum and dad. It was being passed up the line.

'Looks like they've got you down for their new daughter-in-law,' said Bet.

Liz blushed. 'Mind you, that wouldn't be such a bad move. They live in a smashing house.'

Mary looked at her friend. 'Do you really mean that? You hardly know him.'

'I know. But I do like him and his mum and dad.'

'You sure it's not more about where he lives and what they've got?'

'Mary, don't be so ... No. It's because I like him. Don't you believe in love at first sight?'

Mary couldn't answer as she felt the same about Billy, but she was pretty sure he didn't feel the same way about her.

On her way home Mary called in at Sadie's first. 'Hello, Rosie.'

'Come in. Me mum's found yer photo. It was in the passage under the pram.'

As Mary followed her along the passage, she could have hugged her.

'Mum was gonner give it to yer mum, but she ain't seen her.'

'That's all right. I'll take it.'

Sadie was standing at the table doing the ironing when Mary went into the kitchen. 'Hello, Mary love.' She took a black iron off the hob and spat on it, making it sizzle. 'Rosie told you I found that photo?'

Mary nodded.

'It's up there on the mantelpiece,' she said as she flattened out what looked like a pair of pants. 'Don't know why I bother to iron these. They're in the wash more times than they're on our Ron's bum.'

'Mum,' yelled Ron. 'Don't say things like that in front of Mary. It's cos I play football and keep falling over.' He hurried from the room.

Sadie was laughing. 'I shouldn't tease him, he's a good lad.'

Mary picked up the photo. She wanted to cry. It was creased and the corner had been chewed.

'You all right, love?' asked Sadie. 'Want a cuppa?'

Mary sat down in the tatty armchair and shook her head.

'What's wrong?'

'The photo.' Mary handed her the picture. 'It's all crumpled and chewed.'

'I know. Was it like this when you lost it?'

Again Mary shook her head.

'Must have been young Brian, he puts everything in his mouth.' Sadie started to straighten it out. 'I'm really sorry about that. Shall I run the iron over it?'

'No.' Mary jumped up and took the photo. She sat back down and looked at it.

'I'm sure your friend's got another one. Don't get so upset.'

Mary looked up. Tears were sliding down her cheeks. 'What am I to do?'

Sadie got down on one knee and put her arm round Mary. 'What is it, love?'

Iris came running into the room. 'Mum, Brian wants the pot.'

'Get Rosie to sit him on it. And stay out for a minute or two. I'm talking to Mary.'

Mary had turned away when Iris burst in.

'Is Mary all right?' asked Iris.

'Yes, now shoo.' Sadie stood up. She went over to Iris and, gently smacking her bottom, edged her out of the room.

'Now, Mary. What's troubling you? Do you want to talk about it?'

Mary nodded and wiped her eyes. She then explained about the photo and how she'd found it.

'Oh dear,' said Sadie when she'd finished. 'So you don't know who this is.' Sadie was studying the picture. 'The simple thing would be to just ask him.'

'But he told me it was me mum. Besides, that picture was taken in Portsmouth, but she ain't ever been there. And when I was going down there to see Billy, *he* said he'd never been there either.'

'P'rhaps he ain't. Someone might have sent him this.'

'Then why won't he tell us who it is?'

'I don't know, love.' Sadie handed the photo back. 'If I was you I'd tackle him about it.'

Mary shook her head. 'No, I couldn't do that. I don't want to cause any trouble. I wish I could go to Portsmouth and find out who she is.'

'Why? Is it that important?'

Mary shrugged.

'I think you might be reading more into this than you need to. Why don't you have a word with your mum? After all, she's a very understanding woman.'

Mary stood up and wiped her eyes. She gave Sadie a watery smile. 'Thanks. I'll sort it out somehow. Don't say anything to Mum about this, will you?'

'No, not if you don't want me to.'

As Mary made her way next door, her thoughts were churning round and round. Was Sadie right? Was she trying to read something into this that wasn't there? She hadn't told Sadie that she was worried that Eddie's condition could be hereditary and that it could have come from Ted's family. The picture was in such a bad state that she couldn't put it under the bed. It'd be best if she threw it in the back yard: that would explain its poor condition, and Ted would think he'd lost it going out to the lav. Mary brightened up. Yes, that was it. But she still wouldn't know who the young woman was. It was then that another thought struck her. If only Billy were home, she would have an excuse to go to Commercial Road, Portsmouth, and see the photographer. She clasped her fingers round the photo. If she threw it away she wouldn't have it to show the photographer. No, she'd keep it. That'd be best. There would come a time when, with any luck, she'd be going to see Billy. It might not be for several months, but she could wait. Mary pulled the key though the letterbox and went inside.

The usual scene met Mary's eyes when she walked into the kitchen. Eddie was playing on the floor; Ted was sitting reading his newspaper; and her mother was bustling about getting the dinner.

'All right, love?' asked Sarah.

'Yes, thanks. Had a good day, Dad?'

'Not bad. How about you?'

'I'm fine.' Mary smiled and felt surreptitiously for the photo.

# Chapter 15

Winter was over and with the arrival of spring everyone's spirits were lighter. It was Easter Monday and Mary and Liz were at Blackheath wandering around the fair.

'Not the same, is it?' said Mary.

Liz shook her head. 'Didn't think it would be.'

'See, I said we should have gone to Portsmouth.'

'Didn't see the point, not if Pete wasn't there.' Liz stopped and watched some fellows at the shooting gallery. 'We did have a lot of fun with them, didn't we?'

'Yes, but it would have been nice, just going down there for two days.' Mary still had at the back of her mind the idea of going there to find out more about the photo that she had secretly hidden away. She had been disappointed she hadn't been able to persuade Liz to go. Ted had never mentioned the photograph again, so she assumed that he thought he'd lost it at work. 'We could have stayed the night with Mrs Johns.'

'I know. But I can't really afford it.'

'Fancy a go?' said the stallholder, holding out a gun to Liz.

'No, thanks,' she said, shaking her head.

'What if I have a go for you?' said a young spotty lad who was standing nearby.

'No. It's all right.'

'Might win you a furry toy.'

Liz smiled at him. 'That's nice of you but me and me mate are just going on the chair-o-planes.'

'We'll come with you, won't we, Tom?' said the spotty lad, pushing his mate forward.

'No, it's all right. Besides,' Liz whispered, 'our boyfriends're waiting for us.' And she and Mary walked away, grinning.

'Still got the old charm then, Liz,' said Mary.

'I wouldn't mind if they weren't still at school. Blimey, I'm nearly old enough to be his mum.'

Arm in arm, the girls continued to wander round, but Blackheath would never hold the same excitement for them as it had before Portsmouth.

Easter had come and gone and now the excitement that was rippling through the country was the forthcoming Silver Jubilee of King George and Queen Mary. Mary continued to get letters and cards from Billy and she carefully followed his progress on her map of the Mediterranean. The last card she'd had had been a picture of Malta. Liz still got letters from Pete but was very cagey about the contents. Billy hardly mentioned him; as they were different ranks, he had told her that they didn't socialise that much now they were on board.

Tomorrow, Monday 6 May 1935, was the day the whole country was going to celebrate the Silver Jubilee. Today every able-bodied person in Doyle Street was out helping to put up the bunting and flags. The kids were running about wildly and getting in the way. Everybody was happy and the air was full of excitement. Mr and Mrs West in the grocer's shop had been in charge of all the arrangements and Doyle Street had been saving for weeks for the children's party to be held in the afternoon. Tables, chairs, anything that could be used was going to be brought out of every home and placed down the centre of the street. Everyone was helping to do something. The children were going to have sandwiches, cakes, jelly and lemonade by the jugful and all of them were going to be given paper hats and a commemorative mug. In the evening the grown-ups would be supping beer from the barrels that had been carefully placed on trestles in the grocer's to settle. There was sure to be a knees-up to the three-piece band that had been put together. There was a lot of musical talent in Doyle Street.

Mary went into their front room to gather up all the bunting her mother had been busy making for weeks. The floor was covered with brightly coloured triangles of red, white and blue material all sewn together on yards of tape. In the middle of it all sat Eddie giggling and throwing it up in the air.

'All right if I take this lot? Mary asked her mother, who was busy treadling away on her sewing machine.

'Yes, of course,' said Sarah, cutting the tape and breaking off the cotton. 'How are the men getting on?'

Mary laughed. 'That old Mr Coxen at the end nearly fell out of his window trying to reach for the flags that were being thrown up to his window. That was till someone went and fetched the ladder.'

'Oh dear. I do hope they don't have any injuries. Where was Ted?'

'The last I saw of him he was hanging out of a window tying a flag to a pole.'

Sarah laughed. 'I hope someone was holding on to his legs.'

'The street's starting to look really lovely. Everybody's so pleased at what you've done,' said Mary.

'Well, it's nice that we can all do our bit.'

'Come on, Eddie. Up.'

He scrambled to his feet and Mary bent down to gather up the flags.

'Say flags.'

He giggled and hid his head.

'Say flags.' Mary waved one in front of him.

'Mary, I think you deserve top marks for trying.' Sarah went back to her sewing. Her daughter would never stop trying to teach him to speak.

Mary walked out into the bright sunlight with her arms full of bunting. She felt so happy. This was going to be one of the best days of her life.

The following morning, the first thing Mary did when she jumped out of bed was to go to the window and look out. It wasn't raining. She ran downstairs and opened the front door. She looked up and down Doyle Street; it looked so different and lovely. The flags were criss-crossed across the street from every bedroom window; high above the road they gently waved back and forth. One or two of the neighbours were out already making sure everything was as they'd left it last night. This was going to be a day no one would forget.

All morning the preparations continued. Mrs Mann's piano was pushed into the middle of the road and a drum kit was set up next to it.

Excitement was running high and parents were having trouble keeping their kids under control. Then at long last it was time for the festivities to start.

Mary held Eddie's hand tight as they sat on the coping that ran round their bay window. Sarah had been worried about him joining the other kids at the tables so Mary sat with him while her mother helped the other women dish out the food and drink. She was also busy watching Mr Fellows. He had been hanging round the beer all morning.

'Everything all right, Mary?' asked Sadie.

'Yes, thanks.'

'This is great, ain't it? And I can't tell you how pleased and grateful I am that your mum made the girls those frocks.'

Mary looked across at Rosie, Iris and the twins in their red, white and blue striped frocks. There had even been enough leftovers to make the girls hairbands.

'They're that proud of 'em that Rosie don't reckon she's ever gonner take hers off!'

Mary smiled. 'Remember, Mum don't guarantee that they won't run or shrink in the wash – it was only cheap material.'

'They don't care. Mind you, I'm a bit worried about me old man.' She nodded towards Wally, who was holding up a pint of beer to the light and having a big discussion about it with a neighbour. 'He's gonner be well and truly plastered before the night even starts.' Sadie moved Brian from one hip to the other. 'Mind if I sit down? He's getting such a lump. I daren't let him go – he'll cause chaos pulling at everything.'

Brian grinned. He was only two but he was a big boy. He was turning this way and that, fascinated by all he could see, calling out to his brothers and sisters.

'He talks really well,' said Mary.

'Has to in our house, otherwise he'd get nothing. Look at those bloody twins, I've told 'em not to stuff so much in their mouths – and they're wiping their hands all down the front of those frocks.'

Mary smiled. It must look like a feast from heaven for Sadie's kids.

Gradually the food disappeared and the kids started to get restless. At the far end of the street, where there weren't any tables, someone had set up the games. There was to be a tug-o'-war, a sack race, an egg-and-spoon race and much

141

more. Judging by the shouts and screams from the kids, they were enjoying themselves.

Rosie came running back, red-faced and happy. 'Look,' she yelled out, coming up to her mother. 'I won the sack race and I've got a prize.' Rosie held out the book she'd been given.

'It's not fair,' said Iris. 'I want one.'

'You gotter be as fast as me,' said Rosie, smugly clutching her prize to her chest. 'Come on, they're gonner have the tug-o'-war next. Mind this for me, Mum. Don't let anyone pinch it.'

Sadie looked proudly at her children. 'This'll be a day they'll remember all the rest of their lives.'

As the sun slowly disappeared behind the rooftops, one by one the children started to get irritable and the parents knew it was time for them to go home and to bed.

Rosie came up to Sarah and Mary. 'Look, I didn't get any food down me.' She gently smoothed out the front of her dress, then kissed Sarah's cheek. 'Thank you for me lovely frock.'

'It was my pleasure.' Sarah smiled as she watched Sadie take them indoors. 'What a day they've had,' she said as she sat back down on the coping.

'It has been good,' said Mary, sitting next to her. 'Did you see Eddie jumping up and down when he was watching the kids running?'

Sarah smiled. 'I'm glad Ted's putting him to bed. I feel whacked.'

'I know you've been busy, but I hope not too much so, Mum, the best is yet to come.'

'Just give me a moment or two and then I'll get me second wind.'

'Thought you might need this,' said Ted, coming out balancing three cups of tea on a tray.

'You're a life-saver,' said Sarah.

'All part of the service, madam.'

It was at that moment the band struck up. Old Mrs Mann was seated at the piano and was pounding out 'Tip-toe through the Tulips'. As she thumped the keys the tops of her chubby arms wobbled, making Mary laugh. The man on the drums was bashing away enthusiastically and Mr Penn was playing his accordion. The cheerful sound filled the air and soon everybody was singing and their feet were tapping; many grabbed their partners and started to dance.

When darkness fell and the drink was flowing the singing got louder and the laughter even louder. There was one group of men, all of whom seemed to be holding each other up. Mr Fellows was in the middle of it. Sadie was having a knees-up with Sarah and Mary. When it finished, they plonked themselves, gasping and laughing, on chairs that had been brought out.

'That was good!' said Sarah.

'Don't know when I've enjoyed meself so much,' said Sadie breathlessly.

'You should have joined in, Dad,' said Mary, collapsing next to Ted.

'Dancing's not really my thing. But the drinking is. Can I get anyone another?'

'Can I have a lemonade?'

'Certainly, Mary. How about you, Sadie, what can I get you?'

Sadie giggled. 'Now that would be telling.'

'Mrs Fellows,' said Sarah. 'I hope you're not giving my husband any naughty ideas.'

The loud shrieks of laughter had Mr Fellows looking over at them.

143

'Oh Christ, here comes trouble,' said Sadie, suddenly looking afraid as her husband started to lurch towards them.

'Was you laughing at me?' he asked, spilling his beer as he stood rocking in front of Sadie.

'No, why should we?'

'Just thought you was taking the piss.' He was having a great deal of difficulty standing.

'Well, we wasn't, so go back to your beer-swilling mates.'

'Don't you talk to me like that, you old slag. I'll give you a bloody good hiding if you ain't careful.'

'Now come on, mate,' said Ted, standing up and taking his arm. 'Don't spoil a good day.'

Wally brushed Ted's arm away. 'Don't you lay a finger on me, you stuck-up ponce. She's me wife and I can do what I like with her.' He went to gesture with his hand and spilled beer all over Sadie. 'Just remember, she belongs to me,' he yelled out.

The music had stopped and everyone was looking at them.

'Trust you to make an exhibition of yourself,' Sadie hissed. 'You're only happy when you're causing trouble.' She stood up and, pushing him out of the way, went inside their house.

He staggered and almost fell. 'You cow, just wait till I get me hands on you,' he shouted, going after her.

Ted went to follow them but Sarah put her hand out. 'No, Ted. Let them sort it out. Tell them to start the music again.'

Ted did as he was told, but nobody moved.

Mary was so upset. They had been having such a wonderful time, how could one man stop so many people enjoying themselves? But what about poor Sadie, what would happen to her?

Gradually the musicians began playing again, songs everyone knew, and that got them singing and they started to get into the party spirit again.

It was close on midnight when the beer ran out and everybody began to make their way indoors. The chairs had been taken inside and those who had had too much to drink had been put to bed. With great difficulty and a lot of giggling Mary helped Sarah to get Ted upstairs; they left him on the bed snoring his head off. They were sitting quietly having a cup of tea talking about the day's events when somebody banging on the front door startled them.

'Who's that?' called out Sarah.

'Tell 'em we're out of beer,' said Mary, giggling.

The banging carried on. 'Mary. Mrs Harding. Come quick,' Rosie was shouting through the letterbox.

Mary and Sarah looked at each other and for a moment or two they didn't move.

'Oh my God,' said Sarah. 'Something's happened.'

They both jumped up and rushed along the passage. Sarah threw open the front door.

Mary stood dumbstruck as she looked at Rosie. The girl's dark eyes were huge in her ashen face. She had blood all down the front of her frock: the precious frock that had been her pride and joy.

'What's happened?' asked Sarah softly.

'It's Dad. Ron's killed him.'

Mary felt her legs buckle. She couldn't believe what she'd just heard.

'I'll come and see what's happened,' said Sarah, gently ushering Rosie from the front door, through the gate and into next door, with Mary following close behind.

# *Chapter 16*

Sarah, followed by Mary, hurried inside, with Rosie close behind. The front door was wide open; Iris and the twins were sitting bunched up on the stairs and holding on to each other, crying.

'Mum and Dad're in the kitchen,' said Rosie when both Sarah and then Mary hesitated in the passage for a moment or two.

Sarah slowly pushed open the kitchen door. Ron was sitting at the table with his head in his hands. He looked up. The front of his shirt was bloody.

Rosie went to her mother who was huddled on the floor.

'I didn't mean it,' sobbed Ron. 'I didn't mean it.' His face was wet with tears. 'He kept bashing her.'

'We know you didn't,' said Sarah, going to him and hugging him. She held his head to her chest and his tears flowed. She looked at the floor. 'Mary, see to Sadie.'

Mary very cautiously went over to Sadie, who was softly groaning. She was curled in a ball and holding her stomach. Rosie was gently stroking her mother's hair, her tears falling on Sadie's face. Thank God she was alive. Her face was swollen and a pulpy bloodied mess, her left eye had closed up and blood was trickling from the corner of her mouth. Mary fell to her knees and put her hand under Sadie's head. 'Sadie, can you hear me? Where do you hurt?'

'Everywhere,' she mumbled.

Mary looked over at Mr Fellows who was sprawled out on his back in the doorway between the kitchen and the scullery. The front of his shirt was wet and soggy with blood. Against his face, from which colour was beginning to drain away, it was a very bright red. Mary shuddered. His mouth had dropped open and his eyes were wide and staring. The carving knife was next to him.

Mary sat on the floor and cradled Sadie's head on her lap. 'Should I go and get Dad?' she asked her mother in a hushed tone.

'I really don't think he's in a fit state to be of any use.'

'So what we going to do?'

'First things first. Ron, I'm going to get Rosie here to make you a cup of tea. Have you got any tea and milk?' Sarah asked.

Rosie nodded.

'Make Ron a cuppa and put plenty of sugar in it.'

'What we gonner do?' Rosie asked, her big eyes swimming with yet more tears.

'We'll get your mother sorted first. Now go on, get to it.'

'Will Ron go to prison and be hanged?'

'Rosie. See to the tea.' Sarah's voice was calm but forceful.

The young girl wiped her nose on the bottom of her precious frock and carefully stepped over her father. Pressing herself against the wall she inched her way past him. 'He kept punching and kicking Mum,' she sobbed. 'We all told him to stop and tried to pull him away.'

The thought that was uppermost in Sarah's mind was: What had these poor children witnessed? 'Where's Brian?' she asked.

'He's in bed.'

147

Sarah opened the kitchen door. 'Iris,' she called softly. 'Go up and bring me down a sheet from off the bed, any bed, and make sure Brian's asleep and don't wake him. Then you and the twins go up to bed.'

Mary sat rocking Sadie. Her thoughts were also focused on the children. They had just had the best day of their lives, and now it had ended like this. This was certainly going to be a day they and everybody else in Doyle Street would never forget.

Sarah went into the kitchen and came back with a bowl of water. 'Sadie, I'm just going to wash your face. It might help to make some of the swelling go down.'

'Ron. Where's Ron?' Sadie had her eyes closed, her voice was soft and hard to hear. They were having difficulty in making out what she was saying; she had lost a couple of her front teeth as well.

'I'm here, Mum.' Ron fell to his knees and took hold of his mother's hand and pressed it to his pale cheek.

'Ron,' she whispered. 'There's some money in the pot in the kitchen.' She stopped and her face filled with pain; she was finding it difficult to breathe. 'Rosie'll show you. Take it and go away.'

'No, Mum. I won't leave you.'

'You must.'

'Mum, what're we going to do?' asked Mary.

'First of all we're going to tidy Sadie up and make her comfortable, then I'm afraid we've got to get a doctor.'

Sadie's eyes blinked open. 'No. No.'

'I'm sorry, but we must,' said Sarah. 'We have to have a doctor's certificate to pronounce Mr Fellows dead.'

A great scream came from Sadie.

'I'm so sorry,' said Sarah. 'Hush now.' She gently sponged Sadie's face. 'Do you think you could stand?' she asked.

Sadie shook her head.

'Ron, could you help me bring a mattress down here – your mother can't lie on this hard floor.'

Mary was marvelling at her mother, she was being so efficient. 'What do you want me to do?'

'Go and get the doctor. He'll know what's best.'

As Mary pulled the front door to and ran along the road her mind was in turmoil. The flags gently moving above her were a reminder of what a wonderful day it had been. How could a day that had been so perfect end this way? She was glad to leave that house: it was full of death and anger and hurt.

She was breathless when she knocked on Dr Brent's door. When nobody came she thumped again, much harder this time.

'Yes. What is it?' A tall straight-faced woman opened the door. She gave a little gasp when she saw that Mary's frock was smeared with blood. 'The doctor's asleep.'

'Please,' panted Mary. 'He's got to come. Somebody's very ill and somebody else is dead.'

'I suppose it's all this drinking. Tell them to go to the police station.' She went to shut the door.

'No. No,' screamed Mary, throwing herself against the door. 'It wasn't like that. Please. He must come.'

'What's all this racket?' said the doctor, coming to the door; he was tying a cord round a tartan dressing gown.

'Please!' Mary was crying now. 'Please. Mr Fellows is dead and his wife, Sadie, has been badly beaten.'

'Oh dear. I'll just put some clothes on and get my bag.'

'John, you can't go out again, not at this time of night.'

'Beryl, I must. It's my duty. Now go back to bed, there's a dear.' With that he went inside.

'You'd better come in and wait,' Beryl said to Mary.

Mary stepped into the hall.

'Take a seat.'

Mary had never been in here before. The only time she'd come to see the doctor was years ago when she'd had a really bad earache and then they'd had to use the side door that led into the waiting room. The hall was magnificent, with a huge fireplace and flowers on a small table.

'Right, young lady, I'm ready, so lead the way.' Dr Brent picked his trilby from off the table and, placing it on his head, said, 'You can tell me everything that has happened along the way.'

As they hurried along Mary told him all she knew. She carefully omitted to say that Mr Fellows had been stabbed by his son.

'The police will have to be informed. Did you see who did it?'

'No.'

'When I've examined the body you can run round to the police station and ask for PC Pickering. I know he's on duty as I was called out earlier.'

'What will happen then?' asked Mary as they turned into Doyle Street.

'Then, I'm afraid, if it can be proved, someone will be charged with murder.' He looked up at the flags. 'Did you have a street party?'

Mary felt sick. Poor Ron. All he was trying to do was protect his mother from a bully. 'Yes, it was very nice. This is the house,' she said, pushing open the front door.

In the kitchen Sadie was now on a mattress. Mr Fellows had a cloth over his face. Her mother and Rosie were sitting beside Sadie. Sarah stood up.

'Thank you for coming, doctor.'

'And you are?'

'I'm their next-door neighbour.'

'It's very good of you to come in.'

Mary looked about for Ron.

'We're close and, besides, apart from Rosie here, there are four other children to consider,' said Sarah.

'And where are they?'

'Upstairs.'

Behind the doctor's back Mary silently mouthed to her mother, 'Where's Ron?'

Sarah shook her head.

'Oh dear. This is a sorry sight,' said the doctor, going over to Mr Fellows and lifting the cloth. He then turned to Sadie.

Rosie was sitting on the floor next to her mother. She was crying softly and holding her mother's hand.

'Is there anything I can do?' asked Sarah.

'No. Take this one out' – he pointed at Rosie – 'while I examine her mother. But by the looks of things, she'll have to go to the hospital.'

'No,' said Rosie from the doorway. 'She can't. We can't afford it.'

Sarah put her arm round the young girl's slight shoulders. 'Don't worry about that now.'

'There's the Rotherhithe infirmary,' said the doctor, taking off his coat. 'She can go there.'

Rosie was ushered out of the room. Mary followed her and Rosie plonked herself on the stairs.

'Where's Ron?' whispered Mary, sitting down next to her.

'In your house. Your mum sent him in there. She said not to tell anyone till she's sorted things out. Mary, what will happen to him?'

'I don't know. I really don't know.' Mary put her arm round Rosie's shoulders and with her other hand held Rosie's cold hand.

'He murdered our dad, so will he hang?'

'He might not. He's very young and he was protecting your mum. Don't give up hope.'

'What if Mum dies?'

'She won't. Remember, she's very tough.'

'I know. But she ain't ever been beaten like this before. It was awful, Mary. Our dad's rotten.' Rosie wiped her eyes then blew her nose on her dress again.

Mary held her close. She wanted to add: but he's not here any more.

After a while Sarah came out of the kitchen. 'Mary, could you go to the police station and get PC Pickering?'

At that Rosie let out a wail, and the twins rushed down from the top of the stairs where they had been hiding with Iris. Iris followed close behind and fell into Sarah's arms.

'There, there,' said Sarah, gently patting the girl's back.

'What's gonner happen to me mum?' asked Iris, screwing her comfort rag round and round her wrist.

'I wish I knew, love.'

Once again Mary found herself outside, but this time she didn't run: she wasn't in any hurry to get a policeman. She shivered. She was cold, but she couldn't be sure if it was because of the chilly night air or shock.

'Hello,' said the policeman when Mary walked into the police station. 'And what have we got here?'

Mary looked round nervously. 'Dr Brent sent me to get PC Pickering.'

'He's not on duty,' said the officer. 'Can I help?'

'A woman's been badly beaten and her husband's dead.'

The policeman looked at her more closely. 'And where is this?'

'Doyle Street, number fifty-eight.'

'And where do you live?'

'Number sixty.'

'Doyle Street?'

Mary nodded.

'And who did this terrible thing?'

'Mr Fellows beat his wife and then he was stabbed.'

'And who did it?'

'I don't know.'

'I see. And why have you got blood all over your frock?'

'I was holding Mrs Fellows till I went for the doctor.'

'I see,' he said again. He walked away from the counter and called through the back door. 'Charlie, I've got to go round to Doyle Street. Hold the fort till I get back.'

Charlie came to the counter. 'It's a busy night, sarge.'

'Always the same when the beer's been flowing. Come on, young lady, let's get you home.'

The sergeant pushed his bike and as they walked along he asked questions about the incident.

Mary told him again that she didn't know anything about it, just that her and her mother had been called in after it had all happened. He too commented on the flags and street party. That all seemed a million years ago now.

'Hello, sergeant,' said Dr Brent as they walked into the kitchen. 'Didn't know you were on duty as well.'

'It's been a busy night. So what have we got here?'

'Mr Fellows has been stabbed with this kitchen knife.' He held out the knife, which had been wrapped in a cloth. 'Mrs Fellows here has been very badly beaten. I'm arranging for her to be admitted into Rotherhithe infirmary.'

'Has anybody admitted to this killing?'

'Mrs Fellows. Though quite honestly I can't see how she could have had the strength – she is in a very bad way. I've given her a sedative and made her as comfortable as I can.'

Mary couldn't believe it when he said Sadie had said she'd done it. She looked at her mother, who hadn't batted an eyelid. 'Where's Rosie?' asked Mary.

'I've sent her upstairs to keep an eye on the others.'

The doctor and the sergeant went into the scullery and pulled the door to behind them.

'Mary,' said Sarah, coming up close to her and lowering her voice, 'I want you to go home.'

'But, Mum, can't I stay and help in some way?'

'You've done more than enough. Now go on home. We don't want Eddie waking up. I'm going to stay till the ambulance takes Sadie and Mr Fellows away, then I'll have to see about settling the kids down. Not that they'll sleep much. Now go on. I'll be in later. Try and get some rest; we've got a long busy day ahead of us tomorrow.'

'But what about work?'

'I think you will have to give that a miss. We have things to do.'

As Mary wandered back home she wondered what her mother had in mind for her. And what about Ted? What was he going to say? Would he be angry he hadn't been told, or would he be cross that they had got themselves involved with other people's business?

Mary quietly pulled the key through the letterbox and let herself in.

The kitchen door opened and Ron appeared; he had cleaned himself up and put on a fresh shirt.

'Hello, Mary.'

This wasn't the cheeky brash boy who made everybody laugh. He looked older, and desperately worried. At once the terrible thought struck her that he could be hanged. He had just killed his own father.

'How's me mum?'

'Shh,' she said, looking up the stairs and pushing him back into the kitchen. 'The doctor's sending her to the hospital.'

'I ain't sorry I done it.'

'Sit down. I don't know what Mum's thinking of sending you in here.' Ron went to speak but Mary raised her hand. 'I don't blame you for what you did. What he's done to your mum is really dreadful. But you should own up. I don't want my mum to get into any trouble through hiding you here.'

'She won't. I'm going away tomorrow. I don't want to, I wanted to stay and face the law, but me mum said I had to. She said she'd never speak to me again if I didn't go away and look after meself.'

'But what about Brian and the girls?'

'I don't know, Mary. I really don't know. Why did he have to drink so much?'

'The damage has been done now, so there's no use in talking about turning the clock back. Where will you go?'

'I don't know. I've always said I'd like to join the navy, so perhaps that could be the answer.'

'You're not old enough.'

'I'm nearly fourteen. I can always put me age up.'

'Well, you'd better ask Dad about that in the morning. I'll put the kettle on. D'you fancy a cup of tea?'

He nodded.

'My mum's coming back when she's settled the kids down. You'll have to sleep in the front room.'

'That's all right. I don't think I'll sleep anyway. D'you think me mum will be all right?'

'I hope so. I really do hope so.'

'So do I.'

Mary looked up at the clock; it was almost two. Her thoughts went back to just twelve hours ago: everyone had been so happy and laughing. The Fellows kids were having the time of their sad little lives. They had been to the best party they had ever known. Twelve hours later they had witnessed their mother, whom they obviously adored, almost beaten to death and their father murdered by their brother. She then looked at this troubled young man, who had just messed up the rest of his life because of unconditional love for his mother. What was to become of him? They couldn't hang him, surely?

# Chapter 17

A banging on the wall startled Sarah. She sat bolt upright. Iris was standing in front of her chewing her comforting piece of rag. Brian was sitting on the floor looking up at his sister.

'You bin sitting here all night?' asked Iris.

Sarah nodded as she painfully moved in the hard chair.

'Your Mary or your man's bin thumping on the wall. Where's our Ron?'

The banging got louder.

'Can you get Rosie up? Brian's a bit smelly. Can she wash and change him?'

Iris nodded. 'She don't like doing it.'

'Look, I must go home. I'll bring you in some breakfast.'

'All right.' With that Iris left the kitchen.

Sarah straightened her aching back. Sleeping in chairs definitely wasn't good for her health. She looked at the kitchen floor. Even after all the scrubbing she'd done last night after they had removed Mr Fellows's body, there were still remains of the sticky bloodstains that had seeped into the well worn lino. Still, at least Sadie was in hospital and the body had been taken away. Thank goodness that was something the children wouldn't have to confront this morning. What would happen to them now? And what about Ron? So far, neither the police nor the doctor knew anything about him, or that he even existed, but how long would they be able to keep that from the police? It wouldn't be long, surely, before one of the neighbours told them.

Mary was jolted awake. She could hear shouting. At first she felt disorientated; she didn't even remember going to bed. Then everything came flooding back. Eddie was yelling in the bedroom, but it was her father bellowing down in the kitchen that had woken her. She jumped out of bed and, quickly putting on her dressing gown, went in to Eddie first. Picking him up out of his cot, she took him downstairs.

'Sorry if we woke you,' said Sarah when Mary pushed open the kitchen door.

Mary could see her father's face was filled with anger. Ted was pacing the floor. 'I can't believe you've let all this happen without calling me,' he snapped.

'Ted, be fair. Last night you'd had a lot to drink. Mary and me had to put you to bed. As you can see, we didn't even bother to undress you.'

Ted was looking very crumpled in the shirt and trousers he'd slept in. 'I'm sure if I'd known the kid next door had stabbed his father, that would have soon sobered me up.'

'I didn't have time to worry about you.'

'Thanks very much.'

Mary went into the scullery and busied herself getting Eddie a drink. The kettle was gently boiling and she could see that no tea had been made so she set about filling the teapot. She wanted to ask if Ron was still here, but did Ted know he was in the front room?

Sarah came into the scullery. 'I'll just give Eddie some bread for now.'

'Mum, is Ron still in the front room?'

'I don't know.'

'Shall I go and knock on the door?'

'Give your father a cuppa first. It might help to calm him down.'

'How did he know you was in next door?'

'I don't know.'

Mary took the tea into the kitchen. 'Dad, how did you know Mum was in next door?'

'I caught him.' He jerked his thumb towards the scullery door. 'In the lav. I told him to use his own. I don't want him pissing all over the floor and the seat. Then when I dragged him out he told me what had happened.'

'Where's Ron now?' asked Mary.

'I don't know. I told him to sling his hook.'

Sarah gasped. 'You didn't.'

Mary ran up the passage and threw open the front-room door. Ron was sitting on the sofa holding his head and crying. She rushed to him and held him close.

'Mary,' he sobbed, 'I'm so sorry. I don't wanner cause any trouble with your dad. What am I gonner do?'

'I don't know. I really don't know.'

He sniffed and wiped his nose on his shirtsleeve. 'Your dad said he's going to the police.'

'I'm sure he didn't mean it. When he knows all about why you did it, he'll be different. I think it was the shock of seeing you in the lav.'

'What if I go to the police and tell 'em I did it?'

Mary didn't answer.

'If I don't own up I might never see Mum or the kids again.'

'You won't see them at all if you get sent to prison.'

'But look what he did to Mum! I was only trying to stop him. I had to look after her!'

Mary felt so helpless. This young man had only done what he thought was right and now he could be hanged for it. It wasn't fair.

Ron stood up and went over to the window. 'Can I go and see the kids?'

'I don't know. Wait here, I'll ask Mum.'

He looked nervous. 'Don't be long.'

'I'll bring you in a cup of tea.'

'I presume he's still here,' said Ted when Mary went back into the kitchen.

'Yes, I'm just going to give him a cup of tea.'

Sarah followed Mary into the scullery.

'Mum, he wants to go in and see the kids. What shall I say?'

'Tell him to wait a bit. We've got a lot to talk over.'

Mary took in the tea and passed on her mother's message. She went back into the kitchen. Ted was still sitting at the table, his face like thunder.

There was a rat tat tat on the front door. Everybody looked up.

'I'll go,' said Mary.

'Ron. Stay where you are,' said Mary as she passed the front-room door.

On opening the door she was surprised to see Mr West standing there.

'Sorry to trouble you so early,' he said, smiling, 'but is Ted still home?'

'Yes. Why?'

'Some of the bunting's come down and we was wondering if he could give us a hand taking it down before he goes off to work. It's getting in the way and it could be dangerous.' He grinned. 'He's a lot younger than most of us and able to shin up a ladder better.'

160

Mary smiled back. 'I'll tell him. He's just having his breakfast.'

'That's fine. Thanks, Mary.'

Back in the kitchen Mary repeated what had been said on the doorstep.

'See what I mean?' snarled Ted. 'Every time someone knocks on the door we'll be doing a bit. He's a murderer and he's got to go now.'

'But where?' asked Sarah. 'We just can't throw him out.'

'Try me.'

'Ted. Sit down. Let's try and sort this thing out properly.'

'Sarah, *he's a murderer*.' Ted raised his voice and started Eddie crying.

'Mary, get him a biscuit for now,' said Sarah.

'You know you can go to prison for harbouring him.'

Mary looked from one to the other in alarm before she gave Eddie his biscuit.

'Shouldn't you be getting ready to go to work?' Sarah asked Ted, ignoring what he'd just told her.

'I'm not going in.'

'Well, Mary needs to stay home too to help me.'

'He's disrupting this family already!' shouted Ted.

'I think we'd better get Ron in here and ask him what he wants to do. After all, it is this young man's life we are talking about.'

When Mary brought Ron in, Sarah was shocked at the sight of him. His eyes were red and bloodshot. He had aged years. He looked more like an old man than a lad of almost fourteen.

'Can I go in and see the kids?' he asked.

'Not for a moment. Sit down.' Sarah pulled herself together and took charge of the situation.

Ron quickly did as he was told.

161

'So, Ron, what shall we do? Your mother has told the police that *she* stabbed your father.'

Ron let out an anguished cry. 'She didn't. She didn't do it, it was me. I've got to go and tell them.'

'Ron, calm down.' Sarah's voice was forceful. 'I don't think they believe her. So far they don't know you exist, so I think you've got a good chance to get away. This is what she wants you to do. I think you should do what she wishes.'

'I can't let her take the blame.'

'She is very badly injured.'

'Will she die?' His voice was barely above a whisper.

'I don't know,' Sarah admitted in a subdued tone. Mary caught her breath as her mother continued: 'But she's in good hands. Now, what about you? What can we do with you?'

'He can't stay here,' Ted snapped from the armchair.

'I know that,' said Sarah.

'I've bin wondering about joining the navy. What if I go and try? I can always put me age up.'

Sarah smiled in relief. At least he had been thinking. 'Ted, how should he go about it?'

Ted looked up. 'Don't ask me.'

'But you was in the navy.'

'That was years ago.'

'I know. But you must remember how you went and signed on, if that's what you have to do.'

'If Billy was here, he'd tell you,' Mary said to Ron.

'I could go to Chatham,' Ron said.

'That's where you were when you was in the navy,' Sarah reminded Ted.

'That was years ago.'

'But things must still be the same.'

'Sarah, don't keep on. I don't know anything about someone trying to get away from the law.'

'Could you take him to Chatham? Could you help him?'

Ted leaped up. 'What?' he yelled, making Mary jump and Eddie cry.

Sarah went to comfort her son. 'You could go and perhaps see some of your old mates.'

Ted moved towards the door. 'I'm going to work. I'm not staying here listening to this.' He stormed out of the kitchen.

'Don't forget to help Mr West,' Sarah called after him.

For a moment or two it was silent. Then the front door was slammed shut.

'Will he go to the police?' Mary asked her mother.

'I don't think so. But we must try and get this settled before too long. The police are sure to be back today, then someone will tell them about Ron.'

'I'll go to Chatham. I'm sure I'll be able to find me way there.' Ron stood up. 'Thanks for helping. You've been smashing.'

'Sit down. How are you going to get there? You've never even been on a train before and what about money?'

'I don't know. I ain't sorry I done it, but what about Mum? I shouldn't go off and leave her.'

'This is what your mother wants and I think you should do as she wishes. Now, about money . . .'

For the first time since the tragedy happened Ron gave Sarah a little grin. 'Mum gave me the five bob she always kept for emergencies. I didn't know she had it; don't reckon Dad did either, otherwise he would have pinched it.' The grin faded. 'I can't believe I killed him.' He looked at her with sad eyes.

'It's not going to be easy, but you must put that behind you. Remember, it's what your mother wants.' Sarah went to the sideboard and, taking her purse out of the drawer, said,

'You'll have to find somewhere to stay and you've got to eat.'

'I can't take money off of you.'

'Why not?'

Ron looked down. 'I can't, that's all. Don't worry. I'll get by.'

'Ron, why Chatham?' asked Sarah.

'Ain't that where the navy is?'

'I don't know what station you'll have to go to,' said Sarah.

He stood looking dejected. 'I'll find it. Did your boyfriend ever go there?' he asked Mary.

She shrugged. 'I don't know. He only went to Portsmouth as far as I know.' Mary's mind was suddenly going over and over. 'What if I took him to Portsmouth?'

'Now that's a better idea,' said Sarah.

'I know me way there, and there must be a place where he can join the navy.'

'I still think he should go today.'

'I can go today.'

'But what about work?' asked her mother.

'I can take a few days off.'

'No, Mary. I can't let you do that,' said Ron. 'I'll be all right. I can find a job.'

'No, I've made up me mind. I'm taking you to Portsmouth. Nobody will think of looking for you there.' Mary smiled to herself. 'I'll just go up and get a bag packed.'

'Well, if you're made up your mind, Mary, I'll pop next door,' said Sarah, 'and get a few bits together for Ron.'

'I ain't got much,' said Ron. 'Can I say goodbye to the kids first?'

'Course. I'll send them in.'

Mary was devastated about Sadie and Ron and the whole

sorry business, and she wanted to help Ron as much as she could. This was a way she could get him away to somewhere she knew. And as she went up to her room to pack she knew that the thing that would be at the bottom of her bag would be Ted's photograph.

# Chapter 18

Once more Mary was standing on Waterloo Station. This time she was with a very frightened and nervous young boy. Ron was a tall gangly lad and when he spotted a policeman he tried to hide behind Mary; she could feel him shaking.

'It's all right,' said Mary. 'We are just a brother and sister going away for a few days.'

'I feel rotten leaving the kids. What will happen to 'em?'

'I don't know.' But Mary was thinking of earlier and what her mother had said when they were alone. 'They could finish up in a home.' She couldn't tell Ron that.

It had been very tearful and sad when the kids came in and said goodbye. Ron had held them very tight and made them promise to stay together whatever happened.

Eddie too noted the atmosphere and was very clinging. Sarah had to prise him away from Mary when it was time for them to leave. He knew something was wrong and looked about him, bewildered. Mary promised to bring him a boat when she returned, but he didn't know what a boat was.

At the ticket office Mary bought a single for Ron and a four-day return for herself.

'You gonner stay down there for four days?' he asked.

'Might as well. It's very nice. You'll like it. Besides, I want to make sure you get settled.'

'Thanks. I must admit I'm a bit scared. I ain't ever bin on a train. I ain't ever bin out of Roverive before.'

'Don't worry, you'll be all right.' Mary felt guilty that she was using Ron as an excuse to try and find out more about the mysterious woman in the picture, but she knew she was doing him a great favour too. In her bag was her post office book; she had told her mother not to worry as she had enough money to stay for four days. Sarah wasn't happy at that and did question why she wanted to stay there alone, but Mary said she liked it and felt she needed a holiday. She wondered about Liz and what her friend'd say about her being off work. She'll think I'm raving mad, Mary thought. Perhaps I am, but why did Ted carry a photo about with him of a woman he's never told us about? I just have to know the reason.

Soon they were settled on the train and tucking into the sandwiches Mary had brought along. The train wasn't as crowded as before and they had a carriage to themselves. At first Ron sat silent and deep in thought. Mary tried to make small talk but he wasn't in the mood. She tried to understand the pain and heartbreak he was going through. His mother, Sadie, who all her children adored, was at death's door. He didn't appear to have any regrets for his father, who he had just killed. But what about at night? What was to become of the Fellows children and what bad dreams would they all have? At least Mary knew her mother would do everything she could to help them.

It wasn't till they'd long left London behind that Ron's sad face lifted. Mary smiled at his excitement when he saw fields and cows. 'I ain't ever seen a real cow before,' he said as he ran from side to side of the carriage in order not to miss anything.

'You wait till you see the sea. It goes on for ever,' said Mary. 'My boyfriend sends me pictures of all the wonderful places his ship stops at.'

'That must be really good, I'd like to do that.' He sat back and looked pensive, pushing a lock of mousy-coloured hair from his eyes. 'I hope Mum'll be all right. I wish I could have seen her.'

'When you get settled you can write to us. Send your letters to our address. My mum will keep you informed with all the news.'

'I don't wanner get yer mum into trouble. I know your dad don't like me. What if he tells the police about me?'

'I don't think he will. Now, when we get to Portsmouth I'm taking you to a Mrs Johns, she's the lady I stayed with before. Her husband was in the navy and she'll be able to help you.'

'Won't she want to know why I want to go in the navy?'

'We can say that you've just lost your parents and you don't want to go into a home.'

'In a way that's true,' said Ron.

'Yes. Yes it is.'

Once again Ron became very quiet as he sat and gazed out of the window. Mary felt very sorry for him. He was so young and vulnerable; he was heading for a brand-new life all alone.

Portsmouth had also been decorated for the Jubilee; there were flags flying from every building. It looked very festive. Before they went to see Mrs Johns, Mary took him along the front. When Ron first caught sight of the sea, Mary knew she had done the right thing. Forgetting for the moment what had brought him here, he excitedly pointed at the boats bobbing about and chased the seagulls, laughing when they squawked loudly and flew away into the sky. He threw stones into the sea and ran along the beach, calling to her all the time to watch everything he did. She sat down on the stones and laughed with him. In many ways he was still a child. Everything was new and exciting to him.

A large ship was slowly moving along on the horizon.

'Look. Look, Mary.' Ron was shielding his eyes from the sun and pointing. 'I'll be on one of those one day.'

Mary didn't have the heart to tell him that that could be one of the ferryboats.

'Cor, wouldn't the kids love it here?' he went on, breathlessly plonking himself next to her. 'I didn't know there was places as good as this. You wait till I've got some money. I'll bring Mum and the kids here and they can all have a paddle just like those kids over there.' He leaned over and quickly kissed her cheek.

Mary laughed and touched her cheek. 'What was that for?'

'Thanks for bringing me down here. I only hope they let me join the navy. I know I'm really gonner like it.'

'You will write, won't you?'

Ron was staring out at sea. 'I should say so. I'll have so much to tell Mum and the kids.'

Mary suddenly felt sad. If only she could make Eddie as happy as this. She hoped he wouldn't do anything to provoke Ted while she was away.

After a while she said they had to go and get settled before nightfall.

Mrs Johns was so pleased to see Mary when she opened her door that she welcomed her with open arms.

'And who's this young man?' she asked, looking at Ron, who wasn't the best-dressed lad she'd ever seen.

Mary crossed her fingers behind her back. She didn't like telling fibs. 'He's a distant cousin of mine and I'm afraid there has been a tragedy in the family. Ron here lost his father a while back and just a week ago . . .' She stopped.

Mrs Johns gently tapped her hand. 'I understand. You don't have to say any more. But why has he come here?'

'He wants to join the navy.'

A broad smile lifted Mrs Johns's face. 'Well, me lad, you've come to the right place. But how about a cup of tea first? I expect you can do with one after being on those dirty smoky trains.'

'Thank you, that would be lovely,' said Mary. 'Mrs Johns, I was wondering if I could stay here for a few days?'

'Of course, and what about the boy?'

'We're hoping he could go and stay with the navy.'

'Were you now. And what makes him want to join the navy?'

'Think it might be the uniform,' said Mary with a grin. 'He said he liked the look of my Billy.'

'There's a bit more to it than that.'

'Mary said your man was in the navy,' said Ron, looking at the pictures of ships and smart sailors that hung on chains from the picture rail.

Mrs Johns stood up and went over to Ron. 'Yes, he was.' She pointed to a handsome man. 'That's him. In the navy man and boy.'

'So he started as a boy then?'

'Yes. He worked himself up through the ranks and was a petty officer when he was killed. How old are you, young man?'

On the train they had settled for Ron being fifteen. 'Fifteen,' said Ron without hesitating.

'First he'll have to sign on, then he'll go to the naval college.'

'I see. Where is that?' asked Mary.

'St Vincent's. It's over in Gosport.'

'Where's that?' Mary asked again.

'Just across the harbour.'

'How will he get there?'

'On the ferry. But don't worry, the navy will sort all that

out. What about tonight?' Mary was taken aback. She'd expected Ron to go straight away. 'I don't know.'

'He can stay here for tonight, as it's too late to go to the recruiting office now.'

'Thank you. But you've only got two bedrooms,' said Mary.

'I have a camp bed. He can sleep on that in the front room.'

'Are you sure that'll be all right?' asked Mary.

Ron looked from one to the other, concerned.

'Of course. Now don't worry, son, everything will be fine.'

For the first time since they'd left Rotherhithe he gave her a beaming smile.

The next morning, after getting directions from Mrs Johns, they went together to the recruiting office. At the gate, after Ron had told the sailor who was on duty what he wanted, Mary was told to wait outside. She watched Ron go into the dockyard; at the recruiting office he turned and waved. She waited a while then the sailor on the gate told her not to hang about, as if he was accepted, he would be looked after. With a sigh, Mary walked away. If he didn't get accepted into the navy would she ever see him again? She had told him to return to Mrs Johns if that happened. If he didn't have any luck, where would he go then? But Mary got cross with herself for having these negative thoughts. She had to remain positive. She decided to focus on her other problem and made enquiries about Commercial Road. After being told how to find it, Mary swiftly made her way there.

It was a warm sunny day and many people appeared to be on holiday. Mary wandered along looking for Palmer's the photographer's. She had wondered, would it still be there after all these years? It was. She felt excitement rising in her as she stood outside looking at their elaborate window display. Mary could see that they liked taking portraits as well as wedding photos. Would they know who the lady was? Would she be disappointed if it turned out to be someone everybody knew, like a lady who was on the stage – but if that was the case Ted would have proudly told them who she was. As Mary stood trying to get up the courage to go in, a young woman passed her, dragging her son – who was about five and wearing a sailor suit and yelling in protest – inside.

Mary smiled. She knew what it was like to drag a young boy about. After a while she pushed open the door. A bell above gave a tinny ring that could hardly be heard over the boy's shouting. Another young woman came out from the room behind, looking very flushed.

'Yes. Can I help you?'

'I hope so,' said Mary, diving into her handbag.

As Mary searched her bag, the young woman looked anxiously at the door she'd just come out of, where all the noise was coming from. 'Look, I'm sorry, but we are rather busy at the moment. Could you come back a little later?'

'Yes. Do you close for lunch?'

'Not till one.'

'Thank you.' Mary left the shop. She decided to have a cup of tea, then she would call back.

It was very quiet when Mary pushed open the photographer's door for the second time. The young lady was now sitting behind the desk. She looked up, and smiled when Mary walked in.

'I'm sorry about this morning, but the lad was a bit of a handful. It took Mr Palmer and me all our skill to amuse him. His mother wanted a picture of her son to send to her husband who is in the navy.' Her blue eyes twinkled. 'Now, what can I do for you?'

'I was wondering if you could tell me anything about this?' Mary handed her the photo.

'Take a seat. It's not a recent one. She's very pretty, isn't she? I can see that our Mr Palmer took this.'

'How do you know?'

'The pose. It's his speciality.'

Mary couldn't see it was any different from any others she'd seen. 'I don't suppose you know who she is?'

'No. Sorry, but I can't help you.' She passed the picture back. 'Is it important?'

'Well, yes.' With her fingers crossed Mary went through the story she had carefully rehearsed. 'You see, I found it when I had to go through my late father's things and I didn't recognise her. I wondered if she was part of his family; I think there could have been a rift and they didn't speak. I would like to know if she's still alive.'

'You don't come from round here.'

'How do you know?'

'Your accent. Where're you from?'

'London.'

The young lady went all dreamy-eyed. 'Lucky old you. I'd love to live in London. It looks so exciting.'

'Parts of it are.' Mary stood up. 'So you can't help me then?'

'No, sorry.'

The back-room door opened. 'Miss Dennis, could you make out this bill? Sorry, I didn't realise we had a customer.'

'It's all right. I was just leaving,' said Mary, going to the door.

'Just a minute,' Miss Dennis said to Mary. 'Mr Palmer, you don't happen by any chance to remember the lady in this photo? This lady thinks it could be someone in her family. I think you took it.' She turned to Mary. 'Show him the photo.'

Mary handed him the picture.

Mr Palmer was a tall thin man with wiry grey hair and

173

steely grey eyes. He studied it for just a brief moment. 'Yes, I did. You say she could be a family member?'

'I don't know. I don't know who she is.'

'I see,' he said very slowly. 'So how did you get this?'

Mary plonked herself down on the chair. 'I found it among my father's belongings. You know her?'

'I should say so.'

Mary sat upright. 'Who is she?'

'You don't come from round this way, do you?'

Mary shook her head.

'Do you really want to know?'

'Yes, please.'

'There was a great scandal about ten years ago. I did take this picture but that was about five years before all the trouble. This was the picture the papers used.'

Mary sat dumbfounded. 'The papers? What happened?'

Mr Palmer placed the photo on the counter. 'She was such a lovely-looking young woman.'

'You said "was". Is she dead?'

'I don't know.'

Miss Dennis was sitting with her blue eyes wide open. 'What happened?' she asked eagerly.

'She was married to a sailor. I don't remember her surname as everyone called her Darling Daisy. She was a real beauty,' Mr Palmer continued, studying the picture. 'The story went that they had a little boy and when the boy was about two or thereabouts they found out there was something wrong with him. He was a bit backward.'

Mary felt the colour drain from her face. 'You don't remember her surname?'

'No, sorry.'

'You all right, miss?' said Miss Dennis. 'You've gone ever such a funny colour.'

'Yes, I'm fine, thank you. Please go on,' said Mary to Mr Palmer.

'Well, it appeared that when the husband came home on leave he blamed the wife for the boy's condition. After a big argument – I think he knocked her about a bit – she said she gave her son to some gypsies who were travelling through.'

A gasp came from Mary and Miss Dennis.

Mr Palmer paused. He was enjoying every moment of telling this tale.

Miss Dennis and Mary were hanging on to his every word.

'But why would she do such a thing?' Mary asked.

'She was mad, I think,' replied Mr Palmer.

'What happened then?' asked Miss Dennis.

'You said, "she said". Who did she tell?' asked Mary.

'The police. You see, the boy was never traced and everyone thought she'd killed him and hidden the body. She was tried for murder and found to be insane and put in St Mark's.'

'What's St Mark's?' asked Mary softly.

'It's the loony bin,' said Miss Dennis. 'It's not far away.'

'Is she still there?'

'I would think so – don't think they ever get out of there,' said Miss Dennis nonchalantly.

'What about her husband?'

'Left as soon as the trial was over. Never seen again,' said Mr Palmer.

'Didn't he try to find his son?' asked Miss Dennis.

'Don't know. He might have done. We all lost interest.'

Mary's mind was on a rollercoaster, trying to make sense of all this. What if this woman was Ted's sister – the black sheep her mother had told her about, whom Ted never mentioned? Ted had been a sailor. He might have known the woman's husband. Was it possible he was still in touch with him? Had he ever wanted to look for Daisy's son – his nephew?

'Do you think it could be a relation?' asked Miss Dennis, interrupting Mary's thoughts.

Mary shook her head. 'I don't think so.'

'It's a very sad story,' said Miss Dennis.

'Yes. Yes, it is.'

'I'm sorry I couldn't be of more help,' said Mr Palmer. 'But I really must go. I have to prepare the studio for another appointment.'

'Can people visit St Mark's?' Mary asked Miss Dennis when he'd gone.

'I should think so. You're not thinking of going there, are you?'

Mary stood up. 'Don't know yet. Thank you for all your help.'

'My pleasure. I hope you find what you're looking for.'

'Thanks. I hope so too.' Mary left the shop and wandered along Commercial Road, deep in thought. Could this Daisy still be alive? If she *was* Ted's sister, perhaps he didn't want anything to do with her because she'd caused a scandal all those years ago. But what about the boy? What if Daisy was telling the truth and he was still alive? Mr Palmer had said he was a bit backward. Did this explain why Eddie was too?

Mary went back into the photographer's. 'Could you give me directions how to get to this St Mark's?' she asked Miss Dennis.

'I thought you said she wasn't a relation?'

'Now I've come all this way I might as well follow it through.'

'You've got to go along this road, then at the bottom you have to turn right. Anybody will tell you. I think the trams run there. Are you sure you want to go on your own?'

Mary nodded as she put the photo back in her bag.

Miss Dennis laughed. 'You could be another Sherlock Holmes. You will come back and tell me how you get on, won't you?'

'If I can.'

Once again Mary was out in the sunshine. At least now she had a name. Daisy. She had to find her.

# Chapter 19

Mary was full of anticipation as she made her way along Commercial Road. Was she doing the right thing? The directions hadn't been that clear and when she asked one woman where St Mark's was, all she got was a very funny look as the woman hurried on.

'Don't wonner go there,' said another. 'All loonies in there.'

Mary continued on her way. As she walked on she saw a large building ahead; when she saw an ambulance drive in she guessed that it could be a hospital and made her way towards it. They would be able to tell her. She suddenly stopped. What if Daisy was dead and this was all a waste of time? But Mary knew she couldn't give up, not now. She had to find out who Daisy was.

At the reception the smell of disinfectant almost took her breath away.

'Yes?' a very upright woman seated behind a desk asked. She wore a smart dark blue uniform and had a tiny white hat perched on top of her head. 'Can I help you?'

'I hope so. I'm looking for St Mark's. Could you tell me how to get there?'

The woman hesitated before speaking. 'You do know what sort of hospital it is?'

Mary nodded.

'You go out of here to Lake Road.'

'I'm sorry, but I don't know my way round these parts. Would you be kind enough to write it down? I've been told I can get a tram.'

'Yes, that's right.' Without another word the woman took some paper and pencil and gave Mary the directions.

Outside and clutching her piece of paper, Mary made her way to St Mark's.

She stopped when she reached her destination and peered through the large ornate black iron gates at a red-brick building that was set well back from the road. A young man shuffled up to the gates and spoke through the railings.

'Yes?'

'Please, I've come to ask about a patient.'

'Yes. What's the name?'

Mary looked at the ground. 'I don't know her full name, she was called Daisy many years ago,' she whispered just as a tram rattled past.

'You'll have to speak up.'

'I'm sorry. I don't have a name, just a photo.' Once again she brought the picture from her handbag and handed it to the man.

'Who is it?' he asked as he scrutinised the photo.

'I think it's a distant relation of my father's. I was told she is in here.'

'I'll go and ask someone. It ain't visiting time though.' With that he went off, leaving Mary to hang about outside.

It was a while before he came back and, without a word, opened a small gate that was set in the large one. He didn't return the photograph. 'Go to that building over there, a nurse is waiting for you.'

Panic filled Mary. What if she got in and couldn't get out? Nobody knew she was here. She looked about her. As she got nearer the building she noticed a young nurse smiling at her.

'Hello,' she said, holding out her hand. 'I'm Nurse Bentley. You want to know about this patient, Daisy?' She was holding the photograph. 'Are you a relation?'

'I don't know.'

At that, the nurse looked puzzled. 'You'd better come into my office and explain.'

Mary followed her along the corridor. Although the weather was warm and sunny outside, inside it was cold and dark. Tiny windows high up let in little light. The bottom half of the walls had been tiled with brown tiles, the top half with cream ones. The floor was also tiled and shouts and yells coming from behind closed doors echoed and seemed to be magnified. Mary was petrified. What had she got herself into?

'In here.' The nurse pushed open a door; inside was another door. When Mary stepped in she closed both of them behind her.

'Before I tell you anything I want to know what you know about Daisy.'

'She's here?'

'Yes. But this is a very old photo.'

'I know. You see, I found that photo in with me dad's belongings and I want to find out if she's a relation.' She had told this tale so many times now that she was almost beginning to believe it herself. Indeed, in some ways it was true.

'I see. How did you know Daisy was in here?'

'The photographer told me. The one who took that picture.' Mary pointed to the photo, which was on the desk.

'What else did he tell you?'

'Not a lot really. Just that she, Daisy, had murdered her son.' Mary was still standing and she shifted uneasily from one foot to the other.

'That was never proved. They never found the body. You

understand I have to be very careful whom I let in to see my patients. They can be very sensitive and I don't want them upset.'

'Yes, I can understand that. And I understand that you don't want me to see her.' Mary went to turn away.

'Just a moment. You seem to be a sensible young lady. I don't think it would do Daisy any harm to have a visitor. She never has visitors. Have you come far?'

'From London.'

'Finding Daisy must be very important to you.'

Mary nodded.

'Are you down here on holiday?'

'Sort of.'

'Now, although we don't normally allow visitors till the afternoon I think I can make an exception today.' The nurse smiled. 'Would you like to follow me?'

Mary's heart was thumping as she followed the nurse along the cold soulless corridor again.

Nurse Bentley unlocked a door at the end of the corridor. She stopped in front of one of the many doors that led off it and handed Mary back the photograph. 'I don't think it would be a good idea to show her this. I don't want her upset.'

Mary quickly put the picture in her handbag and out of sight.

As they walked into the room a number of women scurried away and sat in the assortment of chairs that lined the wall.

'Daisy, come here. You have a visitor.'

One old lady sitting in the corner rocking back and forth started to sing. 'Daisy, Daisy . . .'

'Thank you, Ethel. That's lovely.'

Ethel grinned a toothless grin.

Slowly, a woman whom Mary took to be Daisy came towards them.

'This is Daisy,' the nurse said. 'I'm afraid I didn't get your name.'

'I'm Mary.'

'Daisy, take Mary into the kitchen and get her a cup of tea. Then, as it's a lovely afternoon, you can go and sit outside and have a little talk.'

Although Mary smiled at this slight grey-haired woman, she was also very shocked. Could this be the same woman, the pretty woman in the photograph? Was this the Darling Daisy the press had called a beauty? Was this Ted's sister? This woman had a gaunt sallow face and with her short grey hair she wasn't at all like the dark-haired beauty she once must have been. Her grey frock hung on her slight frame; she had a tired, lethargic walk. Her blue eyes appeared to be lifeless and she looked beyond Mary. Mary could see there was a resemblance between this lady and the photo, but only a slight one. 'Hello, Daisy,' she said softly.

Daisy didn't answer, she just shuffled away.

'Just go with her,' said Nurse Bentley.

Mary followed her into the huge kitchen and watched as, in complete silence, Daisy went mechanically through the business of making a pot of tea. She placed the metal teapot, milk jug and sugar bowl and two thick china cups and saucers on a tray and made her way outside. Not a word had passed her lips.

Outside there were a few men tending the well-kept gardens. Chairs and small tables were dotted about and Daisy slowly made her way to one in the far corner of the grounds. She put the tray on the table and sat down.

Mary also sat down. There were so many things she wanted to ask this woman, but where could she start and would Daisy know what she was talking about? Mary noted that the woman wasn't wearing a wedding ring. She must have tried to erase all memories of her husband. Mary wondered where her husband was now.

'You're back early,' said Sarah when Ted walked in.

'Yes. Had to go somewhere for the boss so rather than go back to the office I decided to come straight home. Is Mary back?'

'No, she must be staying down there for a few days.'

'What d'you mean, she's staying a few days in Portsmouth? You didn't mention this yesterday. Why?'

'I don't know, I thought she might have come home. She only said she might; she does like it there.'

'What about her job? She just can't up and go like that. Besides, where's she got the money from?'

'She does have her savings.'

'Well, I don't think it's right, a young girl on her own in a place like that.'

Sarah sat at the table. Since Mary had left, every time Ted was around it had been one row after another and she had had enough of Ted shouting and Eddie screaming. First there had been all the trouble over Ron being in here, then last night when she fed Sadie's kids Ted had had another go at her, but what could she do? She couldn't let them starve. Eddie clambered up on to her lap. How could she tell her husband that she had offered to look after the kids till something was sorted out?

A sharp tapping on the front door made Sarah jump up. She put Eddie down and made her way along the hall. She hadn't told Ted but the police had been here and next door asking questions off and on nearly all day long and she was tired. She didn't want to talk to them any more.

'Yes?' she said on opening the door.

An elderly man and woman were standing there. The

woman was wearing a severe navy suit and sensible shoes. Even her hat was the no-nonsense kind. She looked at the note in her hand. 'Mrs Harding?'

'Yes.'

'I wonder if we could come in for a moment.'

'What for?'

'It's about the Fellows children next door.'

For a moment or two Sarah froze. Had they found out about Ron? Had someone told them there was a son? 'What about the children?' she asked.

'I think it's better we talk inside,' said the man.

'You'd better come into the front room.' Sarah stood to one side as they walked in. She opened the front-room door. 'Just go in there and I'll tell my husband you're here.'

Sarah hurried into the kitchen. 'Ted, it's a man and a woman who want to talk about Sadie's kids.'

'Well, you're the one that's involved. Don't drag me into any of this.'

Sarah closed the kitchen door and went into the front room.

'Please, sit down,' she said.

'This is a very nice room,' said the woman, looking all around as she and the man sat down on the sofa of the green velvet three-piece.

'Thank you.' Sarah quickly glanced around. She was always pleased with this room. The sparkling lace curtains moved slightly in the breeze. The fireplace had a brightly polished brass fire-screen in front of it. Yes, all in all it looked very smart. It was a room she had no hesitation in showing anyone into.

'What is it you want to know?' Sarah sat in the armchair opposite them.

'I don't suppose you are aware that Mrs Fellows has died.'

184

Sarah took a sharp breath and visibly shrank in the chair. 'Oh no,' she cried. 'Poor Sadie.' Her tears spilled from her eyes. 'After all that woman has been through. Those poor children, they're orphans.'

'We're from the welfare and our interest *is* the children. They will of course have to go away.' There wasn't an ounce of sympathy in the woman's tone.

Sarah sat back. She felt sick. 'What's going to happen to them?' she asked in a whisper.

'They will be taken to a home for orphans.'

'You're not taking them to the workhouse?'

The man smiled. 'No, of course not. It will be a proper children's home. Believe me, they will be a lot better off there: they'll have food and clean clothes.'

'Sadie always did her best.'

'I'm sure she did.'

'Those kids were her pride and joy.'

'I'm sure they were.'

Sarah watched him twirling his trilby round and round in his hands. She could see he'd never done a manual day's labour in his life. She didn't like this man: with his pencil-thin moustache and smarmy grin, he gave her the creeps. 'When will they have to go?' she asked.

'As soon as we can get the paperwork settled and find a place for them.'

'Why have you come to tell me all of this?'

It was the woman who spoke then. 'We understand you have been looking after them. In fact, the eldest girl said she wants to live here.'

Sarah smiled. 'Yes, I know. Couldn't they stay in their own house? I could carry on looking after them.'

'Does your husband get a good wage?'

'Why?'

'It will mean another five mouths to feed. And the rent to find.'

'I'm sure we could manage. And I know some of the neighbours would be willing to chip in.'

It was the woman's turn to smile, but hers was a condescending smile. 'That is very kind of you but I don't think so. You see, this is now a problem for the welfare. No, they have to go into a home.'

'Will they be split up?'

'I don't know. That's not up to us, we're simply here to make sure we have all the proper documentation ready.' The woman stood up. 'We shall need them to be clean and presentable.'

'When are you taking them away?'

'In the morning.'

'So soon?'

'It's for the best.'

'Do they know?'

'No, we don't want them doing anything silly like running away tonight. Can we ask you to break the news to them in the morning?'

'What can I tell them about their mother?'

'We'll leave that up to you. But if you want my advice, I shouldn't tell them too much. They have a knack of putting two and two together and we don't want them running off.'

Sarah nodded and stood up. Silently she showed them out. She closed the front door and for a moment she stood in the passage unable to move. Tears were welling up. She knew she should go in next door and comfort those children. They were orphans, their mother had died. But at the moment she felt too upset. She had let them down as well as Sadie. And what about Ron? What would he say when he found out about his mother and the kids being put in a home? He'd be back looking for them. What a mess. If only Mary were here. Sarah said a silent prayer: Please Mary, come home soon.

After a while she felt a little more composed, but when she went into the kitchen and saw Eddie quietly playing on the floor her tears welled up again. She sat at the table and began to cry in earnest. 'Sadie's dead.'

'That's a shame, but I dare say it's for the best. That family would never have amounted to much.'

'How can you say that?' sobbed Sarah.

'I don't know why you're getting yourself so upset, or got yourself so involved with that lot. I would have thought you had enough looking after him.' Ted pointed to his son.

Sarah looked up. She wiped her eyes on the bottom of her apron. 'Ted, sometimes you can be so heartless. How would you feel if your child had been made homeless and taken away from you?'

Ted looked down at his newspaper. 'I hope I look after mine better than that bloke did.'

'Yes, you do. But what would happen to Eddie if anything happened to me? Would you let them put him in a home?'

'Don't talk silly, woman. Nothing's going to happen to you. Besides, you've got Mary. She'll never let anything happen to the boy.'

'That's true,' said Sarah. 'But what about when she's married and has children of her own?' She stopped. 'Ted. I don't think Eddie will ever be any different. I really think he should see a specialist of some sort.'

Ted went white with anger. 'Why? What are you saying?'

'I do wonder if there might be something in our background—'

Ted thumped the table. 'Are you saying that *that* is my fault?' He pointed at Eddie.

'No. No. It might be my side of the family.' Sarah had

187

never told him about her father.

Eddie sat carefully lining up his wooden trains, completely oblivious of what was going on around him.

Ted stood up. 'I've had enough of this. I'm going out.'

'Please, let's talk about it.'

Ted stood at the kitchen door and, turning, gave Sarah a look she would never forget. It was as though his eyes were full of hate. But why? What had she done?

When the front door slammed Sarah knew she'd pushed him too far.

Eddie looked up and grinned.

# Chapter 20

Mary could see Nurse Bentley coming towards them. Mary had been talking for the past hour but Daisy hadn't said a word. Mary had told Daisy all about herself, where she worked, her friend Liz and Billy, her boyfriend, who was in the navy. She told her that she lived in London, Ted was her stepfather and that she had a half-brother whose name was Eddie. Mary was hoping that some of it might have registered, but there hadn't been any sign of life in Daisy's eyes at all. At times Mary was very tempted to show her the picture, but thought better of it; she didn't want to upset her and she certainly didn't want this woman, who was getting closer, throwing her out.

'I'm sorry,' said Nurse Bentley. 'I'm afraid you have to go.'

'Can I come back tomorrow?'

'Do you think it will do any good?'

Mary shrugged. 'I don't know. Does she ever speak?'

The nurse smiled at Daisy and took her hand. 'She has been known to utter a few words. Come on now.' She helped Daisy to her feet. 'Mary will come and see you tomorrow. You can come in the afternoon at the proper visiting time. Is that all right?'

'Yes. Yes, that'll be fine.'

'I don't think you'll get through to her, but you never know and it is nice for her to have someone who visits. Say goodbye to Mary.'

Daisy only looked at Mary with her blank eyes.

'I'll see you tomorrow,' said Mary. She stood and watched the nurse lead Daisy away. Mary began to wonder if she was wasting her time being here? But she would come back tomorrow; she had to find out about Daisy.

'Did the lad get signed on?' asked Mrs Johns as soon as Mary walked in.

'Yes. And the sailor at the gate told me that he'd be looked after. I don't think I'll be seeing him again for a while.'

'He seems a nice boy. I dare say he'll write as soon as he's settled. And what sort of day have you had? Didn't do a lot of shopping by the looks of it.'

Mary hadn't brought any bags in. She sat at the table and her eyes filled with tears.

'My dear, don't worry about him. I'm sure he'll be all right. He might find it a bit strange at first, but I'm sure he'll enjoy the life once he settles down.'

'It's not Ron I'm worried about. Mrs Johns, can I talk to you? I need to talk to someone.'

Mrs Johns looked concerned. 'Of course, my dear. You're not in any trouble, are you?'

Mary shook her head.

'Would you like a cup of tea first?'

'Can we have it after?'

'Just as you like,' said Mrs Johns, sitting down next to Mary.

Once again Mary took the photo from her handbag and showed it to Mrs Johns.

'She's very pretty.'

'Yes, she was.'

'Is she a relation? Oh my dear, you said "was". I'm sorry. Is this – *was* this Ron's mother?'

'No. I don't really know who she is.' Mary then went into great detail about the photo and where she'd found it and how she'd used Ron as an excuse to get back down here. She didn't mention the real reason Ron was here. When she started to talk about St Mark's and how she had found Daisy, Mrs Johns looked shocked.

Mary stopped and said, 'Can I have that tea now?'

Without a word Mrs Johns left the table and shortly afterwards brought in the teapot. 'The kettle was already simmering,' she said, taking the cups and saucers from the dark oak sideboard that stood next to the fireplace.

'I'm sorry. I shouldn't have told you all my troubles.'

'No. No, it's not that.'

'Did you know about that court case?'

'No. It must have been before we moved here. Why do you think this Daisy could be related to your stepfather?'

'Well, for one reason he carries her picture around with him. Also, Daisy had a son who was backward. Ted also has a son who's backward – my half-brother Eddie – so you see, they could well be related.'

Mary knew she shouldn't be telling this woman all this, but she needed someone to talk to. She needed some advice.

'Have you told your mother about this photo?'

Mary shook her head.

'She might know all the answers.'

'I don't think so. She would have told me.'

'What do you hope to find out from this woman?'

'I don't know. I don't even know if she can speak. I'm going to see her again tomorrow.'

'Would you like me to come with you?'

Mary shook her head. 'Thank you, but I'll be fine. And

191

you never know, she might say something.'

'I shouldn't get your hopes up. Sometimes when they go like that through shock it can last for ever.'

'Do you think it was shock?'

'I don't know. You could ask her nurse.'

Mary gave her a weak smile. 'As I'm going to stay for a few days, in that time she might get used to me.'

'Those sort of cases can be difficult, so be careful.'

'I will.'

Mary sat back and studied the photograph. What a different Daisy it was to the one in St Marks.'

Today, Thursday, was the day Sarah had been dreading. She had been awake for hours; all night she'd been tossing and turning; now at long last the darkness was lifting and it was beginning to get light. Last night when she'd bathed the Fellows kids, they'd thought it was funny having a bath and clean clothes when it wasn't even Friday. Rosie was a bright child and had been very curious.

As she'd sat in the tin bath she asked, 'Why have we got this posh soap? We always have the green washing soap and a handful of soda.'

'I thought it would be a nice change for you.'

'It's ever so nice,' said Iris. 'Makes you smell all lovely.' She had sniffed her arm. She'd had her bath and was sitting wrapped in a large fluffy towel Sarah had brought in.

Rosie had persisted with the questions. She particularly wanted to know why they had to have a bath at all. Sarah had made up some excuse about hoping they could see their mother. She had felt guilty at telling lies, but what else could she do? When they were all in bed Sarah had collected their clothes and washed them. Ted had complained about them hanging everywhere to dry. This morning they had to be ironed and Sarah had told them she would bring them in their breakfast. She felt she was giving them the Last Supper. If Ron knew this was happening, would he want to come back and tell the truth? And what would happen when he learned about his mother? How could so many lives be messed up like this?

Slowly and quietly, Sarah slid out of bed. She could start getting the breakfast while Eddie and Ted were still fast asleep.

Sarah put the flat iron on the stove and folded the clothes that had been draped all around all night. She could hear the children next door moving about. What would be going through their minds? After making their porridge she quickly ran the iron over their bits and, bundling them up, took them next door.

'Do you really think they'll let us see Mum?' asked Rosie as she sat spooning the porridge into Brian's mouth.

Sarah pretended she hadn't heard the question.

'Why you done our washing?'

'You want something clean to wear, don't you?' Sarah was finding it difficult to look at Rosie.

'How we gonner get to the hospital?'

'Some people are coming here this morning. They're going to take you. Now I must go and see to Eddie.'

As she left the room Rosie took hold of her arm. 'You wouldn't let 'em take us away, would you?'

Sarah bobbed down and held Rosie close. 'I will do everything in my power to keep you here, but I don't think that's going to be possible.' She was having difficulty keeping her tears at bay.

'Our Ron don't want us to go away,' said Iris, who had joined them in the passage.

'Iris, you mustn't tell anyone you've got a big brother.'

'I know. Ron told us. When we gonner see him again?'

'I don't know. Rosie, when those people come send Iris or one of the twins in for me.'

Rosie nodded, her eyes full of tears. She threw her arms round Sarah's neck and held her tight. It was as if she knew. She whispered, 'I love you.'

Sarah's tears slowly slid down her cheek. Gradually she eased Rosie's arms away and stood up. 'And I love you. Now I must go and see to Eddie.'

Outside, she burst into tears. What was to become of these children? How sad and long today was going to be.

That same morning Mary wandered up and down Commercial Road. Should she go and see Daisy again? But what was the point? Perhaps she should just go home. She stood looking across at Palmer's shop; in the end she decided to go and see Miss Dennis.

'Hello.' Miss Dennis's face lit up when Mary stepped inside. 'I was hoping you'd come here again. Did you find that lady in the photo?'

'Yes, I did, thank you.'

'Well, what did she say?'

'She didn't say anything.'

'What, nothing? Nothing at all? What about the photo? What did she say about that?'

'I didn't show it to her. Look, can you come out for a cup of tea or something?'

'I'll just ask. You're lucky, he ain't got a lot on today, so he's spending his time doing some enlargements. I'll just pop out the back.'

After only a moment she was back. 'Right, I'm ready.' Miss Dennis took Mary's arm and led her outside. 'Now, I want to hear all about this mysterious Daisy.'

'There's nothing to tell. I'm going back again this afternoon to see her. Perhaps she'll talk to me then.'

'Why don't she talk?'

'Don't know.'

'What's it like in there? Are they all daft? Do they sit dribbling and rocking backwards and forwards? Do the people who look after them knock 'em about?'

Mary laughed. 'No, it's not a bit like that, and they've got lovely gardens. Daisy made me a cup of tea.'

'What? They're allowed to do things like that, handle hot things? Don't they throw things about?'

'No.'

'I think you're ever so brave going in there on your own. I wouldn't like to walk past there just in case one of 'em got out and chased me. Are they dangerous?'

'I don't think so. I never really thought about it.'

Mary was careful what she told Miss Dennis, whose first name she found out was Jean.

After a while Jean had to go back to work and Mary said she was going to see Daisy again.

'What're you doing tonight?' asked Jean.

'Nothing. Why?'

'Fancy coming to the pictures?'

'Yes, I'd like that.'

'Meet me outside the shop about six and then we can go together.'

'All right.'

Jean went back to work and Mary made her way to St Mark's.

This time the young man at the gate recognised her.

'Nurse Bentley said it was all right for me to come again this afternoon.'

'I'll just go and check.'

He was back very quickly and opened the small gate. 'You know where to go.'

Mary made her way to Nurse Bentley's office.

'Before I take you to see Daisy I want to know what you said to her. She wouldn't eat her lunch and she had to be sedated. What did you say?'

Mary was shocked. 'I just told her about my family and who I was.'

'Did you mention anything about the trial?'

'No. I don't know anything about that.'

'I see. Well, I'll let you see her, but only for a short while. She's still in bed.'

Mary felt guilty as she walked along the corridor. She had come into this woman's life and upset her. But what had she said that could have made her distressed?

The nurse stopped at a door. 'Now, be careful what you say.'

'Yes.'

They stepped inside a large dormitory. Daisy's bed was halfway down and she had her back to them.

'Daisy. Mary has come to see you again.'

'Hello, Daisy.'

Daisy didn't move.

'I'll leave you for a while. But remember, don't upset her.'

'No, I won't. Thank you.' Mary went round the other side of the bed and sat on a chair. 'I'm sorry you're not well. If you want me to go away, just say.'

Daisy had her eyes tightly shut.

Mary looked about at the sparse room. Daisy's bed, like all the others, was covered with a blue bedspread. Blinds hung at the windows and the floor was covered with grey-coloured lino. There was nothing warm or homely about the space. It was sad that people had to live like this. After a while, Mary realised she was wasting her time, so she picked her handbag up off the floor and made to stand up. 'I think I'd better be going.'

Daisy's hand shot out and clamped on to Mary's. Mary quickly sat back down. 'You want me to stay?'

Daisy still had her eyes shut.

'Well, if you want me to stay at least look at me.'

Daisy's eyes immediately opened. They didn't look so far away this time. They darted about and seemed alive. Mary couldn't believe the change.

'Are you going to talk to me?'

Daisy closed her eyes again, but she was still holding on to Mary's hand tightly.

For the next half-hour Mary talked about anything she could think of. The weather. The boats. The fact she was going to the pictures with the girl from Palmer's the photographer's tonight. Mary was hoping that name might have brought a spark of life. She never mentioned the family. She told her all about Mrs Johns and Ron who was joining the navy. All the while Daisy silently held on to Mary's hand and kept her eyes firmly closed.

'I've got to go now,' said Mary when Nurse Bentley opened the door. 'But I can come back tomorrow, if you want me to.'

Daisy opened her eyes. 'Please,' she whispered.

Mary smiled at her. She had got her to talk, and hopefully she would say more tomorrow.

# Chapter 21

It was twelve o'clock and it was with a heavy heart that Sarah was preparing some soup for Sadie's children. She didn't know what time the welfare people were coming, but surely they would let them have something to eat before they took them away? This morning when she'd taken the porridge in she'd known she should tell them about their mother but she hadn't known how to.

A sudden uproar at the front door sent her rushing along the passage. She opened the door just as the woman who had called on her yesterday was physically dragging Rosie towards her car.

'You told us lies,' screamed Rosie when she caught sight of Sarah. She struggled to get free. 'You told us lies. We ain't gonner see Mum. She's dead.'

The twins were standing silently on the pavement looking confused, their big eyes darting from Sarah and back to Rosie. Iris was sucking on her piece of rag and tears ran down her cheeks as she held tightly on to Brian's hand. He was also crying. Mr and Mrs West from the dairy were out of their shop and staring at the scene. Gradually other neighbours joined them and, whispering amongst themselves, they all looked over at Sarah who was trying to talk to Rosie as the woman continued to pull her towards the car.

'What could I say, Rosie?'

'I never want to see you again.'

'I want my mum,' cried Iris.

The man got out of the car and bundled first the twins, then Iris, along with Brian, who was now screaming for Rosie, inside the car. The man turned to Sarah. 'I hope you're happy now. Interfering with welfare business and making promises only brings trouble.' He then climbed inside the car and slammed the door.

Sarah held on to the woman's arm. 'Can't they stay?' she pleaded.

The woman shook Sarah's arm away. 'Now, Rosie, in the car and no more nonsense.'

Sarah went to hug Rosie, but the girl pushed her away and got into the car. 'I hate you.' It was said with such venom that it took Sarah aback. She let her tears fall.

As they drove away, the tear-stained little faces looking out of the car's rear window melted many of the neighbours' hearts and a few dabbed at their eyes with the bottom of their aprons.

'What was all that about?' asked Mrs West, coming over and putting her arm round Sarah's heaving shoulders.

'Sadie's dead and they're putting them in a home,' sobbed Sarah.

'Oh no. Poor Sadie. I'm so sorry to hear that. Didn't have much of a life, did she? And those poor kids. It's a shame, but let's face it, Sarah, it could be the best place for 'em. There's no one to look after them now, is there?'

Sarah shook her head. 'I would have. What if they split them up?'

'I don't know. They've had a hard life and you've been a good friend to them.'

'I've let them and Sadie down,' she sniffed.

'You've done your best. Didn't see Ron. He done a runner?'

Sarah was trying to think fast. 'I don't know. They might have come and taken him away earlier as he's older and probably going to a different place.'

'Could have. I don't reckon he would have made so much fuss: he would have seen it was for the best. How's your little lad these days? He certainly enjoyed the party.'

'Yes, he did.' Sarah looked up at the few sad decorations that were still draped from some bedroom windows. 'I can't believe so much has happened in such a short while. We had a really lovely day.'

'Yes, it's a shame. Has the lad stopped his wandering now?'

'Yes. Ted put a bolt high up on the kitchen door so he can't get out.' Sarah wasn't going to tell her that the house was like a prison with bolts on most of the doors.

'He's not any better then?'

Sarah shook her head.

'And where's our Mary? Thought she would have been out here.'

'She's gone away for a few days.'

'That was a bit sudden.'

Sarah had to think fast. 'She promised a friend she'd see her after the Jubilee.'

'She's gonner be really upset when she finds out about Sadie and the kids going. Did she know about the murder?'

'No. She went off first thing Tuesday.' Sarah wanted to get away. She didn't like all these questions. 'I really must go in and see to Eddie.'

Mrs West smiled, but Sarah was worried. Did she suspect anything?

'I'm really surprised about Ron though. I would have thought he would have stayed with the kids, or at least made a bit more fuss.'

'Could be he didn't get the chance. Those welfare people can be very forceful.'

'That's true. Rum do that. A rum do all round. As you said, such a lot has happened in a short time. Who'd have thought that Mr Fellows would end up dead? Stabbed on Jubilee Day as well. Well, it'll certainly be a day none of us round here will forget in a hurry. A terrible thing.' She bent her head closer to Sarah. 'We heard the police think Sadie did it. So in some ways it might have been a good thing she died. A trial would have been awful for her.'

Sarah quickly looked up. Who had told them that?

'Mind you,' continued Mrs West, 'she had good reason, the way he beat her up. Poor girl, she had a rough life. You feeling any better now?'

Sarah dabbed at her eyes. 'Yes thanks. Now I really must go and see to Eddie.' She was pleased to get inside her front door. She didn't want to discuss this any more. But what *would* Mary say when she got home? Sarah needed her here. Why did she have to stay away this long?

That evening Mary felt happy as she stood waiting for Jean. In many ways, it had been a lovely day. The weather was still fine and she was off to the pictures with a new friend, but best of all, Daisy had spoken to her. True, it was only one word, but it was a start.

Jean came out of the shop and they made their way along to the cinema.

'D'you fancy *It Happened One Night* with Clark Gable and Claudette Colbert?' asked Jean as she slipped her arm through Mary's.

'Sounds good.'

'Right you are then.'

They walked along Commercial Road talking and laughing

together. Mary was pleased at how at ease they were with each other. Some sailors called and offered to take them out; they giggled but both politely said no, thank you.

'Have you got a boyfriend?' asked Jean.

'Yes, he's a sailor. He's my friend's brother. What about you?'

'I did have, but he went off with someone else.'

'Oh, I'm sorry.'

'I'm not. You want to be careful of sailors; they all seem to want a girl in every port. And they're only after one thing.'

'I hope my Billy's not like that.' Mary couldn't tell her that Billy had tried it on.

'So do I. But be careful.'

As they talked Mary found out that Jean had two sisters who were married and had moved away. She lived here in Portsmouth with her mum and dad, but wanted to get a job on one of the big liners that sailed out of Southampton. She wanted to be a photographer, which was why she worked for Mr Palmer. He was teaching her all about the trade. To Mary that sounded a very glamorous job, much more interesting than just packing biscuits.

'Is this the first time you've been to Portsmouth?' asked Jean.

'No, I came down last August. My Billy's ship was here then and me and Liz, that's my friend, came to see him. We went up on the hill to the fair. That was really lovely and it's so big. Does it come here very often?'

'Bank holidays mostly, and it was here for the Jubilee.'

'I'd like to go to it again.'

'Well, when it does come here why don't you come and stay at our house? You won't have to pay for lodgings then.'

'I couldn't. You don't know me.'

'I know you're a caring person, who wants to help people.'

Mary gave her a silly grin. 'No, I'm not.'

'So why are you down here then if it wasn't to help your mum find out about your dad's family?'

Mary felt guilty that she had given Jean that impression, when all the while it was to satisfy her own curiosity.

There was a queue outside the cinema and some sailors who were standing behind them got very close and started up a conversation. They wanted the girls to sit near them although they didn't offer to pay for them. Jean got cross, but Mary quite enjoyed the attention.

After the pictures, which they both enjoyed, Jean and Mary walked along Commercial Road. Jean had told Mary that she lived in Arundel Street.

'That was a good film,' said Jean. 'I really enjoyed it.'

'So did I,' said Mary. 'That Clark Gable is really nice and Claudette Colbert was so lucky to be kissed by him.

Jean laughed. 'It might not be. He might have bad breath or something.'

'Oh you. Don't shatter all me dreams.'

After they parted company, Mary made her way back to Mrs Johns's. She couldn't help smiling to herself. All in all, it had been a very good day.


Mary knew she couldn't stay in Portsmouth for much longer so she decided to go and see Daisy first thing in the morning, planning to get the train home that afternoon. She hoped she would know more about Daisy by then.

When she arrived at St Mark's the man at the gate let her in right away. Nurse Bentley was busy and she had to wait to be let into the ward. Mary was sitting outside her office when a young man of about twenty came up to her. He was tall and his clothes were much too big for him. He smiled at Mary, showing his chipped and broken, badly stained teeth.

'Hello,' he said, snatching off his cloth cap. 'I saw you talking to Daisy. I was doing the gardening.'

'The gardens are very nice.'

'I like gardening.'

'That's nice.' Mary didn't know what to say; she really didn't want to get into a conversation with him.

'Our Daisy don't say much, does she? My mum said I mustn't talk to her.' He bent closer. 'My mum said she done a murder.'

'I don't think it was ever proved.'

His face filled with anger. 'If my mum said she did, then she did. You ask my mum.'

Mary looked about her, frightened. Where was Nurse Bentley or anyone?

'Peter. Go back to your work,' said a young nurse, quickly coming towards them. 'I'm sorry, my dear,' she said to Mary. 'He thinks the world of his mother.'

Mary's mind was racing. His mother knew all about Daisy. Would she be able to help her? 'Excuse me,' said Mary to the nurse as she was leading Peter away.

'Yes.'

'Would it be possible to have a word with Peter's mother about Daisy?'

The nurse smiled and came closer. 'I'm sorry, dear, but his mother passed away many years ago. He still thinks she's alive and will visit him one day. We find it's much better and easier to go along with him.'

Mary sat back down, defeated.

'If you like to come with me I'll take you to see Daisy.'

'Thank you.'

'Do you have special permission to visit in the mornings?'

Mary felt guilty. She knew she shouldn't be here but she didn't want to waste any of the few days she was going to be here. 'I have to go back to London this afternoon, so I thought I'd just pop in to see her before I go.'

'I see. That should be all right. Daisy doesn't get any other visitors.' The nurse led Mary outside.

She was pleased to see Daisy was sitting in the garden, where it was more private.

'Hello,' she said, going up and sitting next to her.

Daisy quickly looked about her.

'I've brought you some sweets.'

'Thank you,' she whispered.

Mary smiled. 'So you can talk?'

Daisy didn't answer. She cast her eyes down and began picking at her fingers, but Mary had noted that her eyes looked more alive today.

'I can only come to see you today. I've got to go back home tomorrow.'

Daisy's head shot up. 'No.'

Mary smiled. 'So you don't want me to go, but you won't talk to me.'

Daisy looked all around her. 'I mustn't talk.'

'Why?'

'They might put me away.'

Mary could feel the excitement welling inside her. How far should she go? This woman was frightened of being put away, but she was already in an institution. What else was she worried about? She put out her hand and held Daisy's. 'You don't have to be afraid of me. I only want to find out all about you.'

Daisy looked up and swiftly pulled her hand away.

'I thought I told you visiting was only in the afternoon.' Nurse Bentley had come quietly up behind Mary.

Mary quickly turned round and jumped to her feet. 'I'm sorry.'

'I told you only in the afternoon.'

'I'm sorry,' repeated Mary.

'The patients have tasks to do in the morning and some of them have to attend clinics. Now, I would like it if you came back later.'

'But Daisy's only sitting here. Can't I stay?'

'No. If I break the rules for one I'll have to break them for everybody.'

Reluctantly Mary picked up her handbag. 'I'll see you this afternoon, Daisy. Goodbye.'

Nurse Bentley walked across the grass with Mary.

'I don't know what you hope to achieve, but I don't want Daisy upset. I don't want the trial and all the trauma that went with it brought back to her again.'

'I don't want to upset her,' said Mary. 'But I'm sure she'll speak to me.'

'Well, I wish you luck. It's something the doctors have been trying to do for years.'

'Yes, but I'm not a doctor and she might think she can trust me.'

Nurse Bentley smiled as she opened the door. 'We shall see.'

Mary didn't want to leave Daisy. She was sure Daisy was about to speak to her. Now she'd have to come back this afternoon. Nurse Bentley had mentioned the trial. Did they have records? She might learn something about Ted if she could have a look at them.

# *Chapter 22*

Mary was cross that Nurse Bentley had made her leave just as she thought she was getting through to Daisy. Although she'd wanted to go home today she knew now she would wait till tomorrow; the extra visit this afternoon might help her to gain Daisy's trust and encourage Daisy to be more confident with her. Mary looked at her watch. She had three hours to kill. Where could she go? She couldn't go back to see Jean, as she would be working. A tram came trundling past and it was going to Portsdown hill. Mary decided to go there.

The view from this hill almost took her breath away. Mary loved sitting here just staring at the sea glinting in the sunlight. This was one place where she would love to live. Her thoughts went to Billy and the night they were here at the fair. What was he doing now? She hugged her knees. As Jean had said, sailors had a girl in every port and his letters weren't very loving. She hoped he didn't think she was just another girlfriend he could play fast and loose with. Should she have let him have his way the last time she saw him? She knew she loved him, but she didn't know if he loved her. She smiled to herself when her thoughts travelled to Ron. She reckoned he'd look handsome in his uniform, as he was already a nice-looking lad. He'd certainly break the girls' hearts and have a girl in every port. But what future did he have? And what about the terrible secret he would have to live with for the rest of his life? She felt a great sadness for him. Mary thought about the other Fellows kids and hoped they were coping with all that life was throwing at them, but she knew her mother would help them as much as she could. She suddenly felt homesick. This was the longest she'd ever been away from home and suddenly she realised how much she missed her mother and Eddie.

That made up her mind. Even if Daisy didn't talk this afternoon she would definitely go home tomorrow.

Once again Mary walked through the gates of St Mark's and headed towards Nurse Bentley's office. She gently tapped on the door.

'Come in. Oh Mary, it's you,' she said as Mary opened the door. 'I'm sorry about this morning, but rules are rules. Daisy is in the garden. I'm pleased to say that she certainly has livened up since you've been visiting.'

'That's good.' Mary hesitated. 'Nurse Bentley, I hope you don't mind me asking, but do you know anything about Daisy's past? You know – the trial?'

'I'm sorry, but I'm not allowed to say anything. Patient's confidentiality, you do understand.'

'Yes. Of course. But what about her family? I would like to find out if she is a relation.'

'I'm really sorry. It's strictly forbidden to give out any information to anyone. I'll just unlock the doors.'

Once again Mary followed her into the garden and walked across the grass to Daisy, who was sitting in the same place as she'd left her this morning.

'Hello, Daisy,' Mary said as she sat next to her. Her voice wasn't as soft and as sweet as it had been every time she'd visited her previously. She wanted Daisy to know that she wanted answers to her questions.

As there was no reply Mary went on, 'I won't be staying long. I'm going back home tomorrow.' She looked around. Peter the gardener was watching them and he gave her a wave. 'It has been nice meeting you. I'll leave you my address and if at some time you feel you want to write to me, I'll be very pleased to hear from you.' Mary went into her handbag for a pencil and paper. As she pulled the paper out so the photograph came out as well and fell to the ground. Daisy bent down and picked it up. She stared at it silently for a long while.

Mary sat speechless. She hadn't wanted this to happen. Would Daisy recognise herself? Mary was getting worried. She didn't want her to be hurt.

Daisy's eyes hadn't left the photograph and she said softly, 'This is me.'

Mary was shocked. This was the first whole sentence she'd heard Daisy speak. 'Yes, I know it's you.'

'I was very young and beautiful then.'

'Yes, you were.'

'This was before I had my little boy. Everybody said I'd killed him, but I didn't, I loved him, I really loved him and I would never have harmed him, he was my pride and joy.' Daisy was still staring dreamily at the photograph.

Mary was almost beside herself with excitement. She wanted to ask so many questions but knew Daisy had to tell her in her own time. 'That must have been a long while ago.'

'Yes it was.'

'Do you want to talk about it?'

'I was courting when this was taken.'

Mary looked nervously at Daisy. She had put the photograph in the pocket of her shapeless floral frock. 'What happened to your little boy?'

Daisy returned Mary's gaze. Tears were running down her

cheeks. 'I gave him away.' With that she burst into uncontrollable sobbing.

Mary put her arm round Daisy's shoulders. She felt terrible knowing she'd upset Daisy, and she was worried that someone would see them and take her away. 'Please, Daisy. Don't cry. I don't want to distress you.' Mary quickly glanced all about her. She could see Peter leaning on a fork and staring at them. She prayed he wouldn't go and get a nurse.

Daisy wiped her eyes and looked at Mary. 'I think I'll go to my room. Can I keep my picture?'

Mary nodded. 'Shall I come with you?'

'No.'

'I'll come and see you tomorrow.'

'You said you was going home.'

'I can stay another day.'

Daisy didn't register any emotion at that remark. She stood up and, without another word, walked away.

Daisy had remembered what she'd said. Was she getting through to her? Mary wondered. Peter was watching them and came trotting up.

'What's wrong with Daisy?' he asked.

'Nothing, she just fancies a rest.'

Peter took her hand and started telling her in great detail about his roses. Mary tried hard to be interested, but she just wanted to get away.

When she got back to Mrs Johns she excitedly told her all that had happened.

'So you're going to see her tomorrow?'

Mary nodded. 'Yes. I can't let it go now, can I? I'm so close now, I can feel it.'

All Saturday morning Mary was beside herself. She desperately wanted to see Daisy again, but knew she mustn't break the rules and had to wait till the afternoon. To kill time Mary made her way to the dockyard; she was hoping to find out about Ron. She had to have something to tell Rosie and the rest of them tomorrow. How was he? She hoped he'd settled in.

When Mary got to the gate she asked the sailor about Ron, having explained who she was. He went into the recruiting office, returning after a while to tell her that Able Seaman Ronald Fellows had been taken on and was now over at St Vincent's and that he was very busy. With a smile he added, 'Tell your aunt not to worry, he should be getting in touch very soon.'

'Thank you,' said Mary and moved away.

As she wandered along the seafront she wondered if Ron had written to her mother. Mary stood watching all the activity. The paddle steamers and the ferryboats going backwards and forwards to Gosport and the Isle of Wight intrigued her. She thought about Eddie. He would love all this. She hoped she might be able to bring him here one day.

At twelve sharp Mary was at the gates of St Mark's again. The man – a different one this time – who let her in asked her name, and when she told him he said that Nurse Bentley wanted to see her. Why? Had Daisy refused to see her? It was with a heavy heart that Mary knocked on the office door.

'Mary. Come in and take a seat. I don't know what you've said to Daisy but she doesn't want to see you. She was very disturbed yesterday and had to be sedated.'

Mary sat down. She was filled with guilt. She had barged into this woman's life and upset her. 'I'm very sorry. She saw the photograph.'

'I know. We can't get it away from her.'

'I *am* sorry, but it was an accident. It fell out of my bag when I was writing my name and address down.'

Nurse Bentley gave her a look that said she didn't believe her. 'I don't think it would be very wise to visit her for a week or two.'

'I shall be going home this afternoon now, so could you give Daisy these chocolates? I brought them as a going-away gift.' Mary was finding it hard to speak, she was so upset. 'She does have my address and when I come down here again I'd like to see her, that's of course if she wants to see me. Would that be all right?'

Nurse Bentley smiled. 'If she wants to see you I'm sure that could be arranged.'

Mary walked away from St Mark's with a heavy heart. But she knew she would be back soon. She was determined to find out more about the mysterious Daisy. But should she tell her mother what she knew? Or should she confront Ted?

Although Mary had only been away four days, so much had happened. When she turned into Doyle Street she felt sad. All the Jubilee decorations had been taken down and even the houses looked dirty and bunched together, something she'd never noticed before.

Sarah was so pleased to see her daughter that she greeted her with open arms and held on to her tight, not wanting to let her go. 'I'm so happy to see you back. Did you have a nice time?'

'Yes, I did. And how are you, young man?' Mary untangled Eddie from round her legs and hugged him. 'Come on, give me a kiss. So, what's been happening while I've been away?'

'He has missed you. He's been sitting in your bedroom waiting for you to come home.'

Mary bent down and cuddled him again. 'And I've missed you. Come on, say I've missed you.' She repeated it very slowly.

Eddie laughed and ran away.

'What about Ron, how did he get on? Is he all right?' asked her mother.

Mary nodded and got to her feet. 'I didn't see him after he signed on to go to the navy college. A sailor took him under his wing. The man at the recruiting office said he would be very busy settling in. I expect he'll be writing to the kids when he can. How're Sadie and the kids, are they all right?'

Sarah looked away. 'I'll make you a cup of tea. I expect you're dying for one.'

'That'll be lovely. How's Dad?'

'He's fine. Your friend Liz came round. She couldn't believe you'd gone off like that. She said she was so worried about you, thought you was ill or something.'

'You didn't tell her why, did you?'

'No. I just said you fancied a few days away. Mind you, she thought it was odd. So you'll have some explaining to do on Monday.' Sarah went into the scullery.

'Yes, I will.'

'What did you do with yourself while you was down there?' shouted Sarah from the scullery.

'I met this girl Jean. She's ever so nice. We went to the pictures.'

'That's nice. What else?'

'I'll just take my things upstairs.' As Mary went into her bedroom her mind was churning over. She didn't know what to do. Part of her knew she should tell her mother about Daisy. But what would her reaction be? And what about Ted? Mary knew he'd be angry with her.

As she came back into the kitchen Mary said, inclining her head towards the wall, 'the kids are quiet.'

'Mary, sit down. I've something to tell you.'

The expression on her mother's face told her it was something awful and Mary quickly did as she was told.

'It was horrible. I was so upset.'

Mary saw her mother's eyes were full of tears. 'What is it? What's happened?'

Sarah sobbed. 'It's Sadie, she's dead.'

'*No*,' wailed Mary. 'When? How?'

Sarah blew her nose, then explained what had taken place on Thursday. By the time she'd finished, she could barely speak for the tears running down her cheeks.

'Poor Sadie,' whispered Mary.

'I didn't want it to happen. I didn't want them to take the kids away. I wanted to look after them.'

Mary went to her mother and they held each other close. 'Don't upset yourself. You did your best . . . *Ron*. What about Ron? He'll go mad when he finds out.'

'I can't believe she's gone,' said Sarah, her words muffled in Mary's frock.

'Where was she buried?'

'I don't know. I couldn't find out anything. I've even been to the Town Hall to see if they could tell me where they took the kids, but they won't let on. I can only pray that one day Rosie will forgive me and write to me.'

Mary didn't know what to say. She knew Ron had had second thoughts about running away, but he couldn't have anticipated this.

'Can you get in touch with Ron?'

Mary shook her head. 'I can write to the dockyard; they might be able to help.'

'What a mess.'

'What has Dad said about all this?'

Sarah managed to summon up a slight smile. 'You know him. He didn't think I should worry about them. Said it wasn't any of my business, but I can't help it. Sadie was a good woman and I liked her. She didn't deserve a bloke like her husband.'

Mary sat at the table and Eddie clambered up on to her lap. How could so much change in just a few days? Mary knew now that she couldn't tell her mother about Daisy, not yet anyway, as she had far too much to worry about.

Ted hugged Mary when he walked in. 'And how are you? We have missed you.' He held her at arm's length. 'Did you have a nice time? So what did you get up to then? I hope you behaved yourself.'

'Ted! What a thing to say.'

'Well, you know what all those sailors are like, especially when a girl's wandering about all day on her own.'

Mary could sense the cool atmosphere between Ted and her mother and knew she had to be careful what she said. She certainly had to bide her time before she mentioned Daisy.

'So, what did you do all day?' asked Ted.

'I met this girl in Palmer's the photographer's. A couple of times we went out together.' Mary emphasised the name Palmer's, hoping to get some reaction from Ted, but there wasn't any. He must have known where that photograph had been taken. 'She's hoping to be a photographer on the liners.'

'I hope you're not getting any ideas!' said Sarah.

Mary smiled. 'What do I know about anything like that?'

'So you had your photograph taken? Let us see it then,' said Ted.

'No, I didn't.'

'What did you go into the photographer's for then?'

Mary crossed her fingers behind her back. 'I had to go there for something for Mrs Johns. You know, that lady I stayed with.'

'She had a cheek getting you to run around after her.'

'I didn't mind. It gave me a chance to find out about the shops.'

'So what happened to the boy you took down there?'

'Ron joined the navy. He's going to the naval college at a place called Gosport. It's just across the river – well, it's the sea really, you have to get the ferryboat.'

'I'm surprised they let him in. Can he read and write?'

'Ted, that's not a very nice thing to say. Sadie was always very proud of what her children could do . . .' Sarah looked at her son.

Mary bent down to Eddie and said, 'You'd like to see all those little boats bobbing about, wouldn't you?'

He looked away and laughed his lovely infectious laugh. Mary kissed the top of his head.

When was she going to find the right time to tell her mother about Daisy?

# Chapter 23

On Monday morning Mary dawdled through the factory gates waiting for Liz to catch up with her. Some of the women called out to her, wanting to know where she'd been and if she was all right.

'Thought you might have been ill or something,' said Bet as she passed her.

Mary was touched at their concern. 'No, don't tell the foreman but I decided to take a bit of a holiday.'

'All right for some. I can't afford to be short in me pay packet,' yelled Lil, who worked alongside Mary.

Mary knew that as soon as she saw Liz she would be bombarded with questions. She would be able to tell her some of it, but not all.

'Where the hell have you been?' shouted Liz, coming up to her.

'You'll have to wait till lunchtime, it's a long story.'

'What was you doing down in Portsmouth?'

'I can't tell you now,' said Mary as she took her clocking-in card from the rack, put it in the machine and pulled the handle.

'It had better be good, that's all I can say,' said Liz, doing the same. 'I thought you was dead or something.'

All morning Mary breathed in the sickly sweet smell of the

biscuits being baked. Funny: the smell had never bothered her before, but now, after the clean fresh air of the sea, it was getting to her. She went off into her own little dream world as she stood at the packing bench mechanically putting packets of biscuits into large boxes. Her thoughts went to Jean: her job seemed more interesting. And what about her future? To work on one of those big liners must be wonderful.

As soon as it was lunchtime Liz grabbed Mary's arm and swept her to the far corner of the yard. 'Well, I'm waiting.'

Mary laughed.

Liz was angry. 'It ain't no laughing matter.'

'I'm sorry, but you should see your face.'

'All week everybody was asking me where you was. Even your poor old mum didn't know why you'd gone off like that.'

'Sit down and I'll tell you.'

Liz plonked herself on the wall next to Mary.

Mary knew she couldn't say too much. She just told Liz that after all the trouble Ron hadn't wanted to be put in a home but to join the navy instead, and that's when she'd decided to take him to Portsmouth.

'Couldn't he have gone on his own?'

'No, he was too upset and, besides, he'd never been on a train before, let alone seen the sea. You should have seen how excited he was at seeing the sea and all the boats.'

'Bit like us, I expect.'

'I was worried that he might have got lost and then Gawd knows where he would have finished up.'

'Poor bloke. Proper little nursemaid, ain't yer? Mind you, that murder was awful. Fancy living next door to a murderer. Do they know who done it?'

'Sadie. His wife.'

'*No!* There wasn't much about it in the papers. The Jubilee took up most of the pages; there was just a little bit about a bloke being done in. When they said it was in Doyle Street, well, you could have knocked me down with a feather. That's why I was so worried. I thought you might know all about it.'

'It wasn't very nice. Sadie was in a bad state. Mr Fellows had bashed her.'

'Did you see her?'

Mary nodded.

'Was it awful?'

'Yes, it was.'

'Then she killed him. I don't blame her,' said Liz, savouring the drama.

'The sad thing is that Sadie died from her injuries and the kids have been put in a home.'

'That's awful.'

'Yes, it is. It's all very sad.'

'So why did you stay so long down in Portsmouth?' asked Liz.

'Well, I do like it down there. The weather was nice and I met this girl Jean.'

'Oh yes. Did you go out together then?' Liz sounded a little put out.

'Only to the pictures.'

'What's she like?'

'She had fair hair and blue eyes.'

'Christ, you had a good look! I didn't mean what did she look like. I meant was she all right? You know, could you have a laugh with her?'

'Yes. She was all right.'

'Did you meet any sailors?'

'No. So what was your Jubilee party like?' asked Mary.

'Great. Could do with things like that all the time.'

To Mary's relief the hooter went for them to start work. At least she didn't have to answer any more questions till it was time to go home. It would also give her time to decide if she should tell Liz about Daisy. She felt she had to tell someone; she couldn't keep this to herself for ever and at the moment it couldn't be her mum – not yet anyway.

Mary and Liz were on their way home when Mary said, 'Liz, could you come to the park with me this evening? There's something I'd like to talk to you about.'

Liz's face went ashen. 'What is it? I knew it – there is something wrong. Did that brother of mine . . . you know? Are you—' She stopped and looked around, then, stepping close to Mary, asked, 'You gonner have a baby?'

Mary laughed. 'No! Whatever made you think that?'

'Well, this Portsmouth business was so sudden. I just thought you might have gone down there to see a doctor.'

'No, I didn't. And I'm not going to have a baby. If you remember I wouldn't let your brother . . . you know. That's why he stopped seeing me for a while.'

'Sorry. Course I'll come to the park, but can't you tell me now?'

'No. We need to be quiet and it's a bit of a story.'

Liz grinned. 'You've got me all wondering now. Here, you ain't marrying me brother, are you? He ain't proposed?'

'No such luck.'

It was time for them to go their separate ways.

'I'll see you about seven, that all right?' said Mary.

'All right.'

Mary watched Liz walk away. If only she had that photo to back all this up but she knew that Liz would believe her.

Liz was at the park gates waiting for Mary on the dot of seven.

'What's so important then?'

'Let's sit over there. Liz, you know I went to Portsmouth with Ron; well, I also went to see someone else.'

'Who? You don't know anyone there . . . do you?'

'I didn't. Let me start at the beginning. At Christmas I bought me dad a wallet.'

'What's that to do with Portsmouth?'

'Will you let me finish?'

'Sorry.'

Liz sat with her mouth open as Mary told Liz about finding the photo and using Ron as an excuse to go to Portsmouth to find the photographer. About meeting Daisy and all that had happened. 'So you see, that's why I wasn't at work.'

'I can't believe all that's been going on,' said Liz, staring at Mary. 'And you said you don't know who she is?'

'No. But I think she's Ted's sister.'

'If she is his sister, why is he keeping her quiet? He must be ashamed of her. Why did she give her son away?'

'He was backward. Maybe her husband forced her to do it, maybe she couldn't cope. I don't know. Liz, I really don't know what to do. Should I tell me mum? Should I ask me dad on the quiet? I'm really in a two and eight.'

'What a time you've had of it. What with that and next door . . .' Liz sat, staring into space. 'I wonder who Daisy gave the boy to? I wonder if he knows who his mum is?'

'I don't know. He must be grown up a bit be now. Would be about twelve, I think. I wish I could have talked to her more.'

Liz eagerly sat up. 'What say we go down there August bank holiday, p'raps you could see her again?'

'What a good idea! We can stay with Mrs Johns; she's a really nice lady. I could talk to her.'

'Does she know why you was there?'

'Yes.'

'Right, that's settled. We'll go down there for a few days.'

'Can you afford it?'

'I shall make sure I can.'

Mary smiled, but August was a long way off.

'I can't wait to see your mysterious Daisy.'

'Liz, promise me you won't tell anyone about this, will you?'

'Course I won't.'

'Thanks.'

'Mary, I do think you should tell your mum. After all, you do get on all right with her, don't you? And you owe it to her to tell her about the boy being backward.'

Mary nodded. 'I feel awful keeping this from her. But what if I'm wrong? I don't want to upset Mum or come between her and Dad. Liz, I don't know what to do.'

'It is a bit of a problem. But I still think you should tell your mum.'

Mary smiled again. 'I feel better already having told you.'

Mary walked into the kitchen and took off her cardigan. 'Is Eddie in bed?' she asked her mother, who was busy knitting.

'Yes, love. Fancy a cuppa?'

'No. Is Dad home yet?'

'No.'

'Mum, can I talk to you?'

'Course you can.'

Mary sat opposite her mother. 'Mum, I had another reason to go to Portsmouth, not just to take Ron there.'

Sarah put down her knitting and said softly, 'Mary, are you in any sort of trouble?'

'No. Why does everybody jump to that conclusion?'

'Sorry. But I was worried about you. It's not like you to go off without a good reason.'

'I did have a reason.' Mary sat in the armchair opposite her mother. 'At Christmas I found a photograph.' Mary then went into the details of all that had happened in Portsmouth.

Sarah sat silently staring at her daughter. When Mary finally finished she said softly, 'And this poor woman is in an asylum for murdering her child who was backward?'

Mary nodded. 'But she said she didn't do it. Mum, do you think Daisy could be a relation of Dad's? His sister, perhaps?'

'Course not.' Sarah was almost shouting.

'So who is she? And why would he keep her photo?'

'I don't know; besides, that's his business. You didn't think to tell Ted or me that you'd found this picture? It would have given him a chance to explain and would have saved you a journey.'

'Why didn't he tell you about her?'

'If it had been important he would have. What happened before we were married was in the past. He must have a very good reason for not having all this brought out.'

Mary went to speak, but her mother rushed on: 'Whoever she is it is no concern of mine, it doesn't worry me and it shouldn't be any concern of yours.'

'But, Mum—'

Sarah's voice was rising with anger. 'I don't believe you could be so underhand as to go down there behind his back to see this woman. What did you hope to achieve?'

It was Mary's turn to sit silently. This wasn't the reaction she was expecting. 'I don't know,' she whispered.

'What was this woman's surname?'

Mary couldn't answer that question. 'She was in a lunatic asylum, Mum. She'd been had up for murdering her baby.'

'But you said she didn't do the murder? I think you are a very deceitful girl. I can't believe that you would do something like this.' Sarah's eyes flashed with fury. 'And what about this poor woman? Did you think of all the hurt you might have caused her? Why didn't you talk to Ted before you embarked on this silly quest? He's a very understanding man. I'm sure there is a reasonable explanation for all of this.'

'Why did he keep her photo?' Mary reiterated.

'I don't know. Now, I don't want to hear any more of this nonsense.'

'Why are you so cross with me?' asked Mary.

'It's because of your lies and deceit. I thought you was trying to help Ron and all the time you just wanted to satisfy your own curiosity. I am ashamed of you, Mary. I really am. As soon as Ted comes home we will discuss this.'

Mary hung her head. What could she say? And what would Ted's reaction be?

Mary was in her bedroom when she heard Ted come home. She sat on the bed full of fear.

For a while it was very quiet, then she heard her mother come up the stairs. Sarah knocked on Mary's door. 'You'd better come down. Ted wants a word with you.' Her mother's voice was cold.

# Chapter 24

When Mary walked into the room she could see the anger in Ted's eyes as they darted about and it frightened her. He was sitting at the kitchen table. Sarah sat opposite him and beckoned for Mary to do the same.

'So, young lady, what's this all about? It seems you've been lying to me and your mother,' Ted said between clenched teeth.

Mary had never seen him this furious before. Her heart was pounding: the sound was filling her ears. Would he take his belt to her as he had done to Eddie at times? 'I'm sorry,' she said softly. 'I should have said something when I found the photo.'

'Yes, you certainly should have. It was mine and you stole it. I never took you to be a thief.'

'Ted,' said Sarah.

He leaned across the table and, pointing at her, said, 'Sarah, be quiet. I don't want you defending her. She's a thief and a liar.'

Mary cringed as he raised his voice and her eyes filled with tears. She didn't want this to happen.

'Ted, I'm sorry, but I don't think you should say those things about my daughter.'

'What? So you're defending her, is that it?'

'No, I'm not, it's just that I don't like you saying things like that. She's a good girl.'

'Is that what you call being a good girl, stealing my property and then going behind my back to find out who it was in the photograph?'

'She's young and inquisitive.'

Ted's voice was getting louder and louder. 'Sarah!' he shouted. The rage in his face was distorting his good looks. 'If you're going to defend her then you can leave this house with this thief and liar.'

'Dad. Stop it. I'm so sorry. I didn't want to cause any rows between you and Mum. What else can I say?' Mary buried her head in her hands and cried.

Sarah put her arms round her daughter. 'Don't cry, love. I'm sure this can all be sorted out.' She looked up at her husband. 'Can't we sit and talk about this like grown-ups? I'm sure you can tell us what this was all about? Ted, why did you keep the photo a secret?'

'What I do is *my* business.'

Mary looked up. Suddenly she became angry too. Why couldn't he tell them the truth? 'Daisy, the woman in the photograph, is in a lunatic asylum. She was supposed to have murdered a child. How can that be any of your business?'

He thumped the table, making them jump. 'That's it. I will not be spoken to like that. Get out. Get out of this house, now.' He stood up, pushing his chair so hard it crashed to the floor.

'What?' Mary sat wide-eyed. She had never witnessed anyone this incensed before. 'Mum, he can't do that.'

He came and stood menacingly over Mary. 'I can and I will. Who pays the rent for this place? Now go up and pack your bags and get out.'

'Ted, you can't do this.'

'I can. And, Sarah, if she don't go, then I will. Remember who pays all the bills round here.'

'But, Ted . . .'

Mary looked from one to the other. She couldn't believe her mother would let him throw her out. 'Mum,' she whispered. 'Don't let him do this.'

Sarah turned to her daughter, her face ashen.

'Sarah!' yelled Ted. 'Get her out.'

'Just do as he says, love.'

Mary was scared now; tears were streaming down her face. 'Where can I go?'

Her mother looked bewildered. 'I don't know.'

Mary stood up; she had nothing to lose and she turned on Ted. 'Why are you so worried about all this? What have you got to hide?'

'Mary,' gasped Sarah. 'Please be quiet. Don't make things any worse for yourself.'

'I can't, can I, he's throwing me out.' Mary was shaking with rage. 'Mum, be careful of him. I don't think he's all he pretends to be.'

Ted walked towards Mary and stood directly in front of her. 'Now you listen to me, young lady. Who Daisy is is none of your business.'

'But it is me mum's.'

He raised his hand.

'Go on, hit me like you hit Eddie. You're nothing but a bully.'

'Mary, please leave. Just go to your room,' Sarah begged her daughter. 'I'm sure we can sort something out.'

Mary looked at her mother, who had tears running down her face. What had she done? Mary felt so ashamed. But why was Ted so angry?

Mary left the room but stopped outside the door; she could

barely hear her mother's voice above Ted shouting her down. She didn't want it to come to this. Slowly, she made her way upstairs, where she looked in on Eddie; he was peacefully sleeping. Mary went and gently stroked his head. 'What will become of you, little feller?' she whispered. Quietly crying, she went to her room, where she lay on the bed, sobs shaking her body. How could things go so wrong? She had lived here all her life; she'd been here before Ted. If he did go ahead with his threats, where could she go?

Sarah sat looking at Ted. His knuckles were white where he was clenching his fists. She had never seen anyone so furious.

'What has upset you so much?'

'Her. She's a menace. I've known all along. She's out to separate us, you know that, don't you?'

'Why? Why do you say that?'

'She never really liked me. She always wanted you to herself. Look how she reckoned she saw me in Oxford Street at Christmas. What was she hoping to achieve then? Go on, tell me. Tried to make out I wasn't working, didn't she? I tell you, Sarah, she's out to separate us.'

Sarah was taken aback; she'd forgotten all about that. 'But why? She's very fond of you.'

'Is she? She's jealous, that's what. She hated me for taking you away from her. You spoiled her. She's always been jealous of me.'

'Don't talk so . . .'

'Don't you tell me what to do.'

'Please, Ted, sit down and stop shouting.'

'I can do what I like. You women are all the same. Get a ring on your finger and you think you can manipulate anybody.'

'Ted, what are you talking about?'

228

'Look at that poor cow next door. She was the same, driving her husband to drink.'

Sarah looked at Ted in amazement. 'Sadie? What's Sadie got to do with Mary?'

'I'm telling you, Sarah, I want her out of this house and out of our lives.'

'I can't do that, Ted. She's my daughter.'

'Well, that's up to you. It's her or me.'

'What is so important about that woman in the photo that you can't talk to me about it?'

He took his jacket from the hook behind the door. 'I'm going out. She'd better be gone before I get back.'

Sarah was thankful he didn't slam the front door when he left. At least he hadn't woken Eddie up. That was the last thing she could cope with. What was wrong with him? Why was he so angry with Mary? Who was this Daisy? Why wouldn't he tell them? 'Why did you have to go to Portsmouth, Mary?' Sarah said out loud and then put her head in her hands and cried. She loved Ted, really loved him. She didn't want him to go. But Mary was her daughter. One day she would get married and leave her, then she'd be all alone. And what would become of her and Eddie? Ted was Eddie's father. She couldn't think straight. Why should she have to make such a terrible decision?

Mary must have cried herself to sleep, as it was dark when she woke up. It was very quiet. She looked at her clock; it was almost ten. Why hadn't her mother been in to see her? Slowly she slid off the bed and opened her bedroom door. The only sound she could hear was Eddie's muffled breathing. She didn't risk going in just in case Ted was in there. Looking over the banisters, she could see that the light was on in the kitchen but she couldn't hear any voices. Very slowly and one by one she made her way down the stairs. Had Ted gone out? It was eerily silent. The only sound Mary could hear was her own breathing and the thumping of her heart. What if he'd injured her mother? What if she was lying in a pool of blood like Sadie? Fear gripped her. She had to go in. She had to see that her mother was all right. Slowly she pushed open the kitchen door.

Sarah was still sitting at the table. Her mind was in turmoil. She had to go and talk to Mary. But what could she say? She looked up full of fear when the door opened. 'Mary?' she whispered.

'Where is he?' Mary looked at the scullery door, waiting for him to burst in.

'He's gone out.'

Mary didn't go to her, she just sat at the table. 'Mum, what's going to happen to me?'

Sarah reached across and grabbed her hand. 'I don't know, my love. I really don't know.'

'Would you let him throw me out?'

'What choice have I got? He's my husband and Eddie's father.'

'He ain't got that much time for Eddie. Mum, why are you sticking up for him?'

'I said for better or worse. And for all these years it has been for the better. I do love him, Mary. I really do.'

'Well, I think you're a fool.'

'What? Don't you talk to me like that.'

'I'm sorry. But can't you see he's the one that's deceitful? Why hasn't he told you about Daisy?'

'I don't know. He must have his reasons.'

'I can see I'm not going to change your mind, so it's me that has got to go.' Mary stood up.

'Where will you go?'

'I'll go and see if I can stay with Liz for the time being.'

'What, at this time of night?'

'What *choice* have I got?' Mary was trying to put on a brave face, but inside she was distraught and wanted to crumple into her mother's arms.

Sarah looked at her daughter. She suddenly appeared very grown-up, and despite her swollen eyes and puffy face she was a lovely young lady. Mary had confidence and Sarah knew she would get on with her life. It was herself and Eddie who would suffer most over this if Ted left her. 'I'll give you some money.'

'Thank you.'

'Mary, please don't walk out of my life.'

'Mum, I'm not walking away, it's you pushing me.'

Sarah broke into tears. 'I'm at my wits' end. What can I do? Oh, why did you ever find that sodding photo?'

'More to the point, why did he keep it and not say anything?'

'Stop trying to be clever.'

'Mum, I'm really sorry. I don't want to leave you and Eddie.' Mary sat back down again and, looking across at her mother, began to cry. 'What am I going to do?'

Sarah jumped up and put her arms round her daughter, holding her tight. 'Promise me you will let me know where you are? I'll be so worried about you.'

Mary shook her mother away. She wiped her eyes with her hand. 'I'd better be off before he gets back.' She walked to the door.

'I do love you, Mary.'

Mary didn't turn round.

In her bedroom she quickly put her few personal items in her case. She went in to say goodbye to Eddie. He looked so

231

serene. Her heart was filled with love for him. Tears softly trickled down her cheeks. 'I know I could have got you to talk one of these days,' she murmured. 'What will happen to you now?' She kissed her fingers and gently placed them on his cheek. He gave a little grunt and turned over.

Her mother was waiting at the bottom of the stairs. 'Here, take this.' She handed Mary some money. 'I'm so sorry, Mary.'

Mary didn't answer or look at the money; she quickly put it in her coat pocket.

'I'll keep all your things safe and perhaps when you get settled I can come and see you?'

'If you like.'

'When he's calmed down a bit I'll try and talk to him, make him see sense.' Sarah threw her arms round Mary and held on to her. 'I do love you,' she sobbed.

Mary struggled free. She wanted to shout out: Then why are you letting him do this to me? But she didn't. She opened the door and walked out. She didn't look back. This had been her home for all of her life; now she had been thrown out. How could her mother do this to her own daughter? Why was she afraid of the truth?

# Chapter 25

As Mary approached Liz's house she could see it was all in darkness. She didn't want to wake them but Liz was the only one she could turn to. She had to stay somewhere tonight.

After she banged on the door lights went on in the two front bedrooms. Mary could hear Liz's dad shouting, 'Who the bloody hell's making all that racket at this time of night?' His voice was growing louder as he neared the front door. 'Yes, what the bloody hell do you want?' he said, flinging open the door. 'Mary. It's you.' His voice was full of shock and surprise. 'What are you doing here? It's very late.'

'Who is it, Stanley?' yelled Mrs Thomas from upstairs.

'Come in, love. It's Mary, Liz's mate,' he called back.

Liz came rattling down the stairs in her nightie. 'Mary! Mary, what you doing here?'

Mary looked up at her friend and tears filled her eyes.

Liz, noting her friend's distress, went and hugged her.

'Liz, take Mary into the kitchen,' said Mr Thomas.

'What is it? What's wrong?' asked Mrs Thomas who, along with the girls, Elsie and Susan, had now joined the little group standing in the passage.

'Me dad's chucked me out.'

'What?' It was a chorus from Liz, Mr and Mrs Thomas.

'Why?' Mrs Thomas asked, adjusting the pink hairnet she

was wearing over her grey hair.

'Over this photo thing.' Mary sniffed.

'Liz, put the kettle on and we'll have a cup of tea,' said Mrs Thomas, ushering them along the passage and into the kitchen. 'And you two,' she said, pointing at her younger daughters, 'back to bed.'

Reluctantly the girls turned and left the room.

'And no listening at the door,' shouted Mr Thomas. 'They can be a crafty pair,' he said, smiling at Mary. 'Now, love, do you want to tell us what happened?'

'Not a lot to tell really. He said I was a thief and a liar and told me to get out.'

'What a wicked sod.'

'Stanley, watch your language. What did your mother have to say about it?'

'Not a lot really. She was in a bit of a state.'

'I bet she was. What made him say that?'

'It's a long story, Dad,' said Liz, walking in with the tea things on a tray. 'I'll tell you all about it sometime. What are you going to do, Mary?'

'Could I stay here the night?'

'Of course you can, love,' said Mrs Thomas. She was a round homely woman with a warm smile that lit up her face. 'You can go in with Liz. It might be a bit of a squeeze in that bed, but I'm sure you'll manage all right.'

The tears trickled down Mary's cheeks.

'I didn't think your dad would do that,' said Liz.

Mary brushed her tears away. 'Just goes to show, you don't really know what people are like.'

Nobody spoke for a while; they just sat drinking their tea in silence. Then Mrs Thomas said, 'Come on, Stanley, let's be off, you've got to go to work tomorrow, remember. See you in the morning, Mary.'

'Yes. Thank you.'

'Don't you two sit down here talking for too long.'

'No, Mum. Goodnight.'

After her parents had left the room Liz said, 'So I assume you've told them about what's-her-name?'

Mary nodded. 'Daisy.'

'And this Daisy? Who is she?'

'I don't know. He wouldn't say. He just got very angry.'

'I gathered that.'

'I hope you didn't mind me coming round here. I didn't know what else to do.'

'Course I don't. That's what friends are for. Fancy throwing you out.'

Mary sniffed. 'I still can't believe it.'

'Now come on, finish your tea and let's get up to bed. This is going to be a long night.'

A rap on the door woke Mary. Her face was pressed against a wall and she was having difficulty breathing. At first she was confused. Where was she? She suddenly remembered last night and moved Liz's arm off her.

Liz grunted and turned the other way. 'It's all right, Mum, we're getting up.' Her voice was heavy with sleep. 'You all right?' she asked Mary as her friend climbed over her to get out of bed.

'Yes, thanks. Did you get much sleep?'

'Not a lot. You was talking and crying.'

'I'm sorry. I don't want to be a nuisance. I'll have to find somewhere to stay.'

Liz sat up. 'Don't talk daft, you can stay here; we'll sort something out.'

'Thanks, but only if you're sure.'

'Course I am. Mind you, we'll have to get some other

235

arrangements sorted out for this bed lark.' Liz laughed. 'Can't say I want you cuddling me all night.'

'Perhaps I could get a mattress and sleep on the floor. That's if your mum don't mind.'

'She won't mind. Now come on, otherwise we'll be late for work.'

Mary touched Liz's arm. 'Don't say anything to them at work. I don't want everybody to know.'

'Course not. Now come on, otherwise we'll have Mum shouting at us.'

For the rest of the week Mary stayed with Liz and her family; they made her very welcome. Mary had told them the reason Ted had thrown her out. Mr Thomas was all for going round and punching him on the nose, but Mary said that wasn't the answer. Mrs Thomas had managed to get a feather mattress from a neighbour and Mary was very cosy. But she missed Eddie and longed to find out how he was.

Mary had deliberately left Liz's address on her dressing table before she left and one day was pleased, but also upset, to find that her mother had been round and left the rest of her clothes.

'How was Mum?' Mary asked Mrs Thomas when she got home from work that evening and saw her things on the chair.

'She was fine. At first I was a bit put out and wanted to give her a piece of my mind, but I could see she was upset. She also said how sorry she was that things had worked out like they did.'

Mary swallowed hard. So her mother *was* sorry. 'How was Eddie?' was all she managed to say.

'He seemed fine. Don't he talk?'

Mary shook her head.

'Why's that, he got some sort of speech impediment?'

236

'No. We don't know why. I've always wanted to take him to see a doctor or someone, but Ted, that's me stepdad, was always against it.'

'That's a shame. This Ted sounds a right one. Has he always been a bully?'

'No, he used to be very nice. It's only since we realised that Eddie was different to other children that he changed.'

'I'm surprised at your mum staying with him. And as for throwing you out, well . . . men.'

'She ain't really got a lot of choice. There's only Eddie and me, of course, and my wages ain't enough to pay the rent and keep us. I don't think anyone would look after Eddie if Mum had to go back to work. They wouldn't have him at school, he was so . . . disruptive, the teachers called it.'

Mrs Thomas put her arms round Mary's shoulders. 'Oh, you poor dear. You have got a lot on your plate.'

'Leave it out, Mum, you're only upsetting her. How about coming to the pictures tonight?'

'That'll be fine.' But Mary knew her heart wouldn't be in it.


On Saturday afternoon Mary wanted to go and see her mum and Eddie, but she knew Ted might be home and she didn't want to cause any more arguments and disruptions. However, she hoped they might go out and that she'd bump into them. So she hung about round Doyle Street for a couple of hours, but there wasn't any sign of them. She must tell Mrs Thomas that if her mother came round again perhaps they could arrange to meet on Saturday afternoon in the park.

It was another three weeks before her mother called again, this time to deliver a letter from Billy. Although Mary had written and told him she'd moved in with his family the letters must have crossed.

'Did she say she would meet me?' asked Mary eagerly.

237

'She said she would try next Saturday,' said Mrs Thomas. 'She thought it was a good idea, but she couldn't say what time.'

'I'll be there as early as I can.' Mary was over the moon. She was going to see her mum and Eddie.

The following Saturday Sarah was singing as she busied herself getting the dinner. Ted had said he would be home about twelve – that would be plenty time enough for her to clear away the crocks and do the washing up before she took Eddie to meet Mary in the park. Although she didn't want to raise any suspicion by changing her routine, she couldn't help getting herself ready to go out, she was so excited. In some ways it was a good thing that Eddie couldn't speak, otherwise he might have given the game away. Ted wouldn't even have Mary's name mentioned. It was as though she had never existed and it broke Sarah's heart. She had missed Mary so much. She would never forgive herself for not standing up to her husband. But what could she do? It had been the worst decision she'd ever had to make. She knew she was a coward and hoped her daughter would find it in her heart to forgive her one day.

Ted was late coming in, but that didn't matter. Sarah was sure Mary would wait all afternoon for her if need be.

'You look very nice,' said Ted when he walked in.

'Thank you.' Sarah had tried not to overdo it, but she wanted to look nice for her daughter.

They sat and ate their meal and it took all Sarah's self-control to do things in a leisurely way. She wanted to rush around and get out.

'That was good,' said Ted, pushing his plate away. He left the table and sat in the armchair. 'Seeing you're all dressed up, what have you got in mind to do this afternoon?' he asked.

Sarah froze. 'Nothing special. Thought I might take Eddie to the park. Why?'

'It's such a lovely day I was thinking along those lines myself. We could all go to the park and perhaps feed the ducks. Have you got any bread?'

Sarah nodded. She couldn't believe this; he never wanted to go out with Eddie – especially to the park to feed ducks. Did he suspect she was meeting Mary? He hadn't asked where she lived but he must have guessed it was at Liz's house. 'Are you sure you want to come with us? You know how cross you get with Eddie when he plays up.'

'He'll be all right if you keep him strapped in his pram.'

Sarah was trapped. She didn't have any choice but to go. She prayed that Mary would see them first. She didn't want any scenes in public. Slowly she got Eddie ready. He got very excited when Sarah told him where they were going. She would have loved to have told him they were going to see Mary; she knew how much her son loved her daughter. Tears filled her eyes. Perhaps she should have stood up to Ted; but it was too late now.

Mary was also getting excited as she hurried home from work at one o'clock.

'What time're you seeing them?'

'Don't know. I'll change as soon as I get in, then I'll be off.'

'D'you want me to come with you?' asked Liz.

'No, that's if you don't mind. I've such a lot to talk to Mum about. And I'm dying to see Eddie.'

'Course I don't, just thought you might have wanted a bit of support, that's all.'

Mary kissed her cheek. 'You're a really smashing friend. I'm so lucky.'

Liz laughed and rubbed her cheek. 'Daft ha'p'orth.'

Later that afternoon Mary had a spring in her step as she made her way to the park. It was such a lovely day and as she passed the church she saw a wedding party having their photos taken. They were all full of joy and laughing. The thought that went through her mind was that one day she would love to be a June bride. A frown wrinkled her brow when she thought of Billy. Did he still want her? When she saw how many letters Liz had had from Pete it did make her wonder if Billy felt the same for her as she did for him.

Mary walked through the park gates. Everywhere there were people. Some older ones were sitting in the sunshine on the striped deckchairs listening to the band. The instruments of the men on the bandstand glistened when they caught the sunlight. It was a very happy scene and it matched Mary's feelings. She wanted to join the children who were running about laughing and shouting; this was going to be a truly wonderful afternoon. She wandered around looking for her mum but there was no sign yet so she decided to sit on a bench near the gates to wait for her. She didn't want to miss a minute of being with Sarah and Eddie.

It was an hour later that she caught sight of them. Her heart sank. Why was Ted with them? They were busy talking and not looking in her direction. Mary wanted to cry. She quickly made her way far from the entrance. Once they were inside the park she could see that her mother appeared to be looking around. Mary knew she wouldn't be talking to her today.

From a safe distance Mary watched them feed the ducks. Her heart went out to her mother. She desperately wanted to be with them; she wanted to talk to Eddie. But today she felt like an outsider. This was her family. This was all she had in the world and now her mother had let her down again. Why did she have to bring that man with her? Tears were stinging her eyes. She wanted to scream out, but what good would that do?

Sarah was trying not to look as if she was searching the crowds. There wasn't any sign of her daughter. Had Mary caught sight of them and gone away? Why did Ted have to spoil today? She could see he wasn't enjoying himself. Sarah tried to smile at Eddie. He was missing Mary so much and was getting even more difficult to handle. Sarah felt so helpless and sad. Would this problem ever be solved?

# Chapter 26

Although Mary knew Liz was out, she also knew Mrs Thomas would be very understanding when she walked in.

'You're back early,' she said. 'Thought you might have been out a bit longer than this. How was your mum and the boy?'

Mary shook her head. 'I don't know. I didn't get to talk to her; she had Ted with her.' Mary felt she could no longer call him Dad.

'Oh, you poor dear. The kettle's boiling so I'll just make us a cuppa. Liz took the girls shopping; they won't be very long.'

Mary sat at the table. 'What am I going to do?' she asked when Mrs Thomas returned from the scullery.

'I don't know, love,' she said pulling the brightly coloured knitted tea cosy over the brown china teapot. 'What would you like to do?'

'I was thinking as I was walking back, I might go to Portsmouth.'

'That's a long way away.'

'I know. But other than Liz, who have I got here now? And I do like it there.'

Mrs Thomas sat at the table. 'I should give it a little while to think about that, love. It's a big step to take. I reckon your mum will soon get this Ted to change his mind and want you back home.'

'I don't know. He's changed so much.'

'Perhaps that was why they was there all together this afternoon. They might have wanted you to go home.'

'You think I should have said something?' Mary felt upset. 'Do you think I did the wrong thing then, by not talking to them?'

'I don't know. Wait and see what tomorrow brings. Who knows, your mum might come round here.'

Mary smiled. 'I hope so. I really do hope so.' She sat back. 'Mrs Thomas, do you mind me staying here?'

'Not at all, love. You've very welcome.' She smiled too. 'And I dare say our Billy will be happy with the arrangements as well.'

Mary was pleased she got on so well with his family. At least she didn't have any problems there.

The front door slammed and the clatter of feet along the linoed passage told them that Liz and the girls were home.

'Mary! I didn't think you'd be back here already,' said Liz, pushing open the kitchen door. 'Any more tea in that pot, Mum? I'm parched.'

'I'll just put a drop of water on these leaves.' Mrs Thomas took the teapot and went into the scullery.

'You don't look very happy. What happened?' asked Liz as she put her shopping on the chair.

'I didn't talk to Mum – she had Ted with her.'

'No. Why?'

Mary shrugged. 'Your mum reckons they might have wanted me to go back home with them, but I'm not so sure.'

'And you didn't talk to 'em?'

'No.'

'That was a bit daft. You going round there to find out?'

'No. If Mum wants me back she can come round here and ask me.'

'You know, you can be such a stubborn cow at times.'

'Thanks.'

'Well, you can.' Liz sat at the table when her mum brought her in a cup of tea. 'Ta.'

'Mary said she's thinking of going back to Portsmouth,' said Mrs Thomas.'

'No. Whatever for?'

'I was happy down there.'

'Yer, for a couple of days.'

'I like it there. Besides, what have I got to keep me here?'

'Me – and what about your job?'

'I reckon I can get a job all right. And I might be able to stay with Jean.'

'Seems like you've got it all worked out then,' said Liz. There was a hint of sarcasm in her voice.

'Our Billy likes Portsmouth,' said Elsie, the elder of Liz's two sisters.

'Is that why you're gonner go there?' said Susan. 'You wonner be with our Billy?'

'You gonner marry him?' asked Elsie.

'You two, stop being so nosy,' said Mrs Thomas. 'Anyway, what did you buy this afternoon?'

'She got a pair of shoes,' said Susan, pointing at Liz.

'That's nice. Well, show us then,' said her mother.

Inside, Mary wanted to cry as she sat watching this happy family. Everything they did they did together, whether with laughter or tears. It could never be like that for her. Her thoughts went briefly to the Fellows family. No matter how bad things were for them, like the Thomases, they always had each other. Even in their darkest moments, they clung together.

'Mary. You was miles away then. I said, do you like 'em?' Liz was holding up a black leather shoe.

'They're lovely.' Mary felt guilty at not taking more interest. 'I like that little heel. Can I try them on?'

'Course,' Liz handed Mary her shoes.

Mary spent the rest of the afternoon and evening with the family, and although they always included her in every conversation, she still felt like an outsider.

When they got back home, Sarah tried hard not to show her disappointment at not seeing her daughter. Had Mary seen her with Ted and walked away? Sarah lifted Eddie from his pram and kissed his forehead. 'Did you like that little outing to feed the ducks?' she asked, but he just pulled himself away and ran down the passage, making his usual funny noises. Still, he looked happier this afternoon than he had since Mary went. He missed her so much. Eddie slammed the kitchen door back, laughing.

'Keep that child under control,' called Ted as Sarah followed Eddie into the kitchen. Ted had already settled himself in the armchair with his newspaper.

'That was nice, us all going out together,' said Sarah.

'Not the sort of thing I enjoy, but if it helps to lift that miserable look of yours then I suppose it's worth it.'

'Well, you know why I'm miserable.'

'Don't start on that again, Sarah. You know I don't want that girl's name mentioned in this house.'

'Why are you so against her?'

'We've been over and over this. She's a liar.'

Sarah knew part of that was right. They had been over and over it and it was always the same. Ted was adamant. If Mary came back he would go. She knew she was being selfish but how would she manage to feed and clothe herself and Eddie, let alone pay the rent, if he left? She couldn't work. Nobody would look after Eddie; he was definitely a problem child.

They could even finish up in the poorhouse. Sarah shuddered at that thought. She knew that one of these days Mary would get married and leave home, but even that thought didn't help ease her conscience.

Sarah couldn't face any more arguments and said, 'I'll make a pot of tea.' In the scullery she watched the flames lick the sides of the kettle. Why did Mary have to take that damn photo and make such a big thing of trying to find out who the woman was? But what if Mary was right and she *was* Ted's sister? The kettle whistling brought her back.

'I shall be going out later,' said Ted, folding his newspaper.

'Anywhere interesting?'

'No.'

'Thought you might be going to the dog track.' Without thinking, Sarah added: 'Mary liked it when you took her.' She cringed, waiting for an explosion, but it didn't come.

'Have you been seeing her?'

'No.'

'Did you plan to meet her this afternoon?'

Sarah crossed her fingers. 'No. What made you ask that?'

'You don't take him out very often.' He pointed to Eddie, who was happily playing on the floor with his trains. 'Well, not for a social afternoon. Just as well he can't talk, otherwise he'd give away all your little secrets.'

'I'll start to get the tea.' Sarah knew she had to busy herself, or she might say something she didn't want Ted to hear.

Tea passed perfectly calmly. As soon as they had finished, Sarah got on with the washing up. Ted walked into the scullery, dressed up ready to go out. He looked so handsome. She knew he could have any woman he liked. He came up behind her and, putting his arms round her waist, kissed the back of her neck.

'I'm sorry, my darling. I don't like upsetting you. I shan't be that long.' He kissed her neck again and left.

Sarah wanted to scream out: If you don't like upsetting me then why won't you let Mary come home?

As she was getting Eddie ready for bed, she began to wonder again where Ted had gone. Did she have time to go and see Mary and explain what had happened today? She looked at the clock; it had just gone eight.

In no time Sarah was in the passage with her hat and coat on. Eddie was dressed and she was just strapping him in his pram when she saw the key being pulled through the letterbox. She froze. Ted opened the door.

'Sarah, I forgot my—' He stopped. 'And where do you think you're going?'

'Ted! I didn't think you'd be home just yet . . . .' Her voice trailed off to a whisper.

'Obviously. Now take him out of the pram, put him to bed and come back into the kitchen. I have a few things to settle with you, woman.'

Slowly Sarah did as she was told. She took off her hat and coat and, after putting a bewildered little boy in his cot, went into the kitchen.

That night, when they were in bed, Mary told Liz that if her mother didn't come round tomorrow and ask her to go back home, she would be handing her notice in at work on Monday.

'You've really made up your mind then?'

'Yes,' said Mary sadly.

'I don't want you to go.'

In the dark Mary smiled, but a tear trickled into her ear. 'That's a nice thing to say. I don't really want to go but what other option do I have?'

'You could stay here.'

'I can't. I've got to make my own way now. I don't want to be forever on the lookout trying to see Mum and Eddie. And what if I bump into Ted?'

'Mary, I really mean it. I don't want you to go. You're my best friend.'

If Mary hadn't been on the floor she would have held her tight. 'And you're my best friend and you always will be.'

'Why must you move right away then?'

'I feel I need to start a new life and a new job and I really think I would fit in down there. I can't be trying to find ways to talk to me mum for the rest of my life.'

'You'll soon forget all about me when you've got new friends.'

'No, I won't. You will write to me, won't you, and send me Billy's letters?'

'If you want.'

'Course I want you to write. Don't forget I'm still going out with your brother.' Mary wanted to add: That's if he still wants me, but instead said, 'You will still come and see me on August bank holiday just as we planned, won't you?'

'I'll see.'

'Please, Liz. Please say you will.'

Liz turned over. 'I said I'll see, didn't I?'

Mary was on her back looking up at the ceiling. She wished she'd never set eyes on Daisy's picture. She'd never wanted this to happen. But if her mother didn't come round tomorrow, Portsmouth had to be the answer.

# *Chapter 27*

It was Saturday morning; Mary stood on the platform thinking about last week. So much had happened. Just seven days ago she'd thought she was going to see her mother and Eddie in the park but her excitement had melted away when she'd caught sight of Ted with them. She'd been upset when her mother didn't come to see her on Sunday and every night she'd rushed back from work, hoping that her mother had been round to the Thomases to explain and to ask her to come home, but it hadn't happened. All week Mary had wondered if she should go and see Sarah, even though Ted would be home, but she knew it would cause too many problems.

On Monday, when Mary had reluctantly handed in her notice, she was touched by the girls wishing her good luck. None of them knew the real reason she was leaving, but perhaps Liz would tell them one day.

Liz was at work that morning and couldn't come to the station with her. In some ways Mary was pleased about that: it could have been too upsetting. She didn't want to hang around waiting till this afternoon for a train, in case she changed her mind. After they had said their goodbyes last night with many tears, Mary hadn't been able to sleep, as her mind was so confused. Was she doing the right thing? But

Mary knew she had to leave Rotherhithe; it held no future for her now.

Sarah looked at the clock. It had gone one. Should she risk taking Eddie to the park today? Perhaps Mary would be there this afternoon as she had missed them last Saturday. If Ted were to come home he would guess where she'd gone. Could she take another shouting and yelling match – that was without the lashing out? Sarah gently rubbed her arm; the bruises had almost gone now. Why was he like this? He had been so sorry afterwards that he had sat and cried like a baby, then they had made love. Sarah sighed. He could be such a gentle man. She knew she should have gone round to Liz's mum during the week when Ted was at work and explained what had happened. Yet what could she say? She felt such a failure. She didn't want people to know she couldn't stand up to her husband who had thrown her daughter out of her home. Her thoughts went to Sadie. She would have stood up to Wally despite the battering she would have got. She wouldn't have let him throw any of her kids out, she always said they were her pride and joy. I'm such a coward. I don't deserve a daughter like Mary, and if I'm not careful I'm going to lose her for good. It was on an impulse that Sarah collected some bread, hastily put Eddie in his pram and made her way to the park. 'We're going to the park to feed the ducks and to see Mary,' she said to her son.

Eddie got very excited and bounced up and down in his pram. Among his funny garbling sounds, Sarah was sure he was trying to say Mary, Mary.

It was well past lunchtime when Mary knocked on Mrs Johns's door.

Mrs Johns's face lit up when she saw who it was. 'Mary!'

she squealed. She moved forward and clasped Mary in her big wobbly arms. 'It's so lovely to see you again, but I thought you wasn't . . .' She stopped when from her shoulder she heard muffled crying. 'Come inside, love, and tell me what's wrong.'

Mary picked up her case and went into the warm inviting house with its familiar smell of lavender polish and baking.

'Now sit down and I'll make you a nice cup of tea. You're lucky, I've just taken some rock cakes out of the oven.'

Mary sat at the table with its brown chenille tablecloth and the usual bowl of flowers in the centre and smiled up at her through her tears. She almost felt she had come home. 'Thank you,' she whispered.

It wasn't long before Mrs Johns returned to the kitchen with a loaded tray. Mary watched silently as she put the tray on the table, then went to the sideboard for the cups, saucers and small plates. Then she sat next to Mary.

'Do you want to talk about it now or later?' she asked as she poured the milk into the cups.

'I can talk about it now, that's if you've got time.' Mary sniffed and searched her handbag for her handkerchief.

'Good. And I've got plenty of time.'

Mary told her all that had happened after she got home. Mrs Johns was a good listener and didn't interrupt.

'So that's it, I decided that, as me mum didn't want me, I'd come down here and get a job.'

'It's a big decision to make.'

'I know. But I'm happy here.'

'You shouldn't have too much trouble getting a job. Are you sure that's what you want?'

Mary nodded. 'I thought I'd go along and see Jean. She might know if a shop or someone wants staff.'

'That's a good idea. What about the young man you

251

brought with you before? Have you heard from him? Has he settled in the navy?'

'I don't know.' Mary didn't want to tell Mrs Johns about Ron's mother. Perhaps one day she would, but not right now. 'Mrs Johns, I don't have a lot of money, so I can't pay you just yet.'

Mrs Johns patted the back of Mary's hand. 'Don't worry about that now. I enjoy having you here and as soon as you get a job you can pay me then. Will you be going to see Daisy?'

Mary shook her head. 'I don't think so. There don't seem a lot of point, not now. What's in Ted's past is his affair and I don't want to upset Daisy again. It's my little brother Eddie I feel sorry for. I'm sure if I kept on with him I could have got him to talk.'

Mrs Johns stood up. 'You're a good girl, Mary. I'll just go in the front room and turn the vacancy card round. I don't want any more visitors at the moment.' She left the room.

Mary looked round. Yes, she was happy here, but what about Eddie? She would miss him so much. In a few days she would write to her mother and tell her where she was, and then it would be up to Sarah if she wanted to stay in touch. Mary gave a little sniff. She had to stand on her own two feet now.

Sarah wandered round and round the park for two hours looking for Mary. Should she go along to the Thomases' house and talk to her? She didn't want to cause a fuss. Perhaps she had seen Ted with her last week and was upset. Does she hate me? Sarah wondered. She knew she ought to get home and face Ted but she didn't care. She collected some veg from a shop and made her way home. 'Well, young man, looks like we've missed her again.'

Eddie looked at his mother. His lovely little cherub face was furrowed with questions, questions that he couldn't ask.

Sarah's heart went out to him and Mary. Would Mary ever see him again? Sarah had to find out how Mary was coping and decided as soon as she got home she would write her a letter. That way she would be able to explain everything. Sarah felt happier as she made for home. At last she could see her way out of this mess.

On Monday morning Mary went to Commercial Road to find Jean. She looked through the photographer's window and saw that as usual they were busy with customers, so she walked along looking in other shop windows for notices saying 'Staff Wanted'. She had only gone a few yards when she saw one in the chemist's window and went in.

The gentleman whom the lady behind the counter said Mary had to see was busy making up prescriptions, so she sat on the bentwood chair and waited. Looking all around her she saw an intriguing array of containers and potions on the shelves. The large bottles in the window filled with coloured liquid fascinated her. Was that liquid ever used for prescriptions these days? The make-up on the stands on top of the counter looked interesting. She crossed her fingers; it would be rather nice working here.

'Sorry I've kept you waiting,' said the portly grey-haired man in a white coat who came up to her. 'I'm Mr Holt. Come through to the back where we can talk.'

Mary followed him through the door at the back of the shop. She noted there was only the older lady on the counter.

'Right. Take a seat.' Mr Holt removed some books from the chair in front of a shabby table, which was also covered with volumes and papers. He smiled and peered over the half-glasses that were perched on the end of his nose. He had a pleasant open face. 'I must get some of this filed away one day,' he said, shifting some of the papers. 'Now, first of all, what's your name?' He picked up a pencil and pushed up his glasses ready to write.

'Mary Harris.'

'You don't come from round this way, do you?'

Mary shook her head. 'I'm from London.'

'Thought I recognised the accent. Well, Miss Harris, I do all the prescriptions and I'm looking for an assistant to work in the shop alongside Mrs Warner. The young lady I did have has gone and got herself married to a sailor and she's moved away. You're not down here to marry a sailor, are you?'

Mary smiled and shook her head.

'What experience have you had in retailing? Serving in a shop?'

'None. I used to work in a biscuit factory.' Mary knew there wasn't any point in not telling the truth.

'Do you think you could manage to add up?'

'Yes. I was good at me sums at school.'

Mr Holt smiled. 'You seem a very confident young lady. When can you start?'

'Right away.'

'You can start tomorrow and be on a month's trial. You start at one pound a week; at the end of the month I can give you another ten shillings, providing it is satisfactory to us both. You have to work all day on Saturdays and have Wednesday afternoons off. Is that all right?'

Mary nodded eagerly. 'Yes. Thank you.' She stood up.

'May I ask what has brought you to this neck of the woods?'

'My mother remarried after my father died and I don't get on with her new husband. I came down here a while ago and liked it, so I decided to come back and start a new life.'

'I presume you have got somewhere to stay?'

'Yes, I'm with a lady in Oyster Street.'

'That's good. So I shall see you tomorrow morning at eight-thirty sharp. Now come and meet Mrs Warner. She's been with me more years than I care to remember.'

Mrs Warner was a tall, slim, older-looking woman who looked very efficient. She took off her glasses and let them hang from the chain she wore round her neck and gave Mary a warm inviting smile when she was introduced to her.

'Lovely to meet you,' she said, holding out her hand to Mary. She turned to Mr Holt. 'Thank goodness you've found someone young and agile. I'm afraid climbing up and down those steps is killing my legs.'

'Go on with you, you're as young as you feel. Miss Harris will be starting tomorrow.'

'That's good. I shall look forward to showing you the ropes.' She went off to serve an elderly man who had asked for a bottle of cough medicine.

'For the wife,' he said with a faint smile.

Mary was over the moon. She had a job and it was going to be fun working in such a lovely atmosphere. While Mrs Warner had been serving it gave Mary a chance to have a quick look around. Mr Holt had returned behind his glass screen where all his lotions and potions were and where he made up the prescriptions. This was a positive wonderland. Mary had never taken particular notice of chemist's shops before, but now things were different. It was going to be hard at first remembering where everything was: there seemed to be so many small drawers at the back of the counter, although she could see that they were all clearly labelled. The counter had a glass top and underneath was a huge array of items. A cardboard head had a display of fine hairnets; there was another that had pink and blue slumber nets on: they had a ribbon you wore under your chin to keep them on in the night. There were cards full of hair grips – oh, and so many things!

Mrs Warner smiled at her when her customer left clutching his brown paper bag. 'Don't look so worried. I'm sure we're going to get along just fine.'

'I hope so. I'll see you tomorrow. Bye.'

As Mary left the shop the bell above the door tinkled. It was a pleasant, happy sound that matched her mood. She felt like skipping along the road. She had to see Jean now and tell her all her news.

Jean looked up as Mary pushed open the door of Palmer's. It took a few seconds for her to recognise Mary, then she screamed out: 'Mary, it's you!' She rushed round her desk and hugged her, then held her at arm's length. 'What are you doing here? You've never written like you promised.'

'I'm really sorry about that, but such a lot has happened. Is it nearly your lunch break? Can you come out?'

'Yes, I'll just tell Mr Palmer. He'll be pleased to see you. What happened about that woman at St Mark's?'

'I'll tell you everything over a cuppa.'

'Right.' Jean disappeared into the studio and came out putting her coat on. 'I'm ready, let's be off. I can't wait to hear all this.'

As soon as they were settled in the café Mary told her in detail everything that had happened. Jean sat silently; her mouth wide open. Only when Mary stopped with the last bit of news that she'd got a job a few shops away did Jean finally speak.

'You're only in Holt's, that's wonderful! I can't believe that all this has happened to you. You certainly don't have a boring life.'

'A lot of it I could do without.'

'But it is good to see you again. Did you want to come and stay with us?'

'No, thanks all the same. I'm very happy with Mrs Johns.'

'Me mum wouldn't charge you much. I bet it won't cost you as much as rent.'

'No. As I'm not just a holiday let she's letting me have a room for seven and six a week, so out of my pound I shall be well off and when I get my rise I shall be rich.'

Jean laughed and then, leaning across the table, touched her hand. 'I mean it, Mary. I am really pleased to see you.'

Mary smiled. She was feeling happier than she had done for a very long while. Tonight she would write and tell her mother where she was, about her job and about her new life.

# *Chapter 28*

It was a couple of weeks later that Mary received a letter from Liz; inside was a letter from her mother and another card from Billy. Mary was full of guilt for, despite all her good intentions, she hadn't written to anyone, not even her mother: she was so busy with her new life. She loved her job and meeting the customers and working with Mrs Warner. She was a widow and a lovely lady. With her white hair in a neat-cropped style she had a certain regal air about her, but she loved to laugh and joke with the customers. She showed Mary where things were and how to keep it all in order and never lost her patience when Mary couldn't find items. After Mary finished work she and Jean went out and about. Jean was very keen to show her Portsmouth.

'Tonight we can go and walk along the front, that's if you fancy it,' said Jean the first night Mary finished work.

'Sounds great. I told Mrs Johns I might be late back. It's such a lovely evening. I feel like I'm on holiday.'

'If you don't feel too tired we can have a walk round the gardens after, they're really nice.'

After that first night they were always together. On Saturdays there were the dances on the pier and at the Savoy dance hall. The dances were usually full of sailors and sometimes Jean got cross with their persistent attentions. Jean told Mary many times that she would never marry.

Mary laughed and said, 'What about when you're on the liners and meet all those rich admirers?'

Jean grinned. 'Well, that might be different.'

Mary didn't mind dancing with sailors; in fact she enjoyed it. She was happy just to have a bit of fun, while knowing that her heart belonged to Billy.

Back in her room Mary settled down to read Liz's letter. It didn't have a lot of news, but she did say she was coming down on August bank holiday Saturday to stay for a few days. That's if Mary still wanted her to. Mary knew she had to answer that letter straight away. It would be lovely to see her friend again. Mary read Billy's card over and over; it only said that Malta was a grand place and that he'd been sightseeing. It wasn't at all loving. She kissed the stamp as she knew that his lips had been there. She put the card in her scrapbook along with the others. When she was low she would look at the lovely pictures of these far-away places hoping that he would be home soon. There wasn't a letter this time. In fact his letters were getting few and far between. Then, full of guilt, she began to read her mother's letter.

It wasn't very long but Mary immediately felt homesick. Sarah started by telling her daughter the reason Ted had been with them that Saturday afternoon. Sarah thought he suspected they were going to meet up. She also said how much both Eddie and herself were missing her and longed for the day when she was home and they could all be together again. She was certain that day would come soon. Her mother told how she'd gone to the park the following week looking for her, but Mary wasn't there. Mary gave a little sob; at that time she'd been on a train being whisked away to Portsmouth. Her mother went on to say that she would try and get to the park every Saturday till they met up. She added that she didn't want to come to Liz's, as she couldn't face her parents; she felt such a failure at being a mother.

A tear slowly slid down Mary's cheek. She desperately wanted to see her mum and Eddie, but knew that all the time Ted was there that would be impossible.

'Mary. Tea's on the table,' Mrs Johns was calling up the stairs.

'Coming.' Mary dabbed her eyes and made her way down to the large kitchen.

'What's the matter?'

'That was a letter from Liz.'

'She's a nice girl. I expect she misses you.'

'Yes, she does.'

'Everything all right at home?'

'I think so. Liz said she'd like to come down here for the bank holiday. Would that be all right?'

'I should say so. Tell her I only want money for food as she can go in with you. That's if you don't mind. That way I can let the other room. Have to make the most of the holiday weekend.'

'That'll be lovely. Thank you. But where will you sleep?'

'I can have the camp bed in the front room. I have to get up early to give the visitors breakfast anyway.'

'Thanks. There was also a letter from me mum.'

Mrs Johns looked shocked. 'Haven't you told her you've moved down here?'

Mary shook her head.

'Now that's a bit naughty of you.'

'She's been to the park looking for me.'

Mrs Johns sat at the table. 'Do you want to go home?'

Mary shook her head. 'Not when Ted's there.'

'I expect she's worried about you. I'm sure things will work out fine for you in the end but you must write to her.'

'I will. Liz also sent me a card from my young man. He's in Malta now.'

Mrs Johns smiled. 'My husband was in Malta; he said it was a very nice place. He liked it a lot. I'll just get your tea.'

Mrs Johns went into the pantry and brought out a plate with a ham salad neatly arranged on it, which she handed to Mary. 'Are you meeting Jean later on?'

Mary nodded as she took a bite out of the bread roll that was on her side plate.

'Is it the Saturday night dance tonight?'

'No. I think she wants to go to the pictures.'

'That's nice. I'm so pleased you've settled in all right.'

'Yes, I have. I'm so lucky I've got a good friend, a good job and good digs.'

Mary answered her mother's letter and she also wrote to Liz telling her that Mrs Johns said she would be more than pleased to see her here for the August bank holiday weekend, which was only a few weeks away.

Mary couldn't believe so much had happened in a year. Was it really only a year ago she was here with Billy? She remembered when they went to the fair and what Madam Za Za had told her. There was going to be another fair on the hill this bank holiday and Jean was already talking about it. Sometimes they went up on Portsdown hill and just sat and admired the view. Those trips were among the many times Mary was so happy that she had moved to Portsmouth.

A week later Mary had another letter from her mother. In it she told her how much she and Eddie missed her and she would try and get down to see her one of these days. Mary knew that was only wishful thinking. Ted would never let her go away on her own, especially to Portsmouth. She then enquired about Ron and if Mary ever saw anything of him. She went on to say a new family had moved in next door, but they didn't talk much and the man had even put a fence between them in the back yard. Sarah didn't know if any letters had come for the kids and suggested, if Mary saw Ron, that she tell him to send his letters to Sarah if he didn't know where the kids were. Her mother added she felt full of guilt over the children being taken away. Sarah said she felt so alone now that Mary had left. Mary wanted to shout out: I didn't leave, I was thrown out, but knew that wouldn't do any good. Mary felt sorry for her mother. A while back she had had it all: good neighbours, a daughter at home and a happy marriage. But she had lost most of that now; even her marriage must be under stress.

Liz was coming to Portsmouth on the Saturday before bank holiday Monday. Mrs Johns had told Mary that she would only charge Liz a few shillings for the extra food. As Mary would be at work that day she told Liz to make her own way to Oyster Street. She was thrilled when, hurrying along the street, she saw Liz, who had been looking out of the window, fling open the front door. They fell into each other's arms.

Liz held her friend at arm's length. 'You look great, you've even got a tan.' She held her pale arm next to Mary's healthy brown one.

'It's all this sunshine,' said Mary.

'I know. It's so hot. We was packed like sardines on that train.'

'Go into the front room, girls, I'll bring your tea in there.'

'You sure?' asked Mary.

'Yes. Tonight's special.'

'Thanks, Mrs Johns,' said Mary.

'Mrs Johns gave me a nice cold drink when I got here,' said Liz.

'I'm so lucky we found her, she does look after me.'

'What we doing tonight? I've got so much to tell you.'

'What do you fancy doing?'

'Dunno. Are you seeing that Jean?'

'Yes. We thought we'd go up to the fair, is that all right?'

Liz grinned. 'I should say so.'

Mrs Johns pushed the door open with her bottom. She was carrying a heavy tray.

'Here, let me help,' said Mary. She took the tray and placed it on the table. 'Don't normally eat in here,' she said to Liz. 'This is only for the guests. I'm normally in the kitchen.' She laughed.

'Liz is a guest,' said Mrs Johns.

'No, she's not, she's me mate.'

Smiling, Liz said, 'I don't mind eating in the kitchen.'

'You can tomorrow,' said Mrs Johns. 'Now I'll leave you two, I expect you've got a lot to talk about.'

'Thanks,' said Mary, pouring out the tea.

'You certainly seem at home here.'

'Yes, I am, but I still miss me mum and Eddie and you. Now, what's been happening at home?'

'Not a lot really. Work's still the same. All the girls send their love and wish they was you. Me mum and dad want to be remembered, and the girls. Mary, do you really like it down here and working in a shop?'

'Yes, I do.'

'What about Daisy? Have you been to see her again?'

Mary shook her head. 'Wasn't any point. She don't talk and even if she was a relation of Ted's he won't let me come home, so there wasn't any point in going to see her. I don't want to upset her either.'

'I can understand that.'

'Now, come on, finish your tea, then we'll be off. There's a lot I've got to show you. These are going to be two great days. I've really missed you, Liz.'

'Not nearly as much as I've missed you.'

'Don't. You might make me weaken and come back with you.'

'I'm gonner try!'


That evening they met Jean and made their way to the fair. It was just as Mary remembered it from last year, noisy and full of fun. They went on rides, had ice cream and laughed and laughed.

'You going in to see Madam Za Za again?' asked Liz when they stopped outside her tent.

'No. I know my fate.' She didn't add that when last year Madam Za Za had said she would have a few problems, she was right and Mary didn't want to be told anything else that might upset her.

They were waiting to go on the dodgem cars when the young man who was jumping on the back of the cars and getting his customers out of trouble came up to them.

'Can't have three in a car, sorry.'

'I'll stay here. You and Liz go,' said Jean.

'You sure?' asked Mary.

'Yes. Go on, quick, before they start up again.'

'I'll take you,' said the young man.

Jean blushed. 'All right then.' She jumped in a car and he stood behind her.

'Looks like she's done all right for herself,' said Liz.

'I hope so.'

'He ain't bad-looking, is he?' said Liz.

'No. She needs a bloke after her sailor went off and married someone else.'

'That's a shame.'

The cars jumped into life and they went round and round bumping into everyone. Jean's escort was very skilled and every time he got her out of trouble. When it was all over Mary could see him talking to her.

'Well,' said Mary when Jean rejoined them. 'Got a date?'

Jean grinned and nodded. 'His name's Danny. D'you fancy coming up here on Monday night?'

'If you want,' said Mary.

'I can't,' said Liz, looking crestfallen. 'I've got to go back Monday. Got to go to work the next day.'

'That's a shame,' said Jean.

Mary tucked her arm through her mate's. 'I wish you wasn't going home, I really love having you here.'

'You know I have to.'

Mary nodded. 'I'll write and tell you how she got on.'

All too soon it was time for them to leave the fair and head back down the hill.

As they sat on the tram Jean asked, 'What're you two doing tomorrow?'

'Don't know,' said Mary.

'As the weather's good, why don't you take a picnic on the beach?'

'That sounds a great idea. D'you fancy that, Liz?'

'I should say so.'

'Jean, you're coming as well.'

'I don't know. I don't like butting in with your mate.'

'Don't talk daft. You don't mind, do you, Liz?'

'No, the more the merrier. Besides, you might have something better than us to eat.'

Jean laughed. 'I'll see what I can conjure up.'

Mary was so happy now she had Liz at her side; that Liz got on well with Jean was a wonderful bonus.

★ ★ ★

The next day Mrs Johns did them up a picnic and Liz and Mary met up with Jean and they made their way to the beach.

'Look at all these people,' gasped Liz. 'I can't see a bit of beach to sit on.'

The weather was warm and everywhere was filled with holidaymakers having a paddle and strolling along the front and eating ice cream.

'Pity you're not here for longer,' said Jean. 'We could have gone over to the Isle of Wight.'

'I would have liked that.'

'Perhaps next time,' said Mary.

'I can really understand you liking it here,' said Liz as they sat looking at the kids playing and their mums and dads watching the youngsters and sorting out any squabbles that flared up. 'Susan and Elsie would really like it here.'

'So would Eddie,' said Mary wistfully.

'Now come on, you two, cheer up. Let's go for a walk along the pier.'

'That sounds good,' said Mary, struggling to her feet.

Again they were walking and laughing together. Mary looked at her two friends. She didn't want this weekend to end.

# *Chapter 29*

All too soon Mary was standing on the platform waving goodbye to Liz as her train pulled out of the station. She wiped her tears away and made her way back down Commercial Road. She was sad at her friend going: in fact, part of her wanted to go with Liz, because all their talk about Rotherhithe had made her a little homesick. As Mary wandered outside into the bright sunshine she thought about her plans to go to the fair with Jean tonight, but her heart wasn't really in it. She sighed. Would she ever be able to go back home again?

The air was stifling at the fair that evening. The heat, noise and smell from the engines was overbearing, but Jean didn't notice any of it as she was eager to meet Danny again. They quickly made their way to the dodgems. Danny smiled and gave them a wave when he caught sight of them. He was tall, dark and very handsome.

'Hello there, girls. Where's the other one?'

'She's had to go back to London,' said Jean, gazing up at him.

'That's a pity. Jump on.'

The girls did as they were told.

When the ride finished Danny went over to another man and while he was talking to him he pointed to Jean and Mary. They saw Danny pat the man on the shoulder before bounding back over to them. 'Well, that's settled. I can spend an hour with you both, but . . .' He looked round. 'I think I'll find someone for you, young lady.' He touched Mary's cheek. 'You see, I don't want to spoil me chances with this lovely creature.'

Jean was smiling fit to burst.

Mary laughed. 'Don't worry about me. You two go off. I'll meet you back here in an hour.'

'No. I won't hear of it. Come on. I know just the lad for you.' He put his arms round their waists and gently pushed them along.

'Where is he?' asked Mary.

'He works the chair-o-planes. There he is. Andy?' he called. When they got closer he said to Andy, 'Can you take an hour off and look after this lovely girl here?'

Andy smiled, his white teeth a sharp contrast to his tanned skin. He had a kind face, not rough and weather-beaten like some of the men who manned the rides. He had his shirt-sleeves rolled up and Mary could see he had very muscular arms. 'And what do you intend to get up to with this other very lovely young lady then, Dan?'

'They've certainly got plenty of flannel,' said Mary, grinning. 'You'll have to watch him, Jean.'

'I can tell you now, he ain't gonner get up to anything,' said Jean indignantly.

'I'm only gonner take you for a drink and a chat,' said Danny. 'I'd really like to know more about you.'

'I bet you would.'

'Go on, Jean. Yell if you want me,' said Mary. She wanted her friend to have fun with other blokes.

Andy stood grinning at them. 'I'll just tell Pa I'm off.' He turned to Mary. 'I'm afraid it'll only be for an hour. Pa gets tired these days.'

'Thanks, pal,' said Danny and, with his arm round Jean's

waist, the two of them wandered off.

Mary watched them go. Andy was talking to an old man who was sitting down at the pay booth.

When he returned Mary said, 'You don't have to look after me, you know. I'll be all right. You go back to work.'

'No, it's fine. Besides, I fancy having an hour off and spending it with a pretty girl like you.'

Mary laughed. 'You blokes certainly know how to talk to the girls. I bet you'd say that to anyone under forty.'

Andy laughed. 'It goes with the job, and I'll butter up the eighty-year-olds as well.' Mary smiled when he winked at her. He had such a cheeky grin. 'But honestly, I don't get time to go out with any one girl.'

'I bet.'

'So, what's your name?'

'Mary.'

'Mary. That's nice. I'm Andy. Pleased to meet you.'

'And I'm pleased to meet you.'

'D'you fancy a lemonade? I can't drink, not when I'm in charge of the chairs. Me pa would skin me alive if anything went wrong.'

'Has there ever been an accident?'

'It has been known to happen, but mostly that's through bad maintenance. Pa's a stickler for keeping everything ship-shape.'

As they wandered around the fair Mary was surprised how easy she found Andy to talk to. He pointed out the names of the people who ran the rides, people he told her he had known all his life. His blue eyes fascinated her; for someone who was so very dark he had the bluest eyes she'd ever seen.

'Have you been to see our Madam Za Za yet?'

Mary laughed. 'Not this time. I did go in last year.'

'Now let me see.' Andy put his hand to his forehead and

closed his eyes. 'I can see in my crystal ball a tall, dark, handsome man for you. You will marry and have lots and lots of children.'

Mary laughed. 'It wasn't quite like that. Is she a real gypsy?'

'Her family might have been way back, just like most of us, but now she's just plain Mrs Winterbottom.'

Mary was laughing till tears ran down her face. 'Stop telling me fibs.'

'It's true. But don't *you* dare tell anyone, otherwise she'll put a spell on me and you.'

Mary wiped her tears away. 'I won't, I promise. I bet I look a right mess now all me mascara's run.'

'You look great. You don't come from round these parts,' he said as they made their way to the top of the hill.

'No, I'm from London.'

'So you're here on holiday then?'

'No, I live here now.' Mary looked out over the city. This view never ceased to thrill her. 'I love it up here.'

'It's a great view and a lot cooler,' said Andy.

'Yes, it is.' She pulled her hair away from the nape of her neck. 'Where—' Mary stopped and giggled as they both spoke together.

'Sorry, what were you going to say?' Andy asked.

'I was going to ask you where your next stop is.'

'Why? You thinking of following us then?'

'No, certainly not. Just making conversation, that's all.'

'Sorry, only joking. It's getting near the end of the season now. Soon we shall be heading back to our winter quarters; after checking over the equipment, doing any repairs and painting, it's all put in store. Then I'll be back visiting me ma.'

'Where's that?'

'Not too far from here.'

'She's not part of the fair then?'

'No, not now. She used to help Pa run the chairs but it got too much for her after she had Patrick, my young brother, although Pa's getting on a bit now.'

'How do you make a living in the winter?'

'You can always scratch around for odd jobs.'

'It sounds a fascinating life.'

He laughed. 'Not when it's pouring with rain and hail and you get all the heavy stuff stuck in the mud. Then you don't get any punters. It can be very hard at times.'

Mary smiled. 'How long are you here for?'

'The rest of the week. Any chance of you coming up here again?'

'I don't know. It depends on Jean.' Mary hoped deep down that Jean was getting on with Danny. She liked Andy but reminded herself he was just someone to talk to, her heart belonged to Billy.

'If you can make it, come over and see me. I'll give you a free ride.'

She laughed. 'Well, thank you. Now that has got to be a very good reason to visit again.'

'That's settled then. I shall be seeing you in the week.'

'Could be.'

They continued chatting together, then Andy glanced anxiously at his watch. 'Look, I'm sorry, but I have to get back to Pa.'

'Of course. I understand. I'll try and find Jean.' As they wandered back Mary was surprised how quickly the hour had gone. She watched Andy go over to his pa, who gave her a wave, then she set off to find Jean.

Mary caught sight of her friend laughing as she was being whisked round on the dodgems. Mary had never seen her look so happy. She had a glow about her.

When the cars stopped she jumped out and ran over to Mary. 'That was wonderful, but I think if it was left to me to drive I would never have got away from the side.' She waved to Danny when the cars started up again. 'So, was that Andy nice?' she asked, slipping her arm through Mary's.

'Yes, he was. What about Danny?'

'I'm coming up here again tomorrow. Do you want to come as well?'

'Are you that keen?'

'He is rather nice. So what about it?'

'If you like.'

Every evening during the following week Jean and Mary made their way to the fair. Jean was certainly struck with Danny. She told Mary that she was even having second thoughts about going on the liners.

'What? You can't give up that idea.'

'Danny was saying what if there was a war?'

'He sounds a bit like Ted, my stepfather. He was always on about another war. Jean, you've only seen Danny for a short while. What do you know about him? Where does he live? And, more importantly, is he married?'

'He lives in Essex, it's the other side of London, a place called Southend. And for your information he's not married.'

'I hope not. I know Southend. I've been there once.'

'Have you? Is it nice?'

'Didn't really see a lot of it, I spent most of the day in the big fair. It's permanent. It don't move about like this one.'

'That's what Danny told me. He don't like being in one place too long, that's why he won't work there.'

'Jean, be careful. I've got very fond of you and I wouldn't like to see you hurt again.'

Jean smiled. 'Thanks, but I won't be.'

'I hope not.'

'What about you and that Andy? Although I can't see you getting all silly over him, not the way you go on about Billy.'

'No, I wouldn't. Andy is nice to be with, but my heart belongs to Billy.'

'Hearts can be broken. I should know.'

'I don't know if I'm happy about you and Danny.'

'Why?'

'How can you be sure about him? Please, Jean, think about it.'

'I will. And, Mary, I would prefer to make up my own mind about Danny, thank you. Now come on, let's enjoy ourselves.'

Mary was a little bit upset that she and Jean were having words. She liked Jean and didn't want her to be let down again.

All too soon it was Saturday night again, the last of the fair. Mary was waiting for Andy to have a break. She had spent most of the evening sitting with his pa, talking to him. He was such a nice old man, who clearly adored his wife and other son.

'You must come and see us when we get back from storing and painting the equipment.'

'Where do you live?'

'A little village not too far from here. Horndean.'

'How old's your other son?'

'He must be getting on for, what, ten now.'

'Does he ever come up here and help you?'

'Now and again.' He gave her a wink. 'He's a lovely-looking lad and his mother's pride and joy. Andy, come and take Mary for a lemonade.'

'Only if you're sure,' said Andy.

'Course I am. Been doing this job years before you was born. He thinks I'm getting too old, but I can still show him a trick or two.'

Andy smiled. 'Course you can, Pa. Come on, Mary.' He took her arm and led her away.

Mary couldn't help noting a crowd of young girls gazing at Andy. With his dark hair and good looks he did look a bit like Tyrone Power. She smiled at the girls almost like the cat who'd got the cream. But it was only for tonight. Tomorrow they would be dismantling the rides and be off.

'What are you smiling at?' asked Andy as they sat outside the tent that served drinks.

'Just thinking about what your pa said.'

'And pray tell me, what precious gem did he part with?'

Mary laughed. 'He asked me back to your house when you get back for the winter.'

'Did he now?'

'Don't worry, I wouldn't hold him to it.'

'It might be nice for Ma to meet someone who's not attached to the fair.'

Mary looked away. Although she liked Andy and he was pleasant to be with, there was no way she was going to meet the rest of his family.

After Andy went back to the chair-o-planes, Mary wandered around looking for Jean. She found her busy kissing Danny as the fairground lights went out.

'I'll wait up on the hill,' said Mary quickly, not wanting to interrupt them.

When Jean caught up with Mary she was flushed and excited.

'I do like him,' she said, holding on to Mary's arm.

'Are you going to see him again?'

Jean nodded. 'I've asked him to tea tomorrow.'

'What about your mum and dad? What will they say?'

'They'll be all right.'

'I hope so.'

'I know you don't approve.'

'Are you going away with him?'

'I don't think so. He's going to write and tell me his plans. I really like him, Mary. And I know he likes me.'

'Jean, be careful. These people are travellers, always on the move.'

Jean pulled her arm away from Mary's. 'Do you know, Mary, sometimes you sound like an old woman.'

'Sorry. But you make such a fuss about sailors, yet here you are willing to throw away everything you've planned and worked for, for a bloke on the dodgems. What do you know about him?'

Jean shrugged. 'I expect it's a bit how you felt when you met your Billy. You know when the right one comes along. You know he's the one you want to spend the rest of your life with.'

Mary laughed. 'You sound like something out of a novel.'

'What d'you know about Billy?'

'I know a lot about him, he's my best friend's brother. And I'm not going to jump on a boat and go halfway round the world with him. Is it that serious?'

Jean nodded.

'Are you going to join the fair then?'

Jean laughed. 'Who knows? I could do.'

'Oh Jean, please watch your step.'

'I will. But you know how it is when someone steals your heart, you have no control over it.'

Mary wasn't so sure. Jean had only just met this bloke. Could she really be thinking of throwing up a career for him?

Mary grinned.

'What's so funny?'

'You. I was just imagining you sitting in a tent telling fortunes.'

Jean smiled with her. 'Now that has got to be the best job in the world. No, I don't think so, I wouldn't fancy wearing those dangly things on me head all day.'

They laughed all the way home, but deep down Mary was worried about her friend, and hoped that her parents would make her see sense.

# Chapter 30

On Sunday morning Mrs Johns asked Mary if she was going out with Jean at all today. When Mary said no and then told her why Mrs Johns was a little shocked. Mary also said how she was worried that Jean might change her mind about working on the liners.

'I don't know what gets into these young girls today. Fancy giving up a good career to go off with one of the lads from the fair. Is he a gypsy?'

'I don't think so.'

'What have her parents got to say about it?'

'She hasn't told them yet. She'll know what they think today when they meet him. I don't reckon they'll be that happy about it.'

'Well, I know I wouldn't if it was a daughter of mine. So what are you going to do with yourself today?'

'Don't know. I might have a wander down to the beach. I'd like to see if I could find out where Ron is.'

'He could be anywhere by now. Has he not written to you or the family?'

Mary shook her head. 'Me mum's never said.' Mary knew it was time she told Mrs Johns what had happened. 'Have you got time to talk?'

'Yes, of course, love.' She sat down at the table.

'Ron isn't a relation.' Mary then told her why she had really brought him down to Portsmouth. Mrs Johns was a good listener and didn't interrupt. Tears slid down Mary's face when she explained about Sadie dying and the kids being sent away.

When Mary finished Mrs Johns said softly, 'The poor boy. You say he killed his father?'

Mary nodded. 'Yes, but nobody knows. And now his mum's dead nobody need know.'

'And he doesn't know about his mother?'

Mary shook her head.

'Has he got this address?'

'I don't think so. He was in a bit of a state when we got here so he wouldn't know where he finished up.'

'You must go to the dockyard sometime and try and find him. The poor boy,' repeated Mrs Johns. 'In some ways I wish you hadn't told me.'

'I'm sorry.'

'What if the police come round here?'

'They won't. They haven't any reason to.'

'What about the children? Won't they want to see their brother?'

'I expect so, but only me mum and Ted know he came to Portsmouth.'

'But what about his name? Surely they'll find out through the navy?'

'I don't think so. I shouldn't have told you. I thought you'd understand.'

'I'm sorry. I do understand. You've certainly had a very troubled time of it one way and another.'

'It's me mum I feel so sorry for. She was very fond of Sadie and the kids.'

'What a dreadful man and what a sacrifice that woman's

family has had to make. And your mother has no idea where the children finished up?'

Mary shook her head. 'No. It's very sad and Mum feels awful about it.'

'It sounds as if she did her best and there's nothing you can do for her, so don't you go worrying too much about her. Who knows, she might be down here to see you one day.'

Mary didn't have much hope of that.

'Now I must get on.'

'Yes, I'm sorry I've kept you. Mrs Johns, you won't say anything about Ron, will you?'

She smiled. 'Course not. Don't worry about it. So, will you be in all day?'

'No. I'll go down to the front. I might go along to the dockyard.'

'Good idea. It's such a lovely day it seems a shame to be stuck indoors. Don't know how long this fine weather is going to last, it won't be long before the evenings start to draw in. Do you want to take a sandwich?'

'No, thanks all the same. I'll get something.'

Mary went to the dockyard but was told to come back during the week when someone might be able to help her. She spent the rest of the day wandering along the beach. Without Jean to laugh and joke with she suddenly felt very alone. She couldn't wait for tomorrow when she would be busy at work – and she would find out what Jean's parents thought of Danny.

When Mary saw Jean at lunchtime her friend told her that her parents had been intrigued with the tales Danny had told them.

'Did you tell them that you was thinking of running away with him?'

'No, I didn't. And I wouldn't be running away with him.

The reason I didn't say anything was because Danny don't want me to go with him just yet. He's going to write and wants me to visit him when they're settled in for the winter. Are you seeing Andy any more?'

'No.'

'I thought you might have gone to see his mum; she don't live that far away.'

'No. I'm not interested.'


It was late on Friday afternoon when Mary, who was serving a lady, heard the bell over the door tinkle. She looked up and her heart skipped a beat. Ducking her head back down she mumbled, 'Thank you,' and handed the customer a paper bag containing her purchases. Would Nurse Bentley recognise her? Would she say where she'd met her? Mary hadn't told Mr Holt and Mrs Warner about Daisy.

'Mary!' Nurse Bentley burst out, coming over to her. 'This is such a nice surprise. How long have you been working here? Are you living down here now?'

'Yes, I am.' Mary glanced over at Mrs Warner, who was busy putting some stock on the shelves.

Mrs Warner straightened up and looked astonished. 'Hello, Nurse Bentley, and how are you keeping?'

'I'm fine, thank you. I see you've got Mary working here.'

'Yes, we have.' Mrs Warner looked at Mary, who stood speechless. 'She hasn't been here that long, I'm surprised you know her.'

'I don't know her, just spoke to her when she was visiting a patient a while back.' Nurse Bentley turned to Mary. 'You don't come to see Daisy now.'

'No. I didn't see the point,' whispered Mary. 'She don't talk much and I didn't want to distress her.'

Nurse Bentley smiled. 'She won't let go of that photo you

gave her. And she's told us over and over that it was a picture of her. So you see, you did do some good. Why don't you come and visit her again? I'm sure she'd like you to.'

'No. I don't think so.' Mary was beginning to feel very uncomfortable. She didn't want Mr Holt and Mrs Warner to know she knew someone in St Mark's.

The nurse finished her shopping and as she went to leave she said to Mary, 'Please do your best and find time to come and visit. I know Daisy would be delighted to see you again.'

'I'll try.'

As soon as the nurse left Mary turned to Mrs Warner. 'I was visiting this woman because I thought she was a relation of my stepfather's, but she wasn't.'

'You don't have to tell me, Mary. What you do and whom you see is none of my business.'

'But I don't want you to think . . .'

'A lot of people finish up in St Mark's. Some because they have nowhere else to go and the family disown them.' She shook her head. 'It's very sad. Now, could you bring that other small box of Germolene out for me, then I can get that ointment stacked on the shelves.' She smiled. 'Although now the children will soon be back at school we shouldn't have quite so many grazed knees to contend with.'

Mary went out to the stock room. Her thoughts were on Daisy. Should she go and see her again? That was something Mary knew she would really have to think long and hard about.

That evening she hurried along to where Jean worked. Mr Palmer was just closing the door.

'Has Jean gone?' she asked.

'I'm afraid so,' he said over his shoulder. 'But if you hurry you could catch her up.'

'Thanks.' Mary had been to Jean's house only once before and hoped she remembered where it was. She ran down Commercial Road, and luckily caught sight of Jean in front. She called out her name.

Jean stopped. 'Mary,' she said as her friend came up to her breathlessly. 'What is it? You look worried.'

'What are we doing Sunday afternoon?'

Jean laughed. 'Is that it? You could have asked me tomorrow at lunchtime, or tomorrow night. D'you still want to go to the pier?'

Mary nodded.

'Well, what is it that's so important?'

'Would you come with me to St Mark's?'

'What? Oh Mary, you're not going to start all that again. I thought you said you'd given up on that woman – what's her name?'

'Daisy,' said Mary. 'I had, but this afternoon Nurse Bentley came in. She recognised me and said she thinks Daisy would like to see me again.'

'I don't believe that. Not after what you told me. How could she say that if she don't talk that much?'

'I'm only saying what she told me.'

'And you're thinking of going to see her then?'

'I don't know.'

'Well, count me out. I don't fancy wandering around that loony bin. Look, I've got to go, Mum'll have me tea ready. I'll see you tomorrow.'

'All right.' Mary turned to walk away.

'Mary?' called Jean. 'If I were you I wouldn't stir it all up again. It only upsets you. Remember the last time?'

'I'll think about it.' Mary walked away deep in thought.

On Saturday afternoon Sarah was at the shops when she

caught sight of Liz. She called out her name and hurried along to catch up with her.

'Mrs Harding,' said Liz.

'Oh hello, Liz. Have you heard anything from Mary?'

'Yes. In fact I was down in Portsmouth with her on the bank holiday weekend.'

'How is she?'

'She's fine. She misses you both,' said Liz, looking at Eddie who was sitting in his pram chewing on a crust of bread.

'Not nearly as much as I miss her. Is she happy?'

'Yes, she is.'

'She said she was working in a chemist's.'

'Yes, that's right. She got a friend, Jean, who she goes out with. She seems to be enjoying herself.'

'That's good. What about the woman she's lodging with?'

'Mrs Johns is very nice and she lets Mary treat her place like home.' Liz was feeling awkward. She could understand Mrs Harding worrying about Mary and she wanted to reassure her that her daughter was fine; but at the same time she didn't want the fact that she knew so much more than Mary's mother to make Sarah feel as if she'd been pushed aside.

Sarah held back a sob. 'That's nice. I do write to her, you know?'

'Yes, she told me. She would really love it if you could pay her a visit.'

'I couldn't do that. My husband wouldn't approve.'

'No, I'm sorry. I don't suppose he would. Look, I'd best be going.'

'Yes. Thank you.' Sarah slowly walked away. Would Liz remember it was Mary's eighteenth birthday the week after next? How she would have loved to go and see her, but that wasn't to be: Ted would soon stop that. Sarah started to talk to Eddie. 'We must get a birthday card for Mary. One day we will see Mary. Say Mary.'

He grinned and turned this way and that, as if he was looking for Mary. Sarah wanted to cry as she watched his little face screw up and tears fill his eyes. He began throwing himself back and forth in the pram. People looked at them when he started making his funny noises, but Sarah didn't care; she was too upset to worry about other people. Like her son, she too wanted Mary. Sarah suddenly focused on the noises Eddie was making. Was he trying to say Mary? Or was it all just wishful thinking?

'We will get to see Mary again one day. I promise you that.' Sarah brushed his tears from his cheek. He grabbed her hand and held on to it. Sarah thought her heart would break. She had to think of some way to go and see her daughter, for her own sake as well as her son's.

# Chapter 31

That same Saturday night, as Mary was being whirled round the dance floor, somehow her heart wasn't in it. She wished they had gone to the pictures. There, when the B film was on or the news, she could have sat and thought about what she was going to do tomorrow. The newsreels were full of what was going on in Europe and what those blokes Hitler and Mussolini got up to. It seemed a bit frightening to her. Should she go and see Daisy? Perhaps if Jean wanted to go somewhere tomorrow she'd have a good excuse not to go and she could tell Nurse Bentley that when she next came in the shop.

'Mary,' said Jean as they made their way home from the dance, 'have you decided what you want to do tomorrow?'

'Not yet. What about you?'

'I'm meeting Danny.'

'What? Why didn't you say anything before?'

'I only knew this morning. He phoned the shop and asked me out.'

'You could have told me earlier.'

'Why? What was the point? Besides, you might have got huffy with me.'

Mary knew that was true. 'Where are you going?'

'Don't know.'

Mary wasn't happy about not seeing Jean, but it had made

up her mind for her. She would go and see Daisy in the afternoon, but wouldn't say anything tonight otherwise Jean might try to put her off.

On Sunday morning Mary told Mrs Johns where she was going.

'Are you sure you're doing the right thing? Look how much trouble it caused last time.'

'That was before Ted threw me out. I've got nothing to lose now. And, who knows, it might help Daisy.'

'I only hope you're right. Is Jean going with you?'

'No, she's meeting Danny.'

Mrs Johns tutted. 'You young girls. I can't keep up with you.'

That afternoon Mary went to St Mark's. She had to wait outside the gate to get permission to go in. There was a new man on duty and he'd gone off to see Nurse Bentley for her permission.

'You can come in,' he said, opening the small gate. 'D'you know where to go?'

'Yes, thank you.' Once again Mary was approaching the building where all the trouble had begun. Inside she went along the dark dismal corridor that she had been down before. It was as drab as ever and her footsteps echoed as she walked along. She hesitated outside Nurse Bentley's door. Should she knock? Should she even be here? Half of her wanted to, but there was always that little doubt. She tapped on the door.

Nurse Bentley's face lit up; Mary could see she was very pleased to see her. 'I'm so glad you came. I'll take you along to Daisy.'

Mary gave her a half-hearted smile but was silent as they went to the day room. Daisy was sitting staring out of the window. The gardens hadn't changed. Peter's roses were still in bloom.

'Daisy. I've brought you a visitor. Mary's come to see you,' said Nurse Bentley.

Daisy turned and looked at Mary. She studied her for what seemed like many long minutes. She appeared on edge and all the time she kept fumbling with something in the pocket of her shapeless floral frock. After a while she said softly, 'I've got my picture.'

'Do you remember Mary?' asked Nurse Bentley.

Daisy nodded but looked away.

'Can I see your picture?' asked Mary.

Daisy thrust her hand deeper in her pocket.

'I'll leave you both to have a little chat,' said the nurse.

Mary wanted to laugh. A little chat. She sat next to Daisy and asked, 'So how have you been keeping?' knowing there wouldn't be an answer. 'I've brought you a bar of chocolate.' She handed Daisy the chocolate. Daisy quickly stuffed it in her pocket, then she looked at Mary long and hard.

'You came here before.'

'Yes, I did. I brought you your picture.'

Daisy's face screwed up. 'It's me.'

'I know.'

Mary could almost see the wheels of Daisy's brain working.

'I was very beautiful.'

'Yes, you were, and you still look nice.' Mary felt so sorry for her. She must have been very proud of her appearance back then.

Daisy slowly took the picture from her pocket and looked at it. Mary could see that it was now even more crumpled and creased.

'He gave me my locket.' Daisy gave Mary a quick look at

the photo, then shut her hand.

Mary hadn't taken a lot of notice of the locket in the photo before; now she could just about make it out, hanging on a chain round Daisy's neck. 'It's very beautiful. Who gave it to you?'

There was no answer.

'Daisy, would you like me to take the photo to the photographer? He might be able to get it to look like new again.' Jean had told her what they could do with old photos these days.

'No.' She quickly thrust the photo back into her pocket.

They sat in silence for a long while. Mary didn't know what to talk about. Then suddenly Daisy said, 'I didn't kill my little boy.'

'I know. You told me you gave him to the gypsies.'

She clutched Mary's hand. 'I did. I did. I didn't kill him.'

'You told me that.' Mary desperately wanted to know more but she knew she had to wait for Daisy to be forthcoming.

Daisy looked around her, then she pulled Mary down so her face was only inches from hers. 'Nobody believes me,' she whispered in Mary's ear.

Mary sat up. 'Why did you give him away?'

Again Daisy looked around at the other patients. 'I mustn't tell you.'

Once more they went into a long silence. After a while Mary decided to leave. Sitting here was beginning to depress her. She gathered up her handbag and was about to stand up when Daisy said softly, 'I couldn't stand his shouting.'

'Was he a naughty boy?'

Daisy looked shocked and shook her head. 'He was such a beautiful baby.' She closed her eyes and began to rock back and forth.

For the next half-hour Daisy silently rocked; she kept her

eyes closed and quietly hummed to herself. She was oblivious of everything and everyone around her. Mary knew that was the end of the conversation and stood up.

'Goodbye.'

Daisy didn't open her eyes and Mary walked away.

Nurse Bentley came up to Mary as she was leaving. 'Mary, I do hope you come and see Daisy again.'

'I don't know if there's any point.'

'Yes, there is.' The nurse fell into step with Mary as she walked along the corridor. 'The doctors are very pleased with her progress. She has made great strides since your visits. I thought you wanted to know all about her?'

'No, not now.'

They reached the door to the outside. 'That's such a shame. I know she was interested in you.' The nurse opened the door and once again Mary was outside. She squinted as her eyes tried to adjust to the bright sunshine. 'Mary, please try and come to see her again,' she said as she closed the door.

As Mary walked back to Oyster Street she thought about what the nurse had said. Did she need to go and see Daisy again? It only upset them both. She had lost her mum and Eddie because of it. And what about Daisy? It had only brought back unhappy memories of her baby for her. Mary wished she could find out where the child was now.

On Monday Jean was full of her date with Danny. They had spent the day on the Isle of Wight.

'As soon as he's settled back home I'm going to spend a weekend with him. Don't worry. It'll all be above board. I'll be staying at his mum and dad's place.'

'Jean, what you do is your affair. I just don't want to see you hurt, that's all.'

'Danny is very nice and me mum and dad like him. So what did you do with yourself yesterday?'

'I went to see Daisy.'

'Oh Mary, you didn't. So how was dopey Daisy?'

'Don't be so mean. The same. She didn't say a lot, but she's still got that photo. It's ever so creased. I said you might be able to do something with it, but she won't part with it.'

'I don't know why you bother with her.'

'I just can't forget her. I don't know why.'

At the end of the month, on 27 August, it was Mary's birthday. She had a card from Liz as well as her mother. Inside her mother's card was a postal order for ten shillings.

'So what are you doing for your birthday?' asked Mrs Johns, who had given her a pretty nightie, with which Mary was thrilled.

'I expect we'll go to the pictures and the dance on Saturday.' In some ways Mary wished the fair was still on the hill; that would have been a lovely way to spend her birthday.

Jean gave Mary a box of handkerchiefs. Mrs Warner gave her a hairbrush and Mr Holt said she could have five shillings' worth of cosmetics from the shop. She felt like a kid in a sweet shop, with so much to choose from.

In the end it was a lovely birthday: Mrs Johns had even made her a small cake; but she couldn't help comparing it with last year's, when she'd bought her new frock and Billy was coming home. So much had happened since then.

Time moved on and over the next month Mary received letters from her mum and Liz; she also had another card from Billy. This time he was in Italy. How she envied him visiting all these romantic places. There was still nothing romantic about his cards, however, nor did he always send a letter. He was very surprised to hear she was living in Portsmouth. She had told him about moving there and why. She also told him about Daisy: anything to fill up the pages and to feel close to him. Although she always sent him long letters he never really answered them; lately he'd said he was too busy, that was why he only sent her cards, but at least he was still keeping in touch.

Sarah continued to write to her daughter with any news, but not a lot happened in Doyle Street and she never mentioned Ted. She wasn't happy with her new neighbours and Mary worried as she always sounded down in her letters.

Liz wrote and told her about the girls at the factory; again, none of it was that earth-shattering except that Bet was going to have another baby. What shocked Mary the most was Liz saying that Bet'd told nearly everyone that she didn't want it and was trying to get rid of it. Liz had mentioned that Pete was well and Mary knew his letters were more loving than Billy's. She wondered when they would be coming back to Portsmouth.

Mary hadn't been to see Daisy again and was dreading Nurse Bentley coming into the shop to ask her to pay another visit. This time she would be adamant and definitely say no. There wasn't any point in seeing her now.

# Chapter 32

Jean came bursting into the chemist's shop on Monday morning waving a letter.

Mrs Warner looked up at Jean, startled, then over to Mr Holt, who had his head down behind his glass partition.

'Sorry, Mrs Warner, but I've got to give this to Mary.'

'That's all right. She's out in the back, I'll call her.'

'No, I can't stop.' With that Jean handed over the letter and left.

'Jean's just been in here like a whirlwind,' said Mrs Warner, looking over the top of her spectacles as Mary walked back into the shop. 'I wish she'd be a little more discreet. Rushing about like that. Fortunately we didn't have any customers. She left this letter for you.'

'That's her all over,' Mary explained, grinning, trying to ease the upset Jean might have created. 'I'm sure this could have waited till lunchtime.'

'She still going out with that young man from the fair?'

'Danny? Yes.'

Mary looked at the envelope. It wasn't very fat and she didn't recognise the handwriting. Who could be writing to her? As there still weren't any customers she took the letter into the back room to read. She was amazed when she opened the envelope to see that it was from Andy.

★ ★ ★

Dear Mary,

We shall be back in Horndean next month and Pa would like to know if you'd come to tea on Sunday 27 October, at about three. He says he'd like you to meet Ma as he's told her all about you. It seems you made quite an impression on him.

I had to give this letter to Danny, as I know he writes to Jean.

Look forward to seeing you again.

All my best wishes,

Andy

Mary studied it for a moment or two. He had lovely writing. She smiled to herself. At least his pa liked her.

'Not any more bad news, I hope,' said Mrs Warner when Mary walked back into the shop.

'No. Not at all. You remember I told you about Andy? He's a friend of Danny's. Well, it seems I made a good impression on his dad and he wants me to go to tea with them at the end of the month.'

'That's nice. Where do they live?'

'Horndean.'

'It's really lovely out that way. Beautiful countryside, even at this time of year. Are you going?'

'Yes, I think so. It's a good excuse to see beyond the hill.'

'You'll like it out there. Plenty of places to walk. I loved it when I was young.' Mrs Warner's smile told Mary she must have some very happy memories.

At lunchtime Jean came rushing out of her shop straight over to Mary who was gazing in the next-door store's window at a winter coat. 'Well? What did Andy want?'

'His dad wants me to go to tea.'

293

'His dad!' she screamed out.

'Shh,' said Mary. She took the letter from her handbag and handed it to Jean, who after reading it handed it back. 'So his dad's taken a shine to you!'

Mary laughed.

'Are you going?'

'I think so. I quite fancy going to tea with somebody like that. They might be very interesting people.'

'And they might be very boring. Andy didn't say he'd be there.'

'I expect he will be. But I'm not going to see Andy, I'm going to see his mum and dad.'

'Well, I still reckon it could be boring.'

'Not if they've been fair people all their lives. I should think they've got some very interesting tales to tell.'

The more Mary thought about it, the more she fancied going somewhere different and Andy's dad had been a nice man to talk to.

'I had a letter from Danny. His parents want to meet me,' Jean remarked.

Mary giggled.

'What's so funny?'

'I remember when me mate Liz went to see her boyfriend's mum and dad.'

'Why? What happened?'

'Nothing. They're nice people. Now you're going to do the same. What is it about these mums and dads?'

Jean laughed. 'I reckon they're all worried that us girls are wicked and are going to take their boys away from 'em. You don't reckon that's why Andy's mum and dad want to meet you, do you?'

'What? Don't talk daft.'

'Have you told them about Billy?'

'No. Didn't see the point. It ain't as if I'm going out with him.'

'I see,' said Jean in a very knowing way.

'The reason I haven't said anything is because . . .' Mary stopped. What was the reason? She really didn't have any.

'So. I'm waiting.'

'I didn't think it would interest him and, besides, who I write to is my business.'

'All right.'

'So when're you going to the other side of London?'

'I don't know. Southend is a long way away.'

'It is from here. First you've got to get to London, then round to Fenchurch Street Station. It'll take you nearly all day.'

'It's going to be difficult as we work Saturdays.'

'Can't you ask for a Sat'day off?'

'I can't see Mr P. doing that. That's our busiest day. I suppose I could say I'm ill.'

Mary didn't comment on that idea.

Mrs Johns was pleased to hear Mary was going out to tea at the end of the month. 'You will like it there. In spring it's a mass of wild flowers.'

'Won't be many out now.'

'No, but the woods will be fun to walk in with all the fallen leaves. As a child I used to love kicking the leaves about. What about you?'

'Ain't got many trees in Rotherhithe, but it was fun when we went to the park.' Mary stopped. Going to the park *had* been fun. It brought back memories of that day when she should have met her mother in the park. That seemed almost like a lifetime away now. 'I'd better answer this letter.' Mary left the room, still thoughtful.

★ ★ ★

Sunday 27 October found Mary standing at the bus stop waiting for the bus to take her to Horndean. She was really thrilled at the idea of seeing some more of the area. She had directions on how to reach Andy's parents' house.

As the bus trundled along Mary turned this way and that, trying not to miss a thing as they went through tiny sleepy villages. She was enjoying the ride so much that in some ways she was sorry when it was time for her to get off.

When she knocked on the door of the tiny cottage she was ushered in and Ma, Mrs Turner, introduced herself. Mary was surprised to see Mrs Turner needed a stick to walk with.

'Arthritis,' she said, waving the stick. 'Do come in. It's so nice to meet you.' She had a wide smile that crinkled her dark eyes. 'You certainly made an impression on Brendan. Here, let me take your coat.'

Mary took off her coat and handed it to Mrs Turner. She was a short but trim woman whose dark hair was pulled back into a severe bun; in some ways she reminded Mary of a Spanish dancer, but she had a round rosy face that was wreathed in smiles.

Mrs Turner placed the coat over her arm. 'I'll just pop it into the bedroom. Go into that room.' She pushed open a door.

Mary gazed about her. This room was full of shining brass and in every corner was a table lamp that had a coloured glass shade with glass droplets dangling from it. The whole room was full of knick-knacks and china ornaments. It was as though she'd stepped into a travelling gypsy caravan, just as she'd seen on the films.

'I didn't know you'd arrived.'

Mary spun round to see Mr Turner standing behind her. She almost expected him to be wearing a scarf on his head and a bandanna round his waist and playing the squeezebox. Nearly giggling at that thought, she said seriously, 'This is a lovely room.'

'It keeps Moira happy. She has to be surrounded by her bits and pieces from the past.'

'You've got a lot of books.'

'I'm sorry Andy's not here, they're mostly his books. He's taken his young brother to a birthday party at Petersfield.'

Mary smiled. 'That's all right,' she said brightly, even though she was a little disappointed. There was something very nice about Andy and she would like to meet him again.

Mr Turner took her arm. 'Allow me.' He took her into another room, which had a table laid with a deep red velvet cloth with a lace overlay and pretty china. The plates of neat sandwiches and cakes looked too good to eat.

After they'd finished the delicious tea and the table was cleared, Mrs Turner came back into the room and sat on the sofa. She patted the cushion next to her. 'Now, Mary, come and sit down and tell me all about yourself. Brendan said you're from London.'

'Yes, I am. South of the Thames. Rotherhithe.'

'London's a very exciting place. I've been there a few times. I used to do the fair up on Blackheath with my parents when I was very young. We hadn't been over from Ireland very long then.' She had a lovely lilt to her voice that fascinated Mary, whose face had lit up at the mention of Blackheath.

'So you've been in this business all your life?'

'Yes, and Brendan. That's where we met, much to our parents' approval. The family used to do Derby week at Epsom. Do you know it?'

'No. But I used to go to Blackheath every bank holiday. I might have seen you there. Did you have the chair-o-planes then?'

'No. That was many years ago, before I met Brendan.' She laughed; it was a happy tinkling sound. 'I used to tell fortunes.'

Mary giggled. 'I had my fortune told by Madam Za Za last year.'

'And?' said Mrs Turner, leaning forward.

'She told me I would meet a tall, handsome man, but would have a few problems along the way.'

Moira Turner sat back. She looked up at her husband. 'That's typical of Bella. Always comes out with the same old patter.' She turned to Mary. 'And has any of that happened?'

'Course it has,' said Mr Turner. 'She met our Andy.'

They all laughed together. Mary wasn't going to mention her problems, which had also come true.

Over the next two hours, they chatted happily. Mary was surprised at how easy they were to get on with. They told her of some of the tricks the boxing booths got up to: weedy-looking men on the outside to entice the punters in and huge great brutes inside. She was told how some of the side stalls made sure the punters were quickly parted with their money: they did things like fixing the darts' flights so they didn't hit the target as they were off balance, and ensuring the rifles didn't fire straight as the viewfinders were just slightly off.

Mary was intrigued. 'It sounds as if you have a wonderful life.'

'It does have its ups and downs,' said Moira. 'I don't go with them so much now, not since I had Patrick and this arthritis. This is Patrick.' She picked up one of the silver-framed photos from the side table next to her and handed Mary a picture of a good-looking small boy. The photo frame was like all the others on the table: silver with flowers entwined up the sides.

298

'He's a lovely boy,' said Mary, handing it back. 'How old is he?'

Moira gazed at it lovingly. 'Ten. He's eleven years younger than Andy. I lost one in between. Do you have any brothers or sisters?'

'I have a half-brother, Eddie. He's six next month. My mother married again after my dad died.'

'I can see that you must miss the little lad?'

'Yes, I do.' Mary wanted to get away from this subject; it was far too painful for her. 'You're a bit isolated here, so how do you manage for shopping? The few shops I did see are miles away.'

'We have a lot of delivery vans round this area. In fact, I can get anything we want and when Andy's home he takes me to Petersfield. I love shopping there. So what brought you down to these parts?'

Mary was warming further towards Andy – he was clearly very good to his family – but she was also beginning to feel uncomfortable. She didn't want to tell them why she moved here.

Mr Turner picked up on her distress and said in a forceful voice, 'Moira, don't be so inquisitive.'

She patted Mary's hand. 'I'm so sorry, my dear. I didn't mean to pry.'

'That's all right,' said Mary. She looked up and noticed it was beginning to get dark outside. 'I really should be off.'

'I'll take you to the bus stop,' said Brendan. 'We'd like it if you came again, wouldn't we, love?'

Moira stood up and held Mary close. 'We certainly would. Now you know where we live you can drop us a line and tell us when you'd like to visit. I'm here all the time. It's been lovely to have another female to talk to. Thank you.'

'Thank *you*.' Mary smiled as Brendan helped her on with

her coat. 'I have enjoyed myself.'

On their way to the bus stop, Brendan said, 'You're like a breath of fresh air for Moira. She can't get out and about much and she does enjoy having visitors. I do hope we see you again.'

'Thank you. I would like to come again.'

As the bus came towards them, Brendan took her hand and kissed it. 'The door is always open for you, my dear.'

Sitting on the bus, Mary smiled to herself. Although she had enjoyed this afternoon she had been a little disappointed that Andy wasn't there. It was lovely going out to tea. There was something very nice and traditional about it. It was what families did. She remembered saying to her mother many months ago that she would have liked to have had an aunt or gran to visit on a Sunday. That's what Mr and Mrs Turner felt like: the relations she didn't have, and she would certainly be visiting them again.

Mary was full of the Turners, their small cottage and the lovely things in it when she arrived back at Oyster Street.

'Sounds charming,' said Mrs Johns. 'You didn't see the young man then?'

'No, he'd taken his young brother to a birthday party.'

'What a nice lad.'

It hadn't occurred to Mary before, but in some ways he was a bit like her: taking his younger brother out and about. Mary smiled to herself; at least Patrick would never have tantrums like Eddie.

The following lunchtime Jean raced out of her shop and into the café they always used. Mary was sitting hugging a cup of tea and looking out at the leaden skies that threatened rain. The weather had changed overnight and today a cold wind was blowing, but it was warm and cosy in here.

Jean plonked herself down on the bamboo chair next to Mary. 'Well? What're they like?'

'Very nice, and you should see their house – well, cottage really. Inside is like something out of a picture book. It's like a gypsy caravan with all the brass and bits and pieces they've got.'

'So what did Andy have to say?'

'I didn't see him, he wasn't there.' Mary then told her where he'd gone and about the Turners.

'So you enjoyed it then? You going again?'

'I would think so. Why don't you come with me? I'm sure they'll make you very welcome.'

'I'd have to think about that.'

'Why?'

'Don't know.'

Although Mary thought that was a funny answer, she let it pass. Was Jean worried that they might know something about Danny? Did he have a reputation that she didn't want Mary to know about?

# Chapter 33

The autumn weeks passed and November was now coming to an end. The shop windows had started to display their Christmas fare and decorations. A cold wind whipped up sweet wrappers, paper and various other bits of rubbish round Sarah's legs and she pulled her scarf tighter round her throat. Her mind wasn't on the weather. How could she even think of enjoying Christmas this year with Mary so far away? If only Ted would let her talk about her. She never showed him any of Mary's letters although he must know that they wrote to each other. Sarah was so lonely; she didn't like gossiping in the dairy, because everybody wanted to know where Mary had disappeared to. Since the murder not a lot had happened, so they needed something to tittle-tattle about. She was sure some of them suspected that she was having a baby somewhere.

The death of Sadie and the children being moved away had added to Sarah's depression. She missed them so much. Even Ron hadn't written and she knew from Mary's letters that she'd tried to find out how he was but so far without any success. Her letters were a joy to read and so entertaining. Mary had told her of her visit to the Turners and went into great detail of how she was impressed with them and their cottage. A whole new world had opened up for Mary and in some ways it upset Sarah; it was as if her daughter was slipping away from her. Sarah was a little concerned that she'd met this Andy at a fair, yet didn't say a great deal about him. Was she behaving herself? Was she looking for love while Billy was abroad? She knew that Billy still wrote to her but he was a long way away.

In many ways Sarah was pleased her daughter was enjoying herself; although it broke her heart to say it, she had done the right thing moving to Portsmouth. She looked at Eddie, who was sitting in his pram chewing on a crust of bread. 'You miss Mary as much as me, don't you? Come on, say Mary.'

With his mouth full he could only shake his head and grin. He was such a lovely-looking boy but he was getting much too big for his bassinet, yet this was the only way she could get around. Tomorrow, the twenty-third, was his birthday. Would Mary remember? He should be at school and running around with other children, not stuck in a pram too small for him. Sarah was beginning to feel very sorry for herself.

As she passed a shop window and caught sight of her reflection she noticed how much weight she'd lost. Her coat hung on her, her face looked drawn and scrawny and she always felt so tired. Looking back at Eddie, the thought that raced through her mind was: What would become of him if anything happened to her? These past months Ted hadn't been interested in his son or her. He spent all his time at work. She'd had to remind him that it was Eddie's birthday tomorrow and he'd given her money to buy him something. She had made a cake, but who was there to share it with? A tear trickled down her cheek. If only Mary was here, then everything would be all right.

'Mrs Harding?'

A voice brought her out of her despondency. She turned to see Liz's mum behind her.

'I thought it was you. Recognised the boy. How is he?'

Sarah brightened up. 'He's fine. It's his birthday tomorrow so I'm just out looking for a present for him.'

'That's nice. He's such a good-looking lad.'

Sarah could almost read her mind as she looked at Eddie. She must be thinking: What a sorry sight. He won't talk and she's got a face as long as a fiddle.

'Your Mary writes to our Lizzie, you know. She sounds as if she's happy down there. My Lizzie went to see her last bank holiday. Do you think she might be coming home for Christmas?'

Home! That sounded such a lovely word to Sarah. 'I shouldn't think so,' she said softly. How could she say her husband wouldn't allow it? It was such a feeble thing to admit to. She should have been strong and stood up to him, but it was too late now. It seemed she had lost her fight and her daughter for ever. She let a tear trickle down her cheek.

'I'm sorry, love. I didn't mean to upset you,' said Mrs Thomas, noting her distress.

Sarah brushed her tear away and gave her a weak smile. 'It's all right. Must be this cold wind making me eyes water.'

Mrs Thomas smiled back. 'I'd better get a move on. Got all those mouths to feed.'

Sarah watched Mrs Thomas walk away, wishing it was her that had a lot of mouths to feed. She turned to walk home; she had completely forgotten about buying Eddie a present.

Mary did indeed send Eddie a birthday card and postal order for five shillings for her mother to buy him something. How she wanted to see him. Had he improved? She constantly asked her mother if he said any words yet, but the answer was always the same. She also asked her mother if Ron had written to her. As nobody had heard from him Mary had a dreadful thought: had he given himself up? She had returned to the dockyard but not had any luck in finding out where he was.

Now Mary was telling Jean that she was going to see the Turners once again.

'Looks like you're making a habit of it,' said Jean when at lunchtime Mary asked her along.

'It was a month ago I went there. So are you coming with me?'

'No.'

'Please yourself, but they said you would be very welcome.'

'You don't want me around; besides, I'll be helping me mum make the Christmas puddings.'

Tears stung the back of Mary's eyes. She remembered the happy days when she and Eddie helped stir the puddings. Was that only a year ago? That was before she had found that damned photograph. If only she could turn the clock back. What sort of Christmas would they have this year without her? Where would *she* spend Christmas this year?

Mrs Johns had told her that she always helped at the Salvation Army hostel on Christmas Day and she told Mary she would be more than welcome to join her. It was very nice of her, but Mary didn't think it would be much fun. What about Jean? Perhaps she could spend it with them? 'So what are you doing for Christmas then?' asked Mary, trying to make it sound as light-hearted as possible.

'I expect we'll be going to Audrey's.' Audrey was Jean's eldest sister, who lived in Somerset. 'Can't say I enjoy it that much with her kids. It's so cramped. I have to sleep on a camp bed in me mum and dad's room, and he don't half snore.'

Mary smiled. So that was definitely out.

'What about you? You going home?'

Although Mary had told Jean why she was living down

here, Jean also knew she wrote to her mother.

'I expect so.' This was something Mary really had to think about. Perhaps she could go to Liz's? The Thomases knew how to enjoy themselves.

Sunday saw Mary on the bus heading for Horndean again. The trees were bare now, and the weather was cold and damp, but once again she was warmly welcomed, and this time Andy and Patrick were there.

'Ma said you come from London,' said Patrick. 'That's where I want to go one day.' He was a good-looking lad, tall for his age. His blue eyes sparkled as he pushed a lock of dark hair back from his forehead. 'Ma's told me all about when she used to read palms on Blackheath. That was before she met Dad and they had the chair-o-planes. So tell me about London.'

'It's a very busy place, not as pretty as here,' said Mary.

'It's not as grand as you think,' said Andy. 'Is it, Mary?'

'No, parts of it are very run down.'

'Now come on, help yourself to the tea Ma's spent all day preparing,' said Mr Turner.

'I hope you didn't go to all this trouble because of me?' Mary looked at the table laden with cakes and sandwiches all arranged, as before, on the pretty china set on the lace tablecloth.

'No,' said Andy. 'We have to go through this ritual every Sunday when we're around.'

'I like nice things and I like things to be nice,' said Moira Turner, smiling at her family. 'Remember I don't see a lot of you through the summer.'

'That's true,' said Mr Turner.

'You're very lucky to have a mum who looks after you,' Mary said to Andy.

'What about your parents?' he asked. 'Do you have to endure this every Sunday when you're back home?'

'Yes,' said Mary softly. 'But I like it.' She quickly changed the subject and she asked them about Christmas. 'Will you be at home over the holiday?'

'No. We all go over to see Ma's folks in Ireland, just for a few days.'

'I bet you have a whale of a time there,' said Mary, full of envy.

'We do if we ain't all seasick,' said Patrick.

Again there was plenty of chuckles and everybody nattering at once. Mary was so at home with these happy people.

'Have you got a boyfriend?' asked Patrick.

'I'm sorry, Mary, but he's so nosy,' said Mr Turner.

She smiled. 'It's all right. Yes,' she said to Patrick. 'He's in the navy.'

'Is that the reason you've moved down here, to be near him?' asked Andy, looking away from her.

'No. He's at sea.' What was it about Andy that made her not want to talk about Billy? 'Look at the time. I should really be going. I've had such a lovely time. Thank you so much.'

'It's been our pleasure,' said Mrs Turner. 'And you will come again, won't you?'

'Yes, please.' She stopped. She suddenly remembered Billy laughing at her when she said that.

The wind was blowing a gale when Andy insisted on taking Mary to the bus stop.

'You didn't have to come out with me, you know. I'm all right.'

'I don't mind. I wanted to,' said Andy. He had his hands stuffed deep in his coat pockets and a white muffler at his throat. 'And you don't have to come up here and sit with them. I know Ma can be a bit of a pain going on about how things used to be.'

'I like being here. You see, I never had any relations to visit on a Sunday and to me this is lovely.'

He laughed. 'I can't believe that.'

'Well, it's true. Here's my bus.'

'When will we see you again?'

'I don't know.'

'Ma will write to you.'

The bus came chugging towards them and all conversation was carried away on the wind. As Mary sat down she looked out of the window. It had started to rain heavily but Andy, standing looking at her, made no attempt to move. The rain had flattened his dark hair and it stuck to his head like a cap. He watched the bus till it disappeared into the darkness. Mary sat back. Again she had had a lovely afternoon, but it had been even better this time with Andy and his brother there. Andy was so nice.

Mary had written to Liz and asked her if she could spend Christmas with them. She was over the moon when Liz said yes. Mrs Johns was a little disappointed that Mary wasn't coming with her to the Salvation Army hostel, but appreciated that Mary would have more fun in Rotherhithe. Mary asked Mr Holt if she could go early on Christmas Eve. After a discussion with Mrs Warner he said yes, and added that she would be getting a bonus. She could have kissed him! That meant she could spend two nights with Liz and her family.

Although she was unhappy at not being with her mum and Eddie, she was excited that she was going to be with so many people who liked her. Mary had written to her mother and told her her plans; who knew, she might just bump into them? Mary kept her fingers crossed for that.

Mary was also pleased that the Turners had invited her to tea on the Sunday before Christmas. She had been buying presents to take them. She'd found a sweet little brass cat for Moira, a pair of gloves for Mr Turner, a game for Patrick and a white scarf for Andy.

'Why're you buying them all this?' asked Jean when Mary told her about her purchases as they stood in the queue to see Shirley Temple in *Curly Top*.

'I can't go there empty-handed; besides, they've been very kind to me.'

'What about me?' said Jean with a grin.

'You've been kind and all, and I've got something very special for you.'

'Tell me! Tell me what it is.'

'No, I won't, you'll have to wait till the Saturday before Christmas when we go out.'

'That's only next week.'

'I know. But you've still got to wait. Besides, what have you bought me?'

Jean laughed. 'I don't believe in Christmas.'

'Why's that?'

'It ain't the same since me sisters left home.'

The queue shuffled forward.

'I know what you mean. It ain't the same when you grow up.'

'Come on, cheer up,' said Jean, grinning. 'Course I like Christmas. In fact, I might even buy you a present.'

'You cheeky thing.' Mary hung on to Jean's arm. She was so lucky to have met her and she knew that Jean would be pleased with the bath oil she'd bought her. It was a new line in the shop, and smelt lovely.

By Monday Mary was very excited. Christmas was only nine

days away. The shops were decorated and most people appeared to be in a happy mood. In eight days' time she would be with her old mate and, who knew, she might even get a chance to see her mum and Eddie. When the doorbell tinkled and a cold blast of air came into the shop Mary looked up to see Nurse Bentley walk in. This was something she had been dreading. She was filled with guilt at not going to see Daisy.

'Hello, Mary,' Nurse Bentley said breezily. 'Haven't seen you for a while now.'

'No.' Mary looked across at Mrs Warner, who was busy with an elderly lady who was having trouble with her chilblains.

'We would like to see you again. Is there any chance of you coming next Sunday? We've got all our decorations up and the place looks really nice and festive.'

'I'm sorry, but I've promised someone I'll go to see them.'

'Is it a nice young man?' Nurse Bentley smiled.

'No.' But Mary couldn't understand why she felt herself blushing.

'Well, perhaps another time. I'd like some cold cream. This weather dries my skin something terrible.'

Mary put the pot of cold cream in a brown paper bag and placed it on the counter. 'Was there anything else?'

'No, not for the time being.'

Mary took her money and put it in the drawer behind her. As she handed the nurse her change Nurse Bentley held on to her hand and said softly, 'Please, Mary. Do come and see Daisy. She needs you. She's not that well.'

Mary looked shocked and quickly pulled her hand away. She glanced over at Mrs Warner, but she was still engrossed with the lady and all the different chilblain ointments that were available. 'What's wrong with her?'

'She's got a terrible cough. But it's her attitude that's worrying the doctors. She has lost the will to live and won't leave her bed.'

'What can I do?'

'You were the one that got her to say a few words. You might be able to get her to eat. Please say you'll come.'

'I can come the Sunday after Christmas.'

Nurse Bentley gathered up her purchases. 'It might be too late then.' She walked away.

Mary watched her leave the shop. What should she do? Guilt weighed heavily on her, but she wanted to visit the Turners. What was it to be? Sitting in a lunatic asylum with a woman who didn't speak, or joking and chatting with a happy family? But if Daisy really needed her, she didn't have a choice.

# Chapter 34

When Mary left the shop that evening she was still troubled over what Nurse Bentley had told her. As soon as she arrived at Mrs Johns's, she quickly took off her hat and coat and plonked herself at the table. 'What do you think I should do?' she asked after telling her landlady what had happened.

'What do you want to do?'

'I don't know. Part of me says I should visit Daisy, especially when Nurse Bentley said after Christmas might be too late.'

'She might have only meant too late to be at St Mark's. They might be moving her to a hospital.'

'I didn't think of that.'

'What a pity you work on a Saturday, otherwise you could visit her then.' Mrs Johns put a cup of tea in front of Mary and sat next to her.

Mary sat up straight. 'That's it. I could go on Wednesday, on my half-day.'

'Now that is a good idea.'

'I was going out with Jean but I can see her in the evening.' Mary hated letting people down and she felt as if a great burden had been lifted from her shoulders.

The following day when they met as usual at lunchtime, Mary told Jean of her plan.

'Do you think it's wise going to see her again? What if you get all upset?'

'I've just got to go. What if the poor woman dies? I'd feel awful not having visited her.'

'Please yourself, but don't ask me to come with you.'

'So what will you do with yourself?'

'I'll find something to do. I might even wrap up a few presents.'

'Make sure you wrap mine up then.' Mary laughed. 'By the way, when are you seeing Danny?'

Jean looked down and began stirring her tea. 'Not till next year.'

'That's a shame. Is there a reason?'

'It's just that I can't get away.'

'That's a shame,' repeated Mary. She wanted to ask why Danny didn't come down here to see her, but decided against that. It was obvious Jean didn't want to say any more on the subject as she went on to tell her about the new frock her mum was making her for Christmas.

'It's really nice. Pale green with little flowers over it. Me mum don't do a bad job. I can wear it when we go dancing. I shan't wear it over Christmas, not a lot of point, not at our Audrey's with her kids scrambling all over me.'

Mary thought that was a delightful prospect. She would have loved to have Eddie scrambling all over her.


On Wednesday, Mary once more made her way to St Mark's. The Christmas spirit had got to her and when she saw a small locket on a chain that was similar to the one Daisy was wearing in the photo, on impulse she bought it for her.

When Mary arrived at St Mark's, again there was someone different at the gate and she had to wait till she had permission to go in. Little flurries of snow started to come down. I wonder if we'll have a white Christmas, Mary thought as she pulled her navy-blue beret down over her ears and her scarf tighter at the throat.

'You can go in now. Nurse Bentley said she wants to see you. D'you know where it is?'

This young man had a surly manner about him Mary didn't like so she only replied with a curt, 'Yes, thank you.'

Nurse Bentley was waiting in the corridor for her. 'Mary, I'm so pleased to see you. It's very kind of you to come along.'

Mary was taken aback by her eagerness; in fact, she wondered if she was going to be taken in her arms and crushed to her ample bosom.

'Is everything all right?'

'Daisy is a little poorly.'

'You said after Christmas might be too late. What did you mean?'

'She may have to go into a hospital. We're waiting for another doctor to see her.'

'Poor Daisy. Is she that bad?'

'They can do more for her than we can. It's the not eating that's worrying the doctor.'

'I've got a Christmas present for her. Shall I give it to her or will you take it?'

'I'll take it. It'll be nice for her to have something on Christmas morning.'

Mary handed her the small, prettily wrapped gift.

As they moved along the corridor Mary noted the Christmas decorations were hanging very high near the ceiling. 'They look nice,' she commented, looking up.

'Yes. They have to be high up otherwise they would be down in a few minutes. Even the Christmas tree, which was donated by a local businessman, has to be shut away in the conservatory and the patients are only allowed in there under strict supervision. We never put glass baubles on it, just decorations made out of silver paper, otherwise goodness only knows what some of them would get up to.'

Mary gave a little smile at the thought of these poor people running wild, pulling all the decorations down and trampling the tree underfoot.

They went into the dormitory that Mary had been in before. She looked up the room to where a small figure lay huddled on a metal bed covered with blankets and a navy-blue bedspread. Mary moved quickly and quietly towards her. 'Daisy,' she said softly, coming up close to her. 'It's me, Mary.'

There was no movement.

Nurse Bentley brought over a chair for Mary. 'I'll leave you for now. Call in when you're ready to go.'

'All right.' Mary settled herself down. She took a small box of chocolates from her handbag. 'I've brought you some chocolates.'

Nothing disturbed the small pile of bedclothes.

'The nurse said you haven't been very well. Are you feeling any better now?'

Again nothing.

Mary was beginning to think Jean was right. Was this a wasted journey? She felt like shouting out: If you don't want to talk to me, well, then say so. I can easily go away; but she knew she couldn't do that, it would be cruel.

'Daisy. I come from London. I was living at home till I found your photo. When I told my stepfather I'd found you . . .' She hesitated. 'Well, my stepfather threw me out of the house. That's why I came down here to Portsmouth to live. I left behind my mum and half-brother.'

There was a slight movement under the bedspread. 'Mary?' It was a very faint whisper.

'Yes?' Mary bent her head close.

'Why did you want to find me?' It was very muffled.

'I thought you might have been a relation of my stepfather's. I thought you might have been his sister.'

The silence went on for many, many minutes. Mary sat back. This was it. This was all she was going to say. Slowly Daisy pushed the bedclothes back from her face. Mary was shocked at the change in the woman. Her hair was a tangled mess and she looked old and withered. Loose skin hung on her cheeks and neck; she was a bag of bones. She began coughing. Mary looked about her, feeling helpless. She helped Daisy to drink from a glass of water that was at her bedside.

The coughing stopped and Daisy lay back, exhausted. She looked up at Mary with her watery blue eyes. 'I've got a lot to tell you.'

Mary smiled at this poor woman. What sort of life had she had, shut away in an institution all these years? Had she killed her son? If so, perhaps hanging might have been kinder. This was not living. She took hold of Daisy's hand and was surprised to find a piece of paper screwed up in it. Daisy let Mary open her hand and Mary gasped when she saw it was the photo. It was little more than a scrap of shiny paper now.

'What do you want to tell me?'

'Please find my little boy.' Her voice was rasping and low.

'Where will I find him?'

'The gypsy's got him. I gave him to the gypsy.'

'Why did you give him away?'

Daisy looked exhausted and it took a while for her to answer. 'I was frightened my husband was going to hurt him.'

'Why would he do that?'

'He didn't like him.'

'Do you have any family? Any brothers or sisters?'

Daisy closed her eyes. Her breathing was laboured and to

Mary the silence seemed endless. It was as if Daisy was trying to remember, trying to conjure up images of her past. Daisy's rasping breath as she murmured broke the silence. 'I brought disgrace on the family.'

'What about your husband?'

'He left me.'

'What was your little boy's name?'

Daisy opened her eyes and gave Mary a weak smile. 'He was very beautiful. I loved him so much. I didn't kill him.'

'I know you didn't. Daisy, what was his name?'

Mary could see that talking about her son animated her.

Daisy smiled. 'Edward had lovely blue eyes.'

'Edward?' repeated Mary. 'My half-brother's name's Edward. So is my stepfather's.' She felt a surge of excitement. Was she going to find out more? 'What was your surname? Did you have a brother called Ted?'

Daisy squeezed Mary's hand, her eyes staring. 'I . . .' was all she uttered before a coughing bout hit her again. Blood began to trickle from the corner of Daisy's mouth, Mary was terrified. 'I'll go and get help.'

Mary ran along the corridor searching for a nurse.

A large woman stepped out in front of her, blocking her way. 'Young woman, you're going to get into trouble running like that.'

'Please. Let me pass.'

'No. Not till you say you're sorry.'

'I'm very sorry.'

'No. Not very sorry. Just sorry.'

Mary wanted to scream. 'Let me pass,' she yelled.

'You're a very naughty little girl and you're not going to get any dinner now.'

Mary pushed her to one side. 'Get out of my way, you batty old cow.'

'I'll tell. I'll tell,' the woman called out after Mary. 'You said a wicked word.'

A door opened and a nurse called out, 'What's all this racket going on out here?'

'Quick, nurse. It's Daisy. She's not well.'

'I know that. Who are you?'

Mary wanted to tear her hair out. 'A friend. Please. She's coughing up blood.'

The nurse started to move swiftly along the corridor towards Daisy's dormitory. She stopped and called to Mary, 'Go and get Nurse Bentley.'

Mary hurried along to Nurse Bentley's room and, without knocking, barged in.

Nurse Bentley looked up, astonished. 'Mary? What is it?'

'Quick. Come quick. It's Daisy.'

Nurse Bentley was immediately out of her chair and the room and rushing down the corridor with Mary close behind.

When they got into the room the other nurse was already giving Daisy oxygen. There was a black mask over her pale face and her eyes were closed.

'I think the doctor should be called,' she said to Nurse Bentley.

'I'll do that. Mary, I'm afraid you'll have to leave.'

'But . . . Can I stay for a little while?' she protested as she was being ushered out of the room.

'I'm sorry. We have work to do.'

'Will she be all right?'

'I hope so. She has a bad cold that's gone to her chest. Now please leave us.'

'Can I come back again?'

'Phone my office tomorrow.'

'Thank you.' Mary walked away with a heavy heart. Over

the months she had become fond of Daisy. She hoped she wouldn't die.

Outside the snow had settled. Everywhere looked clean and white. Sounds were muffled and people had their heads down rushing to their destinations. Mary wandered to the tram stop. It seemed that everything she had tried to do for Daisy had been useless and had only brought her pain. If only she could find her son for her. That would really give her a new lease of life. But where could she start? She didn't even know his surname. Had the gypsies changed it? Was he still alive? And would he want to know about his mother?

She clambered on the tram, still in a dream. Tomorrow she would phone St Mark's and hope the news would be better. And at Christmas surely Daisy would be pleased with the locket she had left with Nurse Bentley.

# Chapter 35

Mrs Johns was sad when Mary told her about Daisy. 'I'm sure she'd be better off in a hospital,' she said. 'After all, they can do such clever things now.'

The following morning before she went to work Mary phoned St Mark's. Nurse Bentley told her that Daisy had indeed been taken to hospital. She asked if she could visit her and was told, very firmly, no.

Jean agreed it was best she didn't go and see her when Mary met her at lunchtime.

As they both made their way back to work Jean said, 'D'you want to go out tonight? This weather's awful. We don't normally get much snow down this way.'

A couple of sailors threw a dirty sludgy snowball at them.

'Stop it, you cheeky buggers,' shouted Jean. 'Don't fancy staying out here long with the likes of them hanging around,' she said, putting her arm through Mary's and hurrying her along. 'Let's go to the pictures; it's got to be a lot warmer in there.'

Yet that evening Mary couldn't concentrate on the film as her mind was on Daisy.

The following morning before she went to work she phoned St Mark's again. Nurse Bentley told her there was no change, Daisy was still the same.

'So that's it then,' said Jean when they met up at lunchtime. 'All your efforts to find out who she is have been in vain.'

'Looks like it. I did find out her Christian name, but I still don't know if she's related to Ted.'

'Are you sorry you came down here now?'

'No. Well, yes, in some ways. I really miss me mum and Eddie.'

'Will you be seeing them over Christmas?'

'Don't know.'

'You going to stay with Liz?'

'Yes. She's got a nice family. Mr Holt's been very kind. He said I could go early on Christmas Eve.'

'You're lucky. I expect we'll be working right up till late. It seems everybody wants a picture for a Christmas present. Mr Palmer won't be out of the dark room all day, he's got so much work.'

'It's a shame you couldn't have a few days off to go and see Danny.'

'Well, it's just one of those things.'

'What about after Christmas?'

Jean began fiddling with the spoon in her saucer. 'He said he'll be busy preparing for the new season and I don't suppose I'll be seeing that much of him.'

'Jean, I'm so sorry. Is it all over?'

'Looks like it.'

'You did like him.'

'Yes, I did, but I suppose it was all a bit of a lark. I didn't really know him.'

'Are you sorry?'

'In some ways. But, as me mum said, it wouldn't have worked out.'

321

'So are you still thinking of going on the liners?' asked Mary.

'Yes.' Jean looked up at the clock. 'Oh no, look at the time.' She jumped up and hurried to the door. 'I'll see you tomorrow,' she called out. With her head down against the wind, she disappeared.

Mary sat pondering; she had another five minutes. It was a shame that Jean and Danny had drifted apart. She hoped that it was different in her and Billy's case and that absence would make the heart grow fonder. As she picked up her handbag Mary thought about next year when he would be back. She desperately hoped that he still liked her. She couldn't wait to be in his arms again.

By Sunday the snow had almost gone from Portsmouth but, Mary discovered as the bus chugged its way up to Horndean, it was still lying thick on the ground further inland. She sat gazing out of the window. Everywhere looked like a picture postcard: snow glistened on the rooftops; the boughs of the trees were laden down and animal footprints had dented the pristine white snow. It all looked very peaceful and beautiful.

At the cottage she received her usual kindly welcome. Moira ushered her in and Mary was pleased to see they had decorated for Christmas. Although she had brought them presents, she hadn't been sure of their religion. A large beautifully decorated tree stood in the corner with its glass baubles and fairy lights twinkling.

'I love the smell of Christmas trees,' said Mary, sniffing the air. 'They have such a lovely clean fresh pine smell.'

'Patrick, Andy and Brendan went over to the woods and cut it down a few days ago,' said Moira.

'We had to wait for it to dry out before we could bring it

in,' said Andy as he took her hat and coat.

'That bag looks intriguing,' said Patrick, coming up to her. 'Anything interesting inside?'

'Son, don't be nosy,' said Brendan.

Mary laughed. 'You'll have to wait and see.' She'd felt at home as soon as she walked in. There was something about them that made her relax.

Tea was as usual full of stories and jokes. There was always plenty of laughter. They wanted to know where she was going to spend Christmas.

'I shall be going back home for a few days. I'm spending it with my friend Liz.' She turned to Andy. 'Do you remember Liz? No, she'd gone back to London before Danny introduced us.'

Moira sat up. 'Not that Danny Coleman?'

'Yes,' said Andy. 'Don't go on, Ma. He's all right.'

His mother fussed with the cushion on the sofa. 'That's not what I've heard.'

'What's wrong with Danny?' asked Mary, alarmed.

'Nothing,' said Andy quickly.

'If getting a young girl in trouble is nothing, well then, my boy, you have very different morals from the rest of us.'

Mary was stunned. Had Jean found out about this? Was this why she had cooled towards him? 'Did he marry her?' she asked tentatively.

'No, I'm afraid he loves 'em and leaves 'em,' said Brendan. 'Now let's not talk about Danny.'

'What made you move down here?' asked Patrick.

Mary looked at Moira. 'I had a row with me stepdad and he told me to leave.'

'My poor dear. What about your mother?' Moira asked.

Mary felt she had nothing to lose by telling these people the truth. They liked her for who she was. 'Mum really couldn't say a lot, you see I have a brother who is a little backward and she couldn't be left on her own with him without any support.' She sat back. 'So, it was me stepdad or me, and he won.'

Silence filled the air for a moment or two.

'How old is your brother?' asked Moira.

'He's my half-brother and he's six.'

'What's wrong with him?' she asked.

'Moira.' Brendan's voice was loud and full of anger. 'I've just told Patrick about being nosy. Mary is a guest in this house and I don't want her every move and statement questioned.'

'I'm so sorry, Mary,' said Moira.

'No, it's all right. I don't mind talking about Eddie. We don't know what's wrong with him. He can't speak and has terrible tantrums and throws himself about and bangs his . . .' Mary stopped when she caught sight of Moira looking at her with her eyes wide open. 'What is it?' she asked.

'That must be awful. I remember many years ago there was a young boy who belonged to Gypsy Velma the fortune-teller who was like that.'

'You said a gypsy?' Mary's voice was low.

'Yes. She always said a lady gave him to her, but we never believed her. We did think she might have stolen him.'

Mary gasped and said softly, 'How long ago was that?'

'Let's see. Must be all of what? Ten, twelve years, I would think. It was before I had Patrick. In fact, I used to think that he was a dreadful child, out of control. I always wondered why, if he had been given to Velma, she didn't give him back. I was quite proud that even though Patrick was younger he overtook him in everything.'

Mary had let her mouth fall open.

'Mary. Mary! What is it?' Andy was at her side and holding her hand.

'Where is this Gypsy Velma now?' she whispered.

'Don't know,' said Moira. 'I left the fair and she moved on. Why? What is it, Mary? Is it very important?'

Mary nodded and wiped her eyes. 'Do you remember the boy's name?'

'No. I'm sorry. It was a long while ago.'

'If it's the same boy and gypsy . . .' Mary stopped. 'She couldn't have known, but she might have saved a woman from being locked up in an asylum for these past ten, eleven years. You see, nobody believed her. They said she had murdered her son but they never found the body.'

Moira gasped, 'No,' putting her hand to her mouth and opening her dark eyes wide. She whispered, 'That's dreadful. You remember Velma,' she added, nudging her husband. 'She stayed till the boy must have been about six. Where would she be now?'

'I don't really remember. Mary, how do you know about all this?'

Mary then told them the whole story: about the photograph, Ted, Eddie, and Daisy. Not a word was uttered till she had finished.

'Is this why you left home?' asked Andy. 'To find this woman?'

Mary nodded. 'In a way. But my stepfather threw me out when I told him about Daisy. Now she's ill and has been taken to hospital.'

'That's awful,' said Andy.

'And she don't talk?' said Moira.

'Very little.'

'I seem to remember that kid,' said Andy thoughtfully. 'He was a handful. At first we all took the mickey out of him, then as he got a bit older we all tried to help him talk.'

Mary sat on the edge of the sofa and asked eagerly, 'Did he talk? Did you get him to speak?'

'A few words, but then Velma moved on.'

'But you got him to talk,' Mary insisted.

'Only a few words, as I said. I expect he's better now. Is it important to you?'

Mary nodded. 'If he eventually talked, there may be hope for my brother Eddie.'

Moira patted her hand. 'I shouldn't build your hopes up too much.'

Mary brushed away a tear. 'No, I mustn't. In any case, Ted won't let me go back home.'

'I'm sorry, Mary,' said Mr Turner.

'I remember that kid,' said Patrick suddenly. 'I used to play with him. He was a funny thing. He'd never look at you and he didn't talk much. I think his name was Teddy.'

Mary gasped. 'Then it must have been him!'

'I do remember he was a very beautiful boy,' said Moira. 'Blond with big blue eyes. So you think this Daisy is a relation of your stepfather's?'

'I think she must be.'

'Why are you so worried about her, Mary?' asked Brendan.

She looked down at the handkerchief she was threading through her fingers. 'If she is my stepfather's sister, it shows that Eddie's condition could be hereditary, passed down from my stepfather's side of the family.' She stopped and scrunched up the handkerchief. She gave a big sob. 'I'm sorry. I shouldn't have come here with all of my problems.' She wiped her eyes. 'This is Christmas, we should be happy.'

Moira came over to her and held her tight. 'I know we've not known each other very long but I feel you are like a daughter. Your mother must be very sad at losing you.'

'I wish I could find Daisy's son, then they would have to let her go.'

'Brendan,' said Moira. 'Could you find out anything for Mary? Would anyone know where Velma went?'

'Why didn't she come forward at her trial? It was in the papers. She must have read about it,' said Mary.

'Not many Romanies of her generation could read,' said Moira.

'I don't know who would know about her now,' said Brendan. 'I can ask when we start getting the rides ready. Someone might remember her. But what if she wasn't telling the truth? What if the baby was hers and she had read about this woman in the paper and used it as an excuse?'

'But he was blond and she was very dark.' Moira was certainly intrigued about all this.

'Well, we don't know about the father, do we?'

'Brendan, you can be so annoying at times. Just do your best.'

'Who would look after Daisy if she did come out?' asked Andy.

Mary looked up. 'I hadn't thought about that. Even if she is Ted's sister he wouldn't want her.'

Brendan stood up. 'Mary, sometimes these things are best left as they are. You say she's been in an institution all these years. Could she cope with the outside world?'

'I don't know. Perhaps you're right.'

There was silence for a moment or two.

'I'm sorry, I'm spoiling things. I'd better go.'

'No. No, don't go just yet,' said Andy.

Brendan gave everyone a smile. 'Now I think it's time for a toast.'

'Good idea, Pa,' said Patrick.

'Not you, young man,' said Moira.

Brendan was still grinning as he went to the sideboard and poured some port into pretty engraved glasses. 'Here's hoping you find all the answers you need, Mary.'

'Thank you.'

'Merry Christmas, everyone,' said Brendan.

'Merry Christmas,' they all said together.

'And a very happy New Year,' said Moira.

When it was time for Mary to go, Andy walked her to the bus stop.

'Mary, you will come to see us again?'

'Yes, your mum said I must. You have all been very kind and I didn't expect to come away with a bag of presents.'

'We are all very fond of you and think a lot of you.'

'Even now you know all about my murky past?'

He laughed. 'I know you are a very caring person. I like that and I hope everything works out for you.'

When the bus arrived Andy gave Mary a hug and kissed her cheek. 'Merry Christmas,' he whispered.

'Merry Christmas.'

'Promise you'll come and see us again?'

'I promise,' she said as she climbed aboard the bus.

Mary watched him waving till he was out of sight, then she sat back. They were all so nice to her. She clutched the bag containing the brightly wrapped presents they had given her. How easy it had been to talk to them about Eddie and her fears. When Andy told her how he had tried to help Teddy to talk she knew he was indeed as kind as he appeared. It wasn't necessarily what you would expect from someone who worked on a fairground.

Her thoughts went to Daisy. Although she had bought her a locket, would finding her son be the best Christmas present she could give her? But Mr Turner did have a point. If this Velma did have her son and she came forward with the evidence and Daisy was released, who would look after her? And how could she ever look after her son? Mary dismissed these questions. She knew it would most likely never come to that.

She sat reflecting on this past year. What would next year bring? A tear ran slowly down her cheek. Talking about Eddie and her mum made her realise just how much she missed them. If only she could see them again. If only she was there she would be able to teach him to talk. She closed her eyes and wished.

# Chapter 36

Mary had come back from Horndean very excited. She told Mrs Johns all about the Turners helping to find the woman who they thought might have Daisy's son. Although Mrs Johns was astonished, she agreed with Mr Turner that to release Daisy now might do more harm than good.

Daisy had been on Mary's mind most of the night. Everything that had been said was going over and over in her brain. Was she doing the right thing in trying to find out about her son?

On Monday morning, as she made her way to the shop, Mary was almost beside herself at the thought that tomorrow she was going back home, back to Rotherhithe. Uppermost in her mind was the idea that she might even be lucky enough to see her mother and Eddie. That would be the best Christmas present ever.

'I'll give you your little gift today,' said Mrs Warner as she put on her overall and went and unlocked the shop door. 'Then you can take it with you.'

'Thank you. I'll bring yours in tomorrow.' There was so much happening in Mary's life at the moment that she could hardly keep the glee out of her voice.

'Good morning,' said Mr Holt as he emerged from his office. 'I expect we'll be busy today with folks getting their last-minute bits in time for Christmas. Should think we'll sell plenty of chilblain ointment if this weather continues and the Andrews liver salts will be needed for all the hangovers. Mary, you may well have to work through your lunchtime, do you mind?'

'No, not at all.' Mary didn't mind what she did for Mr Holt; he was a kind and pleasant man to work for.

'That's fine. On Christmas Eve most of the trade drifts off in the afternoon as folk start to prepare for the big day.'

The bell above the door tinkled as the first customer arrived.

'Looks like it's started already.' Mr Holt disappeared behind his screen to make up the prescriptions.

All morning Mary and Mrs Warner were run off their feet. Jean came in to find out if she would see her at lunchtime. She was disappointed when Mary explained she wouldn't be able to.

'Won't see you tonight as I've got to wash me hair and pack,' Mary said, very carefully removing a very fine hairnet from the cardboard head.

'I'll see you tomorrow then. Got to give you your pressy.'

'All right,' said Mary, concentrating on the job in hand.

'Mind how you go, love. Don't go putting your fingers through it,' said the customer. 'I want to look nice on Christmas Day, me husband's coming home. Ain't seen him for months.'

'Is he in the navy?' asked Mary.

'No, prison. They're letting him out.'

Mary looked shocked. 'They let them out for Christmas . . .?'

The customer chuckled. 'He works there.' She took her purchase and as she left the shop she called out, 'Merry Christmas,' still laughing.

★ ★ ★

Today was Christmas Eve and Sarah had been wandering round the shops all morning. It was drizzling rain, cold and miserable. In fact the weather matched her mood. Her heart wasn't on shopping. She knew she had to prepare tomorrow's dinner but it wouldn't be the same without Mary around and giving Sadie and the kids a cake and pudding. She often wondered about them. How were they getting on? Were they together? Would Rosie ever forgive her and write to her? Sarah had been pleased as well as sad when she'd received a Christmas card from Ron. He'd also sent one for the kids. There was a letter inside asking for it to be passed on to them. That had upset Sarah, as she couldn't do anything about it. She knew Mary hadn't seen or heard from him. He hadn't put an address on it, as he didn't want anyone to know where he was. He must be worried about them. But what would he do when he found out about his mother? Perhaps he would get leave soon, but he had no one to come home to.

Sarah knew that her daughter was spending Christmas with Liz and her family; Mary had written and told her she would be here in Rotherhithe on Christmas Eve. The thought that was filling Sarah's mind was: If only she'd said what time then perhaps she could have met her somewhere. Sarah was also trying to think of ways she could get out on Christmas Day. But she knew deep down that that would be impossible. Ted was far from reasonable these days – that's when he was actually home. She used to be so happy; now her whole life had fallen apart. She pulled her scarf tighter at the throat and looked at Eddie. For once he was sitting quietly. Did he sense her mood? Sarah walked quickly home. Life was unfair all round.

★ ★ ★

Mary was going to the station straight from work at lunchtime, so she wouldn't be seeing Mrs Johns till after the holiday. 'I'll only be gone two days.'

'Yes, I know, but the house won't be the same without you! Now, you will come back, won't you?'

'Of course!' Mary kissed her cheek. 'I've got to find out how Daisy is and if Mr Turner can track down the gypsy's son.'

Mrs Johns hugged her. 'You're such a good girl.'

After she finished work, Mary called into the photographer's on her way to the station. As soon as Jean saw her she darted round the counter and crushed her to her.

When they parted Mary gave Jean her present. 'I hope you like it and remember, you mustn't open it till Christmas Day.'

'Wait just a moment.' Jean rushed into the cloakroom and on her return gave Mary a small packet. 'I hope you like *this*.'

'I'm sure I will. Now I must go.'

'Mary, you will come back, won't you?'

'Of course. Why do people keep asking me that?'

'Well, when you get home you might decide to stay there.'

'I don't think I will. I've got things to do.' Mary didn't want to go into detail about what she'd found out at the Turners; it would take too long and she was eager to get away.

'Merry Christmas.' Jean held her close again.

As Mary hurried along to the station all she could think was: I'm going home.

Once again she sat on the train and watched the green fields give way to the houses. It was drizzling with rain and everywhere looked dirty and grey but Mary didn't care. This was London. Waterloo Station was crowded with people on the move. They all seemed to be loaded down with shopping and parcels. Mary pushed her way to the Underground. There were people everywhere; it was all very claustrophobic.

It was dark by the time Mary was standing at the top of Bray Street, where Liz lived. It seemed shorter than she remembered. The lights in the houses looked warm and inviting. In the still night air smoke curled upwards from every chimney. Many houses had Christmas trees shining in their front-room windows. She hurried along. Liz should be home from work by now.

The front door was flung open the minute she rapped with the knocker.

'Mary!' screamed Liz, hugging her so hard she almost knocked Mary's new felt hat off. She grabbed her bag and pushed her into the house. The kitchen door was open and the family was standing in the doorway.

'Lovely to see you again, Mary.' Mrs Thomas kissed her cheek, then, holding her at arm's length, said, 'Don't she look well, Stanley?'

'Yes, she does. How are you, love?' He too held her close.

'Very well.' Mary was a little overwhelmed at this reception.

'Hello, Mary,' said the younger girls together.

'Come on, let's take your things upstairs,' said Liz.

Mary followed Liz, smiling; she was so happy to be here.

'So, what's been happening?' asked Liz, sitting on her bed.

'Is this for me?' asked Mary, pointing to the mattress on the floor.

'Yes, is that all right?'

'I should say so. Thank you for letting me spend Christmas with you.'

'I'd be most upset if you didn't want to come here. What do you want to do tonight?'

'I don't mind.'

'We could go to a dance or the pub with Mum and Dad.'

'What do you want to do?'

Liz grinned. 'The pub has got this old girl who bangs away on the piano. It's a good laugh and we know all the words to the songs.'

'That sounds good. So the pub it is then.'

Once that was settled, they began telling each other their news. Mary told Liz about Andy's family and them knowing the child that could be Daisy's. 'Mr Turner's going to look into it for me.'

'What a turn-up for the book. It sounds like something out of a novel.'

'Do you still read those sorts of books?'

'Yes. I like 'em.'

'Well, let's hope this one has a happy ending.'

'Will you be able to see her and tell her?' asked Liz, intrigued at the latest developments.

'I don't think so. Well, not just yet, perhaps when she gets better and comes out of hospital.'

'Oh, I'm so pleased to see you again,' said Liz. She was genuinely happy to see her friend again.

'So am I. I don't suppose you or your mum's seen anything of my mum?'

Liz shook her head. 'Not since the last time I told you about.' Mary knew about their last meeting, but there hadn't been any details. 'Mum would have said. Mary, it must be really hard for you. I know how I'd feel if I couldn't see me mum or me sisters, even if they can be a pain at times.'

Mary could only smile her response. Words wouldn't come.

'Tea's ready,' shouted Mrs Thomas up the stairs.

'Come on then,' said Liz. 'I bet you're dying for a cuppa.'

As they sat round the table the giggles and chatter were non-stop. Mrs Thomas asked if Billy had told her when he was coming home. She told them she didn't know. Mr Thomas wanted to know if Portsmouth still looked the same.

Mary told him it didn't look so good in the winter but the countryside over the hill was lovely. The girls enquired about the Turners; it seemed Liz had told them all about their home.

'Is it really like a caravan?' asked Susan.

'Not in size, just all the knick-knacks and brass.'

'Liz said you met the son at the fair.' Mr Thomas was stirring his tea after putting three spoonfuls of sugar in it.

'Yes, I did. It was Mr Turner who invited me back.' Mary didn't want them to think she had deserted their son. 'It seems Mrs Turner don't have a lot of visitors and he thought it would be nice for me to see her. I quite enjoy it; it's like having relations to visit on a Sunday afternoon. They make me very welcome.'

'What's Andy like?' asked Liz.

'Don't always see him. He's very good to his young brother and he takes him out most Sundays. Remember, he don't see a lot of his mum or Patrick during the summer.'

'Why's that?' asked Susan.

'He works on a travelling fairground, him and his dad run the chair-o-planes.'

'Cor, I'd like a job like that,' said Elsie. 'Mary, could you ask him if I could work for him when I leave school?'

'I don't think so, young lady,' said Mrs Thomas. 'It's bad enough one member of the family being away, we don't want two.'

Elsie sat back, pouting.

'I love the paper chains,' said Mary, looking up. 'Did you make them, Elsie?'

Elsie nodded. 'Sue helped me and Dad put 'em up.'

'You wait till you see the tree,' said Susan. 'It's ever so big. Dad put the lights on it and me and Els put on all the balls. Mum made the fairy doll's – she's sitting on the top – frock out of crêpe paper. She looks ever so nice.'

Mary was grinning fit to bust. Oh, she was glad to be here.

The evening in the pub proved to be just as good as Liz had predicted. The singing and impromptu dancing left them laughing and exhausted. Finally, after a lot of shouting 'time' from the landlord, who threatened to lock them in all over Christmas (which many of the men thought was a good idea), they had to leave.

'I ain't enjoyed meself like that since the Jubilee,' said Liz, slipping her arm through Mary's as they walked along together, still chuckling.

'Nor me.' But Mary stopped laughing as she recalled that dreadful night again.

'Did you ever find out what really happened that night? You know, the murder?'

'No.'

'It must have been awful.'

'Yes, it was.' Mary's thoughts went to Ron. Where was he? Where were the kids? As far as she knew Ron hadn't written to her mother. Sarah had told her that she'd never been able to find out where the family had finished up. That made up her mind. When she got back to Portsmouth she would make more of an effort to find out where Ron was.

That night Liz and Mary lay talking again, despite being told off by Mrs Thomas for too much giggling. They were finding it hard to keep their voices down.

'So, is Pete still loving in his letters?' Mary knew she was being nosy, but couldn't stop herself asking.

'Yes, he is. What about my brother?'

'He don't seem the romantic kind. Well, not on paper anyway.'

'Mary, remember I told you not to get your hopes up, didn't I?'

'Yes, you did.'

They were silent for quite a while and Mary thought about what Liz had said. Was she hoping for too much?

She thought Liz had nodded off when she suddenly whispered, 'Would you like me to call on your mum tomorrow?'

Mary sat upright. 'Would you? Do you really mean it?'

'Shh. Course. Look, we'll go round there in the morning. I've go a few jobs to do for Mum first—'

'I'll help,' interrupted Mary.

'All right. When we've finished we'll walk round there, you can wait up the road and if yer dad's out—'

'He's not me dad.'

'Will you stop interrupting? And keep your voice down.'

'Sorry.'

'As I said, if yer dad's out then you might be able to see her and your brother.'

'What if he ain't out?'

'He likes a drink, don't he?'

'Yes. I've got a present for me mum and Eddie.'

'Well, that's it then. If be any chance he ain't out then I just give her the present and let her know that you're just up the road. What d'you say to me bright idea?'

'It sounds good. Let's hope he goes out.'

'Right, that's it. I'm going to sleep. I hope I ain't missed Father Christmas calling. I'll be most upset if me stocking's empty in the morning.'

Mary giggled. 'Daft ha'p'orth. Goodnight.'

Mary lay thinking about Liz's plan. If only it all worked. It was a long while before sleep came. She was so excited about the prospect of seeing her mum and Eddie.

'Merry Christmas, girls.'

Mary blinked as Mrs Thomas pulled back the curtains.

'It's freezing out there.' She scraped the ice from off the

inside of the window, making a hole large enough to peer through. 'No snow, though. There's a cup of tea on the side for you both. Don't let it get cold. Did you sleep all right, Mary?'

'Yes, thanks.'

'Has Father Christmas been?' asked a very sleepy Liz.

'Not to you, girl. Not with all that racket you two were making last night. I think you must have frightened him away.'

'What time is it?' asked Liz.

'Time for you to get up,' said her mother, going out of the room.

'Thanks for the tea,' called Mary as Mrs Thomas closed the door.

'Please. Don't sound so cheerful in the morning, it ain't natural,' said Liz as her head emerged from beneath the bedclothes. 'Christ, it's freezing.'

'It's Christmas. Come on, don't be such a sleepy head.'

'Go away,' groaned Liz. 'I need me beauty sleep.'

'Come on, get up. We've got a lot to do today.'

Slowly Liz sat up. Her dark hair was all tousled and over her face. Her mascara was smudged round her eyes and she looked like a panda in reverse. Mary started giggling.

'What's so funny?'

'You. You wait till you see yourself.'

'I don't know what you're laughing about, you don't look so good.'

Soon they were dressed and downstairs with the family.

'Look what Father Christmas brought us.' Sue was dragging her pillowcase behind her.

'I've got books, games and lots of sweets,' said Elsie.

'That's what I've got as well,' said Sue, diving down into her pillowcase and proudly displaying her goodies.

'We ain't told Mum and Dad that we don't believe in Father Christmas in case they stop giving us a pillowcase,' laughed Elsie.

'I heard that,' said Mrs Thomas.

'It ain't fair,' said Sue. 'Mum said we've got to wait till this afternoon for our big presents. I've just seen Maisie Douglas go riding past on a new bike.'

'Well, I can tell you now, young lady, you ain't got a bike.' Mr Thomas was sitting in front of the fire making toast. 'Fancy a bit of toast, Mary?'

'Yes, please.' Mary looked at the clock. It had just gone nine. In a couple of hours she could be with her mum.

# Chapter 37

Despite helping with as many chores as they allowed her to, for Mary the morning seemed to go on for ever. At long last Liz said she was ready to go out.

'I'll just get our coats,' said Liz to Mary.

'Where're you going?' asked her mother.

'Round to see if Mary can see her mum.'

'Do you think that's wise?'

'Mary's got presents for 'em. I'll knock first and if her stepdad's in we'll just give Mrs Harding the presents and go away.'

'What if he opens the door?' asked her mother, obviously anxious.

Liz quickly looked at Mary. 'Dunno, I ain't thought that far ahead yet. We're hoping he's going for a drink.'

'Now, that's what I call a very sensible idea and just what I'm about to do,' said Mr Thomas, putting on his checked cap and wrapping his white scarf around his neck.

'Don't you be late for your dinner.' Mrs Thomas waved a large spoon at her husband. 'It'll be on the table at two sharp. And if you ain't here, we'll eat it for you.'

'Yes, dear.' He winked at Mary and Liz, then left the kitchen.

'What's the betting he'll be there till chucking-out time?'

said Mrs Thomas with a toss of her head.

'So what time is dinner then, Mum?'

Mrs Thomas grinned. 'Like I said, two.'

'Come on, Mary,' said Liz. 'Let's be off. Won't be long, Mum,' she shouted as they walked up the passage.

'I know it sounds silly, but I'm ever so nervous,' said Mary. 'What if he does open the door?'

Outside Liz tucked her arm through Mary's. 'He don't know me. You've always met me at the door or out somewhere. I'll just say I'm looking for next door, what was their name?'

'Fellows.'

'Don't worry, after all it is your mum.'

Mary had suddenly had second thoughts and was dragging her feet. 'What if he recognises you? What if he sees me? What if . . .?'

'What if pigs fly? Now come on. I wanner get back for me dinner.'

When they turned into Doyle Street Mary's heart skipped a beat. It seemed almost a lifetime ago that she was last here. The street where she'd grown up. The street where she'd played games. The street where she'd been so happy with her mum and Eddie.

'You all right?' asked Liz, catching her friend wiping her eyes.

'Yes. Must be the cold making me eyes water.'

'Right. Give me the pressies. You wait here. You can see the front door from here.'

Mary handed over the two parcels and stood back in Mr and Mrs West's doorway. She looked at the dairy's familiar goods in the window. She was sure some of the things on display had been there before she left. Mary blew her nose and watched Liz cross the empty street. No kids were riding their new bikes round here. *Were* there any kids living round here now? Mary's thoughts went to Rosie and the rest of the little Fellowses. What had happened to them? Where had they finished up? Perhaps one of these days Rosie would forgive her mother and write and tell her where they were and then she could tell Ron. She *must* try to find out how Ron was getting on then her mum could tell Rosie.

Liz turned and smiled as she lifted the knocker.

It was a while before the front door was opened. Mary's heart was beating like a hammer. The pounding was filling her ears. She could see Liz talking to someone – was it her mother? Liz turned and pointed to Mary. When her mother stepped forward and looked over at her, she quickly put her hands to her mouth. Mary wanted to run to her and hold her. She wanted to be with her. Yet Mary knew that if she did that, Ted could make life unbearable for her mother and Eddie. Tears ran down her cheeks, clouding her vision. She gave her a little wave. Her mother waved back. She turned and looked in the house. She blew a kiss to Mary and closed the front door.

Liz bounded over to Mary and grabbed her arm. 'Come on, quick. Don't look round, he might be looking out the front-room window.'

'He was in, then?' said Mary as Liz swiftly propelled her along the road.

'Yes. I could hear him shouting. He wanted to know who was at the door.'

'I wonder what Mum told him?'

'I'm sorry,' said Liz when she slowed down. 'I didn't mean to upset you. I shouldn't have suggested it. Me and my big mouth.'

'No. Don't say that. I'm glad I got a glimpse of her.' She wiped her eyes and gave Liz a smile. 'At least she did get my

343

present. She looked like she's lost a bit of weight.'

'I think it was the pinny she was wearing. She had it pulled round her very tight.'

'You was quick,' said Mrs Thomas as soon as they walked in. 'What happened?'

'Give us time to get our hats and coats off,' said Liz.

'I've made a pot of tea, so pour yourselves out one. You both look as if you could do with it. By the look on your face, Mary, it wasn't very successful?'

'No, it wasn't.'

'Give me your coat. I'll take it upstairs,' said Liz.

Mary sat at the table. 'Ted was in and me mum could only give me a wave.'

'I'm so sorry, love. I know how much you was looking forward to seeing her.'

'Yes, I was. Still, I did see her and she saw me and Liz gave her the presents.' A faint smile lifted Mary's sad face. She knew now that she could never come home all the while Ted lived there.


When Sarah closed the front door she had tears running down her cheeks. What could she do with these presents? Ted mustn't see them. He would know then that Liz or Mary had been round. As she passed the coalhole under the stairs she quickly tossed them in. She just prayed that there was nothing breakable in them, and she'd have to make sure that Ted didn't get any coal today.

'Who was that calling on Christmas morning?' shouted Ted from the kitchen. 'If it was the Salvation Army looking for handouts, tell 'em to go on their way.'

Sarah wiped her eyes on the bottom of her pinny. 'It was a girl from up the road asking for some change for the gas meter. I told her I didn't have any,' she said as she walked into the kitchen.

She looked at the table that had been set for dinner. A lovely smell of cooking came from the scullery. Two days ago Ted had brought home a large chicken. On the sideboard the fruit bowl was full to overflowing and nuts filled another bowl. It looked as if they were expecting company but Sarah knew it was just for them. He had said they mustn't let their standards slip even if there were only the two of them. For some reason he didn't count Eddie as part of the family now. It upset her.

Sarah couldn't get Mary out of her mind as she went about her chores.

'Sarah, have you made enough mince pies?'

She didn't answer.

'I said, have you made enough mince pies? Are you going deaf?'

'Sorry. I was miles away.'

'So I could see. Well?'

'Yes. I've made a dozen but I don't know who'll eat them.'

He laughed. 'Well, now we haven't got that lot next door to feed, it'll have to be me.'

Sarah didn't answer. She missed Sadie and the family. I wonder what sort of Christmas the children are having? she thought. If they're together it could be a lot happier than mine. Then she smiled. But I have seen Mary. She looked so smart in her nice coat and hat. If only she could see her way to talking to her, but Sarah knew that was impossible.

The Christmas dinner at the Thomases' was great and after they'd cleared away they made their way into the front room. Their Christmas tree stood proud in the window, and the presents were neatly arranged round the base. Mary admired the fairy doll sitting on the topmost branch. The fire was glowing and there was a tray of chestnuts close by. Mary guessed they were for this evening. It was a comfortable room with a brown Rexine three-piece and an oak sideboard, which had a bowl of fruit and a vase of flowers on it. The aspidistra with thick dark leaves that always stood in the window on its stand with long spindly legs had been pushed to the side. Mary sat next to Liz and the girls had to make do with cushions on the floor. The matching armchairs were for their parents. It was such a warm homely atmosphere. Mary couldn't get the thought of her mother out of her mind. What sort of Christmas was she having? If only she were there with her and Eddie.

They settled down to listen to the King's broadcast on the wireless. Then it was time for the presents. Paper was thrown everywhere and great whoops of delight rang out as everybody kissed and thanked everybody else for the handbags, scarves, socks, gloves and other practical things. These families didn't waste their money on fripperies. Mary's gifts brought great gasps of joy. She had brought them luxuries from the shop, which included lovely smelly soap for Mrs Thomas, bath salts for the girls and a hairbrush for Mr Thomas. Liz was overjoyed at her make-up and threw her arms round Mary's neck in glee.

'It's very handy working in a chemist's,' laughed Mary when she was released. She only hoped her mother would be pleased with her soap and expensive bath salts. 'And I love this picture of Billy,' she added, looking at the photo in a smart wooden frame.

'Well, we knew he didn't give you one so Liz here thought she'd get it done from a negative we had. It was taken a few years ago, but he ain't changed that much.'

'It's lovely.' Mary smiled. Now she had something to kiss goodnight every night.

It wasn't long before the dinner and beer sent Mr Thomas

to sleep. His paper hat had fallen over his eyes and his snores were making them all laugh.

'Stanley. Stanley. Wake up.' Mrs Thomas prodded him in the ribs with the poker.

'What is it? What's wrong?' He pushed his bright red paper hat up. 'What's happened?'

Everybody was laughing.

'Nothing. You was making so much noise we couldn't hear the wireless.' Mrs Thomas settled back in her armchair.

When it was time for tea everybody lent a hand to lay out the food. Bottles of beer were brought in and with a great flourish a bottle of port was proudly displayed on a tray on the sideboard.

Mr Thomas carefully poured a little port out for his wife, Liz and Mary. There were moans from the younger girls, but they still had to make do with lemonade. 'Good health to you all,' he said. 'And to absent friends.'

Mrs Thomas gave a little sob. 'My Billy,' she said softly, raising her glass.

Silently and to herself Mary said, 'To me mum and Eddie. I hope I can find a way to talk to you soon.'

Later that evening the games were brought out and after endless noisy games of ludo, snakes and ladders and cards it was time for bed.

'Have you enjoyed yourself today?' asked Liz as she jumped into bed.

'Yes. Thank you so much. And it was nice getting a glimpse of me mum. At least she knows I still care.'

'Course she does. I wish you could have got to talk to her.'

'So do I.'

Liz's voice was beginning to sound sleepy. 'I like being a lady of leisure. I wish I didn't have to go to work ever again.'

347

'Me too.' But Mary knew she enjoyed her job far more than Liz did hers.

The following afternoon Mary would be back on Waterloo Station. She was going back to her second home. This time she would really feel sad. That glimpse of her mum was tearing her apart. She had so much wanted to be with her and Eddie. Would that time ever come?

As soon as Mrs Johns opened the door she grabbed Mary and held her tight. 'I know it's silly but I was really worried about you. I did wonder if you'd come back.'

'There's nothing for me up there now,' said Mary, releasing herself from Mrs Johns.

'So you didn't see your mother then?'

'Yes, I did, but only from across the road.'

'I'm so sorry, Mary. I know how much you were looking forward to seeing her and your little brother.'

'I didn't see Eddie at all.'

'That's a shame. I'll let you go up and put your things away. Dinner's ready.'

'Thanks.'

Mary went to her room. She felt terribly alone. Her mother didn't look well. Mary choked back a sob. How would she know if her mother were taken ill? And who would look after Eddie?

When Mary went to work the following morning both Mr Holt and Mrs Warner showed they were pleased to see her.

'I was a bit worried you might not have come back,' said Mr Holt.

'I wouldn't let you down.'

'Did you have a nice Christmas?' asked Mrs Warner.

'Yes, thank you.'

'Was your family well?'

Mary was putting on her overall. 'Yes, thank you.' She had never told them the real reason for her move down here.

As soon as it was lunchtime Jean rushed in. 'You're back. Can we go out tonight?'

'No, sorry, but I've got a few things to do at home.' Mary stopped. She was calling Mrs Johns's house home. Was that how she was thinking now? 'I'll see you at lunchtime tomorrow then we can sort something out. Is that all right?'

'Course. It's great to have you back.'

That evening, when Mary left the shop, her thoughts were full of the New Year. Would things get any better in 1936? What did her future hold? She knew she had to find out about Daisy. And there was Ron to think about too.

# Chapter 38

The next day, when Mary and Jean met up at lunchtime, they talked excitedly about what they'd done over Christmas.

'Sounds as if you had a great time at Liz's. She's nice, I like her. Did you see your mum?' asked Jean.

'Yes, I did, but not to talk to.'

'Why was that?'

'Ted was home.'

'Oh, I see.'

Mary was pleased Jean wasn't going to pursue that. 'What about you, did you have a good time?'

Jean screwed up her nose. 'Not really. My sister's kids are still as horrible. You should see the state of their place now. Even me mum said Audrey's was a disgrace. I'm glad we was only down there for a couple of days.' Jean laughed. 'I certainly ain't having any kids. What about you?'

'I'd like some one day.'

'No,' said Jean, wiping crumbs from her mouth. 'I've made up me mind. It's a career for me.'

Mary hadn't told Jean what the Turners had said about Danny. Had Jean found out about his past? Mary tried to sound innocent as she asked, 'So what's happened? Is Danny really out of the picture now then?'

'Yes. His older sister wrote and told me all about him. She

got my address somehow. She thought I ought to be aware that he was a bit of a heart-breaker and had lots of girl-friends.'

'What did she want to do that for?'

Jean shrugged. 'Don't ask me. She might have thought I sounded a nice person by me letters.'

'She had a cheek reading your letters.'

'She might have stolen them, or he may have shown them to her.'

'Sounds funny to me. Why didn't you tell me this before?'

'Didn't like to. I didn't want you to think that I always manage to pick a wrong 'un.' She sat back with her teacup in her hand.

'You don't think she was jealous and didn't want her brother whisked away?'

Jean laughed. 'I shouldn't think so. Anyway, it's all over now. When I thought about it I realised I wasn't that keen on going round the country with him and spending me days sitting in a bumper car. He was just a bit of a laugh really. Me mum and dad are pleased. Although they liked him they didn't think that was the life for me. I'm gonner start writing to the liners to find out about that job now. I really do fancy that.'

'That'll be nice. Lucky old you.' Mary was surprised at Jean's attitude over Danny but very pleased for her sake. Or was she just trying to put on a brave face? Mary didn't want to show Jean how upset she was at the news that she may soon be going away. It was good for Jean but she would miss her friend.

As she walked home that evening she had never felt so alone. She had looked forward to Christmas so much. The joy she'd had with Liz and even the brief glance of her mum had brought her a great deal of happiness. Was that where she should be, in Rotherhithe? Gloom hung over Mary like a dark mantle.

After going with Jean to a dance heralding the New Year Mary's life settled down to a pattern. She had phoned Nurse Bentley but the nurse hadn't any news of Daisy: she told Mary she would let her know if any was forthcoming.

She received a letter from her mother thanking her for her presents. It upset Mary when Sarah said that Christmas without her had been very sad and she was sorry she hadn't been able to speak to her. Sarah also said she thought Mary had looked well, she liked her hat and coat and that she and Eddie were fine. She went on to say that Ron had sent her and the Fellowses a lovely Christmas card. It had a picture of the *Victory* on it. She said it upset her that she couldn't pass it on. Ron hadn't given his address, so was there any way Mary could find out if he was well?

When she finished reading it, Mary put the letter down and went to ask Mrs Johns, 'Can you think of any other way I can find out about Ron? Mum had a Christmas card from him of the *Victory*, so he must still be here.'

'You could go to the recruiting office, they may be able to help you.'

'Thanks, I'll do that.' As Mary walked away she wondered about Ron. How was he coping with life?

The following Wednesday afternoon she was told she would have to go to Gosport to find out about Ron. She would do that one day soon.

Later in the month, Mary made another trip to see the Turners. She was really looking forward to spending Sunday afternoon with them. She was dying to hear about their Christmas.

After the usual hugs of welcome, Mary told them about her Christmas and Moira told her about their Christmas in Ireland.

'The journey really took it out of me this time but it was wonderful seeing the family again. Everybody has grown up,' she said.

Mr Turner laughed. 'I keep telling her it's not only all the kids growing up, but it's all us old 'uns getting older.'

'That's true,' said Moira. 'When my generation has passed on there won't be any reason for the youngsters to get together.'

'Well, we ain't got that much in common,' said Andy.

'Don't know though, bruv. You was getting on really well with that Bridget. Thought you might have stayed over there, you both looked so cosy.'

'We were just being friendly.'

'Is that what you call it?'

'Take no notice of them,' said Moira. 'As Andy said, he was just being friendly.'

Mary looked at Andy and smiled. Why should she feel a pang of jealousy?

'Did you go out much?' asked Mary.

'Only to the pubs. Ireland's great for pubs,' said Brendan.

'I'm surprised you remember,' said his wife. 'Still, it was great seeing everybody again.'

After they finished tea, with all the usual chat and laughter, it was time for Mary to leave. She didn't want to, but time was getting on and it was very dark outside.

'I really must go,' she said at last.

'I'll walk you to the bus stop.'

'No. I'll be fine. It's too cold for you to hang about.'

'I insist.'

It was cold and icy underfoot and when Mary slipped Andy grabbed her arm.

'You see, you do need me. Mary, there's nothing between Bridget and me.'

'Andy, what you do with your life is up to you. You know I've got a boyfriend.'

'Yes. You did mention you wrote to a sailor. Is it serious?'

Mary couldn't answer that. 'I hope so.'

'Mary, I do like you. Like Dad, I think you've brought a breath of fresh air to Ma.'

Mary wanted to keep this conversation light. 'You sound like my mate. She's always talking like a book.'

'I do a lot of reading.'

'I gathered that from all the books in your house.'

'I shall be leaving soon to start getting the equipment ready for the new season. Could I write to you?'

'Of course. Do you think you'll be able to find out anything about that gypsy, what's her name?'

'Velma. I can't promise, after all it was a few years ago.'

'Will you be here next month when I come?'

'I'll try.'

Mary looked up. 'Look at all the stars, the sky seems full of them.'

'Look. Look.' Andy took her hand and pointed upwards. 'A shooting star. You must make a wish.'

Mary closed her eyes. There were so many things she wished for. 'Did you make a wish?' she asked Andy.

'Yes. I hope it comes true.'

When the bus came in sight Andy took her in his arms and kissed her lips. It was a warm, gentle kiss, and very unlike Billy's wild, searching kisses.

She sat on the bus and looked out on the cold night. She waved goodbye, then gently touched her lips. She liked Andy. He was different. He wasn't just some brash fairground bloke, he was warm and caring. She wondered what his wish had been . . .

The following day the country was stunned at the death of the King. For Mary it brought back so many memories of his Silver Jubilee and the aftermath of what happened on that day. Her thoughts went straight away to Ron. She felt full of guilt because she hadn't made an effort to find him. That made up her mind: on Wednesday afternoon she would go to Gosport to enquire about him.

It was a cold, blowy crossing. Mary hadn't been across the water before and had to keep asking directions as to where St Vincent's was. When she finally found it she was told by the sailor on the gate that they couldn't help her as most of the cadets were practising to accompany the King's coffin.

'If you'd like to leave your address, miss, I'll see what I can do.'

'Thank you.' Mary began writing on the paper he gave her.

'Long-lost boyfriend, is he?'

'No. He's the son of a friend of my mother's. I've just come to live down this way and I thought it would be nice to see him again.'

'I see.' As he took the paper his eyes had that I-don't-believe-you look. 'We get a lot of young ladies here looking for the father of their kids.'

'I can assure you I'm just a friend.'

He looked at the paper. 'See you're over Pompey way then.'

'Yes. Thank you very much.' As she walked away she didn't think for one moment she would ever see or hear from Ron again.

'Do you think Ron will get the message?' she asked Mrs Johns.

'I don't know, love. Let's hope the sailor passes on your

address, then who knows, perhaps one day he'll pay you a visit.'

'I hope so.'

January was a very sombre month. Every shop window was draped with black and pictures of the King. In fact even the weather matched the mood of the nation.

The following month Andy wasn't at home when Mary went on her usual visit to the Turners, as he and Mr Turner were beginning to get ready for Easter. She missed him but didn't know why. Was she falling for him? Or was it just because he was around, and Billy wasn't?

That week she'd had a letter from Billy to say his ship was coming home at the end of next month. She was overjoyed and wrote and told Liz. Liz wrote back saying she couldn't wait to see Pete again and hoped she could get some time off to come to Portsmouth. Mary knew Liz liked Pete, but how serious was their romance?

Everything was moving fast for Mary. Andy had written and told her nobody remembered anything about Velma. Although she was disappointed, it was still a lovely letter and Mary was able to show it to his mother. And at the end of that week in February, after she'd been to the Turners', Nurse Bentley came into the shop.

'It's so nice to see you again,' said Mary, genuinely pleased to see her. 'Have you any news about Daisy?'

'She's been moved to a sanatorium down Devon way.'

Mary felt sad. She knew now that she would never see her again.

'She has TB,' said Nurse Bentley.

'Will she ever get well?'

'I don't think so. The sad thing is that she's lost the will to live.'

Mary looked over at Mrs Warner, then at the clock. 'I'm very sorry about that. Could you wait till one when I'm at lunch? I have something to tell you.'

The nurse also looked at the clock. 'Half an hour. I should really be getting back. I'll hang on if it's that important.'

'Thank you.'

The next half-hour dragged for Mary. Would the nurse wait? She had to tell her about finding the gypsy.

At one o'clock on the dot Nurse Bentley walked back in. Mary looked up. 'Is it all right if I go off now?' she asked Mrs Warner.

'Of course. Just make sure you're back in half an hour.'

Mary smiled as she took off her overall and, rushing into the cloakroom, grabbed her hat, coat and handbag.

Outside Nurse Bentley asked, 'What's so important?'

'Shall we have a cuppa? It's warmer in there.' Mary steered her across the road and into the café where she ordered two teas. Mary feared that Jean might burst in on them so she had to get her piece over quick.

'I've found out about the gypsy Daisy gave her son to.'

Nurse Bentley looked stunned. 'How?'

'I've met some fairground people and the mother remembers a gypsy with a little boy and she said a woman gave him to her.'

'Are you sure they're not telling you a tale – you know, stringing you along?'

Mary felt deflated. 'Why should they?'

'I don't know. But what good would it do Daisy now? Have you spoken to this gypsy?'

Mary shook her head.

'I know you mean well, but it's too late now.' She drank her tea, and gathering up her bag, stood up. 'I'm sorry, Mary. But I do have Daisy's address, would you like it?'

357

Mary nodded, 'Yes, please,' and added softly, 'but will it be, worth writing to her?'

'I should think so. It'll be nice for her to know that you haven't forgotten her.'

Mary knew she would never forget Daisy. She was the reason Mary was here in Portsmouth.

'I'll pop it in the post for you sometime next week,' said Nurse Bentley as she collected her purchases and left.

Nurse Bentley was true to her word and a week later Mary had Daisy's address. However, although she wrote to her, she never expected – or received – a reply.

It was the middle of March. Mary was very excited. She'd had a letter from Billy telling her that the *Marley* would be home in just two weeks.

'I've got to get meself a new frock,' she said to Jean after she'd told her.

'I'm looking forward to meeting this bloke if he's anything like his photo.'

Mary smiled. 'He's even better than that.'

Liz had written and said she was going to take time off from work, but as they were coming into port on a Wednesday she could only come down for the day.

Mary was happy. Everything was going to be perfect.

# Chapter 39

When Mary went to see the Turners as usual on the last Sunday in March she knew that only Mrs Turner and Patrick would be there.

Mrs Turner sighed. 'Even after all these years I never really get used to Brendan being away. I really think he should start thinking of retiring soon.'

'Can't see Pa doing that – well, not just yet,' said Patrick. 'I'll be glad when I've finished school, then I can join Andy and Pa can retire.'

Moira smiled. 'That's what I'm waiting for as well. That and August bank holiday when they come to Portsmouth.'

Mary knew from the letter she'd had from Andy telling her that nobody could remember where Velma had gone to that he and Mr Turner were now in Kent. 'You've got a long wait,' said Mary.

'Yes, I have. Now, what about your news?'

Mary told them about Billy. 'According to the local paper his ship docks next Wednesday round about lunchtime. My friend's coming down from London to meet it.'

'So is he your boyfriend, then?' asked Moira.

Mary smiled and nodded. 'In a way, I suppose so, but I haven't seen him for ages. He's been in the Mediterranean Sea.'

'Is it serious?'

'I don't really know. He does write to me.' Mary wasn't going to admit that for a while now she'd only received postcards. And she didn't want to say too much, as she really didn't know what Billy's feelings towards her were.

'You say he lives near to where you used to live. Does that mean you'll be going away?'

'I shouldn't think so. I stayed with Liz – that's his sister – at Christmas, but it'd be a bit crowded if I was there now as well. Besides, he'll want to be with his family. And I don't think Mr Holt will let me have the time off.'

'That's a shame.'

'Billy said he'll have two weeks' leave. I'm hoping he might come down here and spend a few days with me.' Although Mary knew that could be wishful thinking on her part.

Although she liked Mrs Turner and felt at home with her, without Andy and Mr Turner around, somehow the visits weren't the same.

As she sat on the bus she found she was comparing Billy and Andy: they were so different. Billy was a rough diamond, brash and worldly; although Andy was brash at work, at home he was kind and considerate. Not that Billy didn't think the world of his family, but it was different somehow.

On Wednesday morning Mary took extra special care with what she was wearing and when she walked into the kitchen Mrs Johns smiled.

'Well, what do you think?' Mary asked as she twirled round in front of her. 'Will I do?'

'You look really lovely, my dear. Your young man should be very proud of you.'

'You haven't forgotten Liz will be coming to the shop first? She may not have time to come and see you.'

'As if I could. I'm not getting a meal for you tonight as you will probably eat out.'

'I'm so excited,' said Mary.

'I can see that. Now be off with you. And have a good time.'

'I don't know how I'm going to concentrate on work this morning. I hope I don't give anyone the wrong change.'

'Just as long as you don't give anyone the wrong ointment or pills!'

Mary laughed. 'Bye.' She picked up her handbag and left.

She had such a spring in her step. And she knew she was smiling at everyone. She didn't care. Today she was going to see her Billy and one o'clock couldn't come fast enough.

When Liz walked into the shop Mary's grin spread even wider. 'You look lovely,' she said, dashing round the counter and hugging her friend. 'Mr Holt said I can leave at twelve, so we should be able to see them come in.'

Mrs Warner was smiling. 'It's so nice to see you youngsters all dressed up. Cheering the ship home is great.'

At long last it was midday and Mary and Liz rushed out into the warm sunshine.

'Thank goodness it ain't raining,' said Liz. 'These shoes would probably fall apart if they got wet.'

Mary laughed. 'And my hair would hang down in rat's tails.' She held on to Liz's arm and squeezed it. 'I'm so happy. And it's so nice to have you here.'

'I only wish I could stay longer. You're so lucky living here. I really envy you.'

The smile left Mary's face. 'But don't forget, you've got your mum and dad there.'

'Yes, I have. Sorry about that.'

Mrs Johns had told them where to stand for the best view. As they were jostled by the crowd the atmosphere was exhilarating: you could almost feel the electric charge all around. Mary had never witnessed anything like this before. When the babies in their prams started yelling, mums stuffed dummies of sugar tied in cloths into their mouths to shut them up. Toddlers who were trying to escape from the leather reins keeping them in check were yanked off their feet unceremoniously, so the smaller ones dangled in the air. There were a few older couples patiently waiting too. One old man excitedly put an arm round his wife's shoulders to point out to sea and almost knocked her hat off. She straightened her hat and, dabbing at her eyes, turned and smiled affectionately up at him.

Mary swallowed hard. This was a wonderful sight.

The first excitement after the ship had been sighted died down as they waited while it was being manoeuvred into place. Then everybody was making their way to the dockyard entrance.

Sailors hurried down the gangplank into eager waiting arms, as wives, mothers, sisters and brothers all yelled out names as soon as they caught sight of their loved ones.

Liz was screaming out, 'Pete. Pete. Over here.'

He looked up and a grin spread across his tanned face as he raced towards Liz. Throwing his kit bag to the ground he swept her up in his arms and kissed her lips long and hungrily.

He then turned to Mary and, giving her a hug, kissed her cheek in a brotherly way. With his arm round Liz's waist he said, 'It's so lovely to see you both. God, how I've missed you.' He kissed Liz again.

'Where's Billy?' asked Mary, looking all around.

'He'll be off in a moment.'

She looked up and saw a tall handsome tanned sailor

coming towards them, grinning. His sailor's gait very pronounced.

'Billy.' She rushed over to him and threw her arms round his neck. Holding him tight, she kissed his lips long and hard.

'Hello, sis,' he said, breaking away from Mary and kissing Liz. 'You look good.'

'So do you,' said Liz, still holding on to Pete.

'Right, where shall we go?' asked Billy.

'I'd like to make my way home, if it's all the same to you, Liz,' said Pete.

Mary saw Liz's face drop.

'Couldn't you stop and have a drink or something?'

'I'd much rather get home.' He took her arm. 'Will you excuse us for a moment?' he asked Billy and Mary.

'Yes, of course,' said Billy as they moved away.

Mary could see Liz and Pete were immediately deep in conversation.

'So. This is a turn-up for the book, you living down here.'

'Yes, it is.'

'D'you know, your letters have been very interesting. Sorry I ain't been that good at answering them. D'you like the cards I sent?'

'They were lovely. I expect you're too busy to sit and write long letters.'

'Yer. That's true. Fancy that Dolly, is that her name?'

'No, Daisy.'

'Daisy could be related to your stepdad. What's he got to say about it? Has he been down to see her?'

'No. She's been moved to Devon now.'

'So there's nothing to stop you going back home then?'

'I don't think I could.'

'I reckon your old man would have you back now.'

Mary wasn't sure how much she'd told Billy, especially when she was feeling low and lonely and needed to pour out her woes.

'Right, that's settled,' said Pete, coming back up to them. 'What say we take the girls for a spot of lunch, then Liz and I must be off.'

'Sounds good to me. We can all travel to London together,' said Billy, picking up his kit bag and hoisting it on to his shoulder.

Mary could feel her jaw drop. But what else had she been hoping for? She knew they would be eager to get home to their families after all this time.

'Is that all right, Mary?' asked Liz.

Mary only nodded. She knew the right words wouldn't come.

They went to a café along the seafront. Everywhere was full of holidaymakers, sailors and their families. Everyone was happy and laughing, but as much as Mary tried, she couldn't join in the fun with very much enthusiasm, as she wanted to get Billy on his own. She wanted to be alone with him.

Pete couldn't take his eyes off Liz. Mary noted that Liz had a glow she'd never seen before. Was this really love?

'So what do you think then, Mary?' asked Liz.

'Sorry. I was miles away.'

'So I could see. I was saying, is there any chance of you coming up home for the weekend?'

'I have to work all day Sat'day. It could only be for a few hours on Sunday. Would that be all right?'

'We're due back on the sixteenth,' said Pete. 'So if you could make it say on . . .' He took a small book from his pocket. 'Sunday the twelfth, we could meet you at the station. Let Liz know what time train and we could all have a day in town. What do you say to that?'

'I could come up this Sunday.'

'I'll be busy,' said Liz. 'I'll be going over to Pete's place.'

'What about you, Billy, will you be around?' asked Mary.

'Don't know what Mum's got in store for us. No, as Pete said the Sunday after would be better all round.'

Mary was disappointed that Pete was making the suggestions and not Billy. Did he want to see her?

'If we meet you up West, that way you don't have to traipse all the way over to us.' Liz held on to Pete's arm and looked adoringly into his eyes.

Mary wasn't happy with the arrangements but it looked as if everything had been taken out of her hands.

All too soon Mary was at the station once again saying goodbye. Although Billy had walked along with his arm round her waist he seemed to be talking to Liz and Pete most of the time. When he kissed her it wasn't the wild passionate kiss she had known before. He hadn't said anything about coming down here to see her. She could feel the tears stinging her eyes but she wasn't going to cry. She wasn't going to let him know what effect he had on her. He was making it very obvious that he had cooled off; it almost seemed as if he was just being polite to please her.

Liz hugged her. 'It's been lovely seeing you again. I'm sorry we've got to rush off, but Pete has got quite a journey in front of him. I'll write when I get home. And, Mary, give Billy time.' She got on the train and waited by the open window.

Slowly the train moved away; she waved and Mary waved back. So even Liz had noticed Billy's indifference. Mary could feel the tears trickling down her cheeks. This wasn't how she'd planned it. This wasn't how she wanted it to be. If she were home she would be seeing much more of Billy. After all this time she was only going to see him for one day and then they would be in a foursome. She brushed her tears away. If she were still living in Rotherhithe things would have been so different. This was something else she could hate Ted for. She walked out of the station into the bright sunlight but a big black cloud had descended over her.

# Chapter 40

Mrs Johns looked up when Mary walked in and Mary could see the look of surprise on her face.

'Mary, I didn't expect . . .' She let her voice trail off when Mary's tears began to fall. 'My dear, whatever's happened?'

Mary sat at the table and, blowing her nose and dabbing away her tears, told Mrs Johns how disappointed she was that the others had gone home.

Mrs Johns patted her hand. 'Mary, you shouldn't get so upset. Don't forget the young man has been away for a long while. It's only natural that he should want to spend some time at home with his family.'

Mary sniffed into her handkerchief. 'I know. But I thought he might have said something about coming down here to see me. This is all Ted's fault.' She banged the table. 'I'd still be at home if it wasn't for him. I hate that man. I *hate* him.' Mary was angry, but also felt guilty: if she hadn't tried to be a Sherlock Holmes with that photograph she would still be at home.

'Now come on, Mary. This is not like you. I'm sure your young man will be here to see you one day.'

Mary wiped her eyes. 'I hope so.' But deep down Mary didn't hold out much hope.

★ ★ ★

The following morning at work Mary tried to be cheerful when she told Mrs Warner that after a meal they'd had together Billy had had to go home to see his parents.

'That's only natural; after all, he's been away a long while. When's he coming down to see you?'

Mary crossed her fingers behind her back. 'He's going to write and tell me.'

When Mary told Jean at lunchtime that she wouldn't be seeing Billy till that Sunday, Jean had that I-told-you-so look on her face.

'So you're going up next Sunday?'

'No, the Sunday after.'

'Cheer up. He might come down for this weekend if he gets fed up with being at home.'

'D'you think he might?'

'I don't know. I don't know the bloke. You know me. I'll say anything to see that miserable look wiped off your face.'

Mary smiled. 'Thanks. You're a real mate.'

Jean waved her spoon at Mary. 'And don't you ever forget it.'

Mary knew she would never forget Jean even when she was sailing the seven seas. They had a special bond.

On Sunday Mary didn't go out. She hung around the house all day hoping Billy would arrive out of the blue. But he didn't, so Monday was another miserable day for Mary.

After a full week without a letter from Billy, the following Saturday Mary walked back to the place she now called home thinking about what she was going to wear tomorrow. She'd written and told Liz she was catching an early train so they could spend all day together.

When Mary put her key in the door, she couldn't believe her eyes. There, resting on the hallstand, was a sailor's hat.

She burst into the kitchen and sitting at the table was Ron.

Mary tried hard to hide her first reaction of disappointment, even though she was pleased to see him. He jumped up and embraced her. He was now head and shoulders taller than her and very good-looking.

'Ron. Ron!' she cried and, holding him at arm's length, asked, 'How are you? Why haven't you written?'

'I'm fine. As you can see I got your note with your address on. I was so surprised you're down here. I'm sorry I've not been in touch before but they do keep us busy. I was given your note when we got back from London. I kept it and now I decided to pay you a visit.' He quickly glanced at Mrs Johns. 'I hope that's all right?'

'Course it is,' said Mary. 'I'm so pleased to see you. I was a bit worried that bloke might not have passed it on to you.'

'Look, why don't you both go into the front room,' interjected Mrs Johns. 'I expect you've got plenty to talk about. I'll bring you in some tea.'

'Thanks.' Mary gathered up her hat and coat. 'I'll just take these upstairs.'

She threw her clothes on the bed and rushed back down. 'Now, tell me all that's happened to you,' she said, plonking herself down next to him.

'Mary, first could you tell me if the kids and Mum are all right.'

As Mrs Johns brought in the tea she quickly looked at Mary. 'I'll let you see to it, Mary.'

As Mary poured out the tea she swallowed hard. 'Ron, I don't know about the kids, but—'

'Course,' said Ron, slapping his forehead with his hand. 'I'm daft. Course you don't know if you live down here.' He looked at her quizzically. 'Why do you live down here? Have you run away?'

She nodded. 'Well, got thrown out really.'

Ron looked alarmed. 'Was it because of me?'

'No, Ron. Please let me finish.'

'Sorry.'

'I can't tell you anything about the kids, but, Ron,' she said softly, 'your mum's dead.'

'No. How? Not me mum. Me poor mum. She had so much to put up with.'

Mary didn't interrupt as he silently wept.

After a while he lifted his head and asked softly, 'How did she die?'

'From her injuries.'

'So where'd the kids finish up?'

Ron was silent all the time Mary went into the details of what had happened.

'So you see my mum was heartbroken when they came and took the kids away.'

Ron put his head in his hands. 'What am I gonner do,' he whispered.

Mary put her arm round his shoulder. 'Nothing. We've just got to hope that Rosie will write to my mum one day. Your mum would be so very proud of you. Look at you, you're not that skinny kid next door, in fact you're quite a handsome young man now. I'll bet you'll soon have all the girls running after you.'

His eyes sparkling with tears, Ron managed a slight grin and ran his fingers through his hair. He then sat back with a serious look on his face. 'What can I do? How can I find out where they took the kids?'

'I don't know.'

Mary could see Ron was deep in thought.

'We have a padre, perhaps I could talk to him.'

Mary considered this young man. He had grown not only

in stature but in mind as well. Fancy Ron Fellows talking about going to see a priest. He was so different to the frightened boy she had brought to Portsmouth. He was now a man.

'I don't want the kids to think I've let them down. I've wanted to go and see them so many times. I wanted to write to them but knew I couldn't. Was it wrong of me? Was I being selfish?'

'Course not. Remember this was what your mother wanted for you.'

'I still can't bear to think of that night, you know. When I was in London for the King's funeral, I kept thinking about the Jubilee. I'm told that sometimes I talk in my sleep.'

'You must try to put it out of your mind.'

'D'you think Rosie ever talks about me?'

'I would think so but only to the others, she knew she wasn't to tell anyone that she's got an older brother.'

'She's a good kid.'

'You were all very close.'

'They wasn't bad kids. Why did Mum have to marry a bloke like that?'

'I think they call it love.'

'I would have thought he knocked all the love out of her.'

Mary could see he was getting very sad so she asked, 'Ron, are you enjoying being in the navy?'

At that, a smile lifted his troubled face. 'I should say so. It's the best thing I've ever done, but I don't know how I'll feel if we go to war.'

Mary was taken aback. Although she had seen all the trouble in Europe on the newsreels, she'd never thought about war. 'You don't think there'll be another war, do you?'

'Wouldn't like to say. But we have to be prepared.'

Mary sat back and let her thoughts come out loud. 'Ted

was always talking about the possibility of war.'

'Never really liked that bloke. I can't believe he chucked you out.'

'That's all in the past now.'

'And this woman in the photograph, do you think she's a relation of your dad's?'

'She must be. Otherwise he would have told Mum about her.'

'I bet you miss young Eddie.'

'Yes, I do. I expect he's grown. He still don't talk though.'

'That was a shame.' Ron smiled. 'He was a funny little thing.'

'Where do you live?' Mary asked him.

'Over the water in Gosport. I've met some smashing blokes. I tell you, Mary, I've learned things I couldn't even have imagined before. I'm surprised me brain ain't bursting with all I'm pushing into it.'

They sat talking for hours. Mrs Johns brought them sandwiches and more tea and only when darkness fell did Ron say he had to get back.

At the door Mary held him close. 'Please keep in touch.'

'I won't promise. I'm not very good at that sort of thing.'

'Give me your service number and if Mum ever hears anything from Rosie I can always get in touch.'

'Thanks.' He quickly kissed her cheek and left.

Mary stood at the door and watched him walk down the street. Somehow she knew that would be the last she would ever see of Ron Fellows. Although he was troubled about the kids he knew he had to leave his past behind him. And if he saw Mary she would be a constant reminder of that dreadful night.

She closed the front door.

After a fitful night Mary was up early the following morning. All night Ron had filled her mind. But today all she could think about was Billy.

It was almost eleven o'clock when the train snaked its way into Waterloo Station. Mary stood at the door eagerly looking for Billy. The first person she saw was Liz. She scrambled off the train and rushed up to give her a hug.

'It's lovely to see you,' said Liz.

'And you. Where's Billy?'

'He's gonner meet us up West. Pete will be there as well.'

'Have you seen much of Pete?'

'Yes. In fact he's been staying at our place for a few days.'

'That's nice. So it looks like this is the real thing then.'

Liz put her arm through Mary's. 'Before we go down the Underground I've got something to tell you.'

Mary stopped dead. This was it. This was what she was dreading. Billy didn't want to see her any more. All these years of hoping and waiting . . .

'Mary, you all right? You've gone ever such a funny colour.'

'I'll go back. I don't see the point in staying up here if he don't want to see me. Why didn't he write and tell me instead of dragging me all the way up here?' Mary's voice was rising with anxiety.

'Mary, what's wrong with you? It ain't nothing to do with you and Billy; well, it is in a way. You see, me and Pete are getting married.'

'What?'

'Me and Pete are going to get married.' Liz was grinning as she said it again, very slowly and very precisely.

'Oh Liz. When?'

'Oh his next leave. So today you are here to celebrate our engagement.'

'Have you got a ring?'

373

Liz removed her glove and wiggled her fingers. 'Mary, I'm so happy.'

'A sapphire and two diamonds, it's beautiful.' Mary hugged her friend tight once more. 'I'm so pleased for you.'

'Who knows. It could be your turn next.'

Mary felt her knees go weak. Was Billy also planning to propose? As they walked along the long Underground corridors and down the escalators, Mary's head was in the clouds. By tonight, she might be an engaged woman.

# Chapter 41

Mary's heart was beating like a hammer as she and Liz emerged from the Underground.

'Look, there they are,' said Liz, pointing.

Mary could see Billy was busy talking to Pete. She was hoping that when Billy caught sight of her he would rush towards her and, sweeping her up in his arms, smother her face with kisses.

He turned and grinned and as she got near to him he said casually, 'So you made it all right then.'

'Yes, thanks.'

'Hello, Mary. Good journey?' Pete asked, giving her cheek a kiss.

'Not bad.' She stood close to Billy hoping he too would kiss her, but he didn't. He appeared distant and ill at ease.

They went to a posh place near Hyde Park for a meal and towards the end Mary asked Liz, 'When's the great day going to be?'

'I want to be a June bride,' said Liz.

'June this year?'

Liz nodded.

'But that's only a couple of months away.' Mary was stunned.

'Yes, we know.'

'What's your mum and dad got to say about this?' she asked.

'Mum and Dad are really pleased. Although I expect Mum will have a few tears on the day.'

'And I can assure you, Mary, that my mother and father are equally thrilled. They think the world of Liz.' Pete smiled at his bride-to-be and kissed her hand.

Mary wanted to cry. Not that she was jealous: she was thrilled for them. They both looked so happy. 'Will your ship be here in June?' she asked hopefully. If it was then that meant Billy would still be around.

'No. I'm leaving that ship. I'm going on a course to become an officer.'

'Always said you was officer material,' said Billy.

'That's why we can't wait. We want to get married before Pete gets another ship, so we can have some time together before he goes away again. It could be for a long while.'

Mary looked at Liz. Her eyes were shining with love.

'We've settled for June twenty-seventh. You will be me bridesmaid, won't you?' asked Liz. 'I couldn't bear to get married without you with me. I'm having Elsie and Sue as well. Not sure what colour yet.'

'Course. I'll ask for that day off as soon as I get back to work.'

'Mary, I was wondering if your mum would make me frock. I know how good she was at making your clothes.'

'I don't know. You'd have to go round there for fittings.'

'That should be all right. I'd want her to make me brides-maids' frocks as well.'

'Now that might be a bit awkward as far as I'm concerned.'

'Well, I'll go and see her and find out how she feels about it first, before we start making any decisions.'

For the next couple of hours they laughed and talked.

Mary noted that although Billy joined in there was definitely a coolness about him.

When she and Liz were in the Ladies, Mary asked, 'Liz, what's wrong with Billy? Why is he ignoring me?'

'Are you sure? I don't think he is. It's probably my fault for taking over the conversation. Look, I'll get Pete and we'll go for a walk and leave you two alone, how would that be?'

'Great.'

'What time train're you catching?'

'Dunno. About seven, eight, I ain't that worried.'

'We'll meet you back here at, say, five? Will that do? That gives you a couple of hours to be with Billy on your own.'

Mary smiled. 'Thanks, Liz.'

'Right, that's settled.' With that Liz went and had a quiet word with Pete.

'We're going to leave you two in peace for a while,' said Pete. 'We'll meet you back here at about five. We can have a bite to eat and that will give you plenty of time to catch your train, Mary. Is that all right?'

'That's fine,' said Mary, looking at Billy.

Liz kissed Mary's cheek, took Pete's arm and they walked away.

'They seem very happy,' said Mary.

'Yer. He's a great bloke. She's done all right for herself.'

'Shall we have a walk round the park?'

'If you want.'

There was no walking along arm-in-arm; in fact they ambled apart in silence. Inside the park Mary stopped at a bench 'Shall we have a sit-down? Good job it's not raining.' She was trying hard to keep the conversation going but his silence was driving her mad.

'Billy.'

'Mary.'

They both spoke at once.

'You first,' said Mary.

Billy looked down at his hands. 'I feel awful about this.'

'You don't have to. I'll make it easier for you. I know you don't want to be here with me. I wish you'd said something in your letters. Although I ain't had many of those, but thanks anyway for the cards.' Mary was getting angry; she was also hurt. Why had she been wasting her time mooning over someone who clearly didn't want her? 'Why, Billy? What have I done?'

'Mary, I do like you.'

'Well, you've certainly got a very funny way of showing it.'

'I'm sorry.'

'So what is it about me that has made you . . .' Mary couldn't find the right word. 'Is it because . . . you know, I won't let you do it?'

'No. Well, not now. I feel rotten saying this. Mary, I really like you. You're fun and I know you are a very caring person.' He stopped and lit a cigarette. 'I'm finding this very hard.'

Mary stood up. 'Don't bother making excuses. I know you don't care for me. Have you found someone else?'

'No. Please sit down.' He took a long drag on his cigarette. 'You see, it's like this. We've got a bloke on board and his wife's younger brother is a bit, well, mental.'

Mary looked at him in astonishment. 'So what—'

'Let me finish. He had a letter while we were away to say his wife is now in an asylum. He said it was hereditary. I was telling him about your brother and he told me to be careful as it could happen to you, or any kids you might have.'

Mary sat back down with her mouth open.

'So you see when you was staying with me mum I was worried. I thought that before you thought . . . you know?'

'No, I don't know.'

'This is very awkward for me. I thought that, before we got too involved, it'd be better if we, well, you know, just drifted apart.'

'I don't believe what you've just said. I can't believe you'd listen to a lot of gossip. You're worse than a load of old women.'

'I am sorry, Mary. I do like you.'

She stood up again. 'Well, at least I found out before I got too fond of you.' She went to walk away but Billy held on to her arm.

'Let go of me.' She shrugged his arm away.

'Mary, I am sorry.'

'Tell Liz I'll write to her.'

'Where are you going?'

'Back to Portsmouth. There's nothing for me here.' As she quickly walked away, tears stung the backs of her eyes, but she wasn't going to cry. She wouldn't let him see how much he'd hurt her. Billy made no attempt to follow her or beg her to come back. Would this be the story of her life now? Would nobody ever care for her? It was so unfair. If Eddie's condition was hereditary, it was probably from Ted's side of the family, not her mother's. There was no reason she should ever carry it. But she wasn't going to tell Billy that. He obviously had never cared for her the way she'd cared for him.

On the train Mary's thoughts had been turning over and over. Why hadn't she cried? Was this something that deep down she'd been expecting?

When she stepped off the train there had been an April shower and everywhere looked clean and fresh and glistened in the sunlight. She didn't want to go back to Mrs Johns just yet. There would be so many questions as to why she was back so early when Mary had told her not to wait up as she could be back late. So she made her way along the seafront; the sound of the surf was always comforting.

Liz opened the front door and, when she saw Billy's cap hanging on a hook in the passage, went storming into the kitchen. 'And where the bloody hell did you get to?'

The whole family looked up.

'What's wrong, love?' asked her mother.

'I don't know. Ask him. We waited for them to come back and they didn't turn up.' She pointed at Billy, who was sitting at the table. 'What happened to Mary?'

'She went back to Portsmouth.'

'Why?'

'Liz, for Christ's sake sit down and stop shouting,' said her father.

'I want to know what he said to Mary to make her go off like that without saying goodbye.'

'We had a few words.'

'You mean you've dumped her?'

Billy looked embarrassed. 'What I do is me own business.'

Liz was angry and she wasn't going to let it rest. 'Is it because she won't let you get inside her knickers?'

Elsie and Susan giggled behind their hands.

'Liz, I think you and Billy had better go in the front room and sort this thing out,' said her mother sternly.

Liz looked at Billy. 'Come on. I want an answer.'

He followed her into the front room.

'Well?' said Liz, standing at the door like a sentry.

'It's no good you getting on yer high horse. What I do is me own business. If I don't fancy a girl, well, then that's up to me.'

'But I thought you liked Mary?'

'I did – do. But I don't want to tie her to me. Not with the sort of life I lead.'

Liz glared at him for a moment longer, then suddenly sat down. 'I'm sorry. Yes, I suppose you're right, it is your business, but I'm very fond of Mary and I don't like to see her hurt. She's had more than enough trouble already.'

'And I don't want to hurt her, but I think she was looking for more than just being friends. I stopped writing letters a while back hoping she'd get the hint.'

'But you still sent her cards.'

'Yes, cos she said she liked them and wanted to see some of the places we went to. I'm really sorry, Liz. Will you write and tell her?'

Liz nodded. 'Not got a lot of choice, have I?'

'I'll always like her and I hope she finds another bloke soon.'

'Come on, let's go and have a cuppa.'

Billy smiled as they went back into the kitchen.

# Chapter 42

Mrs Johns was her usual sympathetic self when Mary told her that she was back early as Billy was busy with his family.

'So what time will the young man's ship go on Thursday?'

'I don't know. I didn't ask as I won't be able to see him off, I'll be in the shop all day.'

'That's a shame. Don't worry, he might pop in during your lunchtime.'

'I hope so,' Mary said to ease the situation, although at that moment she didn't really care. As far as she was concerned it was over. Mary went on to tell Mrs Johns about the wedding and how she was going to be bridesmaid.

'Never been one before: I'm so excited. And if me mum makes the frocks, that'll be really great.'

'So is your mother good with a needle?'

'Yes. She used to make all me clothes.'

'Could do with someone like that round here. Dressmakers are like gold dust, and they charge the earth.'

When Mary went to work she knew she would be asked questions about Billy. She told them the same as she had Mrs Johns, that she'd had a lovely day, then added more about how excited she was over Liz's forthcoming wedding.

'Is it possible that I could have that Saturday off?' she asked Mr Holt tentatively.

'I think that could be arranged. What do you say, Mrs Warner, could you manage without Mary for one day?'

She smiled. 'I think that would be all right. The customers will just have to wait that little bit longer.'

Mary could have kissed them. That was the first hurdle over. Now, if her mum made the frocks then that would be a bonus. Despite losing Billy, Mary had a defiant spring in her step and couldn't wait to tell Jean all her news.

That same evening, Sarah was waiting for Ted to come home when a knock on the front door startled her. Ted always used the key. She looked up at the clock. It had gone eight. Ted was late. As she hurried along the passage she hoped it wasn't someone with bad news.

'Liz!' she said on opening the door. Sarah stepped forward and looked up and down the street.

'It's all right, Mrs Harding. I'm alone.'

'Mary. My Mary. Is there something wrong? Has something happened to her?'

'No, she's fine.'

Sarah was flustered. 'I'm sorry. I can't ask you in. What do you want?'

'I've come round to ask you if you still do a bit of dressmaking?'

'I do if I'm asked. But not many round here can afford to have things made.'

Liz smiled. 'I'm getting married and was wondering if you'd make me frock?'

'That's very kind of you to think of me.'

'I always remember how well dressed Mary was and I thought of you.'

'Thank you. But I don't know. It could be very awkward.'

'That's all right. I understand. I just thought . . . It doesn't matter.' Liz turned to go.

Sarah put out her hand. 'No, wait just a moment. Who will you have as bridesmaids?'

Liz grinned. 'Me sisters and me best mate, Mary, of course.'

'That's lovely. I would dearly love to make it, but it could be very difficult.' Her eyes lit up. 'But it would mean I would get to see Mary again.'

'As you say, it might be difficult, but I'm sure we could get round that. So what do you say?'

'Of course I'll have to ask Ted. I'll let you know. Will that be all right?'

'Yes.'

'I'm sorry I can't ask you in, you see I'm expecting him home any minute.'

'That's all right, I understand.'

'So when's the wedding?'

'June.'

'June!' repeated Sarah. 'That's not long.'

'I know.'

'So who's the lucky man?'

'Pete. He's on my brother's ship.'

'How is your brother?'

'He's fine.'

'Is he still seeing Mary?'

'I think it's cooled off a bit now.'

'That's a shame. She was very fond of him. Have you seen her lately?'

'Yes, she was up here on Sunday.'

Sarah was really upset. Her daughter had been here in

London and she hadn't seen her. Mary never even said she was coming.

'I'd better be going. You've got my address; you can always pop round to Mum during the day if you want to. Anyway, let me know what you want to do.'

'Yes, I will. Thank you. Bye.' Sarah watched Liz go and after she closed the front door her spirits soared. If she made the frocks she would get to see Mary. Somehow she had to persuade Ted that this would be a good thing for her to do. He didn't have to know who it was for or that Mary was going to be her bridesmaid. She could do the fittings round at Liz's.

For the first time in months Sarah began singing along with the wireless.

As Liz walked away she thought how sad it was to see Mary's mother, who used to be such a strong woman, so thin and old-looking. She must always be in fear of that husband of hers. Fancy having to ask him if she could make a wedding dress. Mary must really be worried about her. But what could she do? Mary had told Liz that she could never manage to look after her mother and Eddie. Not on her wages. Liz was still mad at Billy for letting Mary down, but perhaps it was for the best. He couldn't have cared for her that much, but she knew there was more to it than what he'd told her. She was sure Mary would tell her one day. Liz let a little smile lift her face. If Mrs Harding did make her frock then Mary would see her mum. It was a pity that Billy would be back at sea when the great day came and couldn't be Pete's best man: it would have been lovely to see Mary and Billy walk back down the aisle together. Liz glanced up at the sky: it had darkened and it looked like rain, but then it was April, after all.

Sarah waited till Ted had finished his meal and she had

cleared the table before she broached the subject. He was sitting in the armchair reading his newspaper when she said casually, 'Ted, a young lady came round here today to ask if I would make her wedding dress.'

'And?'

'I said I would have to ask you before I committed myself.' Sarah had her fingers crossed behind her back.

He put his paper down. 'Thanks. That makes me sound a right tyrant. What did she say?'

'She's waiting for an answer.'

'I see. Do we know this young woman?'

'No.'

'So how does she know you used to make clothes?'

'Her mother has seen some of my work.'

'Where do they live?'

Sarah knew she would be asked a lot of questions so she was ready with the answers. 'They come from Southwark. They used to live round this way years ago.'

'Don't they have any dressmakers round Southwark way?'

Sarah smiled at him sweetly. 'I expect they do, but she wants me to make it and her bridesmaids' dresses as well. I shall really enjoy doing it. It'll keep me occupied.'

'Well, I suppose it'll be all right. As long as you don't neglect any housework or my meals.' He pointed his finger at her. 'And I don't want to find pins and bits of material all over the place.'

'Don't worry. I'll work in the front room.' Sarah went into the scullery hardly able to control her excitement over her good fortune.

It was the last Sunday in the month and as usual Mary was going to see Mrs Turner. She knocked on the door of their cottage. 'Andy!' she said when the door was opened. 'What a lovely surprise. I didn't expect to see you. Is everything all right?'

'Mary.' He smiled briefly. 'Come in. Ma's not here. Sorry I ain't had a chance to write to you.'

Mary could see he looked troubled. 'What's happened? What are you doing home?'

'Mary, there's been an accident.'

'Oh no. Where's your mother? Is she badly hurt?'

'It's not Ma, it's Pa. That's why I'm here. A week ago some yobs loosened some of the bolts on the equipment overnight and when we started the ride up as we always do at the beginning of the day one of the chains broke and a chair swung and hit Pa in the back and legs.'

Mary felt the blood drain from her face. 'Andy, I'm so sorry.'

'In some ways it was a good thing it happened when it did. It would have been disastrous if there had been a lot of people around. The police are looking into it, but I don't think they'll find them.'

'That's awful. How is your pa? Is he badly hurt?'

'He's got lots of fractures, legs mostly; it's going to be a long job.'

'I am sorry. Where is he?'

'Kent. I've come here to look after Patrick while Ma's at the hospital with him.'

'Will he be all right?'

'He won't ever work again. We just hope he'll be able to walk again.'

Mary choked back a sob. She loved these people. 'Andy, I'm so sorry. Your ma was so looking forward to him retiring as well.'

'Well, that's it now. Fairground work's definitely finished for him.'

'What about you?'

'I don't know at the moment. I'm too worried about Pa. It won't be so bad when he's home, but Ma's in a bit of a state.'

'I expect she is. Is there anything I can do to help around the house?'

He smiled. 'Thanks, but being on the road all summer and living in a van you do get very efficient at things like washing and ironing and even cooking.'

'Well, remember, I'm only just down over the hill. So if you want anything drop me a line, or if I give you the shop's phone number you can always phone me. Mr Holt won't mind.'

'Thanks. I told Ma not to worry.'

'Could I have her address? Then I can write and tell her how well you're managing. By the way, where's Patrick?'

'He's gone off for the day with some of his mates. He's trying to put on a brave face, but I think he's taking it very hard. He's worried that his future working the rides is over.'

'Is that such a bad thing?'

'No, not for him. He's a very intelligent young man. I'm sorry, I haven't even offered you a cup of tea.'

'I'll make it.'

'No, you're a guest in this house, but you can come into the kitchen and talk to me. So what have you been up to lately?'

Mary stood in the kitchen and told him about Liz's forthcoming wedding. She also mentioned that she and Billy had finished.

Andy put the teapot down. 'Did he say why?'

Mary nodded. She felt relaxed with him and knew she could tell him. 'He said he was worried that what was wrong with my brother could be catching or hereditary.'

Andy laughed. 'I'm sorry. He don't know much, does he?'

Mary smiled. 'I think it was just an excuse to dump me.'

She was surprised how easy it was to admit this to Andy.

He came over to her and held her at arm's length. 'Don't he realise what a great girl you are?'

'Thanks.' Mary felt a tingle but she still moved away. 'But there it is, it's all over now.'

Andy stepped back. 'Well, he's the loser. Are you sorry?'

'In a way. I was very fond of him and had lots of silly schoolgirl ideas about my future with him. But I've grown up a bit since then.'

Andy didn't comment.

For Mary there was something warm and comforting about Andy.

'I am looking forward to Liz's wedding though. I'm going to be her bridesmaid and the best part is that me mum's going to make the frocks. So I'll be able to see her again.'

'What about your stepfather, won't he object?'

'I'm sure Mum and Liz will work it out.'

All afternoon they talked. Mary laughed when they sat down to tea. It wasn't quite the same as when Moira was in charge.

'So where are the delicate sandwiches and fancy cakes?'

'I said I could manage, but this is man's stuff.'

'I am enjoying it though, just the same.' Mary was happy being here with just Andy and asked, 'Would you like me to come here next Sunday? Or better still, why don't you come down to me and we can have a picnic. Bring Patrick, I'm sure he'll enjoy himself.'

'That's a great idea. I'll bring—'

Mary stopped him. 'No. This is my treat. Kind of my way of saying thank you for all the lovely weekends I've had here with you and your family.'

Andy grinned. 'And there was me hoping it was me you came to see.'

'I'm always pleased to find you here.'

'That's good.' Andy sat back and, putting his plate down, said, 'Mary, I know this is a bit soon, but I'd really like to take you out sometime. You know, on a proper date. What do you think?'

Mary blushed. 'I'd be very happy to go out with you. But not because you feel sorry for—' She didn't finish as Andy was about to kiss her – when the back door burst open and Patrick came barging in. 'Hello, Mary. Cor, we've had a great game over in the woods. Tea ready, bruv?'

Mary grinned as they quickly moved apart.

'I've saved you some sandwiches,' said Andy, obviously annoyed.

'Good. I'm starving. It's rotten luck about Pa,' he said to Mary with his mouth full of sandwich.

'Yes, it is. Let's hope he's home soon,' said Mary.

'He won't be happy stuck in all the time. And I don't reckon Ma will be all that pleased to have him under her feet.'

'I don't know. She'll be happy to have him around.'

Patrick shrugged. 'Let's hope he won't be too much of a pain.'

When it was time for her to go Andy said, as they walked to the bus stop, 'Don't take too much notice of Patrick. He's young and they talk before they think. When he sees Pa he'll realise just how close we were to losing him.'

'Sometimes boys talk like that to hide their true feelings.'

Andy stopped. 'Mary, I don't want to hide my true feelings about you. I know you've just finished with Billy and I don't want you to think I'm sweeping you off your feet on the rebound. But I am very fond of you and I'd like you to be my girl. You don't have to answer me today, but please, think about it.'

Mary stood and looked at him. 'Andy. I do like you. And I

would be very flattered to be your girl.'

'You mean it? You really mean it?'

She nodded.

He took her in his arms and kissed her. This time it was long, hard and passionate.

When they broke apart Andy let out a loud yell.

'Shh,' said Mary. 'People will look.'

'I don't care.'

When the bus came along Andy kissed her again.

As was their custom now, she sat on the bus and waved till he was out of sight. She did like him and she knew it wasn't on the rebound. He knew all about her family and he wasn't worried; he was kind, gentle and a considerate person and it wouldn't be hard to love him. She felt a warm glow inside. Life has a funny way of turning things round and in this case it was for the better. She couldn't wait till next Sunday when she would be seeing him again.

# Chapter 43

At lunchtime on Monday Mary was eager to tell Jean all that had happened yesterday. Mrs Johns and Mrs Warner had been very sorry to hear about Mr Turner and angry that young men would put people's lives in danger with some silly prank.

Mary sat at the window of the café. She was worried and a little cross that Jean was late, especially as she had so much to tell her.

As last Jean appeared, flushed and breathless. 'Sorry I'm late but something rather exciting has happened,' she said as she sat at the table.

'That's good. I've got such a lot to tell you as well,' said Mary.

'So go on, what's your news first?'

'You sure? You seem to be in a bit of a state.' Jean did appear to be on edge.

Jean managed to grin. 'I want you to savour mine.'

'I went to see the Turners yesterday.'

'So what's new about that?'

'Mr Turner's had a bad accident.' Mary then went on to tell her about her day and what had happened to Mr Turner, but she omitted to tell her that Andy had asked her to be his girlfriend. She didn't want Jean to think she was jumping out of the frying pan and into the fire.

'And Andy's home? How're they going to manage for money?'

'I don't know. I didn't ask. We're taking Patrick to the beach on Sunday for a picnic. Fancy coming with us?'

'Could do.'

'So what's your news then?' asked Mary.

Jean leaned forward. 'Well, it's not really settled yet; Mr Palmer and his friend are trying to pull a few strings for me. But . . .' Mary could see Jean's eyes were sparkling; she could hardly sit still. 'You know about this new big ship we've been seeing on the newsreels, the *Queen Mary*? Well, he knows the photographer who's going to be on it and they're putting in a good word for me to be his assistant!'

Mary sat back dumbfounded. She'd never really thought this would happen. She always thought it was Jean's pipe-dream. 'You're going on that?'

Jean nodded. 'I hope so. I'm *so* excited about it.'

'When does it go off?'

'It's having its maiden voyage from Southampton to New York at the end of next month. I can't believe it. I feel like running up and down Commercial Road yelling: I'm going to New York!'

'What do your mum and dad have to say about it?'

'They don't know yet. I only found out this morning. That's why I'm late. You see, when Mr Collins, he's the one that's going to be the photographer on board, came in to see Mr Palmer – they're old friends – I was telling him that was my ambition and he said he was looking for an assistant and he invited me along. He's got to sort it out with Cunard, but he don't think there'll be any problems.'

'Mr Palmer don't mind losing you then?'

'I don't think he was very happy about it at first, but I

know he's going to help and give me a good reference. Are you happy for me?'

'Of course I am. I don't want to sound a wet blanket, but what if he can't pull any strings?'

'If I can't get on this trip there'll be plenty of others. At least I could have my foot in the door.'

'What about the assistant this Mr Collins must have already?'

'She's married and don't want to leave her family, I'm glad to say. Although I think she's daft. This is a job of a lifetime. Think of all the rich people I'll meet and Mr Collins reckons we'll be photographing a lot of the film stars when they come over. Mary, I'm so excited. I can't believe this is really happening to me, I keep pinching meself. Just think, I could have gone off with Danny; now that would have been a total disaster.'

Mary smiled at her friend. Of course she was happy for her, but she would still miss her like mad.

Come Sunday, Mary was trying hard to keep her feelings under control. She and Andy were going to the beach.

'Will it be warm enough to sit on the beach?' asked Mrs Johns as she watched Mary prepare the picnic of cheese and pickle and ham and tomato sandwiches, wrapped in grease-proof paper. She added three pieces of home-made fruit cake.

'I'll wrap up.' Although it was early May it was springlike and mild.

'Now you're sure you're taking enough food? I know how much these young boys eat.'

Mary nodded. 'Yes, thanks. It'll be a nice change for me to feed them. I'd better be off. I said I'd meet them at the pier at eleven.'

'Have a good time,' said Mrs Johns when Mary picked up her basket.

As Mary walked along she felt like smiling at everyone. She was going to see Andy and they were going to spend the whole day together. She knew now she could love him.

Andy's face lit up when he caught sight of Mary. Rushing over to her, he hugged her and kissed her on the lips.

'Come on, you two,' said Patrick. 'I hope you ain't gonner be doing that all day?'

Mary pulled away and blushed. 'Hello Patrick.'

Andy took her basket and they walked along the seafront. When they found the right spot they sat on the beach and had their picnic.

'That was good,' said Patrick, jumping up when he declared he was full. 'I'm going for a paddle, coming?'

'No thanks,' said Andy.

They sat watching Patrick running in and out of the sea and telling them how cold the water was.

'You won't catch me in there,' said Andy.

'Nor me,' laughed Mary.

As the afternoon wore on they talked about so many things. There was never a lull in their conversation.

When the sun began to sink, Mary didn't want this perfect day to end. The deck-chair attendant started to collect the chairs and stack them for the night, and for her it was over all too soon.

'I'm really sorry, but I'll have to get back,' said Andy. 'Patrick has to go to school tomorrow and I've got to make sure everything is ready for him.'

Mary touched his hand. 'That's all right. I have enjoyed myself. I wonder why Jean didn't come?'

'Are you sorry?'

Mary shook her head.

'Mary, I don't know what's going to happen. I don't know where I'll be. I'll write and keep you informed.' He held her hand and looked towards his brother. 'I wish we were alone then I'd kiss you.'

'I'd like that.'

He gently squeezed her hand and putting it to his lips, kissed it. Mary had a wonderful sensation that she had never felt with Billy. This really must be true love.

Jean was full of apologies the next day when she dashed into the café. 'I'm so sorry, but me sister came for the day and Mum said I shouldn't go off as I was going away and I should stay and talk to them. I wasn't very pleased about it, I can tell you. I would much rather have been with you. Did you have a nice time?'

'It was fine.'

'Did you miss me?'

'Course,' said Mary, but she hoped it didn't sound too half-hearted.

It was two weeks later that Jean heard she had been accepted for the job. Over the following weeks Jean was constantly on the move and making endless lists and all the time she wanted Mary at her side to help her choose the things she would need. First there was the passport to get, then she could think about clothes.

'What do you think of this?' she asked Mary when they were searching through the clothes rack one lunchtime.

'Do you have to dress up?'

'Yes. Mr Collins said I've got to get evening frocks. I've got to look the part when we take their photos when they go into dinner.'

'Do you sit with the people?'

'No. We eat with the crew.'

'It sounds so exciting, Jean. I really envy you.'

'I'm so glad me dad's helping me out with the money.'

Mary smiled. She was pleased she'd learned how to stand on her own two feet.

Mary had written to Mrs Turner and told her all the news about Liz getting married and Jean going off on the *Queen Mary*. She had replied telling her that Brendan was hoping to come out of hospital sometime in June. She did say things would be hard for them at first, but thank goodness they lived in a cottage with no stairs. Mary had been seeing Andy every Sunday and knew she was getting very fond of him. Liz had written and told her the bridesmaids' dresses were going to be blue. Her mother had also written and asked for all her measurements. Life for Mary was moving at such a fast pace. Then all too soon it was 27 May – the day the *Queen Mary* was leaving Southampton with Jean on board.

They had hugged and kissed and cried on the last night they were together.

'Don't worry, I'll keep a diary so when I get back I can tell you everything that happens,' said Jean, wiping her eyes once again. 'And I may even be back before Liz's wedding. It don't take that long to cross the Atlantic.'

'I can't believe you're really going.'

'Neither can I. Me mum and dad are coming to the docks with me. I wish you was coming as well.'

'So do I, even though it's on Wednesday. I'd never get to Southampton in time and I can't ask for time off, not with the wedding only a month away and Mr Holt letting me have that Sat'day off.'

'I do understand.'

'You make sure you stand close to the rail and wave hard so I'll be able to pick you out on the newsreel next week.'

Jean laughed. 'I'll try.'

★ ★ ★

Liz had written to tell Mary her mother had finished the frocks and that they were beautiful and could she come up at the beginning of June for a fitting.

At the end of May Mary went to see Andy. She helped him clean and do some cooking ready for Brendan's homecoming on the following Friday.

Mary was busy dusting and as she carefully moved Moira's delicate figurines one by one she said, 'Shame on you, young man. These haven't been touched since your mother went away.'

'If you think I'm fiddling with that lot, well, you're wrong. That's definitely women's work.'

She laughed. Even though just a few days ago she had been sad saying goodbye to Jean, she was now happy with Andy. 'Will you have to start looking for work soon?'

'I don't know. Pa's going to sell off all the equipment so that should be a bit of a buffer till something's sorted out.'

'Have you any idea what you want to do?'

'No. Can't say I fancy working for anyone after being almost on my own all my working life.'

'Would you still stay with a fairground?'

'No, I don't think so. That part of my life is over.'

'I thought you enjoyed it?'

'I did. Don't worry, something will turn up.'

When it was time to leave Mary told him that she wouldn't be seeing him for a few weeks, not till Brendan was ready to have visitors.

'You must come and see them. You know they think the world of you.'

'I'll give it a week or so for him to settle in. In any case I've got to go and get a fitting for me frock next Sunday. Andy, I'm so excited about it. I might even see me mum!'

Andy held her close. 'I wish I could make everything all right for you.'

'Thanks.' Mary knew that although she had lost Jean, Andy would always be there for her. But what would happen when he got a job? Would he work away? She hoped it wouldn't spoil their new relationship.

The following Saturday it was a warm afternoon and not many people were out shopping.

'I think most of our customers must have gone to the beach,' said Mrs Warner. 'Not that I blame them. Mary, perhaps we could use this quiet moment to dust some of the shelves.'

'I'll get the duster.' Mary stood on the steps and with her yellow duster gently touching the shelves she was miles away, daydreaming about tomorrow. She smiled to herself. She was going to Rotherhithe and she would be seeing her mother. Mary was sure she would bring Eddie with her to Liz's. It would be lovely to see him again after all this time. Mary began to think about Jean and wondered what she was doing. She hoped she wasn't seasick. Her mind was flitting from one thing to another and she didn't take any notice of the bell tinkling above the door. It was the voice that made her quickly turn round.

'Mary?' said Nurse Bentley.

Mary got off the stepladder and came over to her. 'How are you? I haven't seen you for such a long while. Is everything . . .' Mary stopped. 'Is it Daisy?'

'Yes. I'm sorry I haven't been in before but I've been away on a course. Mary, I'm so very sorry, but she passed away last month at the sanatorium, in Devon.'

Mary picked at the yellow duster she was holding. She was trying so hard not to cry. 'So she's buried now?'

'Yes. I didn't know till a few days ago otherwise I would have told you. I didn't go to her funeral.'

'She must have been all alone,' whispered Mary. 'Would anybody have gone?'

'The staff, I expect.'

'Mary, would you like to take the nurse into the office?' Mrs Warner had obviously sensed Mary's distress.

'Thank you. It's through here,' said Mary, leading the way. She removed some papers from a chair and beckoned Nurse Bentley to sit down. She then took her handkerchief from her overall pocket and blew her nose.

'Mary, I've brought this back to you.' She handed over a small package that Mary instantly recognised.

'This is the Christmas present I gave her. It's a locket like the one she was wearing in that picture.'

'She never got it. You remember she was taken into the hospital just before Christmas? I was always hoping she would come back to St Mark's, then I could have given it to her, but it wasn't to be; then they sent her to Devon.'

Mary was filled with guilt. She hadn't written to her for months. 'If I'd carried on writing someone would have told me before this.'

'You couldn't have done anything about it. Look, I must go. It's been so nice to have met you. Perhaps one evening when I'm free we could go out together and have something to eat.'

'Thank you. I'd like that.'

'And, Mary, despite all the trauma, you did bring a little life back into Daisy and I know she thought a lot of you.' The nurse took Mary into her arms and held her briefly. 'Goodbye for now.'

Mary stood looking at the door after she'd left. She wanted to cry but the tears wouldn't come. All the time she had lived down here she had hoped to find out who Daisy was; now she would never know for sure. And she hadn't been able to tell Daisy about her son. Perhaps she should go and see Ted; after all, if Daisy was his sister, wouldn't he want to know she was dead? Would he let Mary come home? Tomorrow when she saw her mother perhaps she could talk about it and ask her to ask Ted. Although she loved it down here, she wanted to be with her mum and Eddie so much – but now there was Andy. She was torn. She knew she was falling in love with Andy and wanted to be near him.

Mary moved away from the doorway as a customer came out.

'Just got me prescription, love,' said the woman, smiling. 'Cures all this does.'

Mary smiled. That's just what she could do with, a cure-all.

# Chapter 44

To Mary the journey to London seemed to drag. She couldn't wait to be with her mother and tell her the news about Daisy. And what about Eddie, had he grown? She knew from her mother's letters that he still didn't speak, but that didn't matter, she was going to see him.

At last she was at Liz's front door.

'Mary.' Liz hugged her. 'It's lovely to see you again.'

Mary was ushered into the kitchen where all the family were gathered.

After lots of kisses and hugs Mary asked, 'What time's Mum coming round?'

'She's really sorry, but she won't be able to make it,' said Liz.

Tears filled Mary's eyes. 'Why?'

'She didn't say, but she did say she was ever so sorry. She will try to get to the church on the day though, so you'll be able to see her then.'

'She's done a lovely job on those frocks,' said Mrs Thomas.

'You wait till you see 'em,' said Susan.

'I feel like a princess in mine,' said Elsie.

'Let's have a cuppa for now. Dinner will be about two, is that all right, Mary? Will that give you time to get your train?'

Mary nodded. 'Yes, thanks.'

'Come on, let's go up and look at these frocks,' said Liz excitedly.

When they were alone upstairs Mary sat on the bed and asked, 'Did Mum say why she couldn't come round here?'

'No, honest.'

'How did you have all your fittings? Did you go round home? Was Eddie all right?'

'She used to come here on a Sat'day before *he* got home. Yes, she did bring Eddie and he's fine but she never stayed for more than a quarter of an hour. It was just on with the frocks and she was off again.'

'I can't believe she's that frightened of him.'

'I know she was upset about not seeing you.' Liz took her dress from behind the door and removed the sheet that was covering it. 'What d'you think?' She held up the long white dress.

'Liz, it's beautiful.'

'Yer mum's made a lovely job of it and it fits perfect.'

Mary took hold of the dress that her mother had made. 'It really is beautiful.'

'Look at all these tiny pearl buttons down the back and up the sleeves. It must have taken her ages to sew them on and to make the loops for them.'

'Her hand stitching was always very neat.'

'And look, your mum's sewn a penny in the hem. It's a good luck token. It means we'll never be without money all the time it's there.'

Mary swallowed hard. 'That sounds like Mum.'

'Not that we should ever be hard up. Not with the job Pete will finish up with. I'm so lucky. When I walk out of the factory I'll never have to go back there again.'

'You're not marrying him for that, are you?'

'No. I love him, Mary. I really do. He's so . . . I don't

403

know.' She hugged herself. 'Just perfect, I suppose. I'm so very lucky to have met him. If we hadn't gone to Portsmouth that weekend, well, I wouldn't be standing here holding my wedding dress.'

'I'm really happy for you, Liz.'

'I only wish your story had a happy ending.'

'Perhaps it will one day.'

'I'll go and get your frock. It's in Mum's bedroom.'

Liz returned with a powder-blue creation draped over her arm. 'So, what d'you think?'

Mary held it up. 'It's so pretty.'

'It's the same pattern as mine and the same material, satin-back crêpe. They've all got a sweetheart neck; mine's got the long sleeves with a point that comes over me hand. Yours and the girls' have got puff sleeves. Go on, try it on.'

Mary took off her frock and Liz helped her gently ease into the long blue dress. 'Your mum said we've got the same measurements so I tried yours on for the fittings. It fits perfectly,' said Liz, fussing round her and pulling at the hem. 'Come and look in Mum's mirror: you can angle it to see yourself full-length.'

Mary stood in front of the mirror. 'Liz. What can I say? It's really lovely. Mum's made a lovely job of it.' Mary could almost see her mother treadling away, surrounded by a sea of white and blue fabric. She gently ran her hand over the dress. She knew her mother had made this with lots of love. 'I know what the girls mean. I feel like a princess as well.'

'You look wonderful. Let's go down and show Mum.'

Slowly and carefully Mary lifted her long skirt and made her way down the stairs and into the kitchen.

'What d'you think, Mum?' asked Liz as Mary followed her into the kitchen.

'Oh, Mary love. Don't you look gorgeous.'

'I'm a bit worried she's gonner outshine me,' said Liz, laughing.

'I'll never be able to do that,' said Mary.

'Have you seen what we're wearing on our heads?' said Susan.

'Go and get them,' said Liz.

'This is gonner be such a lovely wedding,' said Mrs Thomas. 'You know Pete's wearing his navy uniform. He'll look ever so handsome. It's a pity my Billy can't be here.'

Susan came bursting in holding the headdresses. 'This is yours,' she said, handing Mary a wreath of blue flowers and leaves.

'I've got orange blossom,' said Liz. 'And a lovely long veil.'

'It's all marvellous,' said Mary, overcome with happiness for her friend. 'I can't wait for the twenty-seventh.'

'Neither can I,' said Liz.

'Where are you going to live?' asked Mary.

'We're going to stay at Pete's mum and dad's for a little while, till Pete settles down. He's starting off at Chatham. We're having our honeymoon in Bournemouth. Just for a week.'

Mrs Thomas laughed. 'Your dad and me had a day at the races for our honeymoon. And good it was as well. Mind you, we didn't have any money to have a bet with, but we did have a lovely bowl of jellied eels to celebrate. We was happy and the sun shone all day.'

'Things have changed a bit since then, Mum.'

'Yes, I know, love. And I'm that proud of you.'

Mary swallowed hard. This was how things should be between mother and daughter.

Mary and Liz went upstairs again to take off her dress.

'Will you be seeing Mum?'

'I won't, but me mum will. She said she'll be round

405

tomorrow just to make sure there wasn't any alterations to make to your frock.'

Mary sat on the bed. 'I was really hoping I would see her.' She could feel the tears welling up again.

'I know.' Liz sat next to her and took her hand. 'It must be very hard for you. And for your mum. I know she misses you.'

'Liz. Daisy's dead.'

'Daisy? Was she the woman you went to Portsmouth to see?'

Mary nodded and brushed a tear away. 'She died in Devon.'

'When?'

'I don't know. That nurse came in the shop yesterday and told me.'

'Poor you.'

'Poor Daisy. She was all alone. If it was Ted's sister how could he let that happen?'

'I don't know.'

'I wanted to see Mum and tell her. I was hoping she would tell Ted and that he might let me come back, or at least let me see her. Why is he treating us like this? Anyone would think I've got the plague or something.' Mary began to cry.

Liz put her arms round her friend. 'I'll have a word with her and see if I can help.'

'Thanks. I'm sorry.' Mary smiled through her tears. 'I promise I won't spoil your big day.'

'I should hope not. By the way, how's that Andy's dad getting on? My dad reckons those what did it should be horse-whipped, putting people's lives in danger like that.'

'Good job it didn't come off when all the punters were there.'

Liz laughed.

'What's so funny?'

'You. You've certainly picked up the lingo.'

'Anyway, Andy's dad came home on Friday. I helped Andy get the place ready last Sunday.'

'So you're still seeing him? I thought it was his mum and dad you went to see?'

'I've been helping him keep the cottage clean and we sometimes take his younger brother to the beach.'

'Oh yes? Sounds very cosy.'

Mary hadn't told Liz that her feelings for Andy had changed. 'They've been nice to me.'

'I see.'

'The smell of the dinner's making me hungry,' said Mary, not wanting to say too much about Andy just yet. She thought Liz might still be loyal to her brother.

'Come on then, let's go downstairs.'

Mary kissed Liz's cheek.

Liz touched her cheek. 'What's that for?'

'Cos you're my best friend and I love you.'

'Daft ha'p'orth.'

Sarah looked at the clock. She knew Mary would be trying on her frock now. If only she could see her, but she knew she had to be careful just in case Ted got suspicious. He wasn't the man she married; why had he changed so much? 'I know our Mary will look lovely,' she whispered to Eddie who was playing on the floor. 'Say Mary.'

He ignored her. Sarah smiled. All the time she was making it she'd been thinking of Mary and talking to Eddie, telling him all about it. Sarah knew she had to keep it a secret from Ted. He was already complaining about her spending too much time in the front room machining and running to the woman whose frock it was.

'Why can't she come here for a fitting? I hope she's paying

your fare, traipsing all the way over there.'

If only he knew. Even Eddie was enjoying going over to see Liz and her sisters. Whatever else happened she would go to the church to see the wedding. She longed to see Mary in her bridesmaid's dress.

As Mary travelled back to Portsmouth that day, her thoughts were still on her mother. Hopefully she'd be seeing her in three weeks' time, even if it might only be at the church.

Mary was pleased when she had a letter from Andy asking her to come and see them on the following Sunday and when she knocked on the front door she was treated like a long lost friend.

Mr Turner was sitting in a deckchair in the garden. 'Mary. Come and sit by me.'

She kissed his cheek. 'How are you?'

'Not too bad. They can't keep an old dog like me down for long.'

Mrs Turner was at her side. 'He looks tons better now, we were worried about him.'

'I wish she'd stop fussing.'

'Dad. Shut up,' said Andy.

Moira grinned. 'Now we're a couple of old crocks together. Andy told us how you came up here and helped him keep the place clean and tidy. It looked really nice, thank you. You're a good girl.'

'I didn't do much. Andy really did look after the place.'

'And you took Patrick on a picnic.'

Mary smiled, and her heart gave a little leap when Andy winked at her.

'What did the bridesmaid's dress look like?' asked Moira. 'You said you went for a fitting. Did you see your mother?'

Mary shook her head. 'No. She couldn't get away, but the frock was lovely.'

'You'll have to show us the photos of the wedding.'

'I will. You remember I told you about Daisy, the woman who gave her baby to that gypsy?'

'I'm sorry we couldn't help you find him,' said Mr Turner.

'It doesn't matter now. She's dead.'

'You poor thing. When did this happen?' asked Moira.

'I don't know. It must have been a while ago. She was down in Devon.'

'So is that another chapter of your life closed?' asked Andy.

'Looks like it.'

'Ma, we haven't offered Mary a cup of tea and after all she's done for us . . .'

'I'm sorry, Mary. I must be forgetting my manners.'

Mary laughed. 'I could make it meself now, I know where everything is.'

'You'll do no such thing, young lady. You sit down and be waited on. Like me,' said Mr Turner.

Again tea, which today was held in the pretty garden, was happy and full of laughter.

They were sitting relaxing and enjoying the sunshine when Andy whispered to Mary, 'Shall we go for a walk?'

'I can't. I came here to see your mum and dad.'

'They don't mind. Look, they've having a bit of a doze.'

'Well, only if you think it'll be all right.'

'It will. I told them how I feel about you.'

'Andy, you didn't?'

He grinned. 'Shh. Come on.'

Mary did notice as she shut the garden gate that they were both smiling with their eyes shut.

They were walking hand-in-hand through the fields and into the woods when Andy stopped.

'I really missed you last Sunday. I couldn't stop thinking of you all day, wondering what you were doing and if you'd seen your mother, and would you be staying up there? Mary, I was really worried. You know I love you and don't want to lose you.'

Mary's mind was in a turmoil. She knew she loved him but, like Billy, he worked away from home. Would his feelings for her change when he was travelling? She didn't want to be hurt again – or to hurt Andy; he was much too nice.

'Mary, I've loved you from the first time I saw you but there was always Billy in the background.'

'But, Andy . . .'

He put his finger to her lips. 'I know all about you and your family. And I want to make you happy. I would never let you down, I promise.'

Mary could feel tears beginning to well up. Yes, she did love him. 'Billy's not around any more.' She put her arms round him and kissed him; it was a warm, comforting kiss.

When Andy kissed her back it was with passion. 'I do love you, Mary,' he whispered as he kissed her neck.

'And I love you,' she managed to say between kisses.

'I can't believe I can be this lucky,' Andy said with his arms around her waist.

Mary smiled. 'I'm so happy.'

'Are you? Are you really?'

'Yes. You won't forget me when you go on the road again, will you?'

'I don't think I'll be going on the road again. You see, I've got a job.'

'That's great,' she said, genuinely pleased. 'What and where?'

'I'm a good mechanic – you had to be in our line of business – and I've been offered a job working at a garage at Waterlooville; they repair a lot of heavy stuff. And the money's not bad.'

'Where's that?'

'It's a village not far away. You pass it on the way here.'

'But will you be content staying in one place?'

'Yes, all the time I have you not far away.' He took her into his arms and kissed her long and hard. When they broke apart he whispered, 'Mary, I know you were let down before, but I swear I'll never do that to you. I know this is a bit sudden, but will you marry me?'

Mary caught her breath. 'I don't know.'

Andy began kicking the ground. 'I'm sorry. I'm rushing you. I should have waited. But you do like me, don't you?'

'Yes, I do. I love you and I'm flattered that you want me to be your wife, but . . .'

'You don't want to be married to—'

Mary put her finger on his lips. 'What if my stepfather says I can go back home? I miss my mum and brother so much. I would run all the way there if he ever said I could go home.'

'I see. Do you think there's any chance of that happening?'

'I don't know. I wrote and told my mother that Daisy had died and I asked if I could go back. I'll have to wait and see.'

'If the answer's no, would you marry me?'

'I would love to marry you, but . . .'

'I'm rushing you. I'm sorry.'

'Just give me time.'

They walked slowly back to the cottage.

'Have you told your parents about wanting to marry me?'

'Yes.'

'And what did they say?'

'They would do everything they could to make you their daughter-in-law. They love you almost as much as I do.'

Mary smiled and stopped. She put her arms round his neck and kissed him.

'We can sort something out. I'm sure we can make it work,' said Andy, squeezing her hand as they went into the garden.

Although she had only just got Billy out of her life, somehow she knew this was going to be different.

# Chapter 45

'Did you have a nice day today?' asked Mrs Johns when Mary walked in. 'How is Mr Turner?'

'Not too bad. His leg's still in plaster and he has difficulty walking, but Andy said it would take time.'

'And how is the young man?'

'He's fine.' Mary knew her grin had spread from ear to ear.

'You look very happy. Almost like the cat that's got the cream.'

'I am. Mrs Johns, can I talk to you?'

'Oh dear, whenever you ask that it's usually something not very good. I'll get the teapot, that always helps to smooth things a bit.'

When Mrs Johns sat at the table and began pouring out the tea, she said, 'I must say, by the look of you it doesn't seem as if I'm about to hear bad news.'

Mary smiled. 'No, it's definitely not bad news. You see, Andy's asked me to marry him.'

Mrs Johns dropped the tea strainer she was holding on to the cup with a clatter. 'But you've only known him a few months. It was only a short while ago you were pining over Billy. Mary, this isn't to spite Billy, is it?'

'No. I was never really sure of Billy.' Mary hadn't told Mrs Johns the real reason he'd dropped her.

'What was your answer?'

'I said I would have to think about it.'

'Very sensible. Has he talked about a job? Is he going back to the fairground?'

'No. He's going to work in a garage.'

'I see.' Mrs Johns had her 'we need to be sensible' look about her. 'What do you think your mother will have to say about this? After all, you are under age.'

'I haven't said yes. I told him he's got to wait till I hear from my mother. You know when I didn't see her last week I thought I'd write and tell her about Daisy and ask if I can go back home. I told Andy he would have to wait till she answered. She can tell me when I see her at the wedding.'

'You're thinking of going back?' Mrs Johns looked shocked.

Mary smiled and nodded. 'Do you think I did the right thing asking Andy to wait?'

'I'm sure you did and if this young man is as good as all you've told me about him, he'll wait for your answer.'

'My mind's all at sixes and sevens. What if I do go back home? I'm not sure I would see him again.'

'Why?'

'I don't think he'll like living in Rotherhithe.'

'Yes, you have a point there. But would you want to live there?'

'Yes, if I could be near Mum and Eddie.'

'Have you told him this?'

'He knows I want to go back to Mum.' Mary blushed. 'But I do like him, he's so different to Billy.'

Mrs Johns only smiled.

Mary didn't go to see the Turners the following Sunday as she needed time to think. She was also worried his parents might try to persuade her to accept Andy's proposal.

★ ★ ★

Every day that passed Mary was hoping to see the postman had been and there was a letter from her mother with good news. But by Friday evening when she left to go to the wedding she still hadn't heard from her.

That night when Liz and Mary were supposed to be sleeping they were chatting. Mary knew she should be concentrating on Liz's big day, but she could only think of one thing: 'I'm hoping when I see Mum tomorrow she's gonner say Ted will let me come back now.'

Mary had a restless night and on Saturday morning she woke to find Mrs Thomas standing in the bedroom looking down at her daughter who was sleeping peacefully. Mary sat up and Mrs Thomas put her finger to her lips for Mary to be silent.

'Is everything all right?' Mary mouthed.

Mrs Thomas smiled and nodded. 'I just want to look at my baby for the last time,' she whispered. 'After today she'll belong to someone else.'

Mary swallowed hard and got off the mattress the Thomases had got for her.

Liz suddenly woke. She sat up. 'What's happening? What's wrong? Mum, what're you doing here?'

Her mother smiled. 'I just come in to see if you was awake, that's all.'

'Is it raining?' Liz asked, panic filling her voice.

'No. It's a beautiful day. The sun's shining, look.' She pulled back the curtains. 'And you're going to be a beautiful bride.'

'She don't look very beautiful now,' said Mary with a laugh.

'Right, the both of you, time to get up and get ready.'

All morning life in the Thomas household was hectic.

Flowers were delivered. The postman arrived with good-luck cards. The telegraph boy brought telegrams. Relations and neighbours came with their good wishes and Mr Thomas invited them in for a drink.

'I only hope he ain't having one with everybody that's come in,' said Mrs Thomas. 'Otherwise we'll have to carry him up the aisle.'

'Mum! Don't say things like that, you're making me nervous.'

'Your mum's only joking,' said Mary. 'Your dad's taking his duties very seriously.' She got closer and, keeping her voice down, said, 'I heard him rehearsing his speech and very good it is too.'

'He's been that worried about it,' said Mrs Thomas. She smiled. 'I think it's good as well.'

At last the shout went up that the cars were here.

Mary looked at her friend and, holding her hands, lightly kissed her cheek. 'You look so lovely. Pete will be very proud of you.'

'I hope so. I'm gonner make him a good wife, Mary. I love him so much.' She put her veil over her face.

'Good luck,' Mary whispered. 'See you at the church.'

Slowly Mary and Liz's sisters made their way down the stairs. Mrs Thomas was waiting at the bottom wearing her new outfit. She looked very smart in a navy frock and her matching hat was really charming.

'Do I look all right?' she asked Mary.

'You look lovely.'

'I'm a bit worried, cos Pete's parents have got a few bob and I expect she'll look really posh.'

'You've got nothing to worry about, you look posh as well.'

The crowd of neighbours standing at the gate confirmed what Mary had just told Mrs Thomas with their cries of:

'Doris, don't you look lovely!' 'Like the titfer!' 'And don't you bridesmaids look good. Nice colour.'

When they'd climbed into the car Mrs Thomas settled back and said, 'I bet some of that lot are green with envy. Likes of us don't go in cars.'

Mary knew that Pete's parents had been very generous, and were helping out with this wedding. They had even paid for them to have the wedding breakfast in a hotel.

Soon Mary and Liz's sisters were standing in the church doorway waiting for the bride and her dad. Everybody was now in their seats. Mrs Thomas had been right. Pete's mum did look posh in her grey two-piece; her tiny hat had a spotted veil that covered her eyes. She even had a fox fur draped over her shoulders despite it being June and very warm. Both Pete's parents seemed very nice when they came and spoke to them before taking their seats.

Mary's stomach was full of butterflies. She was nervous for Liz and nervous for herself. She was hoping her mother would come up to her today and say that Ted said she could come back home. This would certainly then be a day to remember. She thought of Andy and wished he was here with her.

The car arrived with Liz and her dad and they all slowly made their way towards the altar.

Vows were exchanged and a plain gold band was put on Liz's finger. She was now Mrs Cooper.

Outside the photographer was busy trying to get everyone into the picture. Kids were running off and old ladies who were busy talking were taking their time to be moved into position. Mary's thoughts immediately went to Jean. She wouldn't be having this trouble with *her* clients. All the while Mary was turning this way and that to see if her mother was in the crowd and she was reluctant to leave the church when there hadn't been any sign of her.

The wedding breakfast was full of fun with noisy speeches. Mary could see that Pete's eyes never left his bride's face. It was obvious to all that he truly loved Liz, who was glowing with happiness. Mary was trying hard not to be sad. Her mother hadn't arrived.

'What do you mean you want to go to the church to see this bride. What for?'

Sarah was nervous. 'I just want to make sure that those frocks look all right and, besides, I might get some more work.'

'You've seen them when you've been over there, so stop fussing and sit down. I hope you made enough money doing that. All the mess we've had to put up with!'

'There wasn't a lot of mess.' Sarah had made sure of that and she hadn't told Ted that she hadn't charged Liz for making them, that had been her wedding present to her.

All afternoon Sarah looked at the clock trying to imagine what was happening now. Why didn't she just tell Ted she was going? Why was she such a coward? She now knew the answer to that question. At least Ted still paid the rent and kept them – as he was constantly reminding her these days – but she was little more than a housekeeper now. His demands were slowly killing her love for him. But without a breadwinner in the house she could finish up anywhere.

She went outside to the lav and took Mary's letter from her pocket. Daisy was dead and Mary wanted to come home. What could she tell her? When she'd told Ted that the woman in the photo was dead he'd gone into such a rage that Sarah had feared for her life. Although he didn't strike her she could see it had taken all his will power to keep his hands off her, and before storming out of the house he'd forbidden Sarah to write to her daughter ever again. That night he came home very drunk. What was it about that woman that provoked all this? Who was she?

After the cake-cutting it was time for the bride and groom to leave.

Mary was helping Liz into her going-away outfit. She stood back and looked at her. 'This is a lovely colour.'

Liz stood in front of the long mirror and pulled at the jacket of her two-piece. 'I like blue.' She put her tiny hat on and tilted it slightly forward, adjusting the veil over her eyes. 'Well, what d'you think?'

'If you think you're going to get away without anybody guessing you're newly weds, well, I think you've got that all wrong. You look beautiful.'

Liz smiled. 'I don't care who knows it. I'm so happy, Mary.'

Mary held her tight and, with a catch in her voice said, 'Now, tonight you've got my permission to do anything that I haven't done.' She couldn't stop the tears from slowly slipping down her cheeks. She dabbed at her eyes. 'Look what you're making me do.'

Liz crushed Mary to her. 'I wish you could be half as happy as me. I'm so sorry your mum didn't make it.'

Mary broke away and blew her nose. 'Go on. You'd better be going, otherwise someone else might steal that good-looking husband of yours.'

'Over my dead body.' Liz kissed her cheek. 'I'll be down to see you as soon as we get settled.'

Mary watched them get into the car and they went off with lots of jokes, confetti and shouting. Then it was all over.

Back inside the hotel the friends and relations were gradually leaving.

'Mary, it's been very nice meeting you,' said Pete's mum.

'Now, remember, I've told Liz that when they get back and have settled down you must come and stay with us for a few days.'

'Thank you. I'd like that.'

Mrs Cooper patted her hand and smiled. 'You looked really lovely today. Your mother made a wonderful job of those dresses. I only wish she lived near me. Was she here today?'

'No, she couldn't make it.'

'That's such a shame. I must go. I do hope we see you again.' She gently kissed Mary's cheek.

Mary watched them get into their car. Liz was right. They were nice people.

'Right,' said Mr Thomas. 'It's back to our place then up the pub for a knees-up.'

'Can we come?' asked Susan.

'I should cocoa. This bit's for the grown-ups,' said their father.

Susan and Elsie each pulled a face.

'Never mind,' said Mrs Thomas. 'You've had a good day and that was a nice locket Liz and Pete bought you.'

Elsie fingered the pretty silver locket that hung round her neck and smiled. 'Yes, it is. Can we be your bridesmaids when you marry our Billy?' she asked Mary.

'I don't think that will happen,' she said, giving them a half-smile.

'I thought you and him was—'

'Come on, Els. Stop asking questions,' said Mrs Thomas.

Mary knew then that Liz must have told her it was all over between them.

Mary also fingered the locket Liz and Pete had given her. She hadn't told her about the one she'd bought for Daisy.

'You girls, bring the flowers,' said Mrs Thomas. She turned

to Mary. 'You sure you want to put yours on their gran's grave?'

'Yes. I don't visit me gran, not any more. Not since Ted married Mum. He didn't like it.'

Mrs Thomas didn't make any comment.

That night as she got into Liz's bed Mary let her thoughts drift. She was worried about her mother. Why hadn't she written and why wasn't she at the wedding? If anything happened to her who would tell her? Should she go round and see her tomorrow? But was that wise? She didn't want her mother or Eddie to get into any trouble from Ted; she had seen what he was capable of. Mary wanted someone to talk to. She did need Andy, he was so understanding and was a comfort to have around, but was this love or was she just using him as somebody to lean on?

She let her thoughts go back to the wedding. It had been a wonderful do. Liz was so lucky to have so many people around her who loved her. If Mary did marry Andy sometime in the future she knew her mother wouldn't be there. She turned over. Liz was now in her husband's arms. Would she ever find such happiness?

# Chapter 46

The following morning Mrs Thomas advised Mary not to go and see her mother.

'I don't think she'd really appreciate it. You remember what happened at Christmas? I'll tell you what I'll do, I'll pop round on Monday when he's at work.'

Mary was so upset to think that they knew how *he* had treated her mother. 'You don't think he hurts her, do you?'

'No, love. She seemed happy enough when she came round here.'

But Mary wasn't so sure.

'After I've been to see her I'll get my Stanley to drop you a line, that will help put your mind at rest.'

Mary smiled. 'Thanks, I feel better already knowing that.'

Mary felt sad when she said her goodbyes. It had been lovely being with the family, but now that Liz had left home it would never be the same.

On Monday Mary was feeling very low after the disappointment of not seeing her mother. She was also missing Jean very much and looking forward to her coming home with all her news. Mary needed someone to talk to. When she finished work that evening she took a stroll along the front. There was something about being beside the sea that was soothing and comforting. Andy was filling her thoughts. She longed to see him again and decided she couldn't wait till Sunday, so she would go tomorrow straight from work.

'Mary?' said Mrs Turner when she opened the door. 'This is a really lovely surprise. Andy,' she called out. 'Look who's here. He's out in the garden with Brendan.'

Andy came into the kitchen and when he caught sight of Mary he gave a yell.

'Mary, what're you doing here?'

His mother had quietly moved outside.

'I need someone to talk to.'

He took her in his arms. 'Talk to me. I'm here for you.'

Mary couldn't control her emotions any longer and burst into tears.

'What is it? What's upset you?' Andy was holding her close and kissing her wet face. 'Look, let's go and sit in the other room.'

'I didn't see Mum on Sat'day. I wanted to go round to see her on Sunday, but Mrs Thomas, that's Liz's mum, she didn't think it was a good idea seeing what happened before when me and Liz went round there on Christmas morning.'

'She could be right. Your mother must have had a good reason for not seeing you.'

'That's what I'm worried about. What if something's happened to her? I'd never know.'

'What could happen?'

'You don't know my stepfather.'

'Is he violent?'

'He can be. I've seen him belt Eddie.'

Andy visibly winced. 'He'd belt a child?'

Mary nodded.

Andy stood up. 'What do you want to do, Mary?'

'I don't know.'

'If you want me to come to their house with you, I'd be more than pleased. You just say the word.'

'What could we do? I don't want to make things worse for Mum. If he walked out I can't afford to keep them on my wages and I don't really want to go back to Rotherhithe and the biscuit factory. I don't want to leave you.' Tears began to fall again.

Andy sat next to her and put his arm round her shoulder. 'Look, give me a day or two to think about this. I'll have a word with Ma and Pa. They say two heads are better than one; we must be able to come up with some sort of solution.'

'What could you do?'

'At the moment I don't know, but I don't like to see you so unhappy. Remember I love you, Mary. I'm very pleased that you came to me.'

She looked up at him with her tear-stained face. She knew at that moment that she loved him so very much, and when she told him so, he kissed her long and passionately.

When they broke apart he said, 'We will sort this out, I give you my word.'

She wiped her eyes and they went into the garden.

'How did the wedding go?' asked Moira.

'It was lovely. Liz looked so beautiful.'

'All brides seem to get that inner glow. What was her dress like?'

Mary smiled. 'Mum made a wonderful job of all of them. She really is very clever.'

'Has your little brother grown?'

Tears filled Mary's eyes again. 'I didn't see them. I'm so worried about them. That's why I've come here tonight. I need a friend to talk to.'

'My love,' said Moira, coming to her and hugging her. 'You

know you are more than welcome here any time.'

'Moira's made the tea, so sit yourself down and, Andy, get the brandy from the cupboard. I think Mary could do with a little bit of Dutch courage.'

She smiled at Mr Turner. These were such understanding people. She would be very happy when she became part of this family. But at the moment there were more important things to worry about.

When it was time for her to leave, Andy took her to the bus stop. 'I'll come to see you tomorrow straight from work.'

'It's my half-day but I'll meet you there just the same. Andy, I'm so sorry, I haven't asked you how you're getting on. What was your new job like?'

'It's going to take a bit of getting used to working indoors, but they seem a great bunch of blokes. Mind you, I'll appreciate it in the cold and rain.'

'I'm glad you're not going away again,' she said, snuggling up to him.

'So am I now that I've found you.' He kissed her tenderly.

As she sat on the bus she wondered what the future held for her. She felt she was being torn in two. She so wanted to be with Andy, but she was so worried about her mother that she couldn't think about her own happiness. She hoped the Turners would come up with some sort of solution.

The following evening Andy was waiting outside the shop for her. She went up to him and kissed him. 'I'm so glad to see you.'

'I told you I'd be here.' He took her arm. 'I think Ma and Pa have come up with something. Look, let's go and have a cup of tea and talk about it.'

When they were settled, he said, 'You know you don't have go to along with this idea.'

Mary was smiling. Was there going to be a solution to her problem?

'Ma suggested that we bring your mum and Eddie down here.'

Mary looked shocked. 'But where . . .?'

He put up his hand. 'Hear me out. We know you don't want to leave your job, so what if you find a little place here in Portsmouth? Your landlady might be able to help you there. I don't think the rents are that high and at least you'll be near your work, and another thing, Ma reckons your mother will find plenty of work doing dressmaking, curtains, all sorts. In fact, she's already picked out a pattern and she's going into town to get some material. So what do you think?'

Mary stared at him. 'It sounds wonderful. If it was a cheap rent then I might just about manage. I never particularly wanted to live in Rotherhithe again. And if Mum was working . . .' She stopped. 'How would she get her things down here? She couldn't afford anything new or even second-hand, especially a sewing machine. She'd have to bring it all with her.'

'We thought about that. Don't forget we still have the van we used to travel about in. That was one thing Pa didn't want to sell.'

'What if she won't come?'

'That's something you'll have to discuss with her. Anyway, that was our way of thinking.'

Mary leaned across the table and took his hand. 'You are so kind to me. I didn't really want to go back to Rotherhithe, not now I've found you.'

'And I didn't want to lose you because I love you and don't like to see you unhappy.'

'I'll have a talk to Mrs Johns and see if she can help find a house, then I'll write to Mum.'

'That's what we thought. Now, if we do go up to collect your mother Patrick will come to help me move the heavy stuff. If your stepfather causes any trouble – well, let's hope it won't come to that.'

'Please, Andy. I don't want *you* to get into any trouble.'

He smiled. 'Don't worry about it. Come on; let's go for a walk. You can take me to the bus stop for a change.'

They laughed as they walked along. Mary was so happy. She knew she couldn't leave Andy, not now. She really loved him.

When she arrived back at Mrs Johns's she eagerly told her of the Turners' plans.

'It sounds a wonderful idea and if you had a spare room, you could take in holidaymakers like I do.'

'I don't think we could do that, not with Eddie being like he is.'

'Oh yes, that could be a bit of a problem. Now all you've got to do is to get your mother to agree. I must say Andy and his parents sound very nice, thoughtful people.'

'They are. Do you think there might be a little house for rent round about?'

'I'll go along and see my landlord and make a few enquiries. People do come and go round this way with so many sailors on the move and young wives wanting to go back home to their parents. I'll see what I can find out. Mind you, I'll miss you. It's been like having a daughter.'

'I'll always pop in to see you.' Mary was on cloud nine. 'Now I'm going to write and tell Mum all our plans.' But her biggest fear was that her mother wouldn't want to leave Ted.

Several days passed, but Mary still hadn't a reply from her mother. Mr Thomas had written and said that Doris had seen her mother and that she was fine. It was just that she wasn't feeling too well on the day of the wedding. But Mary didn't really believe that. She knew her mother would have gone through hell and high water to see her if she could. So what had happened? What had Ted done to her mother?

When Mary next went to see Andy she was disappointed that she hadn't any news for him.

'Not to worry. You've got to give her time to think about it.'

Sarah read and reread Mary's letter many times. As much as she wanted to, how could she just up sticks and go down there with her? Would she find somewhere cheap for them to live? It sounded wonderful. They would be together, but she was married to Ted. Could he come after her and make her go back? She didn't know what to do; she was in a turmoil. But she did want her daughter and her old life back again.

It was the following Wednesday and almost one o'clock when Mary looked up to see Nurse Bentley walk in.

'How are you?' asked Mary.

'Hello, Mary. I'm fine. What time do you finish?'

'One today.'

'Could we go somewhere and have a talk?'

Mary was puzzled. 'Yes. Of course.'

Nurse Bentley didn't leave the shop; she hung about looking at the shelves and various goods that were on display.

'I've got to shut the door now,' said Mrs Warner. 'So I must ask you to wait outside.'

'That's no problem.'

Mary left the shop and, walking up to her, said, 'What is it?'

'I didn't like to say anything inside. I wasn't sure how much they knew about Daisy.'

'They only know I used to visit her and that she's dead.'

'Look, as it's a nice day can we go to the park?'

'Yes.' But Mary wanted to know why she was here. 'Is something wrong?' she asked when they reached the park.

'No. Shall we sit here?'

'If you like.'

Nurse Bentley started to rummage in her bag. 'I have some papers here. You might like to read them.' She brought out a tattered brown envelope.

'What are they?'

'Daisy's papers. Birth certificate, marriage lines: that sort of thing. There are a few photos as well.'

'Daisy's papers?' Mary whispered in complete shock. She sat staring at the envelope resting in her hands. 'Why have you given them to me?'

'We had to send them to the sanatorium when Daisy was sent there. And they have just come back to us.'

'But why give them to me?'

'I have read them and I thought you might like to read them as well. It might answer some of your questions.'

'But don't they belong to her next of kin?'

'She didn't have any.'

'I don't know. I don't want to pry. I know I did once, but that was when I thought my stepfather was related to her, but it doesn't matter now, does it?' She looked up at the nurse.

'I would still like you to read them before I hand them over to the authorities.'

'Won't you get into trouble?'

'Who's going to tell them? You were good to Daisy and I think you should know something about her. Look, I'll go for a walk and leave you. I'll be back later.'

In many ways Mary didn't want to open the envelope. Now Daisy was dead that part of her life was over. She sat for a while just looking and holding it. Nurse Bentley wanted her to read them. But why?

One by one she took the flimsy pieces of paper out. There was her small square birth certificate. She was born in London on 2 February 1898. A photo of her as a young bride, which had been taken by someone with a Box Brownie camera, was faded and out of focus. Mary had a job to see who her husband was; all she could make out was a sailor's uniform. Daisy's death certificate told Mary she died of pneumonia in March this year. Died more of a broken heart, thought Mary. There was a baby's birth certificate. He was called Edward. There were three photos of this smiling happy baby and then one when he was a little boy. Mary took a quick breath. It was like looking at Eddie. Mary sat looking at the photo in disbelief. There weren't any newspaper cuttings about her trial but when Mary found her marriage certificate, she gasped in astonishment. Daisy had been married to a Mr *Edward Harding*. Mary sat back stunned. Studying the photo more closely, she realised the sailor was in fact Ted, her stepfather. He was a lot younger then, but it was definitely him. What would her mother say? She was still staring at the photo when Nurse Bentley came back and sat next to her.

'Did you find anything interesting?'

'I can't believe it. I always thought that Daisy was Ted's sister. But she wasn't – she was his wife. He married my mother when he was still married to Daisy.'

'What? How do you know?'

Mary showed her the photo and the marriage certificate. Mary was beginning to get angry.

'Are you sure it's him?'

Mary nodded.

'That's awful. That makes him a bigamist.' Nurse Bentley was visibly shocked.

Mary stood up and began pacing. 'Yes. No wonder he didn't want me raking it all up. What am I to do?'

'Sit down, Mary. Why would he marry your mother when he already had a wife?'

Mary did as she was told. 'If you knew Ted you would understand. He wouldn't like to be associated with someone like Daisy and the disgrace she would have brought him. And it was his fault that she gave her son away. He didn't want him just because he was different.' Tears were stinging Mary's eyes and her voice was rising in fury.

Nurse Bentley gently patted Mary's hand. 'Shh,' she whispered.

Mary sobbed. 'And my mother had a house and a warm bed.'

'But what about that photo you said he carried around?'

'He must have had some feelings for her at some time,' Mary said softly.

'What are you going to do?'

'I don't know.'

They sat in silence for a while then the nurse looked at her watch.

'I do have to be off. I hope I haven't upset you too much, but I thought you might have liked to see her little boy.'

'Yes, thank you.' Mary handed the envelope back. 'Her little boy is the image of my half-brother. This has answered a lot of my questions.'

'What are you going to do about it?'

'I'm not sure. This is something I'll have to think about. Will all this have to go to my stepfather?' Mary quickly corrected herself. 'Ted Harding.'

'I suppose it should. If you give me his address I'll get in touch with the authorities and put this all in their hands. Now I really do have to be off.' Nurse Bentley held out her hand. 'It has been nice meeting you. I might not see you again as I'm being moved to another hospital. There are a lot of changes being made.'

Mary stood up. 'Thank you for all your help.'

'My pleasure.'

Mary stood and watched her walk away. Her thoughts quickly went to her mother. How would she react? All these years she'd thought she was a respectable married woman. Now she wasn't. And what about Eddie? She had so much to tell Andy tonight.

# Chapter 47

Mrs Johns was out when Mary got home. Her mind was spinning. She was in such a daze, she didn't really remember walking back from the park. What could she do? She had to see Andy tonight.

'Hello, Mary,' said Mrs Johns, coming in and putting her shopping bag on the floor. She began taking out the shopping. 'I've got some good news for you. I was talking to Mrs Searle in the greengrocer's and she was telling me about a house up the road that's just become empty. She said . . .' Her voice trailed off when she turned and saw Mary's face. She dropped the cabbage she was holding and rushed to her. 'My dear! What is it, you look like you've just seen a ghost.'

Mary sat down. 'Nurse Bentley came to see me today.'

'And what did she want?'

'She brought Daisy's papers for me to look at.'

'Why? What's that woman been saying? What's she said to upset you?'

'Ted was married to Daisy when he married my mum.'

Mrs Johns sat down at the table with a bump. 'No.'

'What am I to do?'

'Well, if it's true it could be a matter for the police.'

'How could we prove it?'

'I don't know. Did you see her marriage lines?'

'Yes.'

'But how can you be sure it was him?'

'I saw a snap of their wedding, and it was Ted standing with her.'

'Well, that's it then. What a wicked man.'

'But what about my mum? She really does love him.'

'I don't know, my dear. This is something you'll have to sort out with her.'

'I'm going to see Andy tonight. He might have some ideas.'

Mrs Johns smiled. 'He has certainly captured your heart. I'm so pleased you've found someone who I know will make you happy.'

'Yes, he does. Sorry, what was you saying about a house?'

'Mrs Searle suggested you popped along to see the landlord tomorrow, first thing, but would you like me to go instead? You've such a lot on your plate. He sounds a reasonable man and the rent's seven and six. You can manage that all right.'

'Yes, I can. That would be kind of you, thanks ever so. But now this has come to light Mum might want to kick him out, then she won't want to move. Mrs Johns, what am I going to do?'

'I don't know, love. See what Andy has to say about it.'


Mary waited at the bus stop. She wanted to see Andy first before involving the family.

'Mary!' he said, leaping off the bus and hugging her tightly. 'This is a lovely surprise.'

She stepped back. 'You're all dirty.'

He laughed. 'It goes with the job.' He took hold of her arm. 'Have you been home?'

'No. I wanted to see you first.'

'Of course you do. I could eat you, you look so delicious.'

But Mary was serious. 'Andy. Nurse Bentley came to see me this afternoon. She showed me Daisy's papers. Ted was *married* to her when he married my mum.' There was a catch in her voice.

'What?'

'I said—'

'Yes, yes. I'm sorry, I heard. So what happens next?'

'I don't know. I'll have to go and see my mum.'

'Right, we'll do that on Sunday. Now come on home. We've got a lot to talk about.'

All evening they talked about what they could do. They planned to take the van along with Patrick, hoping Sarah would leave at once.

'And Mrs Johns is looking at a house for me tomorrow morning. The rent's seven and six, so I'll be able to afford it. If she likes it then I'm going to see it in the evening and give him a week's rent.'

'We can help you furnish it,' said Moira. 'I've got far too much stuff.'

'I'll not argue about that,' said Brendan.

'Thank you. You are all so kind. But what if she don't want to come down here?'

'I can't answer that,' said Andy. 'We'll just have to wait and see.'

That night, Mary prayed her mother would come with them on Sunday.

On Friday Mary had a very short letter from her mother.

> I'm sorry but I can't leave Ted. After all, I married
> him for better or worse. It was a very kind offer and
> I'm sure I would like to live beside the sea. But I have
> a duty to him. Me and Eddie miss you very much.
>
> Love, Mum, xxx

Mary showed the letter to Mrs Johns. 'She doesn't know he's a bigamist. What shall I do about the house?'

'You gave the landlord a week's rent last night, and it's not a bad little place. See how things turn out; after all, next week you can always say you've changed your mind. I'm sure she'll change hers when you see her and tell her the facts.'

'I hope so.'

Her comments were echoed by the Turners and Andy when she saw them that evening.

Mary was so excited she could hardly wait till Sunday. At long last she was going to see her mum and Eddie again! She told the Turners about the small terraced house she'd been to see. It was in the same street as Mrs Johns's, but it was a lot smaller.

'It's got two bedrooms and downstairs is a front room and kitchenette and scullery; a washhouse had been built on the back. I've paid a week's rent. It's been a bit neglected but Mrs Johns knows a few women who will help with the cleaning.' She laughed. 'And she said some odd bits of furniture may well find their way inside!'

Although Mary was elated, she was also very worried. 'What if I can't persuade Mum to move down here?'

'We will have to cross that bridge when we come to it,' said Andy. 'We'll be down to pick you up about nine, will that be all right?'

'Yes. Thank you. Mrs Johns said she'll do us up some sandwiches.'

'I wish I was coming with you,' said Brendan.

'You wouldn't be much good hobbling around on sticks,' said Moira.

At last Sunday morning arrived. It was a clear sunny day and as they motored to London they were singing at the tops of their voices. This was far better than going on the train. But Mary felt sick when they turned into Doyle Street.

She left Andy and Patrick in the van and knocked on the door.

Sarah opened the door and stood on the threshold with her mouth open.

'Hello, Mum.' Mary went to hold her but her mother stepped back. It took Sarah a moment or two to speak. Fear filled her face.

'Mary? What are you doing here? And whose is that?' She pointed at the van.

'That's my boyfriend's and we've come to take you and Eddie away.'

'What?'

'Sarah! Who is it?' Ted's voice was loud and strong and Mary's knees began to buckle.

She looked round at Andy who was clutching the steering wheel. He smiled and it gave her courage. She called out, 'Ted, it's me. Mary.'

'Mary. No,' cried out her mother.

'What?' He came storming up the passage. He pushed Sarah to one side. 'You! I told you never to come to my house again.'

Andy was at her side. 'Everything all right, Mary?' he asked.

'Yes, thanks.'

'And who is this?'

Mary grabbed Andy's hand for moral support. 'He's my boyfriend. And we've come to take Mum and Eddie away from here.'

'Mary,' whispered Sarah. 'Go away.'

'No, Mum, I won't do that.'

Ted moved forward. 'We shall see about that.'

Patrick was now at his brother's side.

'If you don't move I shall call the police.'

Mary laughed. 'That's a good one. It should be me that's calling the police.'

'Mary, what are you talking about?'

'Be quiet, woman. This is all your doing. I know you've been writing to her. I said she would bring more trouble. Now leave at once.'

'I don't think so,' said Andy.

'Are you going to leave?' snorted Ted. 'Or do I have to get the police?'

'We'll go when Mrs Harris here is ready.'

'Her name is Harding.'

'No. I think you'll find it's been Harris all along.'

Sarah gasped. 'What are you talking about?'

'I think we should go inside.'

Mary was marvelling at the way Andy had taken over the situation.

'Mum, he was married to Daisy when he married you.'

'What?'

Mary grabbed her mother as she was about to fall.

'What the hell are you talking about?' Ted yelled furiously.

'Inside,' said Andy, pushing Ted along the passage.

When they went into the kitchen Mary rushed over to Eddie and swept him up in her arms. She smothered his face with kisses, laughing and crying at the same time.

Eddie looked bewildered and buried his head in Mary's shoulder.

'Now, what's all this nonsense about?' asked Ted, controlling himself – with difficulty.

Mary put Eddie on the floor.

Patrick sat down with Eddie and began putting his trains in order. Mary was waiting for him to start screaming, but he didn't. Patrick had a soothing voice and Eddie seemed to take to him.

'You're not married to my mother.'

'What on earth are you talking about?'

'I've seen the marriage certificate and the wedding photo of you and Daisy. And a picture of the little boy you forced Daisy to give up. You never came forward when she was accused of murder and sent to the asylum. It was your fault she had a breakdown and died alone.'

'Little boy? What little boy?' asked Sarah, who was sitting at the table. Her face was white as a sheet. 'Mary, what are you talking about?'

'It's all lies. I always knew you were a liar and a thief. You've always hated me,' Ted shouted.

'Sir, I think you should watch your language and listen to Mary,' said Andy.

Mary sat down and told Sarah everything she knew about Daisy. 'I know you are a bigamist, Ted, and I can prove it.'

'Oh no,' sobbed Sarah.

Mary went and put her arms around her mother. 'We've come to take you and Eddie away from him,' she said softly. 'Do you want to come?'

'Mary, I can't. What about the house?'

'He's always telling me that his name's on the rent book, so now he can have it. Please say you'll come, Mum. It's lovely down there. I've got us a little house and everybody's being so kind and helpful.'

'You've got this all worked out, haven't you,' sneered Ted, looking from one to the other.

'I notice you haven't denied any of what Mary's been saying.'

'Who are you, anyway? You look like some diddicoy she's picked up.' Ted drew heavily on the cigarette he'd lit up.

'For your information, she's the girl I'm going to marry.'

'You want to watch it, you could end up with a daft kid like him.'

Sarah stood up.

'Mum, sit down.' Mary turned to Ted. 'Andy knew your other son. He was different – just as Eddie is. Your wife did give him to the gypsies. In fact, they've been trying to trace him, but the woman has moved on. So you see, whatever it is, it's on your side. But we love Eddie and we can help him. With a lot of patience he will learn to speak; there're a lot of people down there who are willing to help.'

Sarah sat in a daze. 'I don't believe this is all happening.'

Ted, standing stiffly with his foot on the fender, was speechless. He studied his foot for a while, then said, 'I'm going out.'

'Off to see another woman, I suppose,' said Mary. With Andy at her side she felt full of confidence.

'What're you talking about?'

'That woman I saw you with in Oxford Street that time.'

He laughed and threw his cigarette into the fireplace. 'That was just one of my lady friends.'

Mary went to hit him but Andy held her back.

'She had a ready smile and a warm bed. Something I wasn't getting here.'

Andy, who was as tall as Ted, looked him in the eye. 'I think you'd better go before I call the police.'

Sarah stood up again, and this time Mary did not intervene. Sarah suddenly looked stronger. 'The disgrace you've brought me! Go on, get out, I won't be here when you get back.'

Ted, his face as white as chalk, picked up his trilby and, without a word, left.

Mary rushed to her mother and held her tight. Tears were running down their cheeks.

'I don't think I'll ever see him again,' sobbed Sarah.

'Are you sorry, Mum?'

Sarah shook her head. 'Not now. What will happen to him?'

'I expect in time the police will catch up with him. That's if he doesn't run off.'

Sarah brushed her tears away. 'I did love him once, you know.'

'That's all in the past now. We're going to have a lovely life in Portsmouth, I know we are. Andy and Patrick are going to help take your things. Mum, I'm so happy. You wait till you meet their mum and dad, they're lovely people.'

'That dinner smells good,' said Andy.

Sarah pulled herself together, smiling bravely. 'In that case, I'll start to dish it up. Make yourself at home, son.'

Mary went back and sat with Eddie for a moment. He looked at her and, grinning garbled something. 'Mum,' she yelled out. 'I'm sure he just said Mary.'

Her mother stood at the scullery door. 'I've been teaching him to say that.'

Mary thought she was going to burst with happiness. 'I can't believe it.'

'I did say you can teach them, if you keep on,' said Andy. 'Now, what have we got to do?'

'I'll make a start on collecting your things, Mum,' said Mary.

They went upstairs. Mary's room was now Eddie's. It looked as if all trace of her had been obliterated.

'What shall we take?' asked Andy.

'Everything. Just leave Ted's clothes and the table and a chair and anything that looks too tatty. Will you get it all in?'

'I should think so.' Andy kissed Mary. 'I love seeing you look so happy.'

'I couldn't be happier. Well yes I could. On my wedding day.'

'That won't be that far away, not now,' Andy pulled Mary into an enthusiastic embrace.

'Come on, you two,' said Patrick, poking his head round the door. 'We've got work to do.'

Sarah listened to the laughter coming from upstairs. It was a long while since there had been merriment in this house, but that was all over now. Ted had gone from her life. She wouldn't worry about the disgrace he had brought her; she was off to a new life, thanks to her wonderful daughter, her pride and joy. Thanks to Mary, Eddie would have a secure and happy future. And he *would* learn to speak, she just knew it.